ALEX SHANAHAN GOES UNDERCOVER

TO EXPOSE A DEADLY CRIME RING

AT 30,000 FEET—IN LYNNE HEITMAN'S

FIRST CLASS KILLING

"This action-filled thriller packs an erotic punch . . . gathers strength as it goes along."

—*The Boston Globe*

"Enthralling. . . . A very compelling crime thriller complete with blackmail, murder, and an internet-run prostitute ring. . . . The well-written storyline [leaves] the audience eagerly turning the pages."

—Harriet Klausner, barnesandnoble.com

"Get ready for the plane ride of your life. . . . Heitman is an excellent storyteller who creates wonderful and believable characters. . . . *First Class Killing* will leave readers eagerly awaiting the next Alex Shanahan novel."

—*Old Book Barn Gazette*

THE PANDORA KEY
IS ALSO AVAILABLE AS AN EBOOK

Turn the page to read more critical acclaim for the Alex Shanahan novels from Lynne Heitman. . . .

D0595661

HARD LANDING

"A confession: I love to have an insider from a field *I thought* I understood show me how I was wrong. Lynne Heitman's debut mystery, *Hard Landing*, delves beneath the ticket counters and departure gates to expose how both a major airline and a major airport really work. The Boston settings are dead-on, and Alexandra Shanahan is credibly tough and genuinely sensitive at all the right times. Highly recommended."

—Jeremiah Healy, Shamus Award–winning author of *Turnabout*

"*Hard Landing* goes down easy, and will keep you guessing—and flipping pages—till three a.m."

—John J. Nance, *New York Times* bestselling author of *Orbit*

"There's something mysterious happening at Boston's Logan International Airport, and the novel's heroine, Alex Shanahan, the new manager of the fictitious Majestic Airlines, is thrust into the middle of it. Fasten your seat belt—this story, written by an airline industry insider, is exciting from start to finish."

—*American Way*, American Airlines' in-flight magazine

"Sometimes a reviewer just wants to read a book because it's good . . . this is . . . a good novel. . . . Heitman leads Alex in a lively dance."

—*The Boston Globe*

"An edge-of-your seat thriller that sweeps you up and carries you along for the ride."

—Lisa Gardner, *New York Times* bestselling author of *Gone*

"Terrific . . . twists and turns and keeps you on the edge of your seat."

—Kate Mattes, Kate's Mystery Books

TARMAC

"Fast-moving and as fascinating as a natural disaster, the novel is suspenseful and electric and has the appeal of any insider story. Ms. Heitman is a former airline employee of 14 years, and her words ring true."

—*The Dallas Morning News*

"A fast-paced thriller that kept me turning the pages into the night . . . you can practically smell the grease and gasoline."

—Kate Mattes, Kate's Mystery Books

"An intricate and explosive thriller . . . evocative prose . . . [a] tightly woven, compelling read. One of the year's most notable thrillers."

—*Publishers Weekly* (starred review)

"Heitman is proving to be an accomplished thriller writer."

—*Bookseller Star Ratings*

"Truly excellent . . . the best white-knuckle ride I've taken in a long time."

—Lee Child, *New York Times* bestselling author of *One Shot*

"[*Tarmac*] needs no blurbs . . . the book can lift off for itself."

—*The Boston Globe*

" . . . the story kept me turning the pages rapidly. . . . Recommended."

—Barbara Franchi, reviewingtheevidence.com

ALSO BY LYNNE HEITMAN

HARD LANDING
TARMAC
FIRST CLASS KILLING

LYNNE HEITMAN

THE PANDORA KEY

POCKET BOOKS
New York London Toronto Sydney

The sale of this book without its cover is unauthorized. If you purchased
this book without a cover, you should be aware that it was reported to
the publisher as "unsold and destroyed."   Neither the author nor the
publisher has received payment for the sale of this "stripped book."

An *Original* Publication of POCKET BOOKS

 POCKET BOOKS, a division of Simon & Schuster, Inc.
1230 Avenue of the Americas, New York, NY 10020

This book is a work of fiction. Names, characters, places and
incidents are products of the author's imagination or are used
fictitiously. Any resemblance to actual events or locales or
persons living or dead is entirely coincidental.

Copyright © 2006 by Lynne Heitman

All rights reserved, including the right to reproduce
this book or portions thereof in any form whatsoever.
For information address Pocket Books, 1230 Avenue
of the Americas, New York, NY 10020

ISBN-13: 978-0-7434-5616-6
ISBN-10:   0-7434-5616-5

This Pocket Books paperback edition March 2006

10 9 8 7 6 5 4 3 2 1

POCKET and colophon are registered trademarks
of Simon & Schuster, Inc.

Cover design by Jae Song

Manufactured in the United States of America

For information regarding special discounts for bulk purchases,
please contact Simon & Schuster Special Sales at 1-800-456-6798
or business@simonandschuster.com.

THE PANDORA KEY

PROLOGUE

MY ASSIGNMENT IS TO KILL THE HOSTAGES. I HAVE GROWN to like some of them over our ten days together, but my duty is clear. The army is gathering outside the airplane. It is time to execute the plan. We all know our places. We all go to our duties. I dig an extra clip out of the bag. I do not know how many rounds it will take.

I stop at the front of the airplane, in the section that we have reserved for ourselves to pray. Then I go back through the curtains, and when they look at me, they know. By the way I hold the Kalashnikov or by the way I stand or by the way I look at them. Something tells them I am there to finish it.

But I've never killed anyone before. I've dreamed of it. I lied about it to be part of this operation, but I have never done it before. I level the rifle. The first one gets down on the floor between the seats and curls into a ball. I point the barrel at his head and fire. The recoil jams my shoulder back. When the bullet hits, it stops him in the middle of a scream. His head ruptures.

The others run like frightened beasts. They climb over the backs of the seats. They stumble and fall and step on each other, but there is no place for them to go. I smell the fear. They should die like men, as we all will soon.

Outside, firing begins. At first it is like rain, a sprinkling against the outside of the airplane. But then the deluge. The first bomb goes off. The floor rises up, then drops from under me. A wave of pressure pushes me down. My ears hurt, and when I get to my knees, I can't hear. One of them is coming. I find the rifle and shoot. He's screaming, but I can't hear, and he keeps coming. I shoot again, and he falls. When I try to stand, there is too much smoke. My eyes burn, but I can still see they are all coming. Their faces look like my son's crayon drawings. I try to raise the rifle again, but they push me down and step on me as they go over.

Another bomb goes off. The seats are on fire. The air feels greasy, like kerosene. Because I can't hear, everything feels slow. I crawl up the aisle. A man with blood on his face and his arms on fire runs toward me. He bumps into something and falls backward. On the floor in front of me, he twists and kicks and turns and screams until he is still. I pull myself into one of the seats. And I wait.

1

HARVEY BALTIMORE'S HOUSE WAS DYING. ONCE STATELY, the Tudor had become an embarrassment to its Brookline neighbors. Glossy black paint flaked off the shutters, the pocked shingled roof covered the house like a disease, and the other half of the duplex, which had long been a source of good, steady income for Harvey, had been vacant and closed off for almost six months. The dwelling, like its owner, seemed to be declining at an accelerating pace.

The doorbell was broken. I let myself in with my key. For someone as private as Harvey, giving me the key to his house had been a monumental concession, but it only made sense. He wasn't exactly mobile anymore.

"It's me," I called out while I wiped my shoes on the welcome mat in his foyer. No response, as usual, but I knew what I would find. If it was a good day, he would be clean-shaven, reading his newspaper by the light of the sun slanting through open blinds. If it was a bad day, he'd be sitting at his computer in the dark, unshaven, playing Minesweeper. Either way, he'd be in his wheelchair, his body ravaged by the multiple sclerosis that had been stealing function from him in excruciating increments. I hoped for a good day. There hadn't been enough of those lately.

"Harvey, your shutters are flaking. We need to get them—" I rounded the corner, walked into the office, and stopped.

Harvey was there, all right, and it must have been a good day—a very good day—because there he sat in his wheelchair, engaged in a passionate kiss with the woman on his lap. At least, until I'd barreled in, at which point they tore themselves away from each other to stare at me.

Too late to back out unnoticed. I was too embarrassed to go in any further. "I'm sorry . . . I'll just . . . I didn't . . ." have any idea what to say.

"Oh, my." Harvey went every shade of red and some from the orange spectrum. Despite his confinement to the chair, he managed to do a lot of fluttering about, mostly with his hands. He encouraged the woman off her perch. She slipped off easily, stepping gingerly so as not to get entangled in the workings of the wheelchair. Of the three of us, she was the only one who didn't look as if she wanted to curl up into a ball and roll out of there.

I took a step back. "I can just leave you two and, um . . . come back later."

"No," Harvey stammered. "Please stay. It is I who should apologize."

"Why should we apologize?" The woman seemed more annoyed than embarrassed, as if I had just tracked mud into her clean house. "We didn't do anything wrong."

She was petite and fragile-looking, a good thing to be if your habit is to sit on the legs of wheelchair-bound men. She was also vaguely familiar, though I couldn't imagine where I might have seen her before. She wore her chestnut hair cut in a short, shaggy bob. Her tight cotton slacks stopped just above her ankles, and her high-top basketball shoes were tied with thick white laces. She could have passed for a twelve-year-old boy except for her eyes. I took a closer look at those eyes, and I knew who she was.

"You're Rachel."

"Do I know you?"

Since Harvey couldn't seem to find his voice, I did the honors. "I'm Alexandra Shanahan, Harvey's business partner."

She smiled down at Harvey. "You told her about me?"

I pointed to the picture on Harvey's desk, the only personal photograph on display in the entire house and one of the few things she hadn't taken when she'd walked out on him six years before, two years before I'd met him. I had caught Harvey making out with his ex-wife. No wonder he couldn't find his voice, and no wonder I hadn't recognized her right away. She didn't look anything like her photo, especially with the flowing locks cut short.

"Would you like a cup?" Rachel must have noticed me staring at the full china tea service set up on the coffee table. Harvey hadn't been able to make his own tea since he'd dumped a full pot of hot Darjeeling in his lap. That meant she'd made it, which meant she'd been there for a while.

"Harvey said you would be coming, so I made enough for three."

"No, thanks. I'm good." I set the cup I'd brought from Tealuxe on the desk. Harvey's favorite blend had gone cold anyway.

Harvey cleared his throat and waded in. "Rachel has a job for us. I asked her to wait until you arrived to detail it."

"Both of us?"

"But of course. Why would you—" He blinked at me and reached up to scratch his head, bumping his glasses in the process. "Oh, my, no. That was just . . . it has been a long time since we have seen each other, and . . ."

"I'm sorry. It's none of my business. I'm just surprised. I didn't know you two were . . . together."

"Together?" Rachel laughed. "This is the first time we've seen each other in how long?" She reached over and straightened Harvey's collar. Then she just went ahead and hoisted one petite haunch up on the armrest of his chair. "Four years?"

"Yes," he said. "Almost."

"We were talking and reminiscing about how much I used to enjoy giving him his back rubs, and one thing led to another—"

And that was all I needed to know. "What kind of a job?"

"I need someone to go to my house in Quincy and pick up a few things. Some family photos, mostly, and some jewelry. Some things my mother gave me." She glanced at Harvey with a shy smile. "Some things Harvey gave me."

"Quincy? I thought you lived around here."

"We moved a few months ago."

"Why can't you get that stuff yourself?"

"Because I'm afraid my husband"—she glanced down at Harvey—"my soon-to-be-ex-husband will kill me."

"Did he threaten you?"

She wrapped her arms around her as if a sudden draft had blown through. "The last time he beat me, he nearly killed me."

I looked for visible bruises or scars. That she didn't have any didn't mean she was lying, but we had done work before for women who had been beaten down by men they loved. The battering didn't always leave physical evidence, but it never failed to leave some part of them shattered, some part they couldn't hide. Rachel looked whole to me.

"What did the police say?"

"You know how that is." She laughed nervously. "I have no real recourse until he kills me."

"Do you have a restraining order?"

"Yes. But he has two legs and a car, and when he's drinking, there's nothing that'll stop him."

"Why come to us?"

"Because Harvey's a private investigator." She stood up, stepped behind Harvey, and settled one hand on each of his shoulders. "I didn't know about his current condition. I wish someone had told me things had gotten this bad." She glared at me as though I were personally responsible for his MS.

Harvey seemed torn between basking in her attention and wanting to dive under his wheelchair. Public displays of affection were not his thing.

"Rachel," I said, "do you mind giving us a minute?"

She looked down at Harvey. He found her hand, pulled it down to his lips, and kissed it. They locked eyes and held that pose until he nodded. I sensed the slightest bit of triumph behind her smile as she passed without looking at me. I had known the woman all of ten minutes, and I couldn't stand her. Of course, I had despised the idea of her and what she had done to Harvey almost since I had known him.

To Harvey, Rachel was an angel, the only woman except his mother who had ever loved him. That she had dumped him for a younger, prettier boy when he'd been diagnosed mattered not, because love makes you stupid. But when I looked at her picture, I had always seen something in her eyes that made me think she wasn't the angel he thought her to be.

"Please, forgive me." Harvey was clearly embarrassed, and yet he couldn't stop smiling. "That was—"

"Look, Harvey, you're an adult, and your business is your business." I went over, sat on the couch, and looked across the tea service at him. "But isn't she still married?"

"Separated."

"How long?"

"Eight months."

The question was, what did she want? Harvey didn't have any money. Neither one of us did. "Do you believe—" Scratch that. He obviously believed her. "Has her husband been stalking her?"

"I did not ask."

"Did you know that her husband was abusing her?"

"No."

"Has she called you even once over the past four years?"

"No." He fiddled with the loose leather cushion on the arm of the wheelchair. I'd been meaning to tighten it and kept forgetting. "Nor have I called her."

"Is she planning on sticking around after we collect her stuff for her? I mean, I hate to be so skeptical, but doesn't this all seem to be coming out of the blue and moving really, really fast?"

He started to huff and puff. "You would expect what? That I would say no? That I would throw her out of my house and leave her to her own devices?"

Her own devices seemed to be in fine working order to me. "If I'm not mistaken, she tried to take this house from you in the divorce proceedings."

"Are you telling me that you will not take this assignment?"

"Is she paying us?" He stared at me as if I'd just poked him in the eye. How had I become the bad guy? "She left you, Harvey. She hurt you. Now she wants you to help her out of a jam with the guy she left you for. I'm only . . . I'm just asking that you be sure before you get involved with her again."

"She came to me because she trusts me." His voice was quiet but firm. "I could no more turn her away than I could turn you away in a time of need."

There it was. In one deft stroke, he had revealed the essence of his relationship with each of us, stated his priorities, and ended the discussion. Rachel could ask him to walk over hot coals in his bare feet, and he would ask me to hold his shoes. I would do it because I would do anything for him. I sat back and started getting used to the idea of working for Rachel.

"I'll do it for you, Harvey. Not for her."

He took off his glasses, found a cloth in his saddlebag, and cleaned them with a determination that wasn't required. He put the glasses back on and looked at me with a steady gaze as he folded the cloth. "Thank you."

I went over to the door and called Rachel back in. Harvey beamed at her. "We will be more than happy to help you with your problem."

She smiled for him, and I got a bad feeling.

2

THERE WERE TWO WAYS TO GET TO QUINCY. YOU EITHER took the red line on the T, or you sat on I-93 along with everyone else trying to go south through the Big Dig construction. I decided not to waste my hour in traffic, so the minute I hit the end of the on ramp and inched into the flow, I grabbed my cell phone and turbo-dialed Dan.

"Majestic Airlines, Dan Fallacaro."

"Hey, what are you doing?"

"I'm working, Shanahan. I don't have time."

"Wait . . ."

"What?"

"You're going to want to hear this." I filled him in on how I'd found Harvey in a clinch with his ex-wife.

"Are you shitting me? You're talking about our Harvey, right?"

I was talking about our Harvey. Dan Fallacaro was the mutual friend who had introduced us. Dan had worked for me during my brief but eventful tenure as the general manager for Majestic Airlines at Logan. The murky circumstances of my departure from that job had left me virtually unemployable in the airline business. The circumstances weren't murky to Dan, and he had worked hard to help me get started in my new life as a private investigator. He knew a forensic accountant who had done some financial work for him in the matter of his divorce from his lunatic ex-wife. Harvey Baltimore needed a partner with fresh legs, or . . . just legs. I needed work. Dan had made the match.

"She was *macking* on him?"

"Sitting on his lap," I said, "right there in his wheelchair."

"Woo-*hoo!* Harvey's getting some. Good for him."

"I don't know about that." I was stuck behind a belching bus, so I started plotting a lane change. "But if I hadn't interrupted them . . ."

"I wonder if he can still do it."

"If you want to know that, you'll have to ask him yourself."

"Is she hot? She never looked hot in that picture he's got. She looked like a girl in my catechism class in ninth grade."

"Rachel is Jewish."

"Yeah, but with that long, wavy dark hair parted down the middle, she looked just like Katey Ellen O'Meara."

"She doesn't look anything like that now. She looks like a tomboy." The Volvo next to me was lagging in the pace, so I nosed the Durango in front of him. "She has really short hair . . . no makeup . . . basketball shoes."

"It's hard to look hot in high-tops." I heard his phone ringing, the one that wasn't cellular, and realized I had caught him in a rare moment in his office. Usually, he was out walking his operation, monitoring the ticket counter, or lifting tickets at the gate. The labor agreement prevented him from performing the union's work on the ramp. That didn't keep him from telling them how to do it.

Molly's voice floated in from the background. "You're late for your ten-thirty, Danny. Get your ass over to Mass-port before they call me again." She hadn't changed a bit since she'd been my assistant.

"Tell Molly I said hi."

There was a pause. "She says to get off the goddamn phone and let me get to my meeting."

"Just start walking. That's what cell phones are for."

His sigh was long and loud, but he didn't hang up. I heard his footsteps echoing down the long hallway, the marked change as he opened the heavy door and emerged into the Majestic concourse, and then the noise of airline travel—thick and anxious and harried and, every now and then, joyous again. I still missed it.

"What do you want, Shanahan?"

"I want to know what you know about this woman."

"Who, Rachel? Not a fucking thing. I never under-stood how those two got together in the first place."

"They met when he was working on an insurance fraud case. She was his contact in accounting at the insur-ance company here in Boston. He saw her, he fell in love, and he never went back to Baltimore. After that, as far as I can tell, he devoted every ounce of his being to her per-sonal and professional fulfillment. He helped her get her CPA, he helped her get a job with one of the big six ac-counting firms, they got married, and I have no idea if it was quid pro quo. Having met her, I wouldn't be sur-prised."

"Did you ever see the asshole she married? He's fif-teen years younger than Harvey, he can still walk, and from the looks of him, he probably fucks like a bull."

"You met Gary?"

"No, I saw him. It was when Harvey was working on my case. I never told you this?"

"Nope." I could feel one of Dan's stories coming on.

"I'm over there in Brookline for a meeting with Harvey. This was maybe five years ago. I drag him out to the taco place for lunch. I'm telling him how my ex is trying to screw me to the wall. He looks over my shoulder out the window, and I think he's bitten down on a jalapeño or something. Turns out he's looking at this cocksucker standing out on the sidewalk talking to some other guido. What's his name? It started with an *R*, or maybe an *F*."

"Ruffielo."

"Yeah. I thought Harvey was going to cry right there in the restaurant. They live in his neighborhood, you know. He probably has to see him all the time. Poor guy."

"Not anymore." I rolled forward about one car length before we stopped again. "They moved."

"Let me ask you something, Shanahan. What the fuck did you call me for? You already know more about these two than I do."

"Well . . ." That was a good question. "I don't know. I'm sitting in traffic heading down to Quincy, and I guess I wanted to talk to someone about Harvey."

"What the fuck's in Quincy?"

"Rachel's family photos and some jewelry. She says her husband's abusive, she's afraid of him, and she needs someone with a firearm to go down and get her stuff out of their house."

"What if you run into him?"

"As I said, someone with a firearm. It wouldn't be so bad, though, if I got a chance to talk to Mr. Rachel. I would feel a lot better if I knew he was beating her."

"Excuse me?"

The traffic had spaced out a little, so I had to pay more attention to what was in front of me. "I just want to know if she's lying. I don't want her to break Harvey's heart all over again. I mean, if she didn't want to take care of him before, why would she come back now that he's sicker? What do you think she wants?"

"It's none of your business, Shanahan."

"Yes, it is. If she's lying to him—"

"You'll what? Smack her around?"

"No, but—"

"Jesus Christ, the guy is on his last legs."

"He's not." The car in front of me stopped. I hit the brakes and lurched forward against my seat belt. "With his medication and his therapy—"

"He's gonna die, Shanahan. Let him have a little fun before it's too late. I gotta go." *Click.*

I snapped the phone shut and tossed it onto the seat next to me. Dan wasn't a doctor. He liked making these proclamations. He wasn't as close to the situation as I was. It wasn't until I heard the horns—long, loud, and angry—that I realized the cars in the lanes around me were flowing smoothly. I was the only one standing still.

Streets in Quincy were much like those in Boston—all one way the wrong way, rotaries to send you flying off in the wrong direction, and street signs that were either nonexistent or well concealed.

After multiple wrong turns, U-turns, and several minutes craned over the steering wheel, squinting through the windshield, I found Rachel's house. It was one in a row of tightly packed two-story boxes with painted siding, tiny yards, and concrete porches. Some had the side-by-side front doors that marked them as two-family homes. Some had front yards fenced with chain link. All had burglar bars on the windows. Rachel's address, 134 Concord, was one of the doubles.

Parking was no easier to find. I ended up at a meter two blocks down on the busy street that crossed Rachel's. I got out and walked past gas stations, liquor stores, pizza joints, and a White Hen Pantry, the local version of 7-Eleven. It was a long way from the large homes and tree-shaded boulevards of Brookline.

On the way to Rachel's front door, out of habit, I looked closely at every parked car. I looked at all the windows in the facing houses. I looked for anyone or anything that didn't belong. It was no comfort that I seemed to be the only one in that category.

No one answered the door at 134 Concord, which didn't surprise me, given how dark that side of the house was. I walked around to the back. All of the windows on Rachel's side had the blinds closed. I looped back to the front door. When no one answered another knock, I slotted the key Rachel had given me into the lock. It wouldn't turn.

I pulled it out, pushed it back, and was trying again when the door at 136 swung open, and a blond teenage girl poked her head out. "Who are you?"

In spite of her droopy eyelids, she managed to look nervous. She had good reason to be wary, because it wasn't even noon, and she was stoned. Her pupils were pinpoints, and the fragrance of the hemp floated out from behind her. I could hear the sound of more like her inside, chattering and laughing, their voices loud over the sound of some kind of reggae rap music.

"I'm not a cop," I said.

"*What?*"

I looked down at the useless key in my hand. "Could I ask you some questions?"

Her eyes were less droopy now. "What about?"

"You can come out, or I'll come in, but if you don't close the door, the whole neighborhood's going to get high. I'm not here to hassle you."

She glanced behind her as she stepped out, pulling the door closed behind her.

"Thank you," I said. "What's your name?"

"Kimberly."

I told her who I was and showed her my license. She didn't seem impressed. "Do you know where the Ruffielos are?"

"I had nothing to do with it. I didn't see her. I didn't hear her—"

"Who are you talking about?"

"Rachel."

"What about her?"

"I went out to party, I came home, and she was gone, and all her stuff was gone, and on account of that I got grounded for a month. It wasn't my job to watch her."

"Are you saying she moved?"

"She snuck out in the middle of the night with three months' rent due. My mom had a freaking attack when she got home and found out."

I started to feel an I-told-you-so come on, which made me feel alternately smug about Rachel and sad for Harvey. "When did she leave?"

"I don't know. Maybe a week?"

"What about her husband?"

"Gary?" A seductive smile crossed her face, and I got a whiff of something unseemly. "He left three days after school started." Which would have been September, almost eight months ago. It was interesting that she remembered it to the day.

I checked the address on the door. I looked at my

scribbled notes. I looked at Kimberly. "That means no one lives here?"

"It's empty."

"Any idea where Rachel moved to?"

"Don't know. Don't care." She had fallen back into that state of mellow induced by the weed, and perhaps thoughts of Gary.

"Why not?"

"Because she was a stone-cold bitch, always pounding on the wall and yelling at me to be quiet. Before Gary left, they made more noise than I did."

"Doing what?"

"Fighting. All the time."

"She told me Gary abused her," I said. "Does that sound right?"

She let out a harsh laugh, one that was much too knowing for someone her age. "The other way around, maybe. Gary's a sweetheart. He was always doing for her, or trying to. She was the one always yelling at him and putting him down." Kimberly had been slowly drifting toward the door. She wanted to get back to her party. "Can I—"

"Yeah, just one more second." I held up the key Rachel had given me. "I would like to get inside to look around. Any ideas on how I can do that?"

"My mom had the locks changed."

"You're mom's the land—"

"You can't talk to her. You can't." It wasn't up for discussion.

"I won't tell her anything. I just need—"

"No, she's working, and she doesn't know any more than I do. But there's—" She crossed her arms, rolled her head back, and went all teenager cagey. "If I give you something, will you go away and promise to leave us alone?"

"Yes."

"Wait here."

She went inside, reached up next to the door, and came out with a set of keys on a ring. She held up the one marked with a blue rubber rim. "These are the new keys. You can go in and look around, but you have to promise—"

"I won't say anything."

"Just leave them inside, and don't lock the door."

I reached for the ring and nearly had my arm severed by the force of the slamming door.

It was, indeed, the blue key that unlocked the front door. I flipped on the overhead light and beheld the empty space. It looked like a place that had been quickly abandoned, which was to say dirty. Dust bunnies floated around the empty hardwood floors, and something in the musty air made me sneeze. Bent nails and long gashes marked where pictures had hung on the walls—walls that throbbed from the pounding beat of the party next door. Rachel might have been a bitch, but she hadn't been wrong about the noise.

A quick spin through the upstairs bedrooms turned up nothing but a couple of lonely wire coat hangers in one of the closets and an explanation for what was making me sneeze. There was a cat litter box in the bathroom. Also a used bar of soap in the shower and a bunch of balled-up tissues and used Q-tips, which might have been of interest if I were a forensic scientist with a lab. As it was, it pissed me off all the more to be looking at Rachel's trash. Needless to say, there were no family photos or jewelry to retrieve. There was no abusive husband. There was nothing that even remotely resembled the story Rachel had told.

By the time I got downstairs and found all the kitchen cabinets standing open, there was no force on earth that could have kept me from going through and slamming every one of them. Childish but necessary. The same for kicking the large garbage bins in the alley that turned out to be empty as well.

I went back inside, through the house to the front room where the window looked out on the street. I split the blinds to peek through. There was a black sedan parked halfway down the block that hadn't been there when I'd come in. It had two guys in it and was just nondescript enough to be cops. Maybe that's what she was doing. Maybe I was supposed to be a decoy.

The small scope I carried on my key chain was about the size of a large pocketknife. I used it to find the sedan's license plate and copied the number in my notebook.

I had to call Harvey, but first I had to think of a delicate way to explain to him that the woman he still cared about was, and probably always had been, a scheming bitch. I pulled out my phone, stood in the front room, and stared at it. I went and stood in the kitchen and stared at it some more. Then I sat on the stairs with my chin in my hand and thought some more. There just isn't much to work with in an empty house when you're trying to stall. I put the phone away. This was news better served up in person.

3

IT WAS LATE AFTERNOON WHEN I PULLED UP IN FRONT OF Harvey's house. I went up the front steps juggling two cups of hot brew from Tealuxe and searching for the front door key. But I didn't need a key. I didn't even need to twist the knob, because the door was closed but not latched. I cursed Rachel for her careless indifference. She had to have been the one to leave it open, because Harvey never would.

Another thing he never did was listen to music, but when I pushed the door open, instead of the usual hospital-grade silence, I was greeted with a big, muscular blast of Motown. The music was loud but distant, echoing through the halls and around the corners of the old house. It was so jarring and unexpected I just stood in the foyer and listened. It was the Temptations singing "Since I Lost My Baby," and it was coming from upstairs, the part of the house Harvey didn't occupy. The part of the house no one occupied.

"Harvey?"

I pulled the door halfway closed and strained to hear his voice or his cough or the sound of his wheels rolling across hardwood. I got nothing but big horns, lush violins, and immaculate backup vocals. I didn't like the feeling.

"Harvey, are you here?"

The last time Harvey had failed to answer my call was the day he fell down in the shower. I found him there, staring straight ahead, with blood and cold water dribbling down his face. He had hit his head in the fall. After being briefly unconscious, he had come to, but without the strength to get up, or even to turn off the water. It had run so long the hot water had run out. That was the day he quit flirting with the wheelchair and surrendered for good. This felt different.

I set the tea on the floor in the foyer, slipped the Glock out, and did a press check. I didn't like pulling the thing out—ever—but nothing about the day had turned out the way I'd expected, and I couldn't shake the feeling that Rachel had opened the door and let something bad blow into the house. The music was giving it voice. A house filled with dance music was such a departure from the way Harvey usually lived. It gave me the feeling he was already gone. I put the thought aside, left the door open, and moved in, staying close to the walls.

David Ruffin's voice, silky and forlorn, drifted through the house as a bead of sweat squeezed out from between my palm and the gun's grip. It ran straight down the inside of my forearm as I got ready to make the corner into the living room.

> *The birds are singing and the children are*
> *   playing,*
> *There's plenty of work and the bosses are paying*

You looked at Harvey and thought polka. Maybe Perry Como if you wanted to stretch it. Not James Brown or

Marvin Gaye or Curtis Mayfield, and certainly not Isaac Hayes. But that's what I had found the day I'd come to help him move his life downstairs. I had sat on the floor, cross-legged, flipping through his LPs until he'd called me on my cell phone from downstairs. When I'd told him what I was doing, he didn't say anything for a long time. Then he told me to put them back, to leave the records as I had found them. As far as I knew, that's where they had stayed, and that's where the music was coming from now—what was supposed to be an empty room upstairs.

I turned into the doorway, trying to stay under control, and scanned the front room. It was a seldom-used space with blinds perpetually closed. Nothing was moving or out of place, so I kept going.

The kitchen gleamed in the bright light of the cheap old onion-shaped fixture that hung overhead. The frosted bowl had a couple of bug corpses lying inside. I'd never seen them because the single small bulb over the stove was what usually lit that room. Harvey wasn't in there, either.

He wasn't in the dining room or his office. I checked his downstairs bedroom suite last, hoping to find his bathroom door closed. It was open. The light was off.

I was coming down the hall toward the stairs when I spotted his wheelchair. It was at the bottom of the steps, and it was empty. The song finished, and the house went quiet. I stared up at the ceiling, listening for the sound of footsteps or voices, but everything I could hear was closer in: the dull, incessant drone of Harvey's air purifier, the ticking of the old mantel clock, the one his great-grandfather had made in Poland. Harvey wound it every day. My own coils were wound pretty tight as I waited and listened.

The intro beat began, then the violins . . . and the

voice again. I had no idea whether Harvey had a record
player with automatic replay. If he didn't, then someone
had lifted the needle to start the song again, the same
song, and it wasn't Harvey. Harvey couldn't make the
stairs.

My heart felt massive. It was pumping hard, pushing
me forward and back on alternate beats. The stairwell
was empty as far as I could see, but that was only halfway
up. I took the first step. My foot caught on the second,
and I nearly pitched forward. The climb lacked grace, but
it was fast as I made my way to the first landing. I
stopped there. The music felt denser up there, and it was
loud enough that I couldn't hear anything else. All of my
other senses went into overdrive, overcompensating for
what the thick wall of sound took away. If someone came
at me, I would have to see him or smell him. I wasn't
going to hear him.

I took the final flight two steps at a time. Once I
started going again, I couldn't stop. I reached the upstairs
hallway and just kept moving. All the doors were closed
except the one at the end. It was the room where I had
left the boxes of albums.

I stopped short of the door and held with my back to
the wall for maybe a second. Then I dropped into a low
crouch and turned into the doorway. I was so wound up I
almost hoped for a reason to fire, for something to empty
the clip into. But there was nothing to shoot at in that
bare space, just stacks of boxes along one beige wall and
an empty canvas folding chair.

I took a couple of steps into the room. A few of the
boxes had been pulled out into the middle of the floor.
One had the lid off. The LPs inside were stacked neatly.
Another served as a stand for the turntable. The needle
was gliding across a 45. An extension cord snaked be-

tween two big speakers that, last I'd looked, had been gathering dust in a closet. Someone had obviously wired everything up. It could have been Harvey. Maybe Rachel had helped him up the stairs. She didn't seem substantial enough to do it, but I was probably underestimating her.

When I reached down to lift the needle, I caught movement in the doorway to my left. I was hoping for Harvey but taking no chances. As I turned, I raised the Glock. The man coming through the door wasn't Harvey. He had a handgun. That was what I noticed as he dropped to one knee and pointed it at me. He didn't shoot, which was good. He yelled, which confused me. He pointed at me and then at the floor and yelled even louder. Another man came in right behind the first. He pointed his gun at me, and things started to slip out of control. I was sure he was about to put at least two rounds into my chest. But then I looked at what he was showing me with his other hand. Then I knew what they were yelling and why, and I couldn't get my hands up fast enough.

The first man skittered in closer, dancing back and forth as if I were on fire. "*Drop* the weapon. *Drop it!* Put it down. Do it *now.* I *will* shoot you!"

He was so hyped I was surprised he hadn't already. Very slowly, I got down on my knees and set my gun on the floor.

"Face on the floor." He grabbed me by the shoulder and yanked me forward. "*Now. Right now!*"

I went down flat on my belly with my arms out, mashed my cheek to the floor, and tried to figure out what the FBI was doing in Harvey's house.

4

THE MUSIC HAD BEEN OFF FOR A WHILE, BUT IT WASN'T gone. It hung in the air and stayed in my head, the aural afterimage pulsing and pounding. It was possible it would always be there, forever burned into my consciousness by the hot blast of adrenaline that had accompanied it.

We were in Harvey's office. Special Agent Eric Ling of the FBI sat across from me with his laptop balanced across his knees. The tea service Harvey and Rachel had shared that morning was between us: two delicate china cups on saucers, the pot, two spoons, and a bowl of sugar. One of the cups had lipstick on it. Rachel hadn't even taken time to wash the dishes.

Ling was tall for an Asian man—I guessed Chinese—and though he was wearing traditional FBI garb, his black eyes and smooth, shaved head reminded me of a lynx—coiled and dark, with a propensity for slinking about gracefully. That's why it was so disconcerting every time he spoke.

"We're going to hang here until Lew finishes checking the rest of the house. Are you cool with that?"

He didn't sound exotic. He sounded like a slacker,

someone whose every utterance either began or ended
with the "dude" salutation. Someone who would have
been more at home working the skate rental shed on
Santa Monica Beach than sitting across from me in
Harvey's office, typing into his laptop.

Something he saw on his monitor drew a mellow
smile. "Wi-fi *rules*, man."

According to Special Agent Ling, he and his partner,
Special Agent Lew Southern, had drawn their weapons
and entered the house when they found the front door
open and no one responded to their calls. He was careful
to point out that they had identified themselves. They
had done a search, much as I had, but instead of finding
an empty wheelchair had found an armed woman.

It hadn't taken long to get things sorted out. I was who
I said I was, and I had a carry permit. They were looking
for Harvey. I was still waiting to find out why.

Ling glanced up at me. "Do you know that your name
comes up more than a thousand times in Google?"

"Doesn't the FBI have anything more efficient than
Google?"

Dude, "There is nothing more efficient than Google."
When he smiled, tiny pleats formed at the edges of his
eyes. They stood out against the smooth, flat planes of his
face.

"I'm going to try Harvey again." I probably didn't have
to announce it, but the circumstances of our meeting had
encouraged me to avoid making sudden moves. I flipped
open my phone, called Harvey's cell number, got voice
mail again, and flipped it shut without leaving yet another
message.

Ling spoke without looking up from his work. "Maybe
his phone is off."

"It probably is." He could never remember to turn it

on. "But he never leaves the house. He hardly ever leaves his wheelchair. I don't even know how he got upstairs."

"You said his wife was here."

"Ex-wife."

"Maybe she helped him. Maybe the two of them were reminiscing, spinning some old tunes, and decided to go out for a mochachino."

"He doesn't drink mochachinos, and he sold his car a couple of years ago."

"What about her car?"

I sat back in my chair, disappointed and annoyed that I didn't know if she had a car. I didn't know how she had gotten to the house. I didn't have her phone number or her address. I knew nothing about the woman, except that she had suddenly appeared just ahead of the FBI and that she had concocted a story to get me out of the house. Now Harvey was gone.

"I told you she sent me off on a wild-goose chase."

"You also said you found them in a clinch this morning. It could be they wanted a little alone time together."

"He wouldn't have lied to me like that."

Ling said nothing, but he wore an expression I had seen before on law-enforcement types, the one that comes from the deep and abiding belief that everyone lies. He wasn't that old, but he must have seen enough already to know that we were all capable of ghastly things and that lying was the least of them. Maybe so, but . . .

"Harvey wouldn't leave the house without telling me."

"Why not?"

"Because he's a fifty-four-year-old man with the body of an eighty-year-old. Because leaving the house is a big deal for him. Because I'm the one who gets him ready. I'm the one who takes him out. I'm the one who makes sure he has food when he's hungry and medicine when he's sick. I'm the one who gets him a pillow when he's sore and a blanket when he's cold. I'm the one who has been with him a good part of every day for at least the past two years, because there is no one else."

Ling blinked at me. "You must really care about him."

"What?" I had somehow ended up out on the edge of the seat.

"You must care about him a lot."

"I do." Of course I did. I cared about Harvey. I cared about him deeply. I unballed my fists and sat back. But our relationship was more complicated than that, and it had gotten more so as he'd gotten sicker. From the beginning, ours had been a bargain built on mutual need, but over the years, his needs had grown to dominate both our lives, and even though I fought for him and protected him and, had it come down to it, might have even died for him, we were as far apart from each other lately as we'd ever been, and it was because of me. When it came to Harvey's emotional needs, he was a black hole, one that grew ever deeper and more fathomless as the disease grew stronger. Sometimes it made me feel cold and unfeeling to keep him distant, but I also knew his emotional needs could swallow me whole. I had to protect myself. Apparently, Rachel didn't have that problem.

"He wouldn't have gone out without his chair," was all I said. "And he wouldn't have gone out without letting me know. Something's happened to him."

The basement door slammed shut. A few seconds later, the second agent came into the office, wiping his hands with a handkerchief. He was taller than Ling. His craggy face made him look at least ten years older, and he had squints for eyes. He was the one who had thrown me facedown on the floor upstairs.

Ling pushed the tea service aside to make space for his laptop on the table. "What'd you find, bro?"

"Nothing." Southern addressed himself pointedly to his partner, not even looking at me. "The house is empty. No signs of forced entry or struggle." He spoke in a slow and measured way, every word a sigh of resignation. He cocked his head in my direction. "What about her? Did she give you anything?"

"We were waiting for you. Come on in and join us."

Southern came into the office but didn't sit. He ended up leaning against one of the bookcases with his arms folded tight across his long torso. As cold a presence as he was, I was still happy to see him. It meant I was finally about to find out what was going on.

Ling turned his laptop in my direction. "Have you ever seen this man?"

On the screen was what looked like an enlarged photo page from a passport. Pictured was a fifty-nine-year-old man—his birth date was right there—trying to look thirty-five. The face he should have had, the one carved with the chisel of experience and the hammer of time, had been so relentlessly smoothed and polished you could look at it for a long time and never see the man he was supposed to have been. His hair was obviously dyed, his sun-tinted face was remarkably unwrinkled, his teeth were perfect, and he looked out through what were undoubtedly LASIK-corrected eyes.

"I've never seen him. Who is he?"

"His name is Roger Fratello. Has Harvey ever mentioned that name?"

"No."

"What about Stephen Hoffmeyer?"

"No. Who are these people?"

"Possibly the same person. Have you come across any files or records with either name?"

"Never."

"Does he keep files anywhere else?" Southern lobbed his question in from across the room. "An archive? Extra storage that you might not know about?"

"I would know about anything Harvey was involved in." I directed my answers to Ling. Southern made me nervous. "I told you, there's nothing that goes on here that I don't know about."

"You wouldn't have known about this. This all went down before your time."

"How do you know what my time has been?"

He nodded toward his laptop. "You haven't exactly kept a low profile since you've been in Boston."

Right. Google, more than a thousand hits, and wi-fi *rules*, man. "What is it that happened before my time?"

"Roger Fratello was the chairman and CEO of a firm called Betelco."

"I've heard of it." I felt a tiny bubble of confidence from having recognized at least something. "It was an electronics firm that went **bust** after the boom."

"They went bust," Ling said, "because Fratello embezzled all the firm's money."

"I never heard that part." I thought they were just one more start-up with no real product, no real market, and too much unearned investor confidence.

"Not many people knew the whole story."

"He raped that company," Southern said. "Turned it inside out and took everything except the potted plants from the front lobby."

"It was grim," Ling said. "We had the guy cold, but before we could indict him, he left the country. He hasn't been seen since."

"How long ago was this?"

"Four years."

"Four *years*?" I looked at Southern and back to Ling. "Did you get lost on your way over?"

Ling ignored the jab. "About a week ago, we found a safety deposit box in Brussels. Inside was a bunch of stacks of banded U.S. currency. We think it's some of the money Fratello used to flee the country. His fingerprints were all over it."

I shrugged at Ling, waiting for the punch line. Southern was the one who dropped it. "So were your partner's."

"My partner's what?"

"Your partner's fingerprints were right there on the cash with scumbag Fratello's."

Ling and Southern both stared at me. It was so quiet I almost longed for the Temptations. "You're thinking what? That Harvey gave this man money to flee the country?"

Ling looked as if he hoped I could explain it. Southern looked as if he hoped I couldn't.

"What would his motive be?"

"I was going to ask him that." Ling turned the laptop back to face him and started tapping offhandedly at the keys. "I thought maybe it had something to do with the ex-wife."

"Ex-wife?"

"She was Betelco's auditor."

"Rachel was Betelco's auditor?"

"She was the partner on her firm's Betelco account." Ling was looking at me now, watching for reactions as he dribbled out his bits of crucial and surprising information in his casually calculating way. His words didn't come spewing at you like rounds from a machine gun or ripping through the atmosphere like bolts of lightning. They drifted out and bobbed lazily like a raft on a turquoise ocean. If you didn't watch out, he could lull you to sleep. I stood up and started moving around. I didn't want to fall asleep. I wanted to start back at the beginning. "Roger Fratello embezzled money from Betelco."

"That's right."

"He took that money and left the country."

"Correct."

"And now, four years after Fratello disappeared, you've found a bunch of cash with Harvey's and Fratello's fingerprints on it."

"All true."

"Rachel Ruffielo, the woman I told you showed up here this morning and sent me on a fool's errand just before Harvey disappeared, was Betelco's auditor?"

"She was the partner on her firm's Betelco account."

"Which means she knew Fratello."

"She worked with him closely."

"Was she involved in the embezzling?" It wouldn't have surprised me one bit. "How could she not have been? If what you say about Betelco is true, she was either involved in the fraud or the world's worst auditor."

"We can't prove any involvement on her part."

"And yet you're trying to connect Harvey to Fratello through Rachel."

"It's the prints on the money that connect him, and so far, the facts say that Harvey helped him run, not Rachel." Ling looked as if he felt bad about the whole situation. Somehow, I didn't think he really did.

"First of all, that makes no sense. Second"—I ended up behind the wingback, leaning over its high back—"Harvey's prints on that money prove nothing. Harvey is a forensic accountant. He handles money all the time, and you can't tell when he might have handled those bundles or for whom. Third, Rachel did this. I don't know how, and I don't know what, but things started to go sideways the second she walked through the door this morning."

"Things went sideways four years ago," Ling said. He was in the process of shutting down his computer. "Before you were on the scene."

"So?"

"Think about it. The ex-wife showed up just after the money was found in Brussels and just before we got here, and now the two of them are gone." He stood up and tucked his computer under his arm. Southern had already headed for the door without bothering to say goodbye.

"What are you saying?"

"Sometimes we don't know people as well as we think we do."

"You're wrong about Harvey," I said. And yet I couldn't shake the image of Rachel perched on Harvey's lap, and the thought of how much it had surprised me. Ling seemed to know it.

"Here's my card," he said. "When he comes home, give us a call."

5

I WALKED THE TWO SPECIAL AGENTS TO THE FRONT DOOR, mostly to make sure they left. Then I went straight back to Harvey's office, pulled the regular rolling chair from the corner, and slid in behind his desk. The desk was old and well used, and it showed. The brass door pulls were tarnished in the middle where they had been touched most. There was a similar bald spot in the finish on top where he used to lean over his work.

I sat for a moment to collect myself. I was trying not to freak out. Ling was right about one thing: there was absolutely no sign that Harvey had been taken by force. Maybe he was with someone he knew. I called Dan at the airport.

"Hey," I said when he picked up. "You haven't heard from Harvey, have you?"

"Since you called? No. Why, have you lost him?"

I didn't know if it was the phrasing or the question that choked me up. I had to take a second.

"What's wrong, Shanahan?"

"He's not home, and the FBI is looking for him."

"The FBI? What did he do?"

"He didn't do anything, Dan. Rachel did something and dragged him into it."

"Jeez, all right. Jump down my throat, why don't you?"

"I'm sorry, but I came home, and his wheelchair was downstairs, and someone had been playing 45s upstairs, and then the feds came in, saying something about a missing embezzler and some cash they found in Brussels that had Harvey's prints, and it happened four years ago, and—"

"Stop, you're making my head hurt. What about Rachel? Maybe he's with her. You said they were making out."

"He might be with her, but not because he wants to be. That trip she sent me on to Quincy was a setup. There was nothing down there. When I got back to the house, he was gone."

"Why would she take him?"

"When I find her, I'll ask her, which brings me to my next point. I need Felix."

"I think he's covering a double."

"Can't you spring him for a few hours? I need him to run some things down for me."

"The guy whose shift he's covering is already out sick, and I've got another one on vacation."

"All I need is for him to run a license plate." The only useful thing that had come out of my visit to Quincy that morning. "He can probably do it between peaks."

"You know that's not how it will turn out. He'll give you what you need, and then you'll have more questions about that, and because he's so fucking good at what he does, he'll figure out a way to get you something else that you don't even know you need, and pretty soon the shift will be over, and I'll have a ramp full of dirty airplanes, a bunch of ticky-tack delays, and a shitload of mishandled bags."

"Dan, it's Harvey."

"Jesus *Christ*, Shanahan. What do you think I'm doing over here? You of all people should know you can't run this operation without supervisors. Son of a *bitch*."

I waited. I didn't know where he was. It sounded like the bag room. Wherever it was, I knew he was striding purposely in circles. That's what he did when he was upset.

"He saved my ass," he said quietly.

This was a hallmark of a discussion with Dan. Just as he often did quick cuts and maneuvers to speed through a crowded concourse, he often did the same kinds of quick cuts in conversation. You had to pay close attention.

"Harvey?"

"My ex's lawyer had her convinced I was hiding assets. Like I've got assets to hide. I work in the goddamn airline business. If Harvey, God bless him, hadn't proved to the world just how fucking broke I was, they would have doubled or tripled my alimony."

Finally, a deep sigh.

"I'll stay and cover Felix for as long as you need him. Give me a few minutes to track him down. But you've got to do one thing for me. You have to call me when you find Harvey so I don't sit and worry all fucking night."

He hung up.

Every once in a while, Dan let his big heart show. That's why I loved him.

Harvey's Rolodex was on the desk. He had no use for Microsoft Outlook. I pulled it over and found the card for Rachel. When both numbers listed turned out to be disconnected, I called information and asked for a listing under Rachel's name. No luck. I turned to Harvey's computer. It was old and slow, with a boxy monitor, but it would still access the Internet, even if it did have to dial in. Harvey and I had subscriptions to all kinds of private information services and databases. I quickly found Rachel's maiden name—Kleinerer—and tried to find a listing under that name. Nope. While I was in the proprietary databases, I searched for and found her marriage licences and her divorce decree.

While those were printing, I sat down with the list of Harvey's doctors and therapists that I kept with me. I went through all of them, dialing the numbers and asking if they'd heard from him. None had. It took a while. Then I checked the major hospitals, worried that I might find him there, but maybe more worried that I wouldn't. I didn't, so I turned back to the Net.

A homicide detective once told me how to look for people on the run. "Focus on three things," he said. "Where they're living, who they're talking to, and how they're funded." With that in mind, I accessed records of Rachel's real estate purchases, pre-Harvey, the names and addresses of her parents and siblings, and other facts and tidbits that might or might not be helpful.

I thought about Rachel's vacant unit and one of the few clues she had left behind: the cat litter box. I got out the phone book and called every vet in Quincy. Of the ones that answered, none had Rachel's cat as a patient. For the others, I left a message saying I was Rachel and that I needed to check on a prescription for my cat. Would someone call me back, please, at this number? Then I flipped over to Brookline and did the same thing. She'd been in Quincy for months. She'd been in Brookline for years, a realization that gave me the best idea of all.

I was halfway out the front door when I remembered the two cups I'd left on the floor. The tea had gone beyond tepid to cold. I took the cups into the kitchen, picking up the tea service on the way. I tossed the paper cups, then washed the pot and the china cups, careful to erase Rachel's lipstick completely. The pieces were too delicate for the dishwasher, and I didn't want Harvey to come home and find anything broken, so I left it all to dry on a towel on the counter.

The Brookline Pharmacy was just a few blocks from Harvey's house. I spent so much time there picking up Harvey's prescriptions that I had gotten to know everyone well, including the pharmacist. Kelly always asked about Harvey, whom she had known when he was still doing his own pickups.

"I need your help," I said to her. "Harvey has taken a turn for the worse, and I need to find his ex-wife, Rachel."

"Oh, no. How can I help?"

"Has she been in recently?"

"I haven't seen Rachel for months. Hold on." She tapped into her computer and stared at the monitor. "We moved her prescriptions to a Walgreens in Quincy. They can probably get in touch with her for you." She jotted what I assumed was the phone number for Walgreens on a scratch pad, ripped off the page, and tried to hand it across the counter to me.

"Would you mind calling? They won't give me information over the phone, and I'm not sure we have enough time for me to drive down there."

"It's that bad?"

I gave her a concerned sigh. She called right away and spoke to a fellow pharmacist. I heard her recite the address of the empty duplex in Quincy. No help there. But she also got two phone numbers, neither of which was the same as any of the ones on Harvey's Rolodex card. She hung up and handed me the notes.

"I hope Harvey's going to be all right."

"Me, too."

Back in the car, I called the first number. Disconnected. I tried the second. When it started to ring, I closed my eyes and squeezed the phone and willed someone to answer.

"Gary Ruffielo." I opened my eyes in disbelief. Hoping and wishing and pure strength of will hardly ever worked. But before I could speak, the voice of the ubiquitous computer woman interrupted. "—is not available to take your call. Please leave your name, number, and the time of your call, and—"

I hung up. Disappointing, but at least it was something to follow up later.

Felix was next on my list. I started the ignition, checked my blind spot, and pulled out into the flow of traffic. I had been trying to cut back on my use of Felix Melendez, Jr., and his black-bag cyberspace skills, but desperate times called for desperate measures. I'd met him on a case in Miami several years before. He'd been trying to fulfill his ambition of working for an airline by taking a job as the breathtakingly underemployed acting general manager at an airport hotel. He helped me on my case, and I got him hired by Majestic Airlines in Miami.

But the airline business went bad, and Felix was a casualty of the cutbacks after September 11, 2001. When I asked Dan to talk to him about working in Boston, Dan had flatly refused. He had neither the inclination nor the authority to hire someone in the days of bankruptcies and billion-dollar losses. I introduced the two of them any-way. Dan liked Felix so much he built a job for him, but it was only part-time hours. That was good with Felix. As long as he was still in the business, he didn't care where he lived or how many hours he worked. It was good with Dan. He had a part-time employee who worked as hard as three full-timers. But it was best for me. I got to use Felix, the smartest hacker in the world, on a contract basis when I needed him. I needed him now. When I got to the next red light, I turbo-dialed his cell phone.

"IIey, Miss Shanahan. What's up?"

Even answering the phone, he sounded optimistic, as if he just knew there would be good news at the other end of the line. It was always good to hear his voice. "How are you, Felix?"

"Great. I'm fixing some handheld radios for the crew chiefs."

"I didn't know you did that kind of thing."

"I don't. I mean, I didn't, but we can't buy any new ones because of the budget, so the only way I could fig-ure out how to have communication on the ramp, which, you know, we really, really need, was to fix the ones that were broken, and that was just about all of them, so I found this site on the Net with, like, diagrams and stuff. Anyway, I'm getting pretty good at it."

That had to be an understatement. Given how fast Felix learned about all things electronic, he could proba-bly build his own radio at this point, if given the tools and the parts. Or maybe just given the parts. He was pretty good at fashioning his own tools.

"I need you to run down a plate for me."

"Right now? Because I'm working a double this after-noon and tonight, and—"

"I already spoke to Dan. He said it was all right."

"Outstanding. What's the plate number?"

"Give me a second. The light just changed, and I have to drive the car again." I dropped the phone into the seat next to me so I could free up a hand to unzip my backpack and get out my notebook. I balanced the little spiral pad on my thigh and flipped through the pages until I found the one I needed.

"Hold on, Felix," I yelled in the general vicinity of the cell phone. I was heading into the short tunnel under Mass Avenue. That little stretch of Commonwealth Avenue required two hands, mainly because the road was nothing but a field of gigantic potholes but also because cabbies liked to fly through it, and they weren't picky about whose lane they did it in. I emerged unscathed on the other side, stopped at the light at Gloucester, picked up the phone, and read off the plate number.

The keys clacked on his end as he took notes the way he always did: straight into his laptop. "The usual time frame?" he asked.

"As fast as you can. Harvey's missing."

"He is? Wow, that's a bummer. What happened?"

I filled him in. "I think his ex-wife might have something to do with it, and I'm trying to track her down. The guys with the plate I just gave you were watching her house."

"Ex-wife? Harvey had a wife? No *way*."

"Way. Her name is Rachel, and they divorced a few years ago. I met her this morning."

"Whoa. If she had something to do with someone taking him, that is harsh."

Harsh was a good word for it. Leave it to Felix to state the situation in the simplest, most powerful terms.

"Does she have a cell phone? Because I could totally track her that way."

"How could you do that?"

"There's a chip inside all cell phones. Most people don't even know it's there, and unless you know specifically how to turn it off, if your phone is on, the chip is on. All it is is GPS technology. Piece of cake."

"How does it work? Caller turns on phone . . ."

" . . . Chip transmits signal to satellite. Satellite transmits location to receiver. Simple."

"Where's the receiver?"

"At the phone company, but that's not a problem. My friend on the network can access what we need." That was the hackers' network he was talking about, a pretty powerful group of guys.

"What you're saying is you need her cell-phone number."

"Big time. Unless she's using a burner. People who know what they're doing usually use those phones you buy at the Store 24. No way to trace those."

Rachel didn't seem like the Store 24 type to me. If that was true, we had another option. "All right, Felix, here's what you do. Query the Walgreens Pharmacy database, and find out what medicine Rachel is taking. Her last name is Ruffielo." That was code for *Please hack in and steal the information.* "Once you get that, call this number." I read Gary Ruffielo's phone number off the note the pharmacist had given me. "That's Rachel's husband. His name is Gary." I spelled *Ruffielo* for him. "Tell him your name is Kelly and you're the pharmacist at Walgreens in Brookline. It's urgent that you get in touch with Rachel because her medicine, whatever it is, has been recalled. Ask him if he's got a number where we can reach her."

"Heh. Sly, Miss Shanahan. Get someone else to do the legwork. I like it."

"Leverage, Felix. It's all about leverage. Call me when you have something on that license plate."

"You got it."

6

BACK IN MY APARTMENT, I CHECKED MY PHONE MESSAGES on the home machine. Nothing but a recorded voice from the Red Cross saying it was time to give blood again. I called Harvey's house and didn't get him. Then I went through the same routine on his cell phone. I thought about calling my friend Bo but dismissed the idea, at least until I had a better sense of what was going on. I didn't want to bring in the big guns until I knew for sure Harvey wasn't at the Coolidge Corner theater catching a matinee with Rachel. I knew that wasn't the case. I could feel in every part of me that Harvey had not left that house on his own. But my Bosnian enforcer friend and colleague was not a resource to be used lightly.

The speed of my DSL connection was liberating after Harvey's poky dial-up service. I started punching the keys, doing searches and cross-references on names and phrases, looking for connections, and trying to find anything that would help me locate Rachel.

The first thing that came up was a piece in one of the smaller trade publications announcing that Rachel Ruffielo had joined a midsize local accounting firm as a partner. This was four, almost five, years ago, so it must have been shortly after she'd left Harvey.

There was a second, splashier announcement three years after that, when Rachel was named managing partner of the firm. The announcement listed several of the larger accounts she had managed during her tenure. Sure enough, one of them was Betelco. The final articles were all about the dissolution of Rachel's firm in the wake of the Betelco scandal. When Betelco went down, it took its accountants with it.

I did a search for *Betelco* and got so many hits I cross-referenced with the name *Fratello* and words like *indictment, embezzlement,* and *fraud.* It seemed that Roger Fratello had inherited the controlling interest of a company founded by his father in 1944. The Lightway Company manufactured parts used to make lightbulbs. Roger found lightbulbs boring, so he used a good portion of the company's substantial pile of cash to go on a spending spree. One of the companies he bought made semiconductors, and that put Roger right in the middle of the tech boom. He took on new investors to shore up his cash position and, when the technology sector went bust, took off with their money. In his wake, he left faked financial reports, fabricated customer lists, and a lot of very unhappy investors.

I searched hard for any reports on the Betelco fiasco that mentioned Rachel. Her company took a few direct hits in articles toward the end, but she was never mentioned by name. Inquiring minds wanted to know where the auditors had been throughout this ongoing fraud. Another good question to ask when I found her.

I hit the enter button several times, stacking up the Betelco articles for printing, then I went into Google Images to see what pictures I could find. Roger and his wife,

Susan, had apparently been quite the presence on the
Boston social scene, back before he had slithered out of
town with other people's money. The two of them had
been regulars at fund-raisers, charity balls, and other ex-
cuses to wear black ties and gowns. Roger looked the
same in all his pictures. More interesting were the pictures of his wife. I put the name *Susan Fratello* in and
found several more recent photos of her. The difference
in the images pre- and post-disgrace were startling. You
could look into her eyes and see that she had suffered
greatly for the sins of her husband. What better source of
information could I hope to find?

I went back to the private databases to see if she was
still in the area. She was not only still in the area, but she
was in the same house in Newton she'd shared with her
husband. I printed out the address. She would be my
next stop.

When I could think of nothing else to search for, I
checked my notebook. Ling had also mentioned the name
Stephen Hoffmeyer as a possible alias for Roger. I put that
into the Google box and got about a zillion hits. When I
tried to cross-reference it with *Fratello*, I got nothing. I
tried a few more combinations. Just when I was about to
give up, I tried *Stephen Hoffmeyer* and *Brussels*, the city
where Ling had found the cash. What I got in return might
have been interesting to anyone, but for a former airline
person, it was fascinating. A man named Stephen Gerald
Hoffmeyer had been one of the passengers taken hostage
in the Salanna 809 hijacking. Salanna Airlines was a small
Belgian carrier that had gone out of business, driven there
primarily by the bloody terrorist hijacking of Flight 809.

I started skimming the articles, refreshing my memory
of the details. Seventy-nine passengers and crew had

boarded their scheduled flight from Brussels to Johannesburg. One hour in, five members of the radical Armed Islamic Martyrs Brigade pulled out ice picks and took over the plane. Unfortunately for everyone, things began to go wrong almost immediately. The plane took a mechanical and ended up making an emergency landing in Sudan. The Belgians immediately ticked off the Sudanese by dispatching an elite military team to take charge. The Sudanese immediately invited in several high-profile terrorist groups, including Hamas, to help with the negotiations. This ticked off the Belgians.

Ten excruciating days later, with only the Western hostages still onboard, the Belgians stormed the plane without permission from the Sudanese government. In the conflagration that followed, seventeen people died—nine passengers and eight hijackers, the original gang of five, plus three that boarded later. The plane was destroyed.

I found a photo array of the storming and the aftermath. It had happened at night, so the pictures of the initial bombing and the fireball that followed were particularly vivid. The pictures shot in the cold and dreary light of dawn were quite a contrast. The grotesquely twisted hulk of what had once been an airplane was prominent. The debris field that surrounded it was blackened.

It was hard to believe anyone had walked away from that, but eight hostages had made it out. I searched several articles for the list of survivors. Once I found it, I checked the dates, then I sat back and tried to figure out what it all meant.

Salanna 809 had happened four years ago. If this was the same Stephen Hoffmeyer whom Ling had asked me about, and if it was an alias for Roger Fratello, then the embezzler had himself become the victim of a terrible crime. He had been caught on a hijacked aircraft, held hostage for ten days, and then killed in the fiery inferno that had resulted from a failed rescue attempt. He had not been one of the survivors.

Talk about karmic retribution.

7

ROGER FRATELLO'S OLD ADDRESS WAS A LARGE WHITE
Victorian down a shady street in the affluent suburb of
West Newton. It had a vast front lawn and a wraparound
covered patio with a wooden porch swing. Susan Fratello
answered the door. It was the same woman I had seen in
those tuxedo-and-gown photos with her once-respectable
husband, plus twenty years and a blue velour housecoat
zipped up the front.

"Mrs. Fratello?"

A small terrier with wisps of brown hair in its eyes
yapped from behind her leg as she scanned the street.
"Have they found him?"

"Excuse me?"

"Aren't you a reporter?" Her voice conveyed nothing
but calm curiosity, a direct contrast to her nearly hysteri-
cal pooch.

"I'm a private investigator. I'm looking for information
about your husband."

"Read the papers."

She started to close the door, but I put my hand on it,
a gesture that made the tiny canine go nuts. He was a

smart dog. He could spring and yap at the same time. Mrs. Fratello stared at me until I took my hand off her door.

"I'm sorry, but I have read the papers. I've done lots of research." I held up my backpack. "It's all in here. But it doesn't give me what I need to solve my case."

"What kind of case?"

"Someone I'm close to was abducted. My partner. I'm trying to find him."

"What does my husband have to do with it?"

"That's why I'm here. I need to figure that out."

She pushed her head out again and looked up and down the quiet street. "Have you seen the FBI? They've been here. And they watch. They're always watching. Did you see them out there?"

"I was questioned by the FBI a few hours ago."

"About what?"

"About your husband. They have some new information about him."

"Down, Trudy. Quiet." The dog went silent. It was miraculous. "What did they say?"

"Perhaps if I came in, I could answer some questions for you as well."

Susan Fratello lived what appeared to be a modest existence in a large house. While she went to change, I perused the photos lined up across the mantel. Her children were handsome and healthy, tan in the summer, red-cheeked in the winter, and always affectionate and close in their poses. It looked as if it had been a comfortable life, easy to be in, and without ever a thought in the world that it could all go away. There were no pictures of Roger.

Susan came in with a tall glass of water. Trudy, the tiny

terrier, was right on her heels, and I wondered if she ever got stepped on or lost in Susan's longer gowns and robes.

I took the glass from her. "Thank you."

She had put on a pair of white slacks, a dark blue, long-sleeved, scoop-necked top, and a string of white beads with matching earrings. She was also wearing lipstick. I sensed that she didn't get many visitors. She sat on her couch and patted her thighs. The springy dog had no problem leaping up there. Then the two of them sat and looked at me. Susan's smile gave her the appearance of one of her photos—posed and two-dimensional.

"I'm sorry," I said, "to bring all this up for you—"

"It never really went away. Besides, you're not the only one. That awful Agent Southern was here. He brought a new one this time. He was completely bald."

"Special Agent Ling," I said. "That's the team that interviewed me this morning."

"That Southern is a sour man. I wonder what makes him so sour. Do you know?"

"I don't." But I had to agree with her. "Why did they come to see you?"

"Apparently, my husband has popped up somewhere in Europe."

"He has?" If true, that put a big dent in the Fratello-as-Hoffmeyer theory. Hoffmeyer was dead.

"They have no proof. They only told me they had found something of his."

"I think I know what that is," I said. "They told me about all this cash in a safety deposit box in Brussels. Stacks of it with your husband's and my partner's fingerprints."

That got her complete attention. "How much money?"

"They didn't say."

"Was it my husband's?"

"We didn't really talk about the money."

Just as quickly, she turned a little glassy-eyed. "How strange this all is," she said, "after so much time has passed. They showed me his wallet. Don't you find that odd? From four years ago. They think he might contact me. That's why they were here."

"Would he?"

"Heavens, no. I would be the last person he contacted. I would turn him in, and he knows that." She offered that same fixed expression. It was strange. At times, she seemed to be completely present behind it. At other moments, she was just gone.

"Who is your partner?"

"His name is Harvey Baltimore."

"How unusual. Is that his real name?"

I nodded, thinking of how Harvey always had to explain his name. "His people came over from Poland. The agents who processed them couldn't say the family name, and they were going to Baltimore, so—"

"They were rechristened at America's doorstep. Yes, I understand." This time, her smile was not forced. Her maiden name was probably something like Kasprzycki. "I don't know a Mr. Baltimore," she said. "I would remember. Is he also an investigator?"

"A forensic accountant."

She sighed. "Unfortunately, I know what that is. After Roger left, I was interviewed by investigators of every stripe. Agents from the Treasury, the IRS, the state's attorney's office, the attorney general's people—"

"But not Harvey?"

"No."

I hadn't considered that Harvey might have been part of a team investigating the fraud. Ling hadn't mentioned it, but that didn't mean it wasn't so. I pulled out a picture of Harvey and showed it to her. "Maybe you know his face."

She looked at it. "He has a nice face. He looks kind." She offered it back to me. "Did you say he's also missing?"

"He's . . . I'm not sure where he is. I'm looking for him."

I put the picture back and came out with the one I had slipped from the frame on Harvey's desk. "His ex-wife showed up this morning. I think she might have something to do with it. Maybe you know her. She worked with your husband." I offered her the picture of Rachel.

Susan looked as if I had just offered her a plate of botulism. Her neck bowed. Trudy, holding otherwise perfectly still, turned her head and looked back at Susan's face. "Of course I know her. She was the ruin of this family. She deserves the hottest corner of hell for what she did to us." Trudy whined. Susan lifted her up to her face and nuzzled her. "Isn't that right, pookie?"

"I'm sorry." I pulled the picture back. "I didn't realize . . . were she and Roger—"

"Sleeping together?" She shrugged it off. "Who didn't he sleep with? It wasn't that." She leaned forward and pointed with a long fingernail at the image of Rachel in my lap. "She brought the Russians."

"Excuse me?"

"Russian *investors*." She did the air quotes. "The Russian mob, the Russian *mafiya*, the red menace. Whatever you want to call them, just don't call them people, because they're not human, they're animals. Those *animals* made our lives a living hell, and she's the bitch responsible for bringing them in."

"Into Betelco?"

"I'm sure you know all about my husband's company."
She still puffed up a little when she described it that way.
"Actually, my husband's father's business—and the source
of our income—that my husband ran straight into the
ground. We didn't know what we were going to do. We
couldn't find any more investors. We couldn't get a loan.
We were desperate when, out of the blue, we found a
buyer for the business."

"A buyer for Betelco?"

"For the old Lightway, actually, the manufacturing
piece. It was an incredible stroke of unearned and unde-
served luck, at least on the part of my husband. A company in Ohio was interested in buying it at a fair price."
The dog, back in her place on Susan's lap, tilted her head
as Susan scratched behind her ears. "It's no surprise that
the only part of the entire enterprise that had any value
was the piece my husband's father had built. But guess
what happened then?"

"I don't—"

"Roger decided that it wasn't enough to get out from
under all that debt. He decided that the small bit of
money we expected to make on the side just wasn't
enough. Nothing was ever enough for him." Trudy's eyes
had turned to slits as Susan began to rub harder behind
her ears. "No, he had to make the big score. He had to be
on the cover of *Fast Company,* and she convinced him
that he could."

"You're speaking of Rachel?"

"The accountant. That bitch accountant. She told him
everything he wanted to hear, that all he needed was a little more cash and that she knew where he could get it
and that the deal with the people in Ohio wasn't good
enough. She talked him into calling off the deal, and once
the buyer was out of the way, she opened the door and let

the pigs come in, and once they were in, there was no way to get them out."

"These are the Russian investors?"

"Investors. Ha!"

"What did they do?"

"What pigs do. They turned our business, our very lives, into their own personal toilet bowl."

She was starting to flush, the heat showing from the scoop-necked shirt up. I hated to push her more, but I needed more facts and fewer metaphors. "Exactly how did they do that?"

"They . . . they brought in dirty money by the boat-load." One of her hands went flying over her head. "They . . . how do you say it? They *pumped up* the income statement. They made up customers. They used Roger to convince everyone he had turned the business around, and when new investors came onboard, they took their money, too, and in the end, when the FBI showed up to arrest them all, they vanished. And so did my husband. He walked out the door and left me here in the *toilet bowl* to *eat* all the *shit* they left *behind*."

The words came out through a clenched jaw, and her entire body shook with the venomous rage that would no longer stay down. That she felt it was understandable. That she felt it so deeply was unsettling. I almost wanted to reach over and snatch the poor animal from her unsteady hands. Trudy must have felt it, too. She jumped to the floor and scurried off.

Without the dog, Susan seemed to have no place to put her hands. She reached around and stroked the hair at the nape of her neck. "They threatened the children." She said it quietly.

"The Russians?"

"After my husband left, they came. They wanted to

know where he was." The rage had dissipated. Now she seemed frightened. "They came into my house. They made us sit on this couch and watch them as they went through here and tore it apart from top to bottom. It was terrifying. We thought we were going to die."

"Why did they tear up your house?"

"They were looking for him, some sign of him. Some-how, I convinced them I didn't know where he was, or we would all be dead, and he would have the blood of his children on his hands along with everything else he's done."

I looked around the house. There were no signs of a violent search. "When did this happen?"

"When he left. Four years ago."

"Does the FBI know?"

"I was told in no uncertain terms that no authorities should ever know. They obviously knew where we lived. What do you think?"

"Have you heard from these Russians since?"

"No." She seemed to remember for the first time that she was without her tiny companion. "Trudy, dear, where are you, sweetie?"

Trudy must have heard in Susan's voice that it was safe to come back. She came bounding into the room and launched herself into her mistress's lap.

"I'm sorry," I said. "I didn't mean to open old wounds. I have just a few more questions." She held Trudy in her arms and hugged her close as the dog lapped at her face. I hesitated, but she had found her detachment again. Her frozen smile had returned. "Why would Rachel bring these people in?"

"Ask her."

Another good question for when I found her. The list

was getting long. "Do you know the names of any of these Russians?"

"They don't have names. They hide behind their companies. TXH Partners and Bonneville Ventures and names like that." I had my notebook out and started jotting down the names. "Don't bother," she said. "They're gone. Those were nothing but shells. Everything is gone."

That seemed like the right place to end. I thanked her for her time. She walked me to the door with Trudy in her arms. I knew the second I was through it, she was back to her velour robe and whatever activities occupied her day. I decided to take one last shot.

"Susan, do you mind one more question?"

"No."

"You asked me when I first got here if I had found your husband. Do you believe he's alive?"

She didn't hesitate. "With everything in me."

"Why?"

"I feel it. If he were dead, I would know it. If he were dead, I don't think it would still hurt this much."

I got halfway down the walk and turned. She was still in the doorway. "If I find him, do you want to know?"

"No. Yes. Please."

I went out to my car and made notes of everything new I had learned. Rachel had been carrying on an affair with Roger. I did the math. Four years ago, Rachel would have been married to Gary. I was just getting to know Roger, but from what I already knew of Rachel, I wasn't surprised that she had been the other half of an illicit relationship. That didn't even take into account the boundaries—ethical and regulatory—crossed by an outside auditor sleeping with her client.

Next item: Russians. I didn't know much about Russian gangsters, but I knew what everyone else knew. They were among the shrewdest, most savage, most conscienceless people on earth. The only surprising thing about Susan's story was that they had not killed her and her children. Ling had not mentioned any Russians, and yet he obviously knew about them. Any decent investigation of Betelco would have turned them up, or at least evidence that they had been there. The fact that he was holding that back had to mean something.

My phone began to ring. I checked the spy window and flipped it open. "Hi, Felix."

"Blackthorne." He never said hello or goodbye on the phone anymore. He was getting to be more and more like Dan every day.

"Are you speaking in code? How come I can never understand you."

He laughed. "Those plates that you gave me? They were on a rental car, and the company that paid for it is Blackthorne."

"I've never heard of it. What is it?"

"It's a private military firm out of Falls Church, Virginia."

"Private military firm?" I thought about what that particular combination of words might mean. "Mercenaries?"

"I don't think so." He paused, and I knew he was scanning his monitor. "It says here that private military firms are a legitimate and growing industry. They contract with the army to provide services the military needs but can't do on its own and . . . blah, blah, blah . . ." He started to hum a familiar tune with no melody, what I liked to call the Felix Thinking Song. It went on for several seconds. I looked out my window at the other houses on Susan's street. The season's new green lawns were just coming in. They were all neatly manicured. By contrast, Susan's looked a little sad.

"Here we go." Felix was back. "Blackthorne was founded by a marine lieutenant colonel named Tony Blackmon and a CIA operative named Cyrus Thorne. That sounds cool."

"What kinds of services are we talking about for the military? Hauling fuel and slinging hash? Because that's not really all that cool."

"Hold on . . . hold on." He mumbled a little more of the Felix tune. "Okay, hauling fuel and meal preparation would be a passive PMF. Passive means providing training and support. Active means providing services up to and including combat operations. There aren't many that are considered truly active."

"Which is Blackthorne?"

"Active." Another pause. "Whoa. *Way* active. It's the fastest-growing one there is. These guys are all over the Middle East, in the Balkans, Africa, South America. Anywhere there's a fight going on and money to be made, you can find Blackthorne."

"What would a . . . a . . . what did you call them?"

"Private military firm. PMF."

"What would one of those want with Rachel?" I thought about it. "Maybe I should call and ask. If there's a private army looking for Rachel, chances are they'll find her quicker than I will."

"Way to leverage, Miss Shanahan."

"Exactly. Do you have a contact for Blackthorne?"

"I've got their main number down in Falls Church, but I called them already, and there's no way to get through the administrative assistants. It's a wall, Miss Shanahan. I've busted through world-class firewalls that were easier."

"Do you have a suggestion?"

"There's a guy in town you might want to talk to. He's a reporter for the *Globe*. His name is . . . let me see. I just had it here. He won some awards for his stories on the Catholic church scandal, and this guy named Whitey Bulger. Who is Whitey Bulger, anyway?"

"Notorious local criminal and fugitive. His brother was president of the state senate."

"State senate?"

"It's a long story. Who is this reporter? What's his name?"

"Lyle Burquart."

When he said the name, I didn't make the connection, but when he spelled it, I knew I'd seen it before. After we hung up, I dug through the piles of printouts I'd stuffed into my backpack. When I found the swath devoted to the hijacking of Salanna 809, I pulled it out and checked the bylines. Lyle Burquart, reporting for the *Boston Globe*. Yet another twist in the road that had already made me seasick. What did it mean that the same guy who had reported on this private military organization also reported on the hijacking of Salanna 809? I had to stop and think about why the hijacking was relevant in the first place. The connection to the hijacking was the name *Stephen Hoffmeyer*. Ling had said that Hoffmeyer was an alias for Fratello. But Hoffmeyer was dead. That was no secret. I had read it on the Internet. So, why was Ling treating him as if he were very much alive?

Maybe Susan's intuition was right. Maybe a woman is the first to know her husband has died, even if he is a sack of shit.

8

LYLE BURQUART WAS AT LEAST SIX-FOOT-FOUR, WITH dark, wiry hair that sat on his head like derelict shrubbery. His stooped shoulders were a perfect complement to his sad, aching eyes. With a gait that was more like a series of connected lunges, he made his way across the WBRS-we-do-sports-better-than-anyone lobby to greet me.

"Who are you?" It wasn't a warm greeting.

"Alex Shanahan. Thank you for seeing me. Can we—"

"What do you want?"

"I'm a local private investigator. I'm working on a case, and I saw in the paper you wrote—"

"What kind of case?"

"Missing person. It's my partner. Can you—"

"Who is your partner?"

"Harvey Baltimore." I stopped there, grateful to get through a whole sentence, even if it was a short one. When he said nothing, I pressed on. "I called the newspaper, and they said you had left and to try you over here. I was hoping I could get a few minutes to talk with you."

"About what?"

"Salanna 809 and a company called Blackthorne. I understand you reported on both."

He took a step back. It put him directly under one of the overhead fluorescent tubes. The unflattering light caught the bags under his eyes and made them look absolutely huge.

"I can't talk to you," he said.

The receptionist was not bothering to hide her interest. I reached out, as if to gather Lyle in, and made a move for a couple of chairs in the lobby, a good distance from prying ears. "Could we just move over here where we can be a little more comfortable?"

There were lots of things going on with him. His jaw was working, and I could hear his teeth grinding. With his elbows locked, he was bouncing the heels of his hands against his thighs. I watched his chest rise and fall at least ten times before he finally agreed to take five steps to his right.

I turned us so that our backs were to the receptionist. "Look, my partner is missing. He's sick. He's got multiple sclerosis, and I'm worried about him. The FBI came to the house and asked all kinds of questions about a man named Roger Fratello. Do you know that name?"

"No."

"What about Stephen Hoffmeyer? Do you know that name?"

I could see in his eyes that he did. He knew it from the hijacking story. I could also see a spark of interest in his pale face. It wasn't much, but I was hoping it could be the thread that unraveled his resistance. I started to pull on it. "Roger Fratello is an embezzler. He ran a company called Betelco. It sounds as if he got into trouble with a bunch of Russian investors and stole some money and disappeared. This was four years ago, right around the time of Salanna 809."

"There was no one named Fratello on Salanna." His voice was tense but controlled.

"The FBI says Fratello might have been going by the name of Stephen Hoffmeyer."

"Why do they think that?"

"I don't know," I said. "They were the ones asking all the questions. Do you think that's true? Do you think Fratello might have been on Salanna?"

"Not under his own name."

"Could he have been Hoffmeyer, in which case he'd be dead, I assume?"

"No. Stephen Hoffmeyer was not an embezzler from Boston."

"Are you sure?"

"I know everything there is to know about that incident. You're wrong about that. So is the FBI, but . . ." He stared at me with the obsessive look of a problem solver who had left the problem only half solved. He was taking this latest piece of data, putting it with everything else he already knew, trying new combinations, and hoping the answer would emerge. But as quickly as the desire had gripped him, it let him go. Or he threw it off. "I've got a different gig now," he said finally. "I can't help you. I'm sor—"

"Wait a minute. You know something else. I can tell. What is it?"

He let out a deeply troubled sigh. "Why are you asking about all this? It happened four years ago."

"The FBI told me that they found a bunch of money with Roger Fratello's fingerprints on it in Brussels. Salanna 809 left from Brussels, didn't it?"

"It originated there."

"On top of that, I just left Susan Fratello. The FBI told her that her husband has turned up again. I don't know where or what the circumstances were, but something is obviously going on. Then I saw these two guys checking out the house of my partner's ex-wife. It turns out they're from a company called Blackthorne. When I looked into it, it turned out you had reported on both Blackthorne and the hijacking. All I'm trying to do is find my partner. These happen to be the leads I've turned up, and they happen to lead to you."

Something about what I'd said took hold with him. He stuffed one hand into the pocket of his corduroy jeans and used the other hand to mash down that thick hedgerow on his head. "Let me think about this," he said as he spun around the lobby talking to himself. "They know I'm here. If they saw you come here—"

"I don't have a tail. I've been aware of that, and I've been checking."

He didn't even look at me. "You wouldn't have seen them. If they know you're here, and they know for sure I'm here, then that means—" He looked at me and let out a sharp and bitter laugh. "That means I'm fucked."

"Excuse me?"

"It's already too late." He turned and swooped one of his long arms toward the wall of windows that faced Soldiers Field Road. "They're out there already, and they're thinking I'm back in it."

I looked where he was looking. All I saw were dozens of cars speeding by in both directions. "Who's out there?"

He put one hand on his hip, hooked the other around his long neck, and dropped his head back. He almost looked as if a weight had been lifted. He cocked his head in the direction of the hallway. "Come on back," he said as he started that way. He was no longer lunging. His gait was far more languid and relaxed. "You might as well get what you came for."

I followed him to the back offices. We had to pass the receptionist's desk to get there. She gave me the fisheye on my way by. She didn't like me. Lyle took us to a control room and closed the door behind us. The cramped space had panels and counters with lots of buttons and dials. It smelled like machines in there and looked like the inside of a cockpit. It also had thick soundproof tiles on the walls to absorb our conversation. He sat in one swivel chair, and I sat in the other.

"What do you do here?" I asked him.

"I host a sports call-in show with my partner."

"Why would an award-winning journalist leave his job at a prestigious newspaper to do sports call-in on the radio?"

"Because I love sports." He gave me a loopy smile. It made me think that some part of him had gone right over the edge.

"Okay."

He checked his watch. "If you want information, ask me now. I'll tell you what I can, but under one condition."

"What?"

"After you leave here today, you will never try to contact me again. You won't call me. You won't come back here. You won't come to my house. Do you agree?"

"What if I have follow-up questions for you?"

"You have to agree to my terms, or I won't talk to you."

"All right. I agree." What choice did I have?

"Good." He sat back and rested his left foot on his right knee. With his long arms and legs, he was all corners and angles. It made him look like the scaffolding on an unfinished building. "Tell me what you know so far."

I went through it all with him again. He listened carefully. When I was finished, he found a pad and pen. He wrote something on the top page, tore it off, and gave it to me. I read what he'd written out loud. "Gilbert Bernays? Who is this?"

"He was one of the hostages. If Fratello was on that plane, it was probably as Bernays."

"Why do you say that?"

"You know what happened, right? How the plane got redirected to Khartoum?"

"I know they took a mechanical."

"The plane had a hydraulic leak. They made an emergency landing, and for all intents and purposes, the plane was dead. It was never going anywhere again until they got the leak fixed, and no one was going to fix it for them."

"They still had the hostages," I said.

"They did, but they had them in the wrong country. They had planned to be in Afghanistan, where they could get advice and counsel from the senior members of the Brigade. If you look at the hijackers who died, the oldest one was twenty-three. That's part of why things spun so far out of control."

"Why did they do it in the first place? What were their demands?"

"They wanted to force Pakistan to release a radical Muslim sheikh named Ali al-Badat. Pakistan wouldn't do it. That's why the thing dragged on the way it did. It was a standoff."

"Who is Ali al-Badat?"

" 'The people's sheikh' is what *Newsweek* called him. He was very popular. The Pakistani army stumbled over him by accident in a Peshawar raid. They had to put him in jail, but they weren't happy about it."

"Why not?"

"Because he had far more support in Pakistan than

President Musharraf did. They were afraid he would cause an uprising against the government. I'm still surprised they didn't let him out. It would have been the perfect excuse, right?"

"I guess so." At the moment, I was more concerned with problems closer to home than a geopolitical debate. "What about Gilbert Bernays?"

"Right. The hijackers needed food and water, so they started freeing hostages. They let the women and children go first. Then the Muslims, then a Frenchman. Eventually, it got down to seventeen Westerners and the eight hijackers. Seven of the hostages were Americans. One of them was this Bernays. I could never find anything on the guy. He was a ghost. No background or backstory. I always thought his identity had been manufactured. Now you're saying he could be this embezzler." He reached up and scratched his right cheek with his left hand. I could hear his nails scraping the stubs of his whiskers. "I think that could make some sense."

"Why?"

"There were stories among the survivors of how he tried to ransom himself off the plane with a laptop computer."

"A computer?"

"He claimed it was worth a billion dollars. They laughed at him, and they didn't let him off."

"How could his computer be worth a billion dollars?"

"I don't know. No one has ever found him to ask him. He survived the storming of the aircraft, and no one ever saw him again. That's why I think he could be your man. And that's all I know." He pushed away from the control counter and started to get up.

"Wait. What about Blackthorne?"

"I won't talk to you about Blackthorne."

"Why not?"

The receptionist knocked on the door and opened it. We both flinched. "Big Man is looking for you," she said. "He wants to know if you resigned and didn't tell him. He needs you on the air right now."

"I'm coming."

Lyle unfolded himself. I stood up, too.

"It's Blackthorne, right? That's who you're afraid of. Did they come after you? Is that why you left the paper?"

"I dug too deep. That's all you need to know. That's all you want to know. But you should know this. If you start looking into Blackthorne in any kind of significant way, you will be at risk. People you love will be at risk. Don't do it lightly." He reached for the door. "And don't ever come back here again."

Back in the Durango, I sat quietly and looked at every car, trying to figure out if there were any I had seen before. If Lyle Burquart had been trying to scare me, he had succeeded, and more. I got out my notebook again. The pages were filling fast. I copied off the Gilbert Bernays name and then started writing in notes on the hijacking. Then I called Dan. When he didn't answer the first time, I hung up and called him again. He was not happy when he finally picked up.

"What do you want, Shanahan? I'm in the middle of an arbitration hearing."

"Let me just ask you something really quickly. What do you know about Salanna 809?"

"Hijacking. Fucked up."

"Have you heard anything about it lately?"

"What do you mean?"

"I'm not sure. It keeps coming up."

"In what way? Wait. Don't answer that. I don't have

time. I'll see what I can find and call you later. Don't call
me again. Hey . . ."

"What?"

"What about Harvey?"

"Not yet."

He hung up.

My phone was still in my hand when it started ringing.
I checked the caller ID and answered.

"Felix?"

"Hey, Miss Shanahan, guess what?"

"What?"

"Someone just turned on Harvey's phone. Do you
want to know where he is?"

9

DJURO BULATOVIC HAD NEVER BEEN TO MY HOME, AND I had never been to his. I didn't even know if he was domiciled in Boston. I knew we were friends, though, because only his friends got to call him Bo, and there hadn't been a single time in three years that I had called for help that he didn't either show up or send a very capable proxy. He was known for his pastel sport coats, but tonight he wore his work clothes—all black.

Bo was an enforcer, a gun for hire, a person who used every tool at his disposal to persuade individuals to adopt his clients' point of view. The first time we'd met, he had wrapped his big hand around my throat and squeezed until I passed out. But that had been a case of mistaken identity. He had been deeply remorseful about strangling the wrong woman nearly to death, which is how I had apparently established my permanent marker with him.

Through me, he had also met Harvey. Harvey did his taxes for him, which provided me with one of the few interesting personal details I knew about Bo. He earned in the mid-six figures annually from Djuro Bulatovic, LLC, which he described as a "consulting company."

Actually, I knew a few more things. He was a big man who came from violence. It was obvious in the way he moved, in the way he always seemed to be looking ahead to the next problem or looking back to make sure the last one wasn't catching up to him. Since he was Bosnian, I suspected he had fought the Serbs as a soldier or part of a militia and probably killed more than his share. He had a soldier's reverence for duty, and he lived by a strict code of honor. Even if he hadn't liked Harvey, he would have considered it bad form to kidnap a man in a wheel-chair.

He opened the car door and slid into the driver's seat next to me. He turned to the back and reported in to his two colleagues, um . . . Employees? Accomplices? I never knew who the men were that he brought along. I was sure Timon and Radik were as strong and fast and skilled at the task that lay ahead as the usual crew he brought.

Bo spoke to his guys in either Bosnian or Croat or Ser-bian. I had asked him one time which he spoke. He said everyone in his country spoke all three, sometimes at the same time. When he was done, he turned to brief me.

"All three are in the kitchen. They just brought food, so they're eating together. No one is standing post." He shook his head. "Stupid."

"Did you see Harvey? Is he in there?"

"He is in a back room on the floor. I saw him through the window."

"Is he alive?"

"I do not believe that three men with an arsenal would be guarding a corpse."

The reference to Harvey as a corpse was disturbing,

but, as usual, he had a point. I had to calm down or at least find a way to channel the energy. I looked through the dark toward the house. Knowing Harvey was in there got me mentally mobilized. My body followed suit. Everything sped up—pulse, respiration, knuckle cracking.

"What's the plan?"

"We take them."

I looked at Bo. "Take them how?"

"Shoot the guards. Find Harvey. Bring him out."

Shoot. Find. Bring. It sounded so simple. "Why do we have to shoot them? Maybe we should just try to—"

"Hit them over the head and render them unconscious?"

I had been about to say "subdue them," but that worked, too. I felt the ridiculousness of that idea, the complete, television-informed naïveté. But Bo didn't treat me as ridiculous. It was one of the things I liked about him.

"To subdue them," he said, "would require that we get close enough to be killed ourselves. Or it might give them the chance to kill Harvey before we can get to him."

"But we don't even know who they are or why they took him. What if they're, I don't know, police? Or some other good guys?"

"They are not the good guys. This much I know." He angled his head and studied me. "You have killed before, killed with your hands."

"The only person I ever killed was trying hard to kill me back."

He nodded sagely. "Then you will have no problem. These men will kill you if you do not kill them first."

"I think I have to know that for sure, Bo. I think we have to give them a warning."

He sighed deeply. I knew he was the expert, but I didn't want him to count on me to shoot a man in cold blood if I didn't think I could.

"We will give them a chance," he said. "It will be up to them. Only if they shoot at us will we shoot back."

"Yeah, but you have to tell them they have a choice."

"Don't worry." He turned and said something to Timon and Radik. Of course, he could have been saying, "Bust in and blow their fucking heads off," for all I knew. I didn't know what else to do. The situation was what it was.

He laid out his plan, first in English for me, then for the guys in back. It didn't seem to take as much explaining for them.

"What about the noise?" I said. "There are people in these other buildings."

"The police will not show up in this neighborhood unless called, and no one will call them over a few gunshots."

He reached back, and Radik passed him a black gym bag. I could tell it was the weapons bag from the heavy, metallic *clank* it made when Bo set it on the seat between us. He unzipped it, plunged in, and came out with what I knew were a couple of clean semiautomatics with suppressors. He offered them both to me. One was a Glock 30, like mine. I took it.

"Be sure to give it back," he said. "Don't take it home."

"What about stray shots?" I looked through the windshield up and down the street. We were in a neighborhood. A very bad one, but a neighborhood nonetheless. Our target was in the middle of the block. The house on one side looked like a boarded-up crack den, but there were lights on in the one on the other side. "We could kill someone in the next house over if we're not careful."

"We must shoot them before they can return fire. You are a good shot. You will not miss. Aim for the—"

"Center of mass." I knew that. I knew how to kill a paper target.

He waited for me to think up still more objections. I couldn't, so I took a breath, adjusted my vest, and gave him the nod. We did a quick radio check. Then the four of us got out and started toward the house. I split off and went toward the back, where I was supposed to watch through the window and make sure they were in the kitchen where Bo's reconnaissance had left them. I was also supposed to cover the door in case any of them got flushed out that way. It was the easiest assignment, which was fine by me. Timon and Radik were going in through the garage entrance. Bo was going through the front door, right up the middle.

I slipped around and started creeping along the side of the house. I had to go slowly, because it was so dark and I didn't dare risk using the flashlight. The stink of garbage wafted up as I maneuvered around the trash cans. Where there was garbage there were rats, so I tried to prepare myself for any unexpected movement at foot level. I got to the backyard and cruised along the fence line until I got as far in as the crumbling brick planter Bo had told me about. It marked the far boundary of a cracked and pocked patio, which meant it wasn't too far out from the back of the house. I had to be careful. I moved in behind it and made myself as small as I could. Then I peeked over the top to look through the back window.

The blinds were closed. Damn. They must have just closed them.

"Blinds closed," I whispered into the radio. "Moving closer. Hold on."

I turned the radio down and crawled on my belly back to the fence and toward the house. When I got there, I flattened against the back wall. As I inched toward the window, I could hear them. There were two distinct voices. They were speaking something besides English. It sounded Slavic and guttural. There was a sliver of space between the sill and the lowest blind. I crept close enough to get my eyeball to the window to look inside the house.

There were two in the kitchen, not three. The one closest to me was balding. He wore the long and greasy strands of his remaining hair in a mutant ponytail that sat too high on the back of his head. The bigger man had on a black Judas Priest T-shirt. He was Bo-sized, if not larger. He was talking on his cell phone, holding the tiny silver device against his massive head. Bo had declared him the priority. I could see why.

I crept back to the cover of the crumbling wall, turned up the radio, and gave my report. "Two in the kitchen in the back. Repeat . . . only two in the kitchen. No sign of number three."

"Positions?"

"Ponytail is standing . . . leaning against the sink with his back to the window . . . facing the inside doorway. Judas Priest is sitting at the table . . . back to the inside doorway . . . talking on a cell phone. Both have their hands occupied with pizza, beer, cigarette, or phone. No third man. Repeat, no third man in the kitchen. Over."

Bo came back. "Third in the front room watching the door and the television. I will take care of this one. On my signal . . ."

I waited. The next thing I would hear would be the go sign. When it came, it was a short but ferocious burst

over the radio that must have been something like *Go!*
Go! Go! in Bosnian.

The shouting started almost instantly. Then came the
shooting. I couldn't see anything, but I could hear. I knew
when the bad guys were firing, because all our weapons
had suppressors. The blinds crashed back against the
window. It must have been Ponytail. Whoever it was,
when he fell, he pulled the blinds down with him. From
my position, it was like a curtain rising.

Judas Priest was hunkered down beside the refrigerator, clutching what looked like some kind of fully automatic, magazine-fed assault rifle. Timon and Radik were
firing from outside the kitchen door. They had him
pinned down, but every time they tried to advance, he'd
step out and blast away. Judas Priest had only one real
chance to make it out of there, and it was through the
back door directly across from his position. He knew it,
too. He kept glancing that way. The only question was
whether they would get him before he ran through it and
right into me.

I got ready.

He jumped out again and laid down another barrage,
but this time, instead of moving back to the safe corner
behind the refrigerator, he crashed toward the door and
opened it, firing the whole way. The second he moved
onto the small concrete patio, both Timon and Radik advanced through the kitchen toward the door. The way he
staggered down the steps made it clear he'd been hit, but
he was still coming straight at me, which meant I either
had to roll out of the line of fire from the house or stand
up and shoot him, but he was still moving with such
power and authority that I had real doubts about whether
I could stop him. An image flashed of me rising from behind the safety of my wall, emptying a clip into him, only

to have him keep coming. But then he saw me and raised his rifle, and the adrenaline surged and instinct took over, and I was standing to take my shot when someone yelled, *"Down! Down! Down!"*

I dropped to my belly behind the wall and rolled. Five straight shots followed, presumably into the back of Judas Priest. The sound of the shots was subdued, like someone blowing five quick darts through a long pole, which is what a suppressor is supposed to do. Make death quiet.

I didn't hear him die. I didn't hear him gurgle or cry out. But he was dead, lying in the yard, facedown with the rifle still in his hand and blood soaking into his black T-shirt. Bo was the one who had shot him. He was coming toward me now.

"Are you all right?"

"Fine," I said, staring down at the corpse. "You?"

"Good. Everything is good. Go inside and find Harvey." He looked around. There was one house that backed up to the alley from which someone could have seen the show. "Go. Go now."

Inside the house, the light that bathed the room was too warm for such a cold scene. Radik was standing over Ponytail. Judging by the blood smears, he must have been blown back against the window, turned; grabbed the edge of the sink, and slumped to the floor.

"We need to turn off the lights," I said. "Anyone can see in here from the back."

Radik didn't understand, so I pulled out my flashlight to show him and flipped off the overhead light. He got it.

With my flashlight in one hand and the Glock in the other, I started toward the side of the house where Bo said he'd seen Harvey. It was a rambling floor plan that didn't make any sense to me. All I knew was that the doors were all closed, and every time I cracked one of them open, I expected to find something bad behind it— either someone coming at me from out of the dark or, worse, Harvey's body. By the time I got to the last door, my heart was pumping out of control and my lungs straining for breath. It was controlled, but it was still panic. I had to stop. With my back to a wall, I leaned over and put my hands on my knees. Generous drops of sweat rolled from my forehead and dripped onto the floor. When I felt a little less likely to collapse, I opened the last door, shone my flashlight across the room, and found Harvey.

He was lying in a heap in the corner, still wearing the suit jacket he'd had on that morning. I stumbled into the doorway, but something stopped me there. It was the sight of him, so still and crumpled, that kept me from rushing to his side, because if I did, if I reached down and turned him, I might find his eyes fixed in a death stare. I might find his skin long cold. Maybe not even murdered, just dead from the stress on his weak system. I was so afraid that I was too late. But when I saw his chest rise, fall, and rise again, I went and knelt beside him. I put my hand on his shoulder and felt the life still in him. He moaned when I turned him. It was the most beautiful sound I had ever heard, and when he opened his eyes, it was a smile that he saw and not just the tears.

"Harvey, it's me. We're taking you out of here. We're taking you home."

He blinked at me, and I knew he recognized me. "Leave me alone." He tried to roll away from me. "Let me go. Let me die."

Not what I expected. It ticked me off. "Goddammit, Harvey, you are not giving up. Not here and not now. Die at home if you want, but right now we're getting out of here."

I grabbed his other arm and pulled him up into a sitting position. His head and shoulders flopped forward. He was in full rag-doll mode. I slid behind him, put my arms under his, and locked my hands across his diaphragm.

"Help me as much as you can," I said, hoping he could—and would. When I finally got him upright, he wasn't steady on his feet, but I needed only a second or two. All in one maneuver, I let go with one hand, slipped under one of his arms, and draped him over my back. I huffed and puffed a few times and lifted. He wasn't as heavy as he used to be, but he was still deadweight, and I staggered until I found my equilibrium. Then I carried him out of there.

When I got to the front room, Timon was gathering weapons into a pile on the floor. Bo was there, standing very still over the body of the third man, the one he must have dispatched when he came through the front. He was looking at the corpse with an expression I had never seen, and I wondered if he knew his victim. Slowly, he crouched and pulled at the man's shirt, baring his chest and an amazing webbing of tattoos that covered him practically from head to toe.

Bo called for Timon. He walked over and looked where Bo was looking, but he didn't say anything. Then Timon crouched, too, pulled out his knife, and did something really strange. He grabbed the dead man's pants at the knees and sliced them open. Timon stepped back, and Bo said something, and there was a rushed exchange that I didn't need to understand to feel the deep concern.

"Bo?"

He seemed almost dazed when he looked at me. "Give me the weapon."

"What? Oh." He wanted the Glock back. "What's going on?"

"You must leave here," he said. "You must take Harvey and leave at once."

10

I WANTED TO TAKE HARVEY TO THE EMERGENCY ROOM, but Bo said we couldn't risk it. He said they would look for us there but didn't bother to tell me who. He said we didn't have time to discuss it and that Radik would take us home and keep watch. Watch for what? The ride home with the sleeping Harvey and the English-challenged Radik was completely silent, leaving me plenty of time to wonder. Also to think about what had just happened. While the adrenaline had been flowing, I hadn't felt much of what I had seen. Now I was starting to.

The bodies. The blood. The smells. I saw the tattooed man lying on his back with both eyes open. They were blue. Pale blue. There was a third hole between them, and there was no weapon in his hand. I didn't have to wonder why. The look on his face told me everything I needed to know. He'd had no warning, but maybe that was part of why we were all still alive and Harvey was in the backseat on his way home.

Or maybe it was just murder.

Bo must have given Radik specific instructions, be-

cause when we got home, he carried Harvey into the
house and put him in his wheelchair, then did a complete
sweep of the inside while we waited in the foyer. Once I
had the all clear, he went outside, presumably to patrol,
and I wheeled Harvey into his bedroom. As I was trying
to work out the logistics of how to get him into bed, he
stirred, and then he opened his eyes and blinked at me.

"Where are my glasses?"

I reached out to pat his jacket. "They're in your breast
pocket. How are you feeling? Are you injured?"

"Just tired. Very tired."

"What can you tell me?"

He looked at me hard, as if he were trying to pick me
out of a Where's Waldo? puzzle. Part of it was the fact
that he didn't have his corrective lenses on, but much of
it, I was sure, had to be due to the trauma he'd just suffered. I wouldn't get much from him before he got some
sleep, but I had to get my basic questions answered.

"Harvey, where's Rachel?"

"I . . . I do not know. Is she not with you? Is she all
right?"

"She's not with me. She sent me to Quincy to an
empty house. There was no husband or jewelry or photos
or anything else. Why did she do that?"

"An empty house?" I hoped that his confused look was
because he hadn't known about it.

"Yes. She moved out last week in the middle of the
night. It seems to me she wanted me out of the way so
that whoever grabbed you could do it without interfer-
ence. Does that sound right?"

"No. Why would she do such a thing? Why would she
have to? I would have gone with her, had she asked."

Sadly, that was probably true. Rachel had to know that.
There would have been no need for the elaborate sub-

terfuge just to get Harvey to go somewhere with her. "Do you know who took you?"

"No. I . . ." He tried to reach up and rub his eyes, but his arm was a little floppy. "I cannot remember much. I have been sleeping."

"What can you remember?"

He looked around his room, as if absorbing the familiar might sharpen his memory. "We were listening to music, Rachel and I, and . . ." He squeezed his eyes shut. One of his arms slipped off the armrest, which caused him to tilt slightly. "She left. She had to go, and then I was alone in the music room—"

"The room upstairs with the turntable?"

"Yes. It was our music room when she lived with me." The thought seemed to relax him, but only for a second. "Someone came up the stairs. I thought it was you, but they put a bag over my head. They put me in a vehicle, in the back of an SUV, perhaps. I was lying flat. I tried to think about how long the trip was, but I was disoriented. I was . . ." His voice trailed off.

"Did they speak?"

"No one spoke. I asked them several times who they were and what they wanted. They would not answer."

I sat on the corner of his bed and looked at him. "Harvey, the FBI was here earlier. They were asking questions about Roger Fratello and Betelco and some cash they found in Brussels." I looked for a reaction. There was nothing but dazed confusion. "They believe you helped Fratello flee the country after he defrauded his company. Is that true?"

"I do not know where Roger Fratello is."

My stomach tightened. "But you do know him?"

"I might. Perhaps a client? I . . ." He looked as if he wanted to answer my questions, but he'd been without food or medicine for hours, and he was fading fast. "Must we speak of this now?"

I gave it one more shot. "Rachel was the outside auditor for Fratello's firm. Could she have been the one involved in this somehow? Is that why she was here this morning? Maybe she was looking for your help?"

"Help . . . yes. But I cannot remember. I cannot . . ." He shook his head. "I cannot go another second without washing the stink of this ordeal from my skin. I must shower."

"I need you to tell me about Fratello. I need details. I need—"

He lifted his hands with difficulty and began to unbutton his shirt. "I can do it myself."

On a normal day, he could have. He had the kind of modified shower with a seat, plenty of handrails for maneuvering, and enough pride that he could still find a way to take care of the deeply personal aspects of his self-care. It was pride and, I suspected, fear that crossing that particular threshold would take him downhill fast. Faster. This wasn't a normal day, but he still had his full measure of stubbornness.

"Just tell me one thing. Do you know where Rachel is?"

He shook his head. I had never had to wonder before if Harvey was lying to me, but I wondered then.

I helped him unbutton his shirt and peel it off. Then I pulled his T-shirt over his head. Without letting him notice, I checked the soft white expanse of his back and then his chest for bruises or cuts. Saw none. I took off his shoes and socks. He unzipped his own fly, and I helped him stand so he could step out of his trousers. It was all very clinical and mechanical until he was stripped down to his boxers.

"Um . . . do you need me to—"

"I can manage from here, thank you." He tried to turn his chair and roll himself to the bathroom. Left to his own devices, it would have taken hours. I pushed him in, turned on the shower, and made sure a fresh towel was in reach. I went back to the bedroom to find his pajamas and robe hanging on a doorknob. When I got back, he was listing to the right in his chair.

"You should have let me go."

"What?"

"I was ready to go." He turned his head slightly. "You should have let me."

I had hoped that his wishing to die had come from the stress of the situation, but he looked like a man who had already given up. I hoped that a shower and a good night's sleep in his own bed would change his outlook. All I said was, "I'll be right out here."

I hung his bedclothes on the inside knob and pulled the door almost closed. The clothes I had stripped from him were piled on the floor across the room. I didn't feel comfortable pawing through them, but maybe they could tell me what he couldn't. Or wouldn't.

There were no coins or keys or wallet in his trousers. Those would all be in the desk drawer in his office. His cell phone was missing, presumably taken by the kidnappers and inadvisably turned on at some point. His schedule of medication was in a side pocket. The only other item was a photograph. It was Harvey in younger, healthier days. He was standing with Rachel at some scenic overlook. The sight of Harvey in sunlight was enough of an oddity, but to see him smiling was stranger still. With his arm around Rachel's waist, he was gazing upon her as if she were some kind of rare hothouse flower. Rachel was gazing at something off camera. The photo paper was soft and fringed around the edges, the way pictures get when you take them out and look at them often. As much as I disliked the woman, he obviously took comfort in seeing her face. I set it on his nightstand, leaning it against the base of his reading lamp so he could look over and see it if he wanted to.

The clothes offered up nothing more beyond the stale and pungent odor of a helpless man stiff with fear. I piled them into a corner and took the medicine list to the prescription stash in the kitchen. I pulled out everything he should have taken and didn't while he was missing. He could figure out what he could skip and what he had to catch up on. I put the pills on his bedside table with a glass of milk, which is what he typically used to push them all down.

For a brief moment, I gave consideration to calling Ling to let him know that Harvey was home. I even took out the business card he'd given me and stared at it. Calling him would have been the safe thing to do, the right thing to do. Instead, the phone rang. Not my cell but Harvey's land line. I went into his office to take the call.

"Harvey Baltimore's office."

"Goddammit, Shanahan, don't you ever return phone calls?" It was Dan. "I left you about a hundred messages on your cell."

"What are you talking about?" I dug into my pocket for my phone. "I don't have any—" Oops. I had turned it off before the big rescue and never turned it back on. When I did, I found seven messages waiting: five from Dan and two from Felix.

"Sorry. We were out getting Harvey back."

"You got him? How is he?"

"A little worse for the wear. I think he's really depressed." I left it at that as I dropped down into Harvey's desk chair. "Did you find something?"

"I've got one word for you. Are you ready? Afghanistan."

"What about it?"

"The U.S. invades Afghanistan, right?"

"We did, yes." I clamped the receiver between my shoulder and ear and began straightening the stuff on the desk. I needed to be doing something.

"In towns and villages and mud huts all over the country, Marines are rolling in through the front door and terrorists are running out the back."

"Is this at all relevant to the case?"

"They're leaving all their shit behind, like bomb-building instructions and maps and computers and memos and all the internal papers and documents and other crap that goes with running an organization, be it an airline or a terrorist ring."

"Memos from Osama?"

"Right, right. Expense reports. Performance reviews. Anyhow, there's this bumfuck little village south of Kabul called Zormat. In Zormat is a house. In the house is a closet. In the back of the closet is a big black Hefty bag."

"If you say so." When the surface of the desk was straightened, I started in on the drawers. I collected a bunch of loose binder clips and put them back in their box.

"Inside this bag are empty wallets, family photos, business cards, a few passports. Nothing of value but things that might mean something to the people who lost them, especially . . . are you listening to me?"

"I'm listening." And trying to refill the stapler. Those replacement strips of staples are hard to handle without breaking them apart.

"Especially if they lost them in a hijacking."

"Uh-huh." I stopped. What? Wait. "What are you saying? Are you saying—" I switched the receiver into my other hand. "You're saying there's a bag in a closet in Afghanistan filled with the personal belongings of the people on Salanna 809?"

"A black Hefty bag."

"From four years ago? You cannot be serious."

"Serious as a fucking heart attack."

"How did it get there?"

"Those shitheads who did the hijacking . . . what the fuck were they . . ." I heard papers shuffling on his end. "Jihads R Us or Jihad Express or—"

"Armed Islamic Martyrs Brigade."

"Those guys, yeah. The ones who took over the aircraft, this was their safe house or headquarters or something like that."

"How did it get there? The hijackers were all killed."

"The ones on the plane. But I told you this thing was fucked up, didn't I? It was a circus. People on, off, on, off. That's how they got their guns, by the way. Those fucking Sudanese let someone onboard who was carrying Kalashnikovs. Stupid motherfuckers. Anyway, one of them must have gotten off somewhere along the way, brought the bag back with him, threw it into a closet, and forgot it was there. You do that, don't you? Put shit away and forget about it?"

"Well, yes, but I'm not an international terrorist." I closed the drawer. Enough cleaning. "Why would they keep incriminating evidence around?"

"I don't think the Taliban gave a flying fuck what these guys had in their closet. Can you imagine the eBay potential for that stuff? Someone is going to make a lot of coin."

I got up and walked to the bookcase, which had been

my next planned stop on the cleaning-and-straightening tour. "This has to be it."

"What has to be what?"

"The reason all this is happening now. The whole thing with Fratello. Susan said the feds showed her Roger's wallet." I started to feel the tingle of a few things finally coming together. "It must have come out of the Hefty bag, and whatever else they found must have led them to that safety deposit box and the money."

"Shanahan?"

"What?"

"I don't have a fucking clue what you're talking about."

"I know. Sorry." I couldn't remember who knew what. The only thing I had told Dan was that Harvey had disappeared. "Roger Fratello is an embezzler. He stole a bunch of money and fled the country around the same time as Salanna 809. I think he was on that plane traveling as Gilbert Bernays."

"Wait, I've got a copy of the manifest. Hold on."

"You have a copy of the Salanna 809 passenger manifest? How did you get that?"

"Majestic used to handle Salanna down at JFK. I know this flight attendant who used to be married to a ramp supervisor down there, and he knew a guy who knew a guy, and I don't know. I just did it. Bernays, you said?"

"Gilbert Bernays."

"Yeah, hold on." I heard pages turning. Whereas Felix's thinking music was a low, steady hum, Dan's was more like a fast rattle, something like "tsetsetsetse," as in *tsetse fly*. "He was in seat 4B. Boarded in Brussels, on his way to Johannesburg."

"Supposedly, he was one of the ones who survived."

"Do you want to talk to him?"

"Why? Do you know where he is?"

"I know where he might be for the next few days. Believe it or not, these Salanna 809 people have reunions."

"The hostages have reunions?"

"I shit you not, and they're *former* hostages. Lucky for you, they're having one this week."

"This week? That's a pretty strange coincidence, don't you think?"

"No. It was scheduled for later in the year, but they moved it up because of a State Department request. State wants to meet with the survivors to give back their stuff. It's happening because of Zormat."

Wasn't everything? One way or another, everything was happening because of Zormat and what was found there. Nothing, I was finding, was coincidence. Coincidence, in fact, was to be regarded with deep suspicion.

"Where is this reunion?"

"Paris. Do you want to go? I can get you in."

"Is it a private affair?"

"It's very private. They don't let anybody in."

I would have asked how he could do that, but the answer was always the same. He knew a guy who knew a guy. "How long is this thing going on?"

"Tomorrow and the next day until noon."

I went back behind the desk and sat down. It had been a rough day, and no matter how good the lead, a trip to Paris in the next twenty-four hours felt overwhelming. Besides, the more I thought about it, the less reason I could find to go there. Harvey was safe, I didn't know what Rachel was up to, and as long as I could protect Harvey from her, I didn't care. Roger Fratello was the FBI's problem. I couldn't afford a walk-up fare to Paris, anyway. That had to be at least a couple grand. But Dan had done a lot of good work for me, as he always did when I asked. I didn't want to just dismiss the idea.

"Let me call you back after I figure out what's going on. Harvey has more to tell me, and I'm still waiting for Bo." I started to end the call but had one more thought. "But if I have to go, you have to give me a break on the fare."

"Jesus fucking Christ."

I would have said thanks and good job, but he'd hung up on me. It was so much fun to push his buttons. I was just about to dial Felix when Bo walked in. I took one look at his face and hung up. Felix would have to wait.

11

WHEN BO LOWERED HIMSELF ONTO THE FURNITURE, IT seemed to sigh. That's what the couch did when he settled his bulk on it. "We have to talk."

"Let me just check on Harvey. I left him in the shower."

"It's important."

"I can see that. I'll be right back." Harvey's room was dark when I got there. He had already managed to get himself into his pajamas and then into his bed. The light that fell across his face illuminated the fact that he had combed his hair and shaved. It appeared that he had also taken his meds. The bottles were arranged next to his nightstand, the milk was gone, and he was sleeping soundly, unbothered by his own loud snoring. I closed the door, leaving it open just a crack in case he needed something.

Bo started the meeting the second I walked into the office. "They were marked."

"Marked?" I sat in the wingback across from him. "Those guys at the house?"

"Yes."

I thought about how he and Timon had checked the bodies with both curiosity and concern. "The tattoos?"

"Yes." He sat with both feet on the floor, one arm resting on his thigh and the other on the armrest. It was an oddly stiff pose. I could feel the tension coming off him in waves.

"What does that mean?"

"It means we never should have taken them." I had never seen Bo regret anything. Things were what they were, and he simply dealt with them and moved on. Not this time. He shook his head. "Never."

"Why not?"

"They belong to a man named Drazen Tishchenko." He looked at me as if I should know the name. As if everyone should know. I didn't know the name, but he sounded Russian, and Russians had already come up in this investigation. Given the lack of sleep and the high stress level, it took me a minute to connect the dots. Betelco. Russian investors. Russian *mafiya*. "This Tishchenko is a Russian?"

"He is Ukrainian. From Kiev. People confuse them, but they are not the same."

"What's the difference?"

"Most people fear the Russians. The Russians fear the Ukrainians. The Ukrainians fear no one."

Worse than a Russian. Excellent news. "Borders notwithstanding, would this guy be considered a member of the Russian *mafiya*?"

"Not a member. A leader. Tishchenko is a *vor*."

"I don't know what that means."

"*Vor v zakonye*. It's Russian. It means . . ." His large forehead showed the effort as he searched for the words in a language not his own. "I do not know how this is said in English, but it is a brotherhood."

"Of criminals?"

"Yes."

"Like the Italian mafia?"

"Worse."

"Is he like a mafia don?"

"Much worse."

"Worse how?" I wished he would just give me the bullet on these guys so I wouldn't have to keep pulling it out of him.

"They come from worse. They come from murder and blood. From the gulags and the work camps. It makes them hard, the things that happen to them and the things that they do. It makes them strong. The strong kill the weak. That is where the power comes from. The last man standing is a *vor,* which makes him a very powerful man."

"And we just pissed one off."

"Yes."

I had one of those how-did-I-ever-get-*here* flashes. I didn't get them much anymore, and when I did, I was able to trample them down. I was here because I chose to be here. But I hadn't signed up for Ukrainian mobsters. I got up and started to pace.

"Those men we killed, the ones who came in here and took Harvey, were they his men, this . . . what's his name?"

"Tishchenko. I'm sure they were. Former KGB . . . Spetznas . . . Russian police . . . Soviet Army. He has all of them. It could have been any of them."

"This guy isn't here, is he? He's not in Boston."

"He is here now. He came to talk to Harvey Baltimore, which is why we found him unharmed. Tishchenko hadn't spoken to him yet."

"Why . . ." I was having a little trouble breathing. "Why would someone like that want to talk to Harvey?"

"I couldn't find that out."

"Okay." I made myself sit down and tried to channel all the energy to the exercise of my brain instead of my feet. "Let's think about what we know. Harvey's ex-wife, Rachel, came here yesterday out of the blue and sent me on a wild goose chase, which got me out of the house and left her alone with Harvey. That's when they took him."

"Do you believe she set him up?"

"It looks that way, but I don't know why she would have. He would have gone anywhere with her if she just asked." A new thought was occurring. "Maybe they took her, too. Maybe they only took Harvey to get to Rachel, or because he happened to be here in the way."

"Why would they take her?"

"It all comes back to this company Betelco. I told you about Fratello, right? This embezzler who disappeared? Fratello's wife told me Rachel brought Russian partners into Betelco."

"There are no such things as Russian partners," he said. "Only victims waiting to be."

"That's pretty much what she said. This Tishchenko must be one of those partners. Maybe he's really looking for Rachel."

"Why?"

"I don't know. I do know that Tishchenko is looking for something or someone. He tore Susan's house apart and threatened to kill her children. And now Rachel is missing, at least to me. Harvey claims not to know where she is."

Bo sat there nodding while I rattled off the facts as I

knew them. I wasn't sure whether he derived as much benefit from hearing them as I did from saying them out loud. It helped me organize the bits and pieces into a coherent story. Well, a story. I sat back in the chair. "Somewhere in all this might be a private military firm called Blackthorne, but we hope not. And Fratello might have been hijacked. That's all I know."

Bo tapped his big fingers on the couch's wide armrest. The thumping seemed loud in the quiet room. He pushed forward on the seat and assumed the tilt of confidentiality. He didn't speak until I did the same. Other than Harvey asleep in his bed and Radik patrolling outside, we were completely alone, yet he still insisted on the cone of silence.

"There is a way," he said. "But it is dangerous, and we must move carefully. You must think about whether you want to be involved with this man."

"With Tishchenko?"

"Yes."

We were very nearly touching noses at this point, close enough that I could see his pores. "Do you know him?"

"We have a professional relationship."

"Then can't you talk to him? He's the one who started this. He took Harvey. He should recognize our right to come and take him back, shouldn't he?"

"It does not work that way."

I hesitated to ask the next question. I wasn't sure I wanted to know the answer. "Are you afraid of him?"

There was no hesitation from him. "I would be a fool not to fear him. So would you."

"What would—" My tongue wouldn't work right. My body, generally smarter than my brain, had already chosen its course. "What would I have to do?"

"We must go and see him. He knows where we are. It is best to go to him before he comes again."

My chest, already tight, was getting to the point of shutdown. "What would happen if I said no?"

"He will come again, but this time he will come for us all."

"Then what choice do I have?"

12

BO HAD OTHER BUSINESS TO ATTEND TO, SO HE TOOK off and left me pacing around the big house. I checked on Harvey several times. He never moved.

Timon had joined Radik for guard duty, so I didn't have to worry about the house being safe. That left me free to devote all my energy to worrying about my meeting with Tishchenko. Before he'd left, Bo said he would set something up for the next day. The sooner the better, he said. Easy for him to say.

I went back to Harvey's office and turned on his computer. It would take a while to get fired up. I checked my watch. I felt as if I'd lived three days in the past twelve hours, and yet it was just after midnight. I thought about calling Dan again but then remembered that Felix had left me two messages. It never bothered Felix to get a phone call in the middle of the night, so I dialed him up.

"Hey, Miss Shanahan. You're up late."

"We found Harvey. He's home, and he's fine, thanks to you. He was exactly where you said he would be."

"That's awesome news. Tell him I said hi when you get a chance."

"I will. I hope you called because you found Rachel."

"No, but I'm working on that. The medicine she's taking is Thyroxine."

"Great." Apparently, the Walgreens firewalls were as porous as expected, at least for Felix. "What does that do?"

"Well, the thyroid hormones, thyroxine and triiodothyronine, are tyrosine-based hormones produced by the thyroid gland. They act on the body to increase the basal metabolic rate, affect protein synthesis, and increase the body's sensitivity to catecholamines, which is, like, adrenaline. An important—"

"Felix."

"It gives her thyroid a boost. Nothing serious."

"Have you tried her husband yet?"

"I didn't get this until a few hours ago. I think it's probably too late for a real pharmacist to call, but I didn't know what time zone he's in because if he's out west, then I could totally call him, or I could have two hours ago. I could call him in Hawaii if he's there. But now it's kind of too late to get him anywhere."

"Sorry, but I couldn't have helped you anyway. I don't know where he is."

"That's cool. I'll just call him tomorrow first thing."

I watched Harvey's desktop laboring to snap to. It reminded me that Felix had a T3 connection. "Are you at home?"

"Yes."

"Can you do a quick search for me?"

"Sure, go ahead."

"Look up something called the *vors*."

"Like V-O-R-E-S? V-O-A-R-S?"

"I don't know." I used the heel of my hand to rub my left eye and then my right. "Throw some options into

Google with *Russia* and *Ukraine,* and see what comes
up."

He started doing the Felix Thinking Song as he moved
through his searches and scanned his screen. It was like
being on *Jeopardy.* I got up and started to wander so I
wouldn't fall asleep. Felix didn't seem ever to sleep. Before he went wireless, I used to find him by following the
cables through his apartment. He didn't own a desk, and
he liked moving around to work, on the theory that some
spots in his living space were luckier than others. The
luckiest spot of all was the balcony. He was probably
there, slumped in a chair so that all you could see from
the back were the tips of his spiky hairdo peeking out.
Dan had made him cut off the bleached tips he had
sported in Miami. No employee of his was going to look
like "some fucking birthday cake." Even without the out-
ward manifestation, Felix was still the accidental anar-
chist, the kid whose irrepressible enthusiasm and daffy
hyperintelligence led him inevitably to places he shouldn't
be to do things no one was supposed to be able to do.

"This is really interesting shit, Miss Shanahan."

Felix had never used to cuss until he started working
for Dan. Since I had introduced them, I felt vaguely responsible for his corruption. On the other hand, the reason I had met him in the first place was that he was a
gifted hacker.

"What's interesting?"

"*Vors v zakonye.* It's Russian for 'thieves in law,' and
they're the real power inside the red *mafiya.* Did you
know that in Russia they spell *mafiya* with a *y?*"

"Thieves in law?" No wonder Bo hadn't been able to
translate. I didn't even know what it meant in English.

"From what I can tell, they're like, um, the Justice
League of criminals in Russia."

"The Justice League?"

"Oh, yeah." His tone changed entirely as he gave his full attention to filling the void in my education. "To be in the Justice League, you have to be Superman or Batman. The best of the best. Not just a hero but a superhero. Green Lantern or the Martian Manhunter. You have to be smarter and stronger and more powerful than the bad guys. Except in this case, they're, you know, the bad guys. The worst of the worst, I guess. Not the Justice League but—"

"The *vors*. I'm following you."

"*Vory*. More than one is *vory*. They live by their own code. That's why they're called thieves in law."

"What are their laws?"

"Um . . ."

I had made it to the kitchen, which was dark except for the dim light over the stove. The china cups, saucers, and teapot I had washed were still sitting on the counter, exactly as I'd left them.

"Well, it goes without saying that you can never rat out one of your brother *vory*, but you also aren't allowed to work. In the old Soviet Union, if you got caught on any of the official work rolls, they'd kill you."

I opened the cabinet where Harvey kept the china service and stacked everything away.

Felix went on. "You couldn't serve in the army. Basically, you couldn't serve the interests of the state in any way. The only way you're allowed to make money is to steal it. Or play cards. Did you know the most revered criminals in Russia were the pickpockets?"

"I did not know that."

"Me, neither, but it's true. And here's the really bad news. Since the Soviet Union fell, the Russian *mafiya* and the *vory* have gone global. They're like Microsoft, spreading their brand of evil all over the world. They can't be stopped."

"Do you see anything there on tattoos?"

"Tons. Tattoos are a really big deal with these people. First of all, you can't just get tattooed with something because you think it's, like, really cool. You have to earn one before you can have it, and the more you have, the more respected you are."

"Like Boy Scout badges."

"Exactly."

"Earn it by—"

"Mostly murder. The other thing is you can also get killed if you get a tattoo you didn't earn. How do you think they keep track of who has what tattoo? Do they have a database or something? They would probably need some kind of a special scanner."

"I don't know, Felix."

"How come you're interested in *vory*, Miss Shanahan?"

"I'm scheduled to meet one tomorrow. I think he might have been the man who took Harvey. He might be a little ticked off at us."

There was a long silence. Felix was hardly ever speechless. It was unnerving.

"I'll be all right, Felix. Bo will be there."

"Oh, I wasn't worried about that. I was just wondering . . . can I come with you?"

13

A PHONE WAS RINGING. THE SOUND WAS LIKE A PATIENT,
persistent worm burrowing ever deeper into the apple
that was my consciousness. The ringing stopped. Maybe I
was dreaming.

I opened my eyes, and I was looking at the elaborate
tinwork that was the ceiling of Harvey's office. What had
apparently been quite an elegant feature back in the day
was just one more thing Harvey couldn't take care of.
The sun streaming in through the east-facing windows illuminated the tarnished and discolored condition. It was
in need of a good polishing or . . . whatever one did to
maintain a tin ceiling. Why had I never noticed before?

I had fallen asleep sitting up. When I tried to lift my
head from the back of the couch, my neck muscles ob-
jected fiercely. I was trying to gather my wits when the
ringing started again. It was my ring tone, but the sound
was muffled. I followed the sound to the crevice between
two couch cushions.

"Hello?"

"It's time to go."

"Bo?"

"The meeting is set. Tishchenko is waiting for us."

Crap. I sat up straight and nearly knocked my laptop to the floor. I'd forgotten about the meeting. That was one of my wits I had failed to gather. "Where are you?"

"Out front."

I wobbled to my feet and peered through the front window. The way the light hit the hood of his silver Mercedes, it seemed pretty early in the morning. "What time is it?"

"Seven."

"*Seven?*" I rubbed my eyes.

"He is a busy man. He will not wait long."

Right. Busy doing what *vory* do at seven in the morning. Maybe getting a new tattoo. "All right. Just give me a second to check on Harvey. I'll be right out."

I hung up and searched for my shoes, black leather lace-ups with thick soles that were kind of clunky and a little hard to misplace. I looked under the couch and behind the desk and found them under the side table next to the wingback. As I put them on and tied them, I wondered what the dress code might be for meeting a *vor.* Jeans, a polo shirt, a windbreaker, and clunky work shoes were all I had to offer.

I found a clean shirt upstairs in a spare dresser where I kept a few essentials. Harvey was facedown in bed with one arm flopped over his head. I couldn't see his eyes, but I could hear him snoring. Next stop was the medicine cabinet. I went with four ibuprofen for my stiff neck and a Pepto-Bismol chaser straight from the bottle. Then I went to the kitchen and poured a glass of grapefruit juice to wash away the filmy pink residue. Feeling marginally fortified, I grabbed my backpack, took a deep breath, and headed out the door to my first-ever breakfast meeting with a Russian mobster.

*   *   *

The name of the café was Grigorii's. It was in a part of
town I had never been to and saw no reason ever to visit
again. Bo got out of the car, straightened his jacket, and
buttoned it. He looked as if he'd gotten himself spiffed
up for his first Communion. It wasn't anything overt, but
he wasn't his usual awe-inspiring self. It made me nervous.

There wasn't much to Grigorii's. It was a dim space
that smelled of bacon grease. The foam tiles that made
up the low ceiling were stained with brown water blos-
soms. The predominant feature was a long bar along one
wall. The tables had no cloths, and the chairs had no
padding or upholstery. It had the look of a campus coffee
bar but the feel of something else. Something defiant and
political, as if the place itself resented even being in the
United States. Almost an entire wall was draped with a
yellow and teal flag, which I assumed was Ukrainian. Another wall was adorned with yellowed newspaper articles
affixed with brittle Scotch tape. They emanated from a
solid center like a newsprint sunburst. I was willing to bet
they were not from the city section of the *Boston Globe.*

Every once in a while, a harsh blast of laughter would
issue from a corner where a group of men who hadn't
shaved in a while sat around one of the larger tables. It
wasn't the fun kind of laughing but the edgy and wicked
and loud kind. There had been an eruption when we
walked through the door.

I leaned in toward Bo. "How do these men . . . how
are women treated in this culture?"

"Not well, but they respect strength wherever they see
it. I know of one Ukrainian hit man who took his wife
along to do his murders."

"Great." I felt much better.

The opposite corner of the place was occupied by a wiry man sitting in a corner by himself reading a newspaper and smoking. He probably knew that smoking in a restaurant was against the law. He seemed to have mighty powers of concentration.

Bo approached the man behind the bar and spoke to him in a language I didn't understand. I didn't know if Bo spoke Russian or if the other man spoke one of the languages from the broken country of Yugoslavia. Either way, they communicated just fine.

As the bartender watched, Bo took the .357 from his shoulder holster and laid it on the counter. The two of them looked at me. I followed Bo's lead and laid down my Glock, which looked puny next to Bo's howitzer. The bartender tilted his head toward the smoking man. We were allowed to pass.

When we got to the booth, Bo did the talking. Again, I couldn't understand, but it felt like some kind of tribute. He gestured first to himself and then to me. I tried to look less terrified and more honored, but it was hard, because at close range, Drazen Tishchenko was a terrifying man.

He looked to be in his late forties or early fifties, with a face made by God but substantially rearranged by man. His nose was too thick, his mouth was a grim, crooked line, and his ears seemed to be too low on his head, as if someone had grabbed them by the lobes and yanked. Most disturbing were the tattoos. They slithered out from under the collar of his tight black V-necked sweater, up both sides of his neck, and into his hairline. They covered both his forearms and even his hands and fingers. If murder was how you earned your badges in this Boy Scout troop, then Drazen Tishchenko was an Eagle Scout.

But I didn't need the tattoos to tell me he was a killer.

He told me with his eyes. I looked into his eyes and felt the value of my life drop to nothing.

"Step out," he said in English. He made a motion with his hands as if he were reeling me closer. "Do not be afraid of me."

I stepped forward so that I was next to Bo instead of behind his right shoulder. "Thank you for seeing us."

"Do you speak Russian like my friend Djuro?" It took me a second to realize he was referring to Bo by his given name.

"I'm sorry, I don't."

"We will speak English, then, so you will understand. Please, sit with me."

Bo and I sat on one side of the booth, Tishchenko on the other. I slipped in first, giving Bo the outside in case he had to make a quick move. It didn't matter. If he did, we were both dead. Undoubtedly, everyone in the place was armed and dangerous and belonged to Drazen.

"What would you like?" he asked me.

"I'm fine."

He sat back so that only his fingertips still touched the table. "What is your name?"

"Alex. Alex Shanahan."

"Short for Alexandra?"

"Yes."

"Sashen'ka." He clasped his hands and pushed them forward on the table. "Please, Sashen'ka, you will order something." It didn't seem like a request.

"I'll have a cup of tea. Thank you."

"Yes. Very good."

He called over to the bartender, held up two fingers, and pointed to his own empty espresso cup. He was ordering for Bo. Interesting. I wondered how well these two men knew each other.

"My friends, what can I do for you?"

I glanced at Bo to see if I was supposed to talk, but he took the lead.

"I lost a friend yesterday. Someone came into his home and took him away."

"This is sad news." Tishchenko shrugged. "But what concern of mine?"

"We made a mistake," Bo said quietly. "We are here to ask your advice."

"What mistake?"

"We took him back."

Tishchenko's gaze slid over to me. Whether he had known all along we had been the ones or whether he figured it out right then, I couldn't tell. But he knew now. "What is this man's name?"

He was looking at me, so I answered. "Harvey Baltimore."

"And who is he to you? Is this man your father?"

"He's my business partner. He's also my good friend. He's also . . . he's sick." I glanced at Bo. I wasn't sure how much to say. "He has multiple sclerosis. We were afraid if we didn't get to him soon, he would die."

A small boy appeared from behind the counter. He had a sucker in his mouth and a tray in his hand. On the tray were two steaming cups of espresso, which he distributed to the men. He put the small carafe of milk, the little pot of brewing tea, and a cup and saucer in front of me. He handled it all like a pro, despite the fact that he couldn't have been even seven years old.

He grasped the tray under one arm, put his other hand on Tishchenko's shoulder, and casually leaned in toward him. Maybe he was there to pull a thorn from his paw.

Tishchenko put his arm around the boy, pulled him

close, and kissed him on the top of his head. "My grand-son."

The boy's face was vulnerable and mischievous at the same time as he whispered something in the older man's ear.

Tishchenko laughed, spoke to the boy in his language, and shooed him away. As his grandson wandered off, Tishchenko called out to the bartender, who nodded in return.

"Such a smart boy. He wants ice cream, but he knows his mother won't permit treats before school."

I looked over. The man at the bar had an ice cream scoop out.

Tishchenko stirred milk into his cup. When he picked up his spoon, Bo did, too, but I let my tea steep. I was afraid to handle anything hot with my unsteady hands.

"Do you think this man, Harvey Baltimore, might have something of value? Is that why he would have been taken?"

"He doesn't have any money."

"Whoever took him, I do not think it would be for money. There are easier ways to get money, you know?" The corners of his mouth quivered into what might have been a smile. "Something he knows, perhaps?"

"We do not know why he was taken," Bo said. "We know that if he had died, whatever he might know would have died with him. Perhaps the people who took him did not know that."

He seemed to consider that. "Djuro, if you were Tishchenko and two people came to you in this way, how would you advise them?"

Bo put his hands in his lap and stared at the table. "I would advise them to find out what it is that Harvey Baltimore has, or what it is that he knows, and to let the man have it, this man who took him. But"—he held for an extra beat—"I would also understand that they meant no disrespect in taking him back. They didn't know."

"Then you believe this man should . . ."

"I would ask that he forgive any disrespect that was shown and accept in exchange the full and true disclosure of whatever it is that Harvey Baltimore knows that he needs."

Tishchenko sat back and scratched his chin. "If he did, that man would be a very understanding man."

"Yes."

"A benevolent man."

"Yes."

"And in line," I said, "in front of the FBI, who also wants this . . . this thing, whatever it is, which . . . which we don't know what it is because . . . because . . ." They had both turned to look at me. "Because Harvey is home recovering and hasn't told us yet." They turned away, and I knew how it felt to get smaller.

"This man who took your friend, Djuro, would he not be stupid to forgive the thief who stole his chicken before he got his eggs? With no chicken and no eggs, he has nothing now. My six-year-old grandson knows this much."

"He would have my word."

Tishchenko picked up his cup and drank down the rest of his espresso. Then he picked up the spoon and dropped it into the cup, where it clanked delicately.

"Sashen'ka."

"Yes."

"Do you have a brother?"

I looked at Bo. He gave me a subtle nod. "Yes."

He put his hand on Bo's forearm. "Djuro reminds me of my brother Vladislav. Vladi was also my business partner. We came here to America together. I miss my brother very much."

"What happened to him?"

"Someone killed him."

"I'm sorry he's dead, but Harvey never killed anyone."

"Perhaps. But this man who took your friend, he might believe Harvey Baltimore knows something about the man who killed my brother, a man who left this country and to this day has never paid the price for what he did."

"Wait a second. Roger Fratello killed your brother?"

Tishchenko sat back abruptly. He reacted as if I'd squirted lemon juice in his eyes. Bo was also staring at me. I had apparently violated the code of vague communication. I tried again.

"Why do you—" I had to pick my pronouns carefully. "May I ask why the man who took Harvey thinks Harvey can help him with his problem?"

"He might have friends who know such things."

Friends in the FBI? That was a scary thought, though not entirely out of the realm of possibility.

Tishchenko aimed his steady, impassive eyes at me. "Would he have your commitment, Sashen'ka?"

"For what?"

"If this man were to let your friend go and forgive your mistake, would he have your commitment to provide a service in return?"

"What exactly is the service requested?"

"Find the man who killed Vladi. Tell me where he is. That's all."

"First of all, I have to be clear. Are we talking about Roger Fratello?"

He offered a curt nod.

As far as I knew, no one knew where Roger Fratello was hanging out. Certainly not the FBI. Maybe Harvey did, maybe he didn't. "If Harvey knows something—"

"I do not believe in *if*. It is a weak word. Something either is or it is not. You either do or you do not."

I was afraid my voice would come out as a squeak, so I made myself calmly reach for the teapot, lift it, and pour the tea into my cup. I put the pot down, picked up the cup, and took a sip. It was strong and hot, and as I settled my cup back on its saucer, I looked at Tishchenko.

"If I did this, then this man we're speaking of would no longer have interest in Harvey?"

"He would have no interest in Harvey Baltimore."

I glanced at Bo. He was giving me no cues. This was apparently up to me. I looked at Tishchenko's dead eyes. "Yes, he would have my commitment. I'll find Fratello."

"Conscience and honor," he said, looking at Bo. "This is the law I live by. Not the laws of this country or my country or any country but the laws of man. You know this, Djuro."

"Yes."

"A commitment means everything. Do you understand, Sashen'ka?" He watched me closely.

"I understand."

He looked straight at Bo. "Make sure that she does."

If I hadn't been in Bo's Mercedes, I would have thrown up on the way back to Harvey's. As it was, I couldn't stop trembling. I heard myself talking to Bo. I heard the words that came out of my mouth, but I couldn't make any kind of cognitive connection to them. My mind was back in that dank café, playing over and over again the moment where I had made the commitment to Tishchenko. Something told me I had just made a very large bet.

"Bo?"

"Yes?"

"What if I can't find him?" That he didn't respond was not reassuring. "Roger Fratello disappeared four years ago and hasn't been seen since. The FBI hasn't been able to find him. Obviously, the . . . the tsar back there hasn't been able to find him, and I'm sure he looked. Both of those organizations would have way more resources than I have."

"He believes that Harvey Baltimore knows where he is. If he believes this, then it is true, even if it is not. Do you understand?"

I did. I opened the window on my side and let the cool air rush over my face. "This is not a good situation."

"He will not kill you if you give him what you said you would give him. He is a man who lives by his commitments."

"What if I can't?"

He stared straight ahead. "As I said, he is a man who lives by his commitments."

14

THE NEWS JUST KEPT GETTING BETTER. BO WAS SUPPOSED to go back to Harvey's with me and strategize, but he got a phone call that took priority. Boston PD was interested in talking to him about a disturbance that had taken place in a local neighborhood in which three men disappeared. He wasn't sure what they had, but he had to go and take care of it. When he dropped me in front of Harvey's, he assured me that Radik and Timon would still be around—as long as the cops didn't want to see them, too, in which case we might all be in big trouble.

I assumed that Harvey would still be in bed, but when I came into his office, he was sitting quietly in his chair in the middle of the room, blinking at me.

I froze. "What's wrong?"

"Nothing is wrong."

I didn't believe him. Something was always wrong. But he had gotten himself out of bed and dressed. He looked much more together than I felt. "You look good," I said. "You look better. Are you feeling better?"

"I am well, thank you. Much better than last we spoke."

"What are you doing?"

"Waiting."

"For what?" The tea service was back out. A fresh pot had been brewed. "Are you expecting company?"

His hands had slipped into his lap, and he was staring at them as if he'd just screwed on a new pair and didn't know how they worked. It was the way he looked when he felt guilty.

"I was hoping to have this done before you got back."

"Have what done?"

"I called the FBI."

"You called—"

He held up a business card, and I had a sick feeling, because I knew whose it must have been. I went over and snatched it from him. Special Agent Eric Ling.

"Where did you get this?"

"It was on my bedside table. I thought you left it for me, either by design or by fate."

"It was neither, Harvey. It was by accident. Why did you call him?"

"You mentioned last night that the FBI had come. Feeling somewhat more lucid this morning, I have an idea of why they were here. I think it is my duty to speak to them."

"About what?"

"Roger Fratello."

I looked at him more closely. It was clear from the way he said the name that he knew who he was talking about. "What about Roger Fratello?"

"You said they were looking for him."

"They are. They said he was a bad guy and that you helped him go on the lam four years ago. I told them you wouldn't do that."

He wouldn't look at me. He kept rubbing the back of

one hand with the other, which was what he did sometimes when they felt numb. My heart started to beat with
purpose, like someone hammering on a door, trying to
wake me up.

"Harvey?"

He started to answer and stopped. He scratched his
head. The clock ticked, he swallowed hard, and I started
to feel numb as I waited to have the last of my illusions
shattered.

"I did it. I did help him sneak out of the country."

Crap. I went over and flung myself down on the wingback. "Why would you do that?"

"He was a danger to Rachel."

That figured. I closed my eyes and tried to stay calm.
But then I opened them, and I was staring at all my casework strewn across the floor in plain sight. "When is Ling
coming?"

"At nine o'clock." We both looked over at his great-
grandfather's clock.

"Dammit, Harvey." I had fifteen minutes. I went down
on my hands and knees and started scooping up all the
bits and pieces of the case that I had so scrupulously fit
together the night before. "A conversation between the
two of us would have been nice before you invited the
federal government over. There are things going on that
you are not even aware of, things we need to talk about."

Without bothering to sort, I shoveled everything into a
couple of file folders. "Besides that, we're partners. We
should be making decisions like this together." Looking
around for a hiding hole, all I could think of was to shove
everything under one of the couch cushions.

"There are some decisions you cannot make for me,"
he said, "or even with me. This might be one. I do not
know. It is confusing."

He sounded genuinely conflicted. Had I not been so angry with him, I would have felt bad for him.

"I know how you feel about Rachel," he said, "but I cannot let harm come to her. If I am to take the heat, I believe that must be my decision alone to make."

"Take the heat for what?" I closed up the laptop and shoved it under the couch. Then I smoothed the seat cover and checked around for anything incriminating. Eventually, my attention landed on Harvey, who hadn't bothered to answer. I stood up and pushed the hair out of my eyes. "Harvey, will you answer me, please? Take the heat for what?"

He hesitated. "I know you do not understand . . . us. Rachel and me. I have never really understood it myself. But I love her, and I always will, and I have a chance to do something for her with the life I have left."

"Harvey—"

"I am dying. I know that is hard for you to accept. It is hard for me to accept. I do not want to die. I do not want to have this illness, but I have it. I do not know how many days I have left, but I know one thing: there will never be another one that is better than the one that preceded it. I am a burden to you—"

"Please, don't start with that."

"Let me finish." He sat as straight as he could and took a deep breath. "When those men came and took me out of my house, I was certain they would kill me, that I would be murdered by people I did not know for reasons I did not understand. I was terrified. But do you know the thing that frightened me most? That it was fitting."

"What was fitting?"

"That a man who had lived such an unremarkable life would die in such an anonymous way."

"Your life has not been unremarkable."

"My life has been remarkable only for the amount of energy I have expended to keep it that way. I have never done anything that would draw notice, I have never caused a commotion, I have never taken a risk."

"You married Rachel." It took him a second or two, but when he got it, he smiled. The moment was fleeting. He went on.

"All my life, I have been offered opportunities that I never took. I have turned away from the things that frightened me. When you came to get me, I was ready to die, but now I feel that God has granted me another opportunity, and I promised myself that when the time came, I would not turn away. The time has come."

"The time for what?"

The clock began to chime. It was nine o'clock. He waited until all nine bells had sounded. "To turn myself in."

"To turn yourself in for what?"

"For the murder of Vladi Tishchenko."

"Vladi Tishchenko? Drazen's brother? Drazen's much-loved and sorely missed brother?" I thought maybe we were joking again, but he seemed perfectly serious. I considered sitting down, but I knew I couldn't stay down. "I thought Roger killed Vladi."

"Roger Fratello did not kill Vladi, and if he comes back here, he will undoubtedly say so."

"Then who did? Because I know it wasn't you. I know—" That was when I got it. I finally got it, and everything made sense. Horrible sense. "Rachel killed Vladi. That's what this is about. Rachel killed Vladi, Roger knows that, and that's why you got him out of town. You did exactly what Ling said you did."

"Yes."

"And you did it to protect her."

"Yes."

I hadn't had much sleep, I was feeling like crap, and I still had a Drazen hangover, but I managed to come up with the relevant question. "Why did she kill him?"

"He tried to rape her. It was self-defense. But that would not matter to a man like Drazen Tishchenko. He will kill Rachel if he finds out. Roger Fratello can never come back here."

"If Drazen thinks you did it, he'll kill you."

His face went slack, and his lips parted. His jaw began to quiver under his jowls. "How do you know what he would think?" His voice was shaky. Drazen had that effect on people.

"Who do you think snatched you? Bo and I killed three of his men last night getting you home. That's where I was this morning, having breakfast with him and trying to make amends."

"What did you tell him?"

A car pulled up outside. I checked through the blinds. Our guests had arrived. "That I would find Roger Fratello. In exchange, he promised to forgive and forget and to leave you alone."

"Why would you do that? I never asked you to do that." He tried to press his lips together. He tried to look stern, but his chin was quivering. "Why would you do that?"

"You are my partner and my friend. There is no other choice I could have made. Don't you get that?"

Two car doors slammed in quick succession. Ling and Southern would be walking up the driveway. I needed time to think.

"All right, look. I can figure this out. I know I can." I

started doing laps around the couch. "There is a way to make this work so that no one gets killed. I know there is, and I know I can find it. But I can't do it if you're in FBI custody, I can't do it if I'm worried about Drazen coming after you, and I can't do it right this second." I stopped in front of his wheelchair. "I need for you to give me a little time."

"How much time?"

"I don't know. But more than the thirty seconds it's going to take for them to get to the door. I need you to stall them."

"What would I say? I am the one who called them."

"I don't know, just please don't say you killed anyone. Don't confess to something you didn't do. At least give me the rest of today."

There was a loud knock on the door. They'd probably been standing out there for a while, not knowing the doorbell was broken.

"What's it going to be, Harvey?"

He seemed a little more crumpled than usual in his chair, and he was starting to wheeze. "I will do what you ask," he said. "Under one condition."

Everyone had conditions. How come I never got to set the terms? "What condition?"

"If it comes down to it and you have to choose, you must promise me that you will choose Rachel." He might have looked crumpled and sounded spent, but his tone was firm.

"If I have to choose between you and Rachel, you want me to choose her?"

"I am sorry. I am truly sorry, and I believe that you can figure all of this out. But I have to know that if you cannot, or if you cannot in time, Rachel will be safe."

The pounding on the door began in earnest. Ling and

Southern had already come in once with guns drawn. It was time to make a decision.

"Fine. I promise. But here's *my* condition. After they leave, you have to tell me what it is about this woman that would make you want to die for her." Because I just didn't get it.

15

SPECIAL AGENTS LING AND SOUTHERN LOOKED LIKE CIRCUS
clowns through the parabolic lens of the peephole, but
when I opened the door, they were all business.

Southern stepped up. "Where is he?"

"In his office."

He brushed past me and headed down the hallway.
Ling wiped his feet on the mat. "Thank you," he said. I
tried to look as if I knew what for. He smiled. "For having
Harvey call."

"Oh, absolutely. I insisted."

He let me lead the way to the office, where I was surprised to find Harvey on his feet. He was leaning on his
cane but mostly upright. After he confirmed that he was
who he was, Ling flashed his ID and introduced himself
and Southern. "We'd like to talk to you alone."

"Excuse me, Special Agent Ling," I said, "but I already
feel involved in this because of our interview yesterday. I
would like to stay."

"I'm sure you would, but have you checked with your
partner?"

Harvey wobbled a little as he blinked at me from behind those thick lenses. My jaw tightened, my stiff neck throbbed, and I knew there was still the chance that he would choose today to throw himself under the bus for Rachel. I knew that's what his instincts told him to do.

"Miss Shanahan is my partner," he said finally. "Whatever you need, I am sure we can both help you." He gestured to the small seating area. "Do come in and sit down."

Ling dropped onto the couch—right on top of my casework—and made himself comfortable. I almost expected him to prop his feet up on the coffee table. Southern, something less than comfortable but not exactly jittery, found a place against the bookshelves and stood there, holding a manila file flat against his chest. Harvey worked his way over and lowered himself into the wingback. I stayed close to the door. Normally, I would have wanted to watch Ling's face, but for this discussion, I needed to keep an eye on my partner.

"We were looking for you yesterday," Ling said to Harvey. "You weren't home."

"Yes, I understand. I am sorry I missed you."

"Where were you?"

Harvey glanced at me. He had never been good with lies, either the commission or the omission kind. He blinked too much or shifted around in his seat. He pushed at the bridge of his glasses or pitched his voice too high. That he exhibited none of these nervous tics as he sat under the watchful gaze of the FBI was alarming. I was afraid he was about to tell them the truth.

"I was . . . shopping."

Southern rolled his eyes, I exhaled, and Ling reached over and picked at a small water stain on the linen covering the arm of the couch. He was precise about it. "Really? What did you get?"

"I have been thinking of investing in a new chair." Harvey nodded in the direction of his old wheelchair across the room. "That one has seen better days. But they are very expensive. I made no purchases."

"You left your music on," Ling said, "and we almost shot your partner. She was very concerned about you."

"Yes." Harvey chuckled. "She made me apologize profusely."

Ling turned enough to show me his profile. "Then there was nothing to worry about after all?"

"He forgot to turn on his phone. I should have known."

Harvey shifted in the wingback. His legs were probably bothering him. "How can I help you gentlemen?"

"You called us. You said you had some things to discuss."

"I did?"

"Yes," Southern groused, "you did."

"Oh, my." Harvey reached up and straightened his lenses. "This is most embarrassing." He turned his head and scratched behind his ear. "I have recently adjusted my medication, and I have been doing some odd things, such as leaving the house without telling Alex. That was quite unusual. I am certain she told you."

Ling seemed quite concerned, though I was reasonably certain he wasn't buying any of it.

"Please accept my apologies," Harvey said. "I know you gentlemen are busy, but I cannot, for the life of me, think of why I might have called you." He looked at me with eyebrows raised, as if I could help.

"We'll have to talk to your doctor. I'm sorry, too," I said

to Ling. "I was out this morning, or I would have prevented this."

"Really?" Ling shifted around. "Where were you?"

"Um . . . having breakfast. With a client. He's an early bird."

Harvey scooted himself to the edge of the cushion and started to pull himself up with his cane. "You have my assurances, Special Agents, that this will not happen again."

"That's okay." Ling was as serene as ever. "We were coming anyway. We had some questions for you."

Harvey looked up at me as he eased back into his chair. Southern stepped up and handed his file to Ling. Ling flipped through it. When he found the item he wanted, he passed it over to Harvey. I went and stood behind Harvey's chair so I could see it, too. It was the same passport photo of Roger he had shown me.

"This man is Roger Fratello," Harvey said.

"Then you know him?"

"He is a seminotorious fugitive from our area. Of course I know *of* him."

"Do you know where he is?"

"How would I?" Harvey passed the picture back to Ling.

"We were thinking that, wherever he is, you might have helped him get there."

"That is nonsense. Would either of you like some tea? I brewed a fresh pot."

"No, thanks. How about the name Stephen Gerald Hoffmeyer?"

Harvey furrowed his brow. "Nothing comes to mind, but I am a sick man. With the medication and the illness, as I told you, my mind is not what it once was."

"Maybe we can give your memory a nudge." Ling passed over another item he pulled from his file. "We found this in a safety deposit box in Brussels." It was a photograph of a single piece of scrap paper. A list of codes was written on it. "We think they might be numbered bank accounts." Ling looked at Harvey. "Check out what's written across the top."

Harvey and I both leaned in. I was the one who almost started wheezing when I saw that it said "Baltimore." Harvey was calm.

"Are you sure that does not refer to a city in Maryland?"

Southern's expression soured even more, but Ling's brightened. He seemed to be enjoying the challenge presented by the elegant stone wall that was Harvey Baltimore. I might have enjoyed it myself had I not been trying so hard to keep up. It was a side of Harvey I hardly ever got to see.

"Good point by you," Ling said. "We can't really tie the list to you because the only usable prints are Roger Fratello's. We don't have the same problem with the cash."

He offered up the next exhibit, a photo of the individual stacks of banded U.S. currency he had spoken of. The stacks were arranged in rows—three across and two down—and wrapped in plastic. "We found that bundle in the same box in Brussels. That shrink wrap is great for prints. Yours were all over it. Can you explain that?"

"I already—"

Ling held up his hand to shut me up. He was polite about it. "If you don't mind."

"I am an accountant," Harvey said. "I handle money, typically other people's money. I am not responsible for where it goes or what it is used for after it leaves my hands."

Good answer. We hadn't even coordinated.

"Do you do business with drug cartels? Because that's where we usually see bills bundled that way."

"I certainly do not."

Ling nestled back against the couch, as relaxed as if he were sitting in his underwear at home watching *The Untouchables* on DVD, or whatever his tastes ran to. Maybe *Bill and Ted's Excellent Adventure*. "By the way, you both understand that you can go to prison for lying to us, right?"

"Title 18," Harvey said. "United States Code, Section 1001, makes it a crime to knowingly and willfully make any materially false, fictitious, or fraudulent statement or representation in any matter—"

"That's the one. Let's talk about motive. That's really the only part I don't get, although, personally, I think it all comes back to Rachel."

"Rachel is not part of this." Harvey's answer came out in a high-pitched voice, too fast to be the truth.

Ling noticed, too, and then he came out with his ace in the hole. He started pulling pictures out of his file and passing them over to Harvey, watching Harvey's face the whole time. They were black-and-white surveillance photos, the kind divorce lawyers get from private investigators who do that sort of work. The only source I could think of was Susan Fratello. Maybe she had finally gotten fed up with Roger's serial philandering.

The first showed Rachel kissing Roger in the front seat of a car. Ling put down a second and a third. Harvey's right leg twitched enough to send the pages on his lap sliding to the floor. I reached down and trapped them against his shin, and I saw it in his face. He wouldn't last much longer.

I collected all the exhibits and handed them back to Ling. "We get the idea."

"Maybe she came to you and asked for help in getting Roger out of harm's way."

"That is not the case." Harvey's forehead was starting to glisten. His breathing was shallower. "Rachel is not part of this."

"Did I miss something," I asked, "or did you gentlemen articulate at some point exactly what it is that you want?"

Southern stared at Harvey. "He knows what we want."

"Then explain it to me."

"We want your partner here to tell us where to find Fratello so we can drag his ass home and nail him for the murder of Special Agent Walter Herald."

"Excuse me? Murder?"

Ling was reassembling his file. "We believe Roger was involved in the murder of an undercover officer named Walter Herald. Walt was Special Agent Southern's partner."

Gauging the look on Southern's face, had I tried to express condolences, he would have pulled out his service weapon and shot me. "Roger Fratello killed your partner?"

"Walt was undercover at Betelco for nine months. He approached Roger about flipping on his scumbag partners. After he agreed to do it, the cocksucker turned around and told them about Walt, and they killed him. We never did find Walt's head or his hands."

No wonder he was so pissed off. "So, the Russians killed him?"

Southern shot right back. "Anyone who was involved in the conspiracy to kill or cover up the murder of a federal officer is in deep shit." He was talking to me and staring at Harvey. "Anyone in that position would be well advised to cut a deal and spill his guts rather than go down for felony murder."

I put myself between Harvey and Southern. "Are you planning on taking him in?" Neither man made a move, which meant the answer was no.

"Here's the thing," Ling said. "One of the chief beneficiaries of Walt's murder was Rachel. After his body turned up, no one wanted to testify. We couldn't bring any indictments."

Harvey looked at him. "Rachel wasn't the only beneficiary."

"That's true." Ling didn't argue with him. "But you're in with some bad people on this one. You don't want to take the heat for them, and you don't want to be screwing with the Russian *mafiya*."

"We'll certainly take that under advisement," I said. "Can I show you to the door?"

"We'll find it." Ling was his affable self as he stood to button his jacket. But Southern had one last shot to take. "An inmate in a wheelchair has a hard time taking care of himself in prison." He stared down hard at Harvey. "All kinds of bad things happen to gimps in the can."

I walked Ling and Southern to the door anyway, and watched them to their car. After they had pulled away, gone down the street, and turned the corner, I went back to the office. Harvey had moved back to his wheelchair. His chin was resting on the collar of flesh that had formed around his neck in the past year or so. It made him look overly jowly. That the stakes had taken a gigantic leap in the past hour had not been lost on him. He was clearly shaken.

"All right, Harvey. I need to know the truth. Did you have anything to do with the murder of that agent?"

He was horrified that I would ask such a thing, but my new policy was to be thorough. I was tired of being surprised.

"Yes or no?"

"No."

"What about Rachel? She and Roger had a thing. Susan Fratello also thinks she was in bed with the Russians."

"In bed with the Russians?"

"Not *in bed* with them." At least I didn't think so. "She told me Rachel brought the Russians into Betelco as investors. Does that sound right to you?"

He looked up at me. I could see he didn't want to think it could be true. I could also see that he wasn't sure.

"We have to ask her," I said. "You have to tell me where she is so I can find her and bring her back here."

"I do not know where she is."

"Harvey, you don't want her out there alone, running from Drazen and possibly the FBI."

"No." He shook his head. "I do not. I wish I could send you to her, but I made her promise not to tell me where she was going. She is supposed to call when she gets settled somewhere."

"All right." I went over to the couch where Ling had been lounging and pulled my casework out from under the cushion. I found my backpack and stuffed everything into it.

"Where are you going?"

"I'm going to see Felix. I have him working on something to find Rachel. The three of us need to sit down and pool ideas and resources. That's the only way I see this working—all three of us together." I reached under the couch and coaxed out my laptop. My backpack had just enough room left for it. Even so, it took me four tries to get the flap zipped up. I was ready to go, but I had one item still open. Harvey had rolled his chair to within arm's reach of the teapot. I helped him pour a cup.

"You have to tell me," I said, "because you promised. What is it about this woman that would make you act this way? As your friend, I would like to know. As a woman, I would really like to know."

"I am not sure I can explain it to you."

"You need to try, Harvey, before I go and find her."

He set the saucer on his thigh. It had a design on it that looked like pink rosebuds, and it occurred to me that Rachel had probably picked it out. He balanced the saucer on the cup and looked at me.

"I asked her to dance and she said yes."

"That's it?"

He sat back, and his gaze drifted to that tarnished tin ceiling. He seemed to be looking for his words up there.

"There is a point in one's life where it becomes impossible not to look back and say, my life has not worked out. It is neither here nor there. One cannot change what he is, but realizing what he is inevitably colors expectations, what he might expect his life to become. I learned to be satisfied with very little. One day, I met Rachel. I asked her to dance with me. I expected her to say no, but she said yes. When I asked her to dinner, she said yes. When I asked her to marry me, she said yes."

"You used to dance?"

"I loved to dance. I loved dancing with my wife."

That's what the music was all about. Now it made sense. It had been something he had shared with Rachel. It had been packed away in boxes, which was where he'd wanted it to stay. That's why he'd told me to pack everything away and leave it alone.

"She said yes for a reason, Harvey. She said yes because you gave her something, too."

"Whatever I gave her, it could never approach the happiness she gave me. I love her because I asked her to dance and she said yes."

16

IN MY EXPERIENCE, HOUSES WERE MOST EASILY BROKEN
into through the basement windows, which were either
unlatched or easy to make that way. The basement window for the house where Rachel was hiding was so low to
the ground I had to lie on my belly in the dirt to check it
out. The window was at ceiling height for the basement
and had a simple latch lock that I could handle easily. I
used my flashlight to look for the obvious signs of an
alarm system. When I saw none, I put on my gloves,
opened my tool case, and went to work.

Not surprisingly, Rachel had found a nice house to
hide in. It was a large, white, brick-front ranch-style, sitting on almost an acre out in Acton. That it was built on a
cul-de-sac made it even more secluded and private. Perfect for hiding, but it's hard to hide from Felix. He had
talked Gary Ruffielo into providing a current cell-phone
number for Rachel. After working the problem all day, he
had finally managed to track her through the use of that
very useful GPS chip.

I finished with the latch, popped the window open,
and gave thanks when no alarm sounded. If it was a silent

alarm, I was in trouble. I cut the flimsy and rusted chains on each side that kept the window from flopping all the way to the wall. I gathered my stuff, turned on my belly, and wriggled in. When my feet hit the ground, I closed the window and did a sweep with my flashlight. It was dark and gloomy and haphazard down there, the way basements are. I saw nothing living or breathing of the human variety, but there was an old kitchen chair in the corner. I moved it to a position under the window in case I needed a springboard to a quick exit.

At the top of the stairs, I put my ear against the interior door, listened, and heard nothing. I heard more nothing when I popped the door open, which was a good thing. No alarm sounded as I stepped into the kitchen. No motion detectors were tripped, so I kept moving. There were no lights on, which made it very dark in the house, but I heard something, and it wasn't just the daily hum of household machinery. It sounded like a shower running upstairs.

I cleared the downstairs as quickly as I could with a flashlight. The rooms were big and open, with few nooks, closets, and alcoves to hide in. But it took forever to get up to the second floor. The stairs creaked. I took each one in slow motion, checking for loose boards as I went. By the time I reached the top, my muscles felt as if they'd fused into one inflexible mass. The hallways were all dark up there, but, like the music in Harvey's empty house, the sound of the shower running told me where to go: down to the room with the closed door.

Given that I had broken in, I had to decide about the Glock. It was one thing if it was Rachel behind the door. It was quite another if it was the law-abiding owner of the house, hiding out, perfectly justified in shooting the home invader. But what if it was Rachel with a gun? I didn't know her. I didn't know how she would react. I decided I needed to go in with my weapon front and center. I twisted the knob, flattened against the wall, and pushed the door open.

It was like a steam room in there, the steam billowing out from behind an interior door across the room. The light from behind the door provided the only illumination. It fell across the bed, where the sheets were twisted and the blanket mostly puddled around it. A rolling carry-on bag sat on the floor with its zippered flap lying open. Clothes were strewn about as if it had exploded. I stayed low and crept in, listening to make sure there was spraying and splashing and not just a steady hum. I got close enough to the bag to read the tag. Rachel Ruffielo of Quincy, Mass. It was good to know all the sneaking around hadn't been for nothing.

I was careful to keep an eye on the bedroom door as I worked my way across the room. On the way, I checked under the bed. I checked the closet on the far wall. When I got close to the bathroom, I stopped.

I could feel my heartbeat in the tips of my fingers when I placed them on the damp door. I pushed. The hinges whined. The steam billowed out. My face got damp, and it was only as I was wheeling into the doorway that I realized there was now no interruption in the water's flow, and unless she was standing perfectly still under the shower head, Rachel wasn't in the shower at all.

She stepped forward, emerging from the thick steam like some kind of poltergeist.

"Don't move," she said, and I didn't, because in her small hands, she held a 45-caliber revolver, and it was pointed straight at my right eye. Her .45 was bigger than my Glock, and her hands were shaking violently. There wasn't much chance my gun would go off by accident, but I couldn't say the same for hers, so I did as she asked.

"All right." I had to make myself heard above the roar of the shower. "Let's calm down here. No one has to get hurt. I didn't come here to hurt you."

"No? Let's see, you track me down, you break into the house, you creep in here with a gun, and you didn't come here to hurt me?"

I knew I should have had Harvey call her first, but I was afraid she'd bolt.

"I came to help."

"With a gun?"

"You never know what you'll find behind a closed door."

She raised one shoulder to wipe away the copious amounts of perspiration dripping into her eyes, and the barrel of the .45 twitched. A defibrillator couldn't have made my heart jump more.

"Be careful, *please.*" I put up my left hand, as if that would stop a bullet. "Let's put the weapons down. We'll do it at the same time."

"No." It wasn't even up for consideration. "You first."

"Why would I do that?"

"You've got no choice. You're not gonna shoot me."

"How do you know what I'll do?"

"Because you're Harvey's partner, and I know Harvey." The barest trace of a smile appeared. "But you don't know me. 'Maybe,' you're thinking, 'she's just desperate enough to do it. Maybe she doesn't care if she lives or dies.' Or maybe—" She pulled the hammer back. "Maybe this thing goes off accidentally."

"Dammit, Rachel, be careful." I pushed my hand farther forward. That would surely stop a bullet. "Do you know what that will do if it goes off?"

"Another good question. Do I even know how to use this?" Her smile broadened. She had slipped into something more comfortable—a Brooklyn accent. Either I had failed to notice it the other day, or it only came out in times of stress. She was also right. I had no idea what she was capable of. I did the high-stakes calculation again. I had a better chance of surviving if I put my gun down, even if she kept hers.

"All right. I'm putting it away." I flipped the pistol around so it was aimed at the ceiling and engaged the safety.

"On the floor. Put it on the floor."

"No." I reached around and slipped it into my waist holster. "I'm putting it away so it's not pointed at you. You do the same."

"Put your hands up."

"Rachel—"

"Put them *up.*" Her stress level was rising. It probably showed on her face, but I was watching the weapon, and all I could think about was the size of the hole a 45-caliber slug left in the targets at the shooting range, particularly from that close. I tried to keep my own nerves from showing as she moved to the shower and turned off the water. The silence was abrupt and welcome.

"Listen to me. If that goes off by accident, you'll kill me. If you don't want to kill me, point it toward the floor."

I didn't think she wanted to kill me, but I also didn't think intent mattered at that moment. How light the trigger was, how twitchy her finger, how good or bad her aim—those were the things that mattered, and the longer she held the gun on me, the greater the chance that something would go wrong.

"How did you find me?"

"Your cell phone has a chip in it."

"Who put it there?" She pushed the .45 at me, and I couldn't help but turn my head slightly, away from the wrong end of that terrible weapon. Not that it would help much. Instead of blowing my face off, the blast would simply blow away the side of my head.

"Samsung . . . Nokia . . . Motorola . . ." She glared at me. "They come that way. We got your number from Gary, and we tracked you with the chip."

I watched out of the corner of my eye as she began, very slowly, to lower her arms. I felt the pistol's sight track down my body. Given the way my luck was running, I expected to be shot through the knee any second. When I was finally out of the bull's-eye, I peeled my tongue off the roof of my mouth.

"Decock it, please."

She did. Without even thinking, I was on her. I couldn't have stopped if I'd tried. I grabbed the revolver and wrenched it out of her delicate hand. With her other delicate hand, she tried to gouge out my eyes. She wasn't very big, and I was really mad, so it was easy to spin her around and give her a hard shove out the door. She ended up sprawled facedown across the bed.

"You bitch." She said it with her face in the mattress. "You lying bitch. I knew I shouldn't have trusted you." She was strangely calm, almost resigned. When she started to turn and sit up, I pulled the Glock again and pointed it at her, but I kept the safety on. Harvey wouldn't like it if I shot the love of his life, accidentally or otherwise.

"Put your hands on top of your head, Rachel." I waited until she sat up and complied before flipping open the cylinder on the .45 and shaking the cartridges out into my palm. I put the gun in the sink and the cartridges in my pocket.

"Can I put my hands down?"

"If you sit on them." She rolled her eyes but slid her hands, palms down, under her knees.

I found a wall switch and turned on the overhead lights. "How did you know I was here?"

"I heard a noise," she said.

Not as stealthy as I thought, perhaps. I was soaking wet from the steam and a little shaky from having nearly died but otherwise okay. I pulled the stiff-backed chair away from the desk, dragged it over to face her, and sat down. We each took in a deep breath. I wanted to start over again. I did not, however, want any more surprises.

"Where are the people who own this house?"

"In Thailand for three months. They don't even know I'm here."

"Why are you still here? Why didn't you leave town?"

She sniffed. "I didn't have anyplace to go."

"No family? No friends to take you in?"

"Haven't you heard? I'm a hot commodity. For the first time in my life, everyone wants me. I can't bring that into the homes of my family or my friends."

"You didn't have any trouble bringing it into Harvey's home."

She leveled her shoulders and smiled. "Harvey gets me. He understands me, and he likes helping me. It makes him happy."

If that were true, Harvey must have been deliriously happy. "He's home recovering from his abduction, in case you're interested."

"His ab—" She stopped herself, but not before her

face had betrayed the slightest bit of surprise. I had been hoping for concern.

"Are you telling me you didn't know that your friend Drazen Tishchenko sent people to pick him up?"

"*My* friend?"

"You brought Drazen into Betelco for a little postmodern plundering. Maybe that makes you more like professional colleagues."

"How do you know about Drazen?"

"We had a power breakfast this morning. He's looking for the person who killed his brother. That would be you, wouldn't it?"

She tried to act blasé, but her fluttering eyelids betrayed her. Her expression then proceeded to anger as she must have figured out who had told me. "I don't know what you're talking about. As far as I know, Roger Fratello killed Vladi."

"Lucky for you, Drazen still thinks so. Now get your stuff together. We're going."

"I'm not going anywhere with you."

"Would you rather talk with the FBI, because that's an option, too?"

She hooted. "Do you think the FBI scares me? The F-B-*eyyyye* can't even protect *themselves* from Drazen. I'm going to trust them to protect me? No, thank you. I grew up near Red Hook. I know what they can do, these people. They're animals." She shook her head, and the laughter stopped. "They're animals."

"So I've heard."

She blinked a few times as if an eyelash might have drifted across her cornea. She found a spot over my head to stare at. "Did they hurt Harvey?"

"Not physically. Emotionally, he's pretty beat up."

Without ever breaking her gaze, she used her pinkie to

flick something from the corner of her eye, pulling her hand from under her knee to do it. I let it go. There was a shred of compassionate concern down deep somewhere. It made her almost human.

I stood up and pushed the chair back in place. "Get your stuff together. We're leaving."

"Where are we going?"

"Back to Harvey's. I can keep you safe there while the three of us figure this out."

"Figure what out?"

"The first thing we need to do is find Roger Fratello. Then we'll figure out how to keep everyone alive, starting with Harvey and me."

"Why would we look for Roger?"

"Because if I don't find him, Drazen will kill Harvey."

"But if you do—"

"I know. He'll spill the beans on you. I've got all that." I started to tell her that Harvey was willing to take her place with Drazen but figured that was information she might be tempted to act on. Better to remove all temptation.

When I looked at her again, I could tell she was running through her options and handicapping each one. She raised a thumbnail to her lips and started plucking at a front tooth. It made a hollow, snapping sound. "I need some guarantees before I help you."

More conditions. Everyone had conditions. "What guarantees?"

"What do you think? I need you to guarantee that Drazen won't kill me. Otherwise, think about it. What would be the point of helping you?"

More thumbnail plucking. She seemed truly frightened, so I walked to the bed and sat beside her.

"Rachel, we all have secrets. I think it's fair to say the

one you and Harvey have been sitting on is bigger than most. Now that I know the truth, there is one guarantee I can make you."

She tilted her head back and looked at me through half-closed eyes. "I'm listening."

"If it comes down to turning Harvey over to Drazen or turning you over, it will be you. I guarantee it. Now, let's go."

Rachel could really move when she wanted to. We were out of there in two minutes. I had to help her get her bag down the stairs, which made me wonder how she'd gotten it up. Then she had to go into the office to get her cell phone, which she had left charging next to the computer.

"Would you quit turning all the lights on?" I followed along behind her, turning them off. We were almost out the door when she remembered she'd left her Thyroxine up in the medicine cabinet. As she was coming down the stairs, the lights went out.

"Hey," she said, cranking up the decibels along with the belligerence level. "At least let me get down the damn stairs, wouldya?"

"Be quiet."

"Excuse me?"

Something was different. It was the silence, the kind you hear when every major appliance or system in the house shuts down at once. "The power's off."

"What?" I heard her racing down the stairs, and then she was right next to me. "What's going on?"

I saw what I thought was a shadow moving outside one of the low windows in the dining room. I went to the wall next to it and mashed my face so I could see around the blinds without moving them.

"What is it? What is going on? What are you looking at?"

Someone in a low crouch, moving along the side of the house, toward the back. Moving fast. I moved pretty fast myself back across the room toward Rachel. I could see her silhouette. When I got closer, I could see how wide her eyes were open. She was staring at my Glock, which was up and cocked and ready to go. When had I even pulled it out? I tried to keep my voice steady.

"Go upstairs. Get that .45 out of the sink, and bring it down here."

"It doesn't have any bullets," she hissed. "You have them."

I thought about it. If something happened to me, it wouldn't be fair to leave her with an empty revolver. I dug the cartridges out of my pocket and put them into her hand. "Load it upstairs, and bring it down. Go toward the front. I'll go to the back. Shoot anyone you see. If you get in trouble, go to . . ."

"The office," she said. "It has a door that locks and windows." She was scared but still thinking. That was good. "Who are they?" she asked.

"I don't know. Go *now*, Rachel."

Good question. Who were these people? They had to be Russians. What had Bo said about Drazen? He had former KGB . . . Soviet Army . . . Russian police. Had Drazen lost patience this quickly? Maybe he had found out about Rachel. Maybe he had found out she killed Vladi. Maybe he had just decided to wipe us all out, and maybe I should stop thinking so much, because I was getting shaky.

I had to talk myself through it, to slow everything down. I had a flashlight. This was why I carried it. I held it to the side, away from my body, but didn't turn it on. With my shoulder to the wall, I felt my way toward the kitchen. I didn't know the layout of the house, but I knew

the back better than the front. I moved the way I had
been trained—both arms up, one shoulder back, my gun
hand resting in the other, both thumbs pointed down the
barrel. Like holding a golf club with a trigger, one of my
instructors had said. What my instructor could not have
explained, and what I could never have experienced in a
thousand simulations, was the roar of adrenaline that
practically had me levitating.

My whole body was like one big sensory receptor. I
felt the darkness against my skin. When the latch on the
back door began to rattle, the sound came into my body
through every pore. I started to back up, but it was too
late. The door opened, someone stepped through it, and
my entire world telescoped down to the assault rifle in his
hands. He saw me and raised the rifle to shoot. I held the
light out, pointed it at the intruder, and flashed it on. The
high-intensity beam hit his face. He flinched but still
fired . . . and missed. I didn't. I put two rounds into his
chest. He yelled and fell back. The second man came in
firing right behind him. I ducked, killed the flashlight,
and hauled ass the other way. Red beams from their
weapons wheeled around the dark hallway, and I knew I
was in someone's line of fire, and I knew I had to get out,
so I fell through the next doorway I found. I landed on
the floor inside. The door slammed shut right behind me.
I used my flashlight and found Rachel, which meant I
had found my way to the office. She threw her arm over
her eyes. "Get that out of my face." The .45 was in her
other hand.

"How many did you see?" I asked her.

"I just heard shooting and came in here."

There were boots on the floor outside the door, more
than one pair. If the first guy hadn't gone down, it was because they had on body armor. I had definitely hit him

twice in the chest. A scarier possibility was that there were more than the two I'd seen.

Then came the unmistakable *cha-chink* of someone chambering a round in a pump-action shotgun. I grabbed Rachel, pulled her behind the desk, and covered my ears against the mighty roar of the blast. Another *cha-chink*. They were blowing the hinges and would follow that by blowing out the dead bolt, and then there would be nothing standing between them and us.

Somewhere it had registered that they were wearing night-vision goggles, which explained why the first guy had reacted as he had to the high-intensity beam. I reached for Rachel's hand and put the flashlight in it.

"When they come through the door, flash this at them, but move it around, like this." I showed her. Keep it away from your head, because they'll shoot at it." Her hand was shaking. "It'll be all right. We'll be fine. Don't worry."

I left her there and scrambled across the floor. There wasn't any better cover than the furniture, so I crouched behind the couch. When the third shot went off, I felt the reverb in my chest. The door crashed in. The red beams came first. I got flat on my belly, aimed for knees and feet, just in case they did have armor on, and fired. One of them went down. I fired at his head until he stopped moving. I popped the clip—I knew I was out—and reached into my pocket for the second one. The shotgun roared again, and a substantial chunk of the back of the couch blew out over my head. Rachel screamed. When I looked up for her, a loud crack sounded. My head snapped back. A stingingly bright light erupted behind my eyes, and I fell backward. The light ruptured, and the pain came with the darkness. I covered my face with my hands and rolled over onto my stomach, wondering in some detached part of myself if I'd been shot through the head.

When I opened my eyes, a figure dressed all in black hovered over me. He wore a black mask and all the gear. He flashed a light in my face, then at a picture in his hand. I was apparently not the one he was looking for, because he took a step back and started to raise his assault rifle. Before he could get his shot off, his body began to convulse. He tried to turn around, but the convulsions began again. When he started to go down, I rolled out of the way. He fell next to me like a redwood.

I felt around for the Glock and found it behind me, but I didn't need it. Rachel jumped down from the desk and leaned over her prey. I heard a buzz, like a mosquito zapper, and he seized again. She was holding a Taser against his neck. She'd Tasered him.

"Come on," she said. "Come on. Get up."

I was wobbly, but I wanted to live. We stepped over the body in the doorway, the one I had shot. On the way by, I reached down for his shotgun. It was a pistol-grip Mossberg. There were a bunch of shells in a pouch Velcroed to his belt. I grabbed it, too.

Out in the hall, I lurched instinctively toward the basement, but Rachel dragged me in the opposite direction to another doorway that led to the garage. When she pulled the door open, I was staring at a monster, a huge black Humvee. Either she had planned for a quick exit, or someone didn't like backing the thing out of the garage, because it was facing out. She circled around to the driver's side. The passenger-side door was so close to the wall on my side I could have practically climbed in from inside the house. She started the engine and then must have stepped down on the accelerator by accident. The engine roared in that dark, close space.

"I'm putting up the door. Ready?"

"Wait until I get this thing loaded," I said, struggling with the Mossberg. "There might be more of them." My fingers were shaking so badly I kept dropping the big cartridges on the floor in front of me.

"Hurry up!"

It was a nine-shot. I got six in and pumped one into the chamber. Then I powered down the window and braced the barrel on the door ledge, facing forward.

"Go."

She punched the opener. The door started to lift immediately, and an overhead light snapped on. She put both hands on the wheel and leaned forward. She could barely see over the dashboard, but she had the focus of a pointer ready to go get her bird.

We both watched as the door came up. My forehead was bleeding. I kept wiping the blood out of my eyes. We both had our necks bowed, looking for feet or legs to appear beneath that slowly rising curtain. The Humvee made a lot of noise in that cramped space, and the door was not quiet, either, which was probably why we didn't hear the man coming through the side door from the house until he was right there.

I tried to swivel the shotgun around, but he was too close. He grabbed the barrel and pushed it straight up with one hand. With the other, he stuck a semiautomatic into the car. I let go of my weapon and went for his. He got a couple of rounds off just as I slammed his arm against the dashboard. The cabin filled with the smoke and the smell and the sound. Rachel was screaming something, and he was trying to pull his arm back. I was kicking at his arm with both feet and feeling around with one hand for the Taser. Out of the blue, his fingers slipped from the grip of the gun, and he started screaming. Rachel had powered up the window and pinned his arm to the ceiling.

"Drive!" I yelled. *"Drive! Go!"*

She hit the gas, and his masked head whipped around, because he could see what I had seen—that there was about three inches of clearance on his side between the Humvee and the side of the garage doorway. The machine roared out of the gate, and the jamb instantly peeled off our attacker. When he stopped and we kept going, his arm whipped past my head and then disappeared completely. Rachel skidded out into the street. She must have hit the remote again, because as we were pulling away, the garage door was coming down.

17

WHEN WE GOT BACK TO HARVEY'S, RACHEL NEARLY RAN me over going through the front door. I found her in the kitchen with Harvey, standing next to him with his face in her hands, staring soulfully into his eyes.

"Baby," she said, "I'm so glad to see you. Are you all right?" Then she kissed his forehead and smiled as she wiped a tear from her eye. If it was a performance, it was a good one. It might also have been a posttrauma realignment of priorities. It was hard to tell with Rachel.

As for Harvey, the way he blushed in her presence made him look more alive than I had seen in ages. He reached up, took her hands in his, and kissed each one. Then he looked at me.

"Oh, my God. What happened?" The alarm on his face told me I must have been a mess.

"I'm all right." I had a skull-pounding headache, but everything else seemed to be working. "Where's Bo?"

"After he got your call, he brought more men over. He is showing them the back."

"Rachel can tell you what happened. I'm going to get cleaned up, and then the three of us have to sit down and talk." I left the two of them gazing into each other's eyes.

Bo came upstairs almost immediately. I had washed the blood out of my eyes, found a clean shirt, and just retrieved the first-aid kit from under the sink in the bathroom loosely designated as mine.

"What happened?" he asked, focusing immediately on my most obvious injury, the contusion on my forehead.

"I think I got whacked in the head with the butt of an assault rifle."

"Let me see." When he looked behind the damp, bloody washcloth, he seemed concerned but not alarmed. It was the sort of thing that qualified as routine in Bo's line of work. But his jaw tightened. Violence against women was another of his deeply entrenched rage buttons, and no matter how hard I tried to change his view, he considered me a woman first and a professional colleague second. He put down the toilet seat cover.

"Sit."

I did, happy to let someone else be in charge. He worked quickly and expertly, cleaning and dressing the wound.

"Drazen's got some technical operators," I said. "These guys were pros."

"How many?"

"Two for sure. Maybe three." I didn't know if the one we had scraped off the Humvee in the garage had been a third man or the Taser man. "They had all the gear. Masks and night-vision goggles and armor. All kinds of firepower. Bat belts. They were definitely Velcro guys. *Owwww.*"

"Hold still." He dabbed at the gash on my head, which had become the primary focus of all my nerve endings. "Voices?"

"I didn't hear any. They weren't talking, and there was too much other noise."

He put the lid on the bottle of peroxide and found the trash can for the pile of bloody cotton balls that had accumulated from his ministering. "They were not Drazen's men," he said. "He knew nothing of what happened."

"What? How do you know?"

"I spoke to him. He told me."

"But they were looking for Rachel. I mean, I think they were. They were looking for someone, and they were ready to take me out, so it must have been her." I started to stand up, but a wave of nausea put me right back down. "He must be lying to you, Bo."

"He wants Roger Fratello. He wants you to find him. Why would he kill you?"

I looked into his face, trying to detect whether he believed what he was saying or whether he believed it because Drazen had told him to. All I saw was a lot of stress in his eyes and deep creases in his thick forehead.

"If they weren't Drazen's men, then who were those guys?"

"I don't know. When my men got to the address you gave me, there were no bodies."

"No bodies? It's been, like, an hour. Are you sure they were at the right place?"

"As you said, technical operators. There were no shells or weapons or bodies. They cleaned up."

I leaned back against the tank and thought about it. If it wasn't Russians, there was only one other possibility. "Blackthorne."

Bo had found a large adhesive bandage. He peeled off the back and centered it over the cut. "Who is Blackthorne?"

"It's a what, not a who. A private military firm. Army for hire."

"Yes, yes. We had many such groups in my country.

That is how the Croats beat the Serbs." He perked up at the memory. "Their militia was trained by one of your American companies."

"Blackthorne had a car parked outside Rachel's house. They're all ex-military and intelligence. These guys must have been from Blackthorne."

"What did they want?"

"Rachel." This time when I got up, I managed to stay on my feet. "And she's about to tell me why."

Harvey and Rachel were still in the kitchen when we went downstairs. I settled in at the table with them with a big glass of cold water and a bunch of ibuprofen. Bo went off to make calls. He was still working his way off the Boston PD's "person of interest" list. Looking across the table at the newly constituted couple, I was almost afraid to begin.

"Rachel, why is Blackthorne after you?"

"Who's Blackthorne?"

"A private military firm."

"Mercenaries?" She looked at Harvey. "French Foreign Legion? That kind of thing?"

"No," Harvey said. "These are private firms that provide military services for profit."

"They can do that?"

"It is sometimes appropriate for governments to transfer some of their public responsibilities to the private sector." Harvey's measured tone was a nice balance to Rachel's increasing shrillness. "It can be more efficient on many fronts, including cost." Harvey looked at me. "Why do you ask?"

"I think that's who came after us at the house."

"That's terrific," Rachel said. "That's just great. First the Russians, and now I get to have a bunch of mercenaries on my ass."

"You have no idea why?"

"Not a clue."

I could have pushed harder, but there was so much to cover. I moved on. "You killed Vladislav Tishchenko."

"In self-defense." They said it in stereo.

"We'll talk about that in a second. Let me just get all the facts out first. You killed him, but Drazen thinks Roger Fratello did it. He's looking for Roger to, I don't know, exact his revenge, and he thinks Harvey can tell him where to find him. It's possible he thinks this because some mole inside the FBI tipped him off. That's pure speculation, but it could make some sense, because we know the FBI also thinks that Harvey can help them find Roger." I pulled out the only unoccupied chair at the table and put my feet up. "The FBI wants Roger because he tipped off his Russian—actually, Ukrainian—business partner, who I assume is Drazen Tishchenko, that there was an FBI agent undercover at Betelco. Drazen then either killed this agent or had him killed. Is that true, Rachel?"

I looked at her, hoping that our fracas in Acton would have convinced her the time for bullshit had passed.

"Drazen was in Betelco," she said. "That part is true, but I don't know anything about the FBI agent except that he died."

"It wasn't natural causes, Rachel. He was missing his head and his hands when they found him, which, according to the FBI, scared off any other potential witnesses in the Betelco case. That sounds like Drazen to me. What do you think?" Her neck stiffened. Either she was surprised by the news, or she just didn't like being reminded.

"Yes." She spoke precisely. "It sounds like something Drazen would do, but I had nothing to do with it. And I wouldn't."

"Even if it meant you would have gone to jail?"

"I wouldn't have done anything like that no matter what." Harvey put his hand on the table next to hers, and the two of them entwined fingers. She did sound convincing.

"Okay, so everyone is looking for Roger. As a way to protect Harvey, I have committed to Drazen that I would find Roger for him. At the time, I had no idea that doing that would put your life, Rachel's life, at risk. Your life would be at risk because Roger didn't really kill Vladi. He knows that you did and would presumably use that tidbit as a way to save his own life, if forced to choose. Is all of that right?"

Neither raised an objection. "Good. That means we have a conundrum. Find Roger and save Harvey, or leave him lost and save Rachel. My goal is to save you both . . . and me, of course."

"How do you expect to do that?"

"First, I need all the facts, starting with Betelco. I want to understand your relationship, Rachel, with the Tishchenkos. Start at the beginning, and don't leave anything out."

She hesitated, so I rephrased. "Susan Fratello says you brought the Tishchenkos into Betelco. She said you talked Roger into killing a pending deal to sell Betelco at a fair price in order to do it. Is that true?"

I thought one of Harvey's almost useless legs would pop up and bang the table. "I beg your pardon?"

He looked at me, I looked at Rachel, and then we both looked at Rachel.

"All right, here it is. The cold, hard truth. It's true. I did bring Drazen in."

Harvey's chin dropped about half an inch as he turned away. It wasn't much, but enough to convey his disappointment. She brought her other hand up so that she was holding his hand with both of hers. "I'm sorry," she said, trying to get him to look at her. "I had no choice."

Gee, that was a shocker.

"It was my husband. My sweet, stupid, degenerate gambler husband. Gorgeous to look at, but . . ." She couldn't suppress a wistful smile before she must have realized it was Harvey's hand she was holding. "I never should have left you, baby. I didn't know what a good thing I had."

"What about Gary?" We needed to stay on point.

"Drazen likes to buy gambling debts. He looks for anyone he considers to be useful to him, like lawyers and accountants and cops. People on the inside of successful companies. Gary had a big debt we couldn't pay. Drazen bought it and then told us he would kill him if I didn't do what he said."

"What did he ask you to do?"

She tried again to make eye contact with Harvey. He didn't seem to be able to look at her, but he also hadn't pulled his hand out of the knot of interlocking fingers and thumbs where she had tied herself to him. "Identify targets of opportunity for him. He had a lot of money coming into the country, and he needed legitimate places to wash it. He wanted it where no one would look for it."

"You did this with other companies?"

"I had no choice."

It made sense. As an auditor for midsize firms, she would have been in the perfect position to know who was vulnerable to a Drazen pillaging. "You figured out how badly Roger needed cash and brought the Russians in. Is that right?"

"Roger begged me to bring them in. He was all upset about the company going down, his father's business and the family legacy and all that crap. At least, that was what he said at the time. He knew I had . . . connections. He asked me to hook him up. I told him he was better off with the deal he had, but he wouldn't listen, and he wouldn't leave me alone, so I did what he asked. I introduced him to Drazen's people. Drazen came in and recapitalized him."

"What did Drazen get in exchange?"

"He got to use the company for various things."

"Such as?"

"What you'd expect. Laundering money. Shipping stuff around the world using Betelco as cover."

"How much did Roger know?"

"Turns out good old Roger knew exactly what he was getting into. Not too long after they came in, he started giving me the cold shoulder. I didn't see him much anymore. If you want to know the truth, I think he used me to get them in there, because once they were in with all their dirty cash, he started stealing it."

"Stealing Drazen's cash sounds like a risky strategy."

"It put me in a very bad position, because if Drazen found out, he would have blamed me."

"Let's see, you screwed your lover, Roger, over by bringing in your Russian investors, then got worried that Roger was about to screw you back?"

"Exactly. I got the feeling he was about to take his dough and disappear and leave me holding the bag. I couldn't let that happen. Drazen would have thought I was in it with him from the start. I had to know what he was up to, so I went through the books and . . . the *books*, if you know what I mean. I figured out where he was hiding the money. That night that it all came down, Roger and I were supposed to meet at the offices to talk about it." She glanced again at Harvey and pitched her voice to him and him only. "That's why I was there. I didn't have any choice, baby. They would have killed Gary."

The implications of doing what she had done to protect the man for whom she'd left Harvey, while she was sleeping with another man, seemed to elude her. "Anyway, he never came, but Vladi did. That's the night it all went down."

"That's the night Vladi died?"

"Yes."

"Keep going."

"Vladi was like Drazen's puppy dog. He followed him around and did errands for him. From what I heard, he was his bodyguard back wherever they came from. Vladi took a bullet for him more than once. Anyway, I was there at the offices working late that night when Vladi showed up. I was by myself, and all of a sudden, this big, hairy, smelly piece of crap whacked out on coke and God knows what else walks in, sees me, and starts drooling. I knew I was in trouble. He'd been up for days drinking and snorting and gambling and whoring. He thought I was just part of the package, a cute young thing sitting right there for the picking. I tried to talk to him, but those people—Russians, Ukrainians, whatever—to them, a woman is for screwing or beating or maybe both at the same time. He was on me before I had time to scream. He bent me backward over Roger's desk and put his tongue down my throat."

Harvey was listening closely. The healthy coloring in his face had been temporary. He was as pale as ever.

"There were so many different ways I thought I would die that night." Rachel's voice had softened. She was sounding as exposed as she must have felt lying across that desk. Harvey patted her on the arm. "I was scared out of my mind, so while he was groping me, I started looking for his gun. I knew he'd be carrying. He was so far gone when I found it, he didn't notice. I shot him."

"What kind of gun?" I asked her.

Her eyes flashed. "What difference does that make?"

"Do you know how to disengage the safety on an automatic? Can you do it while you're bent over a desk being raped?"

"You do a lot of things you didn't think you could when you're about to die. I found the gun, and I stood him up, and I shot him." Her voice had turned brittle, but it wasn't strong. Even though she was angry, there was still something vulnerable about her, and I couldn't tell whether it was harder to feel for her or *not* to feel for her.

"How many times?"

"Three."

"Was he dead?"

"Oh, yes."

I turned to Harvey. "This is where you came in."

"Very well." He shifted his weight, cleared his throat, and began. "It happened four years ago in March. I remember, because it had been a long winter already, and it was still so very cold. It was evening. I was on my way to see a client, a man who owned a chain of dry cleaners. I was doing his taxes."

This might have been one level of detail more than I needed, but too much was better than too little. I let him carry on.

"My coat was on, and my hand was on the knob of the door when the phone rang. It was a rule. Once I had my coat on, I would never answer the phone. For some reason, that day I waited, and when the machine picked up, I heard Rachel's voice." He gave her a shy, sideways glance. "She was crying."

"You broke your rule."

"Yes, thank God. She said she was in trouble and needed my help."

I wanted to ask if he'd bothered to ask what kind of trouble, but there was no point. Nothing could have drawn Harvey in more than having a chance to be of service, especially to Rachel. "What happened then?"

"I went to the address she gave me. It was an office building in Cambridge. Roger Fratello's office. She was on the fourth floor. The elevator was out of order, and I had difficulty climbing the stairs. The more I tried to hurry, the harder it became."

I pictured him trying to make those stairs, crawling on his hands and knees if he had to, to get to her.

"When I got there, she was sitting in a chair, shaking like a frightened animal. Vladislav Tishchenko was dead on the floor. She told me she had killed him. There was blood." He closed his eyes. "There was much blood."

"Keep going."

"It was a nightmare. The entire scene was a nightmare. We rolled the body in . . . in large plastic bags Rachel found in a janitor's closet and carried it down the stairs. We put it into the trunk of the dead man's car. There was money in the trunk, packs of currency and lots of it. I had to move it to fit the body in. I put it in a bag Rachel found that was in the front seat."

"Was this the money that ended up in Brussels?"

"I assume it was."

"Then this explains how your prints got on it. You handled it to put it in the bag." I looked at Rachel. "Did you ever touch it?"

"Harvey handed it to me in a bag. I never touched it."

"And you gave it to Roger when you helped him run. Is that it?"

They looked at each other. "Yes," Rachel said quickly. "That's exactly it."

I made a mental note to come back to that point. Something wasn't right.

"All right, Harvey. You had this body in the trunk. What then?"

"I drove Rachel home. I helped her clean up and dispose of her bloody clothes, and then I drove the body out of town and buried it."

"You buried Vladi?"

"Yes."

"By yourself?"

"I was not so feeble then as I am now. What else was I to do?"

I raised an eyebrow at Rachel. That was all it took to bring her back to her posture of snide self-defense. "I had blood on my clothes. We also had one car too many. We had to take my car home. But while I was there, Gary woke up. There was no way I could go out again."

"That was convenient. Did you ever tell Gary what had happened?"

"I never did."

"You just left Harvey to clean up your mess."

Harvey cleared his throat and waded in. "Nothing she could have done would have changed what I did."

I tried to picture the logistics. If they took her car home, that left them with Vladi's, and Harvey's still at Roger's office in Cambridge. "You said you drove Vladi in his own car. What did you do with it?"

"I drove it to the Alewife Park-and-Ride. I wiped off the fingerprints and took the T into Cambridge. Then I walked to my car and drove it home."

That meant the Cambridge police or the transit authority had found that car. "Neither of you was ever questioned in the investigation?"

Rachel shrugged. "As far as they wanted to know, Roger did it. Vladi disappeared, and then Roger disappeared. They didn't look too far past him."

"What did Drazen think?"

Rachel smiled. "He believed what they believed, and he believed me. I told him I had seen Roger kill Vladi. It was the least I could do to that bastard."

Their story made sense. I couldn't find any major holes. But then the two of them looked at each other, and I saw something pass between them. They no longer shared the same home, the same name, or the same monogrammed sheets, but Rachel and Harvey still had the ability to understand each other without words. It was one of the vestiges that endure after the end of an intimate relationship. There was more they hadn't told me.

"What's the rest?"

Rachel caught the inside of her cheek between her teeth but said nothing. I looked at Harvey. I did not want him to be hiding things from me. Finally, he spoke. "Roger had the incident on video."

"Excuse me?" I sat forward. Perhaps I hadn't heard right.

Rachel pulled her top hand off the pile and used it to straighten her blouse. "He had the whole thing. The shooting. The cleanup. He had it all."

"How did he get it?"

She shrugged as if it should have been obvious. "Surveillance cameras in his office."

"You were the auditor, and you didn't know about them?"

"It was a secret camera. Roger put it in himself. No

one knew. It was like that Nixon thing. Who cares how he got it? He came to my house that same night and showed me what he had. He told me he would give it to Drazen if we didn't give him what he wanted."

"Which was what?"

"To get out of the country with his head, his hands, and his money."

I closed my eyes and pressed the heels of my hands against the bones just above them. "Let me guess. You called Harvey, who had probably just returned home from burying the body of the man you had killed."

I opened my eyes. Harvey looked self-conscious. Rachel looked defiant. Maybe I was getting the hang of this silent communication thing. "Harvey, what did you do for Roger?"

"I alerted several banking contacts I had in Europe. I opened numbered accounts for him in Switzerland. I had several fake IDs made for him and set up credit-card accounts in those names. I did what I could to make sure he would have access to his money anonymously and from a distance."

In short, everything Ling had accused him of, and Baltimore was not just a city in Maryland.

I got up and went to the refrigerator. It had been a while since my cold water had been cold. I grabbed one of the checked dish towels from the oven handle. As I made my own ice pack, I tried to distill the information to its essential elements. I needed to find Roger. If I found him and tried to bring him back, he would no doubt invoke the power of the video. That assumed he still had it after all this time or that it hadn't burned up in Salanna 809. Or that Ling hadn't also stumbled across it in a Brussels safety deposit box. If he had, he was keeping it awfully close to the vest. Too close, I decided.

If he'd had that kind of leverage, he would have used it on Harvey by now. The safest thing was to assume Roger still had his deadly digital weapon and was still willing to wield it.

I checked my watch. What had Dan said about the hostage reunion? That it was on for another day and a half, which meant I had to get to Paris by tomorrow before noon. Dan's next flight to Paris would get me there in time. I had no expectation that Roger Fratello would come to a hostage reunion, as Gilbert Bernays or anyone else, not if he was on the run from Drazen. But if he had been on that hijacked flight, then the last people I knew to have seen him would be there. I went back to the table and eased into my chair. The other aches and pains in the rest of my body were beginning to catch up with my head.

"We need to find Roger."

"Excuse me." Rachel waved her hand. "Are we forgetting what happens to me if we find Roger?"

"Think about it this way. When Roger tells Drazen that he didn't kill Vladi but you did, Drazen has no reason to believe him unless he has the video to back it up. I think the first thing to do is find Roger and find out if he has the video. You can help me find him or not, but that's what I intend to do. Harvey?"

"Yes?"

"You set Roger up for his life on the run. Is there any way you can track him that way? Through these accounts you set up, maybe?"

"I destroyed all my documentation."

"Destroyed it?"

"I never wanted anyone to find him, nor did I envision any reason to find him myself. For him to come back would have meant a death sentence for Rachel."

"All right, look. There's some indication that Roger might have been hijacked."

"*Hijacked?*" Rachel was incredulous. Harvey was intrigued.

"Do you remember Salanna 809 from four years ago?" It didn't matter if they did. "A bunch of people got hijacked to Sudan by terrorists. Some were held onboard for ten days, and most of those were killed. Among the survivors was a man named Gilbert Bernays."

Harvey's eyes opened wide. "That's him. That was one of the aliases we set up for Roger."

"Good. That's good to know." I should have been excited, but I was too worn out. "Gilbert-slash-Roger was on his way to Johannesburg when he got hijacked. Does that give us any clues for how to find him?"

"Forget about all that." Rachel sounded weary. "I know how to find him."

"How?"

"Answer his e-mail."

18

THE CAMBRIDGE CYBER CAFÉ LOOKED LIKE A SHOPPING bazaar in India. The plaster walls were painted the color of Georgia clay. On the floor were baskets full of magazines and throw pillows. If people hadn't been there to use computers, they probably would have all been sitting cross-legged on the floor and drinking organic ginger beer.

I pulled up to the counter and signed in. The pierced, plaited, and tattooed desk jockey looked down at my name and asked to see a picture ID.

"Just to be sure," he said. "You're alone, right?"

I told him I was, and he took me over to a computer in a secluded alcove. A tent card perched on top of the monitor announced that the machine was reserved.

"How did you know I was coming?"

"Dude called." He leaned across the back of the chair to slap at the keys. "Said you'd be coming and wanted you to sit here."

I looked around at the other tables and desks. It wasn't crowded, and the people who were there seemed to be deep into whatever were doing. "Why here?"

"This one has encryption software on it. You're set."

He walked away, and I sat down. He had signed on to a site, clicked on a link to a messaging service, and typed in, "She's here." I waited, feeling naked in that situation without Felix either at my side or on the phone, but my instructions had been specific: "Come alone, and stay alone."

Now there was a response, with the cursor blinking next to it: *"alex shanahan?"* It was weird. It was as if the monitor were a one-way mirror and whoever was at the other end could see me, but I couldn't see him.

I typed in my response. "Roger Fratello?"

"answer the question. is this you?" The cursor blinked, and then this appeared: *" ' . . . representing Rachel Ruffielo. We are in receipt of your last communication but need positive identification. Who are you, and can you prove it? Please contact ASAP. We want to make a deal.' "*

I recognized it as an excerpt from the reply I had made in response to Roger's message, the one Rachel had reluctantly produced after it turned out to be in her best interest. The communication had arrived in Rachel's in-box several days earlier, and had been the trigger for almost everything else that had happened, including her midnight move and the visit to Harvey. It had been short, blunt, and very intriguing. "Tell me," it said, "where Vladi is buried or the video goes to Drazen." Rachel had no idea why Roger would want Vladi's body, especially after all this time. Harvey had refused to tell her where he buried it. He didn't want to incriminate her.

"Yes," I typed. "I am Alex Shanahan, Boston PI representing Rachel. Why do you want location of the body?"

"this is not roger"

I read it, then I read it again. It was a hard sentence to

misinterpret. I typed, "My message was response to blackmail threat. Did you send it?"

"message was sitting in out-box. sent automatically when I signed on"

"Who are you?"

"not important"

"Why do you have Roger's laptop?"

"no comment"

I sat back to contemplate. An e-mail message sits in Roger's out-box and goes out automatically the next time someone—but not Roger—opens the program. I hadn't seen that one coming. "If you're not Roger, how did you sign on?"

"hacked in"

"The account is still active?"

"is that rhetorical?"

Good point. Obviously, it was. I wasn't sure what to say. I hadn't prepared for this particular scenario. "Where is Roger?"

"don't know"

"Just to be clear, you're not blackmailing my client?"

"not for money but watched an interesting video. explanation?"

Now things were getting tricky. I hadn't mentioned any video, so he must have found it on Roger's hard drive. But I had to know his intentions before giving him information. "Hard to give info when I can't get any in return. Who are you? Why do you have Roger's computer?"

I hit enter and waited. I didn't like exchanging information this way. I didn't even like talking on the phone. I liked seeing the face of the person I was speaking to.

"investigative journalist working on story. came into possession of computer by legitimate means. whom did rachel kill?"

Yep, he had definitely seen the video, and he was another reporter, probably looking for a story. "Have answers to all questions. Makes for a great story. Will trade for laptop with video."

who is fratello?

"Former CEO of Betelco, embezzler, and accused conspirator in a murder. Missing for four years. Possibly hijacked." That should get his attention.

hijacked?

"Can tell you more, but would like to meet and get file back."

no way. not even in the country

Here was the problem with written communication. Did that comment mean "No way will I even consider meeting with you," or "There is no way I can arrange a meeting with you or anyone else because I'm not even in the country"? I craved inflection.

"Telephone?"

this is the only way i'll talk to you. spew or get off

That took care of the inflection problem. I sat for a long time with my hands resting on the keyboard, long enough that another entry came up from him, one that simply said "???????????????????"

"I'm thinking," I typed. "Don't bother me." It's amazing how e-mail as a communication medium removes the rules that make us generally civil to one another. I was trying to think of a way to make sure that if I gave him anything, I got what I needed, too. I wanted to be interesting but not informative. I pulled out my notepad and paged through it. I finally went with the obvious.

"The man in the video is a Ukrainian mobster. I'm trying to keep the video out of the wrong hands. It's a good story for a reporter. Will be in Paris within the next 24 hours. Would like to meet." I hit enter. Another long delay. I didn't know how to interpret the silence. Was he thinking, or had he left the building? I got tired of waiting.

"You have my contact info," I typed. "Let me know when and if you want to talk."

I reached down and was about to turn off the computer when his response came back.

"i'm an investigative journalist, not a reporter . . . are you working with blackthorne?"

Blackthorne? My pulse rate jumped. "Working independently, but have information on Blackthorne."

The answer came fast. *"what information?"*

My heart sped up to about two beats for every blink of the cursor. "Will trade for video."

I waited. This was it. Finally, his answer came. *"will meet you in paris"*

I used a self-serve kiosk at the Majestic Airlines counter to check in. The security line moved quickly because the Paris flight was the last of the evening. After clearing the checkpoint, I went straight for the gate where the LA trip was boarding. The second the agent opened the door, I handed over my boarding pass, rolled down the bridge, onto the aircraft, and all the way to the aft galley. Dan was waiting with a ramper's hat and jacket.

"See anybody?"

"No," I said, slipping the gear on over my jeans. "But that doesn't mean they're not back there."

"Who?"

"Russians . . . paramilitary storm troopers . . . FBI."

"Since when did you get so paranoid?"

"Since this case." I put on my ramper's hat. "How do I look?"

"Like I should be reaming your ass for dogging it. Get out of here."

The cabin services crew was just finishing. I joined in and went down the aft stairs. I walked across the ramp to the Paris-bound B767 and climbed the outside jet-bridge stairs. Using Dan's key, I unlocked the door and went inside.

Passengers were already boarding, so I stood to the side and waited. Dan arrived moments later, strolling down the jetway with my bag. He traded it for the hat, the coat, and the boarding pass to LA.

"Here." He put a ticket jacket in my hand. "Don't say I never did anything for you."

Inside, I found a first-class boarding pass to Orly. He had already waived the sixty-day advance purchase requirement on my ticket. I was flying to Paris in style, or at least as much style as airlines provided these days, for the grand total of three hundred dollars. That was damn good news.

"Wow. I didn't expect this."

"You don't deserve it, either. I just didn't want to hear you bitch and moan." He turned to help a stooped woman with long gray hair who had caught her rolling bag on the lip of the aircraft door. "Here you go, ma'am. Have a nice flight."

She thanked him, and so did I.

"Remember the story," he said. "I don't want you embarrassing me with my contacts over there."

"I've got it. Don't worry."

Dan had told a tiny white lie to get me onto the very tightly controlled guest list for the hostage reunion. I was enhancing the customer-care section of Majestic's disaster manual, the one that gets pulled out when you have to turn your maintenance hangar into a morgue or make arrangements for your hijacked passengers, or their bodies, to get home. I was to interview passengers about how they had been treated in the wake of the flight 809 hijacking to find out what had worked and what hadn't, what they had needed and not gotten.

"What do you think you'll find over there, anyway?"

"Someone who can tell me they've seen or heard from Roger lately, or his alter ego, Gilbert Bernays."

"That reminds me." He pulled some folded pages from the pocket of his suit jacket. "Take this with you."

"What is it?"

"It's the 809 manifest and as much updated contact information as I could find. I was going to throw it away, but I thought you might need it."

Like Felix, Dan had a way of coming through with all the things I didn't even know I needed. I gave him a kiss on the cheek. "Thanks for the first-class seat."

"Get your ass onboard. I'm not taking a delay for you."

19

IF YOU DIDN'T KNOW OTHERWISE, YOU WOULD NEVER guess the people talking and laughing at the Paris Hyatt were former hostages gathered to commemorate their hijacking. Considering the outcome, perhaps gathered to celebrate the fact that they were there at all. Nine of them, plus eight hijackers, hadn't come back.

I took a few minutes at the door to review the scene. Straight in from the airport, I'd taken time to shower in my room and change my clothes. Then I'd ordered a room-service breakfast and eaten, so I was feeling all right. I'd put some heavy-duty concealer over the cut on my forehead, pulled my bangs down as camouflage, and come down early to the ballroom.

The room was just beginning to fill. People gathered around twelve round tables with white tablecloths set for brunch. Each table had a bright bouquet of spring flowers as a centerpiece, which struck me as optimistic, given the cold and damp early-spring weather outside.

As people filtered in, I spotted the one man who looked to be in charge. I got close enough to read his name tag. He was the contact Dan had set up for me.

"Dr. Wilson." I offered my hand. "I'm Alex Shanahan from Majestic Airlines."

"Oh, indeed. You're the researcher from Boston. We had a call that you were coming. Welcome."

There wasn't much on Dr. Wilson's tall frame except his suit, and his voice was almost as wispy as he was, but there was substance in his eyes. He seemed to be someone you could count on.

"Thank you," I said. "I feel privileged to be here. I know you don't let a lot of people in."

He shifted his drink from one hand to the other and put the free hand in his pocket. It allowed him to lower his head without appearing to be whispering. "This is a smart thing your airline is doing. Salanna did a very poor job in the area of customer support. We were scattered all across Africa with no money, no passports, and only the clothes on our backs. Everything was taken from us. We had no cell phones and very little information. You never realize how important your identity is in this world until you stand without it in a hostile country."

When I hadn't been sleeping on the flight over, I had been studying the information I had on the passengers, trying to match names on the manifest to stories in the various articles. I knew Dr. Wilson had diabetes. He had been let off the plane early with a group of women and children. His being from Portugal and considering how the ordeal ended, his disease might have saved his life. "You were one of the hostages?"

"We prefer to be called survivors." He gestured to his name tag. It said it right there: "Survivor." Mine said "Guest."

"I'm sorry. I didn't mean—"

"Not at all. How would you like to approach this? Shall I introduce you to some of our group?"

"I know this seems xenophobic," I said, "but would it be possible for me to start with the Americans, since Majestic is a predominantly domestic carrier? Domestic to us, anyway." I pulled out a picture of Roger and showed him. "How about this man? I've been told that he would be a good one to start with. You know, lots of complaints to air."

"Ah, Mr. Fratello."

"Yes, Mr.—" Wait, he wasn't supposed to know that name. "What did you call him?"

"Your American FBI showed me a picture of this man. They have a different photograph, but it is, naturally, the same face. The agent told me this Roger Fratello is or was a notorious criminal in the States. Is it true?"

"I have no idea." I pretended to dig through my bag, as though I might find the answer in there. I should have figured the FBI would be doing exactly as I was trying to do. I looked around at the growing crowd. "Is the FBI here?"

"No. I was interviewed in Lisbon."

"This is embarrassing," I said. "I thought his name was Gilbert Bernays."

"Yes, so did we all." He handed the picture back.

"Whatever his name was, he was on this plane, right?"

"I'm told he was."

"You don't remember him?"

"The takeover happened within one hour of our departure. We were immediately separated on the aircraft into small groups. Much of the time, we were bent over in the crash position or blindfolded. Beyond my own group, the first time I met most of these people was at our first reunion."

"I see. I'm going out on a limb and assuming Gilbert Bernays has never been to any of your reunions."

He laughed. "That's correct. I don't believe anyone— at least, none of us—has seen him since the ordeal ended."

We were being increasingly interrupted as more guests arrived and made a point of saying hello to Dr. Wilson. As he was greeting someone, I pulled out the manifest Dan had given me.

"The other American men who survived"—I checked my notes again—"Voytag, Plume, and McGarry. Are any of these gentlemen here?"

"I'm afraid Peter Voytag died last year."

"That's too bad. How did he die?"

"Very sad. He survived the inferno, only to be felled by prostate cancer. He was young, too. But Frank and Tim are scheduled to be here. Perhaps we can find them." He stretched his body up like a Slinky dog and checked around the room. "I don't see them yet." He was about to comment further when a young woman rushed up to him with the distressing news that a reporter was at the door, agitating to come in. A voice of authority was needed.

"Is it Mr. Kraft again?"

"No," she said. "It's someone different."

Dr. Wilson turned to me. "I do apologize, but I must take care of this matter."

"Who is Mr. Kraft?"

"He's a reporter. Actually, he insists on being called a journalist. An *investigative* journalist."

"Really?" That was very interesting. My cyber pen pal had made the same self-reverential distinction in our chat. "What's his first name?"

"Max." I wrote the name in my notebook, on the off chance that I had just stumbled over the Mr. No Comment in possession of Roger's computer. We were still on for our meeting in Paris, but I had no idea when or where. He had all my contact information. I had none for him.

"What does he want?"

"He's been agitating for a list of names and numbers of the survivors, and I won't give it to him."

"There's no reason you should."

"I agree. I feel an obligation to protect these people." He looked around the room. "We didn't ask to be hijacked. None of us did. We shouldn't have to talk to reporters if we choose not to."

"Is he doing a story?"

"So he says. You must excuse me, but I've told people you would be here, so you shouldn't have any trouble."

"No problem. I can find my own way around."

He apologized again and rushed off.

I surveyed the crowd. A group of seven or eight was gathered around a nearby table. Some were sitting. Some were leaning in with hands on the backs of chairs. With a range of skin color and dress, they looked to be from an array of different countries and cultures. Checking name tags, I saw that many were marked as survivors. I introduced myself as the researcher from Boston. There were several nods of recognition, which made everything easier.

"I'm looking for this man for a project I'm doing for Majestic Airlines. Have any of you seen or heard from him? I believe his name is Gilbert Bernays?"

I handed the picture of Roger to a woman in a sari. She shook her head and passed it on. The group validated a few things Dr. Wilson had told me. First, that no one had seen or heard from Fratello-Bernays since the hijacking. Second, that the group, on the whole, made for very unreliable witnesses. At the time of the hijacking, they had been scared and in shock. Now, four years removed from an event they wanted to forget anyway, they mostly recognized each other from the reunions and not the hijacking.

The same was not true, however, of Frank Plume and Tim McGarry, the two American survivors I stumbled upon in a corner. They were chatting with another survivor named Helene. I introduced myself and listened in as they talked about their meetings with the State Department.

"I got back three pages of an old expense report and my wallet." Tim was crisp and angular, with wire-rim glasses, an efficient haircut, and a pale pallor. "I had a flashback moment when I saw it. It was like this list of things I did on the last day of my old life. I don't even have that job anymore. Hell, I'm not even in that business. After I got back, I quit and started my own—"

"Pictures of my husband were still in mine." Helene didn't bother waiting for Tim to finish. "He's my ex-husband now, but anyway, my license and credit cards were gone. I asked them if they thought my ID had been used to make a fake one. Can you imagine if one of these people got into the country using my name? More and more of those suicide bombers are women now, you know."

"Did you get any electronic equipment back?" That was Frank. Thicker and healthier-looking than Tim, he had coarse, curly sideburns and a comfortable grip on his highball glass. He also talked really fast. "You didn't, didja? Me, neither. That's because they took all that stuff, all the cameras and recorders and laptops, they took it back to that place in Afghanistan, and they reused it."

"Who?" Helene sounded intrigued.

"The terrorists."

"Reused it for what?"

"For whatever terrorists do with those things. They're

not living in tents, you know. They're digital, just like we are. They send e-mails and get e-mails. They have Web sites, which they use to send coded messages. They talk on cell phones. They use video cameras for scouting targets. Just the other day in my neck of the woods, they caught a husband-and-wife team with a videocam on the Chesapeake Bay Bridge and Tunnel. They were taking shots from every angle. Bad things are going to happen." He raised his glass to drink but ended up using it as a pointer. "You watch. It's only a matter of when."

His tone was ominous, but I couldn't blame him. Something bad had already happened to him.

"Are you saying some of our belongings could have been used to set up an attack?" Helene seemed very interested in the idea that her possessions had gone on to participate in some meaningful event.

"That's what repurposing means—using it for their purposes. That could have been your camcorder they were using."

"Oh, I didn't have one—"

"Or my laptop. Did you ever think about that? My laptop sending e-mails to sleeper cells in Detroit." He raised his eyebrows and gulped half of his drink.

Here was an interesting concept, this idea that the passengers' computers had been part of the Zormat stash. I had only been thinking about things like wallets and family photos coming out of the Hefty bag.

"Did everyone onboard have their laptops confiscated?"

Frank looked at me. "Who are you again?" I reminded him. Researcher from Boston, Majestic Airlines . . . "Oh, yeah. Sorry."

"They took everything," Tim said. "Every damn thing we had, they took. Socks. Pencils. Key chains. CDs. They got a big kick out of playing our music. That's something I wish I could have back, my traveling music. A lot of those CDs were hard to find. A bunch of them were signed by the artists."

"Have any of you heard about reporters ending up with these computers?"

Frank shook his head at me. "The government is keeping all that stuff."

"Whose government?"

"Ours. No one would ever know, right? They would just say it all got lost."

"Do you know that's true?"

"Do you know it's not?"

Tim chuckled. "Typical conspiracy theorist. All leading questions and vague accusations and an entire case built on proving a negative." He looked at me. "Here's the thing with the computers. They were in the house in Zormat. The military found them and called in the CIA. In the meantime, the villagers picked the house clean, which is what happens when you leave valuable electronic equipment lying around poverty-stricken, war-torn countries. All the laptops were gone when the spies got there, but there's a reporter named Kraft who got in and got them. Supposedly, he bought them off a kid with a goat. He says he's got a big story from one of them."

Before I could jump on that one, Frank was into it. "Timmy, you talked to him, didn't you? You told me you weren't going to."

"I changed my mind."

I had to work hard to make my tone casual like theirs, because I wasn't supposed to be asking these questions. It wasn't easy, because it was pretty obvious Max Kraft was my guy. "What's the deal with this Kraft? Everyone around here talks about him as if he's not welcome."

"He's public enemy number one around here," Tim said. "He tried to hack into Raul's computer and steal the contact information for all of us."

"Dr. Wilson's?"

"Raul was not happy about that." He looked pointedly at Frank. "That is the full and true story with the computers."

"Okay, okay." Frank was sounding a little desperate. "Forget about the computers. What about what happened that night, Timmy? You saw it, too. You can't tell me there wasn't something going on there."

"All hell was breaking loose, Frank." Tim glanced quickly at me. "I'd been thrown out of a burning airplane, bullets were flying, it was dark, and there was smoke everywhere. We were covered in blood. We all had heavy beards. My own mother wouldn't have known me. I have no idea what I saw, and I would appreciate it if you wouldn't go around telling people what you think I should have seen. Now, if you'll excuse us . . ."

Helene didn't seem ready to move on, but I was glad Tim took her with him. That left me alone with Frank. I moved a step closer. "He seems a little touchy on the subject."

"Yeah, he doesn't like to talk about it." Frank was looking past me. He turned slightly and dipped his shoulder toward me. "Do you know that woman over there to my right? She's wearing that raincoat kind of jacket thing. Be cool when you look."

I glanced over. The woman he described turned away when I glanced her way.

"I don't know her. Why?"

"She's been staring at us."

He could have been right. It could also have been the paranoia talking. Whatever it was, he was agitated. "Maybe we could go outside and talk," I offered.

"Good. I could use a smoke. Who are you again?"

Since he couldn't remember anyway, I dropped the pretense and just showed him the picture of Roger. "I'm trying to find this man. It's important. If you have information that can help me, I hope you'll share it."

He already had a cigarette in one hand. He took the picture in the other and held it at arm's length the way people do who are missing their glasses. "Gil Bernays? That's who you're looking for?"

Apparently. "Have you seen him or heard from him?"

"Nope." He chuckled. "Not likely to, either. Gil's dead."

"What?" I stopped, but he had gone on. I caught him as he was leaving the ballroom. "Are you sure?"

"Hell, yeah, I'm sure. I watched him die."

20

I FOLLOWED FRANK OUT TO THE SIDEWALK IN FRONT OF the hotel. He lit his cigarette. "I like it over here," he said, taking a long drag. "You can smoke." Having cheated death once, he must have felt invincible, because he smoked unfiltereds.

"Are you sure this man is dead?" I held up the picture again. "The records say he's alive."

He tapped the picture. "Nuh-uh. The official record is wrong. Hoffmeyer survived, and your guy died."

"Stephen Hoffmeyer?"

"That's right."

"I'm sorry, I don't mean to be obtuse." I held up the photo of Roger Fratello one more time. "This man, Gilbert Bernays, and the other one you called Hoffmeyer were both on the plane at the end?"

"Right there with the rest of us." He picked a bit of tobacco from his tongue. "The records all show that Gil survived and Hoff died. It's the other way around. It's part of the cover-up. They want everyone to think Hoffmeyer is dead."

"*They* being the government?"

"Yeah. Hoffmeyer was CIA."

"Why do you say that?"

"I'm not just saying it. I know it." He shifted his weight to his back foot and started ticking off points on his fingers. "He spoke Arabic or Farsi or whatever they talked. He said he'd done work as a contractor in Saudi. He wasn't afraid of the boys with the guns. At all. He spent all kinds of time with them. He always said he was trying to get stuff for us, more food or water or whatnot. He kept them from killing a hostage. He wasn't just a normal schlub like the rest of us."

"How did he save a hostage?"

"They were threatening to kill one of us. It turned out it was going to be Peter. Pete Voytag, God rest his soul. It was all so random. It could have just as easily been me." He sucked a little more life out of his cigarette. "They came and got Peter and took him up there screaming and crying. Next thing, Hoffmeyer just pushes the kid watching us out of the way and goes up there. This kid had a Kalashnikov." He shook his head, still impressed. "Anyways, there's a lot of shouting and yelling, not in English. Then the two of them, Peter and Hoff, they both came back. That was it. I don't know what he said to them, but they never tried that again."

I made a note to check out Hoffmeyer's background. It would be easy enough to see if he'd really worked in Saudi. "What else?"

"He knew his way around a situation, I'll tell you that."

"How do you mean?"

"Tim and me, we're not standing here today if it wasn't for him. He saved us. I don't know why Timmy doesn't see that. I think he sees it. He just won't say it, you know?"

"How did he save you?"

"The night that it happened, the kid they had watching went up to the front of the plane and left us alone. He'd never done that before, so I had to think"—he touched his temple with his middle finger—"what is so important? It can't be too many choices, right? Either they're letting us go, or they're not, and I just had the feeling it wasn't that they were about to let us walk. I wasn't the only one, because even though the cabin smelled like piss the whole time we were in there, it started to smell like fresh piss. Everyone was thinking the same thing, that we were all gonna die. After ten days of the worst hell you can imagine, they were about to kill us. It sucked."

He was a little hard to follow, because he was shoving so many words into such a small space. But I had practice. I knew Dan.

"Then the kid came back through the curtain, and I swear to you, the look on his face, he looked exactly like one of those Columbine boys. Slow, mechanical, completely blank. He came down the aisle and started shooting people, but his face, you know, he looked like he was taking out the garbage. I got up and ran, but there were some that fell, and this kid, I don't know, maybe he was seventeen, he walked up and just . . ." Frank put his index and middle fingers together and aimed them carefully at the sidewalk. "He put the barrel up against a man's head, this human being he'd been talking and joking with, and pulled the trigger."

He paused for another long drag, sucking until the insides of his cheeks must have touched. I got the feeling looking at his face that it was easy to launch into this story but not so easy to finish it.

"Anyways," he said, "that was Gil. He was the first one to go."

My mind went blank for a few seconds, the way a computer screen does when things go haywire. News of Roger's death had crashed the system for me. All my assumptions were wrong.

He loosened his tie and shoved one hand into his pocket. Again, he turned his shoulder in toward me, and it was almost as if the two of us were watching the incident unfold on a screen in front of us as he narrated. "Then what happened was a bomb went off. The shooting started outside. All of us stampeded for the door. Everyone was yelling and pushing. There was another explosion. This one knocked me down, and I didn't want to get up. All I wanted to do was hug the floor. There was so much smoke. I couldn't see. I couldn't breathe. Someone grabbed me by the shoulders and stood me up and shoved me down the aisle. Me and the rest."

" 'Stay low.' He kept telling us that, to stay under the smoke, but then another bomb went off just as we got to this crack, this opening. Everything went sideways. He told me to jump. I looked down, and it was too far down, but it was too damn hot to go back, and he said, 'Drop and roll. You'll be fine. Go.' He pushed me, and I was all of a sudden on the ground, and I did roll, because that was the last thing he said to me, and it was what was in my mind. Then he was there again picking me up and pushing me away from the fire. I turned around to look and see who it was. It was Hoffmeyer. He looked me right in the eye and said to me, 'Good luck, man,' and that was it. He ran off."

"Ran where?"

"Into the smoke. I wanted to go with him, because he was the only one who knew what he was doing. But somebody else grabbed me and pulled me behind something."

He shook his head. Now he was looking at his own movie that only he could see. "I could hear the damn thing burning. Do you know what that sounds like? An airplane burning? It was like a roar, but I could still hear the screaming. I knew they were burning to death. I could hear them, and all I could think was it could have been me."

"I'm sorry." I didn't know what else to say. "I'm sorry that happened to you." He shrugged. "It sounds pretty chaotic. As Tim said, a lot going on. You're absolutely sure Roger didn't make it?"

"Are you talking about Gilbert?"

"Yes, sorry."

"I stepped on him. We all did. He was on the floor, and we trampled over him like a bunch of crazed bulls. His head was split open. There was no way he got off that plane alive."

"What about bodies? Dead bodies don't get mixed up these days."

"You can't believe how hot that fire burned. Instant cremation. And I guess our government had some issues with Sudan getting back the remains. Besides that, if Hoffmeyer was CIA and they extracted him, do you think they would admit to that? Hell no. Blood, beards, bullets, smoke. I must have been confused, right? How could I know?"

He certainly sounded convincing, but so did many in the grassy-knoll set. It was because they believed so passionately. "Seven other men survived. Did anyone else identify Hoffmeyer?"

"No. Well, Timmy, but he won't cop to it. He doesn't want to think he's crazy. He already thinks he's crazy because he never sleeps. It just goes to show you, don't it?"

"Show me what?"

"We all burn the same, even the ones with a fortune."

He said it with half a smile that suggested the tiniest bit of schadenfreude. "You're saying one of the hostages had a fortune?"

"Gil said his laptop was worth a billion dollars. He tried to ransom his way off with it. They laughed at him."

"Gilbert Bernays said he had a computer worth a billion dollars?"

"Look, I'm not giving away any secrets here. We all got down and dirty with each other. We thought we were going to die. He told us he stole it off a dead Russian. He just didn't have what he needed to get to the money."

"Like what?"

"I don't know."

"A password?"

"Maybe."

I wanted to grab him by the shoulders and shake him until the answer came out. There was only one dead Russian Roger could have been talking about, the one Rachel had killed, and so far, she had failed to mention anything about Vladi having a computer worth a billion dollars.

"To my way of thinking, a billion dollars wouldn't have made a difference. Whatever those boys were doing, whyever they were doing it, it wasn't about money."

"What was it about?"

"Who knows? I don't think the baby terrorists even knew. They started with this sheikh demand but dropped that pretty fast, so that wasn't the ultimate goal."

"Maybe it was planned as a martyr operation from the beginning. The sheikh would have been a bonus."

"The whole point of a martyr operation is to wreak havoc and spread terror. If these boys were interested in publicizing their cause, why did they insist on a media blackout?"

"There was a media blackout?"

"They gave no interviews and didn't want any cameras around. The whole thing was a debacle from beginning to end. I'm telling you, we don't know the whole story of what happened on that plane."

Something over my shoulder caught his attention. "I think there's someone in there watching us."

"Is it the woman again?"

"No. It's a man this time. I think they've put some people on me, if you want to know the truth. It pisses me off. What about my rights? I'm a citizen. I didn't do anything. Nobody ever told me not to talk about what I saw. I'm going in there and—"

"Let's go in and have another drink, Frank. We don't need a scene here with all these good people, do we? Besides, I need to talk to Tim."

He dropped his cigarette on the sidewalk and crushed it under his loafer. It was only half gone, but it was the third one he'd lit since we'd been out there.

Frank was the one who found Tim. It wasn't hard. They were seated at the same table, and brunch was about to begin.

"Excuse me, Tim?" I pulled him away from the table and from Helene, who seemed determined not to let anything go on without her. "I was wondering if you had a contact number for that reporter Max Kraft."

"He asked me not to give it to anyone."

"I'm sure he did, but he'll want to talk to me." I pulled out the manifest Dan had given me. It had updated contact information for probably seventy-five percent of the survivors. "I've got something he's looking for."

21

MAX KRAFT LOOKED LIKE A SCRAPPER. HE WASN'T TALL.
He wasn't particularly big. His arms seemed a little long
for his body, and he definitely spent more time in front of
his computer than working out. From the looks of him,
though, you would want him on your side when a fight
broke out. He had the look of a man who knew how to
fight dirty, and would. He wore his brown-going-gray hair
just long enough to prove he didn't have to go to work in
an office every day. He probably owned lots of safari
shirts and no neckties.

I had no idea how long he'd been holed up in room 5
at the Novotel, a twelve-room motel on the Left Bank,
but when he opened the door and let me into his room, it
looked as if he'd lived there half his life. The smell of
warm beer and greasy hamburgers lingered. Torn bags of
vending-machine pretzels littered the premises, and carefully arranged light blue Post-it notes festooned the
dresser mirror.

He closed the door behind me and went immediately
to the window, where he had to move the heavy curtains
to peek out. "How did you get here?"

"Cab. I switched twice. There was no one on me."

"Good." He turned and held out his hand. "Where is it?"

"Slow down." I walked over to the dresser mirror and glanced at his notes, mostly names and phone numbers. They looked like contacts. When he saw me perusing them, he scurried over and barged in between the mirror and me.

"How did you get my name?" he asked, snatching the contacts off the mirror, one by one.

"I'm an investigator. I investigated. Do you have the video?"

He pulled a flash drive from his pocket and held it up. "Here's what you want. Where's mine?"

I took the drive, slung my backpack around, unzipped it, and pulled out my laptop.

"What are you doing?"

"Do you expect me to just believe you?" I sat on the unmade bed and turned on the computer. "I'm going to watch it."

He put his hands on his hips, apparently incensed that I didn't just take the word of an *investigative journalist*. "Are you sure that unit will even read this drive?"

"If it doesn't, we have a problem. You're not getting the 809 list until I'm convinced I'm getting what I need."

His mouth crimped around the edges. It actually made him look prim, which I knew he wasn't. He went over and flung himself into the hotel's one seating surface that wasn't a bed—a chair in the corner.

"Tell me where you got this," I said, waiting for my programs to load.

"I told you, I copied it from the laptop that belonged to Roger Fratello, then erased it from the hard drive. As long as that was the only one, this is now the only one."

"Where is the laptop?"

"I'm not saying."

That was a problem. I had been around Felix long enough to know that just erasing a file didn't really kill it. But I was hoping that Roger being dead might buy me some time on full eradication. Theoretically, no one would be looking for the video but me.

I pulled up Explorer while he bounced up and down . . . checked the window . . . wound his watch . . . went to the sink to throw cold water on his face. . . . He had a point about the software thing. If my machine couldn't recognize the drive, I had problems. I opened the small device, inserted it into the USB port, held my breath, and . . . nothing happened.

Shit.

I sat for a moment, considering the options. I could go online and search for the necessary software and download it, but I had never tried to access the Internet in France. I got out my cell phone and started to dial my best option.

Kraft rushed over. "What are you doing?"

"It doesn't work. I'll have to go to plan B."

"Forget that." He ripped the drive from the port. Arrogant prick. Time for a bluff. I signed off, closed down, and started packing to go.

"Wait a minute. I delivered. You owe me that contact list."

"If I can't verify that you delivered, I can't give you the list. Sorry."

"Just . . . just slow the fuck down here." He put his hands on either side of his head as he paced around the small room, eyes to the ceiling. He looked as if steam might start issuing from his ears at any second. "Okay, stop. Let's just stop right here." I hadn't even moved off the bed. He had a way of saying things to me that mostly applied to him. "What can I do to convince you?"

I thought about that. Maybe he was onto something. I spied an unopened bag of pretzels on the dresser. Except for breakfast a few hours earlier, I hadn't eaten much in the past few days. "Can I have those?"

"They're stale. Here . . ." Suddenly very accommodating, he went over to a Styrofoam cooler on the floor, pulled out a full-size bag, the kind you get at the grocery store, and tossed it over. His generosity, though, seemed to go only as far as snack goods, because, when he went in again, he came out with only one bottle of beer. I would have berated him, but I didn't need to be drinking anyway.

The plastic wrapping on the pretzels was still cold from being stored in the cooler. I opened the bag and stuffed a few of the salty delights into my mouth.

"Where did you get Roger's laptop?"

"Bought it from a kid with a goat."

"Where?"

"Afghanistan. What is this? Twenty questions?"

"This is plan C. I need to know more about Blackthorne. You seem to know about them, so let's talk for a while and see if we can find some common ground." If I was right about Max Kraft, Investigative Journalist, he was itching to tell someone his story.

He twisted the cap off the bottle and took a swig, then moved back to the chair, set the bottle on the little, round, fake-wood-grain table next to it, and seemed to settle in.

"The story of a lifetime cost me fifty bucks and an Elton John CD." He savored the thought, much like he savored his cold beer.

"What's the story?"

"I won't tell you that."

"It's Blackthorne, isn't it? Something about the private army? The CIA? Stephen Hoffmeyer." I threw everything out there. Something had to stick, and I knew I was on the right track. The last guy I'd seen nervous enough to be peeking through the curtains was Lyle Burquart.

"I don't think you need to know. You don't want to know."

"How did you know the computers were in Zormat?"

He squeezed one eye shut and looked at me with the other. "I never said Zormat."

"You haven't mentioned Salanna 809, either. But I know that's where you got the machine, from the hijacking victims' stuff in Zormat. Roger Fratello was on that flight as Gilbert Bernays, who seems to be dead. That's how his computer got into the closet."

He stared at me, seemingly confused about whether to view me as a threat or a source. "The locals got into the house before the CIA ever showed up. They stripped it clean. My contacts got word to me. I have a lot of contacts. I went there, I checked out the merchandise, and I bought it."

"Just Roger's?"

"No comment."

That meant there were more, and he had them. "One of the hostages said Roger claimed to have a billion dollars on his laptop."

"A billion dollars? What, are you kidding?"

"It's what I heard." I got out my notebook and flipped to the Frank pages. "He said Roger used the machine to try to ransom himself off, but he couldn't access the money. Something was missing. Maybe a password?"

I looked up at him. This didn't seem to be something he already knew about, which meant he was interested.

"Where would he get a billion dollars? Is that what he embezzled from that . . . that—"

"Betelco. I don't think so. Roger told this other hostage he'd stolen it off a dead Russian, the one on the video." I pointed to the drive he'd ripped from my machine. It was still in his fist. He looked at it.

"The one Rachel killed."

"Yeah. I know that she took cash belonging to Vladi." She and Harvey had pulled it from the trunk of the car. "It ended up in a safety deposit box in Brussels. So far, she hasn't mentioned any billion-dollar computer." That she hadn't mentioned it, of course, did not preclude the fact that she knew about it.

He held up the drive. "This video came off a machine belonging to Roger Fratello. It had an e-mail program, a bunch of files with memos and business-related stuff he wrote. I didn't see anything that looked like a billion dollars, and I looked all through it. It was one of the few I didn't need a translator for."

I leaned back on the bed, bracing myself with my arms behind me. "I wonder what it would look like. What do you think? Secret accounts? Treasure map?"

"Yeah," he said. "That's probably it. A treasure map. Yo-ho-ho."

"Whatever it was," I said, "I don't think Roger could get to it."

"Why do you say that?"

"Think about it. A computer has something on it worth a billion dollars. Wouldn't you encrypt it or protect it somehow, just in case someone boosted it? And whatever that protection was—the password or the code or the key—wouldn't you be likely to keep that on you?"

"Yes on both counts. So what?"

I had a few pretzels. They were good and fresh. "This

e-mail that accidentally fell out of Roger's out-box when you signed on, it was to Rachel, and it was asking for the location of Vladi's grave."

"Vladi, the dead Russian?"

"Yep."

"What, you're thinking the dead Russian still has this . . . this code or key or whatever it is on him?"

"Well, it would have been more viable four years ago, I would think, when Roger actually intended to send the message."

"Hey," he said. "Here's what I want to know. How the hell is this guy's account still active if he's dead?"

I thought about that. If it was a business account, it would have been paid for through Betelco. Since he'd been on the lam at the time he sent it, that wasn't likely. "His wife," I said, remembering the look on Susan Fratello's face when I'd asked her if she would want to know if Roger were alive. "His wife might have kept it open all these years."

He smiled for the first time and pointed the longneck at me. "Grave robbing. I like it. A little creepy but a good angle. Too bad I'm not doing that story." Then he shrugged. "But who gives a shit? Russians . . . obscene amounts of money. It's been done."

"Was Vladi's one of the computers you bought from the kid with the goat? Do you have the billion-dollar treasure map?"

He sat back and stretched with his hands over his head. "Wouldn't you like to know?"

I did want to know. I wasn't sure I needed to know, because I had no plans to dig up Vladi, not even for a billion dollars. But when I didn't jump all over his idea, he got agitated.

"You do, don't you? Don't you want to know if I have a computer worth a billion clams?"

Kraft was a unique personality, to be sure. He was either flush with confidence to the point of overbearing arrogance or anxious and needy to the point of mewling. He didn't seem afraid to be either.

"Why? Are you interested in a trade?"

"You told me you had information to give me on Blackthorne. I need to know what you have and where you got it."

"Yeah, I made that up." I rolled up out of my tilt and pulled my notebook from my backpack. "I don't have much. I heard something about them from another guy who is also scared to death of them." I glanced up at Kraft. "Same as you, right? Isn't that who has you peeking out from behind the curtains? Mr. Black and Mr. Thorne?"

"Tony Blackmon is dead, Cyrus Thorne is running the show, and I have good reason to be careful."

Kraft stood up and started pacing around the room again. He forgot his beer, went back for it, looked in the mirror, then finally turned and sat sidesaddle with one foot on the floor and one dangling. "This guy you talked to, who is he? What's his name?"

"He was a reporter. He said he dug too deep into Blackthorne. Now he's a—" Kraft was about to fall off his perch waiting for my answer. "Now he's not."

"What's his name? I'll bet I've already talked to him."

Max Kraft was a tricky guy, but Lyle had made it pretty clear he wanted nothing to do with Blackthorne. It wasn't for me to be throwing his name around. "All I can tell you is he was doing a story on the 809 hijacking. Somehow he ran into Blackthorne. He told me to steer clear of them. I'm trying to take his advice."

He wet his lips. "I can tell you what he wouldn't."

"Why would you do that?"

"Because I want to talk to him. I want his name."

"I won't give it to you."

"If he dropped the story, he doesn't deserve your protection." He took another swig of beer. Judging from the face he made, either the beer was flat, or he had a deep and genuine contempt for Lyle. "No journalist worth his ink would or should ever drop a story like this. People need to know. But it's his loss. This is Pulitzer time, baby. You watch. My story will blow the doors off."

"Good for you." I stood.

"Where are you going?"

"I don't need a billion dollars, if it even exists. I'm not giving you the name of my Blackthorne source. But I do have this." I pulled out the 809 manifest and held it up. "The names and contacts of most of those people from Salanna 809 are on here. I'm violating all kinds of confidences by giving it to you, and I'm taking your word on the video, but I'll still make the trade."

He opened his hand, looked at the flash drive, and tossed it over. I flipped the manifest onto the bed. Then I thought of one more question. "Do you know why Blackthorne would be tailing Rachel?"

He had been reaching for the manifest. He stopped. "Rachel, the one who got the message from my computer?"

"Well, technically, Roger's computer, but yes. They tried to scoop her up last night. We just got away, and they weren't nice." I brushed away my bangs to show him my forehead. "What would they want with her?"

"Shit." He went back over to the window and peeked out. "Blackthorne is trying to kill me. They've been chasing me all over the world trying to get to me, and you're just telling me this?"

"Why is Blackthorne trying to kill you?"

"Because my story is going to blow—"

"Blow the doors off. You told me, but you won't tell me why. It's a little vague for me to really connect with. What I heard is that it's a private military firm out of Virginia that contracts with the U.S. government and others to provide services up to and including combat. Also intelligence."

"That's how it started, and that's what it looks like, but that's not what it is now. Blackthorne is the CIA on steroids. What the CIA would like to be if it weren't for the Constitution and government oversight and diplomacy and international laws and political infighting and lots of ass-covering."

"I don't know what that means."

"All you need to know is they don't want anyone to read what I'm writing, and the only reason they would be tailing her would be to get to me."

My backpack was getting heavy, so I sat down on the edge of the bed again to try to think that through. Something about it didn't work. "If you're the only thing that connects Rachel to Blackthorne, how would they have known about her? Until an hour ago, neither one of us knew who you were."

"The e-mail. That goddamn e-mail that I didn't even send." He was starting to move around the room with purpose now, collecting his dirty clothes from the floor and throwing them into a canvas bag. "I told you I was using translators? I had one who found out Thorne was looking for me. He copied a bunch of my files and sold them to him behind my back. That has to be it." He tossed his kit bag into the larger canvas bag. "But it doesn't matter. If they know about her, then they know about you, and if they know you're in Paris, then I'm fucked."

Interesting wording. It was exactly what Lyle had said. So far, everyone I knew who was connected to Blackthorne was fucked. But I had to get back to an earlier point. "Did you just say that Thorne had copies of some of your files?"

"Yeah, that's what I said."

I pulled the USB drive from my pocket. "From before or after you erased Rachel's video?"

"I don't know. I guess . . . uh . . ." He leaned over to stuff one of the hotel's fresh white towels into his bag, which was the only reason the round that crashed through the window, twitched the curtains, and flew past my ear missed his head and lodged instead in the cheap hotel wall behind him.

22

MAX KRAFT WAS OBVIOUSLY USED TO BEING SHOT AT. HE hit the deck loudly and promptly.

"Mother*fucker.*"

I was right behind him. Another round came through the window and punched through the drywall, this time around bed height. The window must have been shatter-proof, because it popped with the sound of each shot but didn't break. With the heavy curtains drawn, whoever was out there had to have been firing blind, which was to our advantage.

I reached instinctively for my Glock, which wasn't there. I hadn't even tried to bring a firearm through French customs. Kraft apparently hadn't had the same is-sues. He was holding what looked like some kind of a compact Beretta, maybe nine-millimeter.

"Can you shoot that?"

"I can shoot."

"How many rounds do you have?"

"Two clips," he said. "Ten each. You know, don't you, that that's the only way out." He pointed at the front door. The booming quality of his voice came out under stress, even when he was whispering. "I can't believe you brought these people."

"I'm not the one in trouble with Blackthorne, so be quiet and let me think." I pulled out my phone, but the phone in the room rang before I could dial. I picked up. "Hello?"

"We're not interested in you." It was a man's voice, soft and a little seductive. I looked at Kraft, who seemed alarmed that I was taking calls.

"What can I do for you?"

"You can come out alone. Leave the reporter inside. If there are weapons in the room, bring them out with your hands in the air."

"Uh-huh. Then what happens?"

"You can walk away. We'll take it from there. I'll hold fire for five minutes."

I checked my watch and marked the time. "Can I confer with my colleague and call you back?"

"You have five minutes. If you don't come out, we'll come in."

The line went dead, and he didn't leave his number. I had to count that as a no. I scrolled to the number I had preprogrammed into my cell and dialed it. As it was connecting, I looked at Kraft. "Get ready. We're leaving right now. I'd stay low if I were you."

"*Leaving?* What? Who was that?" To his credit, he didn't just ask questions. He started moving around in a low crabwalk and grabbing his stuff while he asked questions. "What's going on?"

I was busy with another phone call. "They're here," I said when Frank picked up. "Are you sure you can do this?"

"I lived through a hijacking. This is nothing."

"Good." I moved on my belly to the wall Kraft's room

shared with the next. I stood up long enough to grab the end of the dresser and swing it away from the wall and toward the door, the direction that would provide the most cover, at least as much as we would get in that flimsy room. I found a good spot low on the wall and knocked on it quietly. "Right here," I said into the phone.

"Stand back," he said, and hung up.

The second I clapped my phone shut, the banging erupted, and it was loud. Kraft stared at the wall. He was still staring when the sight of the ax blade coming through the wallpaper knocked him backward into a graceless sprawl. "Holy mother of God. They're coming through the fucking walls?"

"He's with me," I said. "I lied about coming alone. Give me your jacket."

"What?"

Kraft had on a lightweight olive-green jacket, the top half of the running suit he was wearing. "Give it to me, *now.*"

He unzipped it and pulled it off. I put it on, then reached into my backpack for my Red Sox cap. By the time I had it on, Frank had broken through, making a passable hole at the base of the wall. When the banging stopped, his face appeared through the drywall dust, then his hand. I put my backpack in it, and he pulled it through by the straps. Kraft still hadn't moved. I grabbed his big canvas bag and shoved it through, but when I reached for his laptop case, he wouldn't let it go.

"Give it to me, Kraft."

"No."

It wasn't a big hole. I was pretty sure I could squeeze through, but Kraft was stouter than I was, and it would be a tight fit for him, even without a laptop clutched to his chest. "Then hand it through to Frank."

"Who's Frank?"

"A concerned citizen who wanted to help." Had insisted on helping, in fact. He had overheard me asking Tim about Kraft and then followed me out to the curb. He had wanted to meet Kraft and set the record straight on Salanna 809 and Hoffmeyer. He was about to get his chance. On the way over, he'd told me he was a volunteer firefighter back in Norfolk, and we had formed a plan in case there was trouble.

"Come on," Frank said. "What the hell's going on in there? Get your ass moving, Kraft."

Kraft looked at me, and he looked at the front door. Then he crawled to the opening.

"Give me your gun," I said. He handed it over, then, still holding his computer, dove through headfirst. Frank must have grabbed him by the shoulders and pulled, because Kraft's top half disappeared into the wall. Then he got jammed.

"Dammit, Kraft, are you willing to die for what's on that laptop?"

"Yes, frankly, I am."

"I'm not." I reached up and grabbed the case with both hands. I had the better angle and could brace my foot against the wall. He was breathing hard, so I waited for him to inhale and gave it a big yank. When it came loose, I fell flat on my back with the case in my arms. But I knew Kraft had slipped through. I could hear him yowling.

Sounds coming from just outside the front door told me they were setting up to come in. I checked my watch. Ninety seconds. That's when I noticed the sirens, the wailing kind that you hear in Europe when the police are on the way. Frank might have called them, or someone might have summoned them when they heard the shots. Either way, it was probably a good development for us.

I spun around, shoved the laptop through the hole, and followed it. From inside the neighboring room, I reached back through the opening, grabbed the leg of the dresser, and pulled. It was not a lightweight piece of furniture—I had to struggle to move it—but I knew it would cover the hole. It wouldn't fool a professional army for long, but it might give us the edge we needed.

I stood up and wiped the drywall dust from my eyes. I looked for Frank and Kraft, but they were already through a door that led to still another room. I hadn't even known the room adjoining Kraft's was a connector. Frank had worked it all out on his own. I followed them through, Frank closed that door behind me and locked it. That put us another room removed from our pursuers.

The sirens were getting loud. If we didn't want to get picked up, we had to move fast. I started toward the front window to check the scene, but Frank grabbed my arm.

"Back here." He led me to the bathroom. I joined him there in time to see Kraft disappear through a window above the toilet seat.

"This one has a window?"

He smiled. "Deluxe suite."

"Cool."

Frank climbed up onto the toilet seat and dove out after Kraft. I was right behind him. I pushed my backpack through and jumped out after it. When I hit the pavement six feet below, Frank was across the alley, banging on an old and rusty slab of a back door to what looked and smelled like a restaurant.

The sirens were upon us now. I expected police cars to

come barreling up each end of the alley any second. It was hard to talk and hard to hear and harder to think. Frank and I decided to split up. We shook hands quickly as Kraft looked on, stunned, confused, and angry. Frank would take Kraft. I would be the decoy.

Shouting came from inside the hotel and then what sounded like gunfire. Kraft took off, but Frank tracked him down, grabbed him by the arm, and pulled him back to the iron door. Frank stared at it as if it might open magically for him. He was about to bang on it again when it did. The big door swung out wide enough to let the two of them slip inside. Before it closed, a man with a chef's hat stuck his head out and looked up and down the alley. Frank had turned out to be a very resourceful guy to have on my side.

I heard a police car coming from one end of the alley, so I took off in the other direction. I covered the half-block easily to the street, made a left turn away from the hotel, and ran almost directly into a woman standing on the sidewalk. Something about her was familiar. She had on a light raincoat. She was the woman Frank had spotted at the reunion. Without thinking about it, I turned and headed the other way, directly into the path of a van that veered up on the sidewalk in front of me.

It screeched to a stop. The side door cracked open, and at least four men came rushing out like a black tide. There was a lot of yelling in French and heavy boots on the ground and the sound of gear moving. Also the sound of weaponry—metal against metal. When the assault rifles came out, I dropped my backpack and threw my hands in the air. Someone came up from behind and grabbed my arms. Someone else grabbed my feet, and then I was flat on my belly on the wet ground with my hands behind me, wrists cuffed, and a boot on my neck.

From my vantage point, I could see the end of the street. There was a lot going on and a lot of people racing around. I looked for the woman in the light raincoat. She was gone.

23

A POLICE LIEUTENANT IN BOSTON, WHO HATED ME ANY-
way, once threw me in a holding cell, basically because I
ticked him off. My first time behind bars had been a
pretty frightening experience, mainly because I wasn't in
there alone. The second was in California, where the
highway patrol picked me up on a warrant for check kit-
ing, a charge that turned out to be totally false and a complete misunderstanding. The West Coast lockup was
nicer, as were the officers. In neither case was I locked up
for more than twenty-four hours, but it made being in jail
not an entirely new experience for me. What was new
was being tossed into a French jail.

The guys who had grabbed me were some kind of flying SWAT team. Once they had pulled me up from the
wet ground, I had seen *Gendarmerie* written across their
backs. Someone had heard the shots in the hotel and
called the police. They'd spotted me running away, and
they'd caught me with Frank's gun in my pocket. I didn't
know much French, but I knew that was going to be a big
problem.

At the station house, I had asked a lot of questions, but

my jailers kept telling me they had to find a translator before anyone could speak to me, which was bullshit. It
wasn't as if I were a code talker.

I sat on the cot in my cell, isolated and waiting and trying to remember to breathe through my mouth. This jail
had something in common with the other two I'd visited.
It was my guess that jails all over the world had the same
thing in common: the pungent smell of mold, greasy skin,
body odor, and every variety of human discharge.

After several hours, an officer came and opened my
cage. He took me through a series of gates and doors
and elevators until we arrived at an open office area, not
unlike the bullpens I've seen in the many different police departments I've had the pleasure of visiting. He
handcuffed me to a chair next to an empty desk and told
me to wait. That's what he said. One word in English:
"Wait."

There was a lot of shouting going on behind the closed
door of an office along one of the walls. It was muffled
French that I couldn't understand. What was easy to understand was the level of vitriol. When the arguing
stopped, the door opened, and a man in a black raincoat
came out. Right behind him was another man, somewhat
younger, in shirtsleeves and tie. They stood in the bullpen
speaking loudly and gesturing. When it was all over, the
man in the black raincoat stalked out. The shirtsleeved
man yelled at a uniform, pointed in my general direction,
then retreated to his office and slammed the door. The
officer came over and uncuffed me, then guided me
through the procedure for release, talking to me the
whole time in perfect English. He answered no questions
about why I'd been released. I asked what would happen
if I demanded an explanation. He advised against it.

On the way out, they returned my personal belongings. I went out to catch a cab, thinking how nice it would be to take it straight to Orly. I could still catch the evening flight to Boston if I hurried. But I had to go back to the Hyatt and get my things.

As it turned out, I didn't need a cab. The man in the black raincoat was sitting in a car at the curb. He leaned over and popped open the passenger-side door.

"Get in."

There was enough room between the car and the curb for me to step down. With one hand on the open door and one on the roof, I poked my head in so I could see his face. "Who are you?"

"Cyrus Thorne."

Nothing screamed success like a private jet. Blackthorne's looked rich without being ostentatious. The seats were big club chairs covered in glove-soft caramel-colored leather. There was carpet, subdued lighting, tables with polished wood-grain surfaces, and individual flip-up television monitors at every seat.

Thorne had taken a right turn into the cockpit after we'd boarded. I was trying to figure out which seat to flop into when a flight attendant approached and asked if I wanted anything.

"Water, please."

I took a big swiveling chair that gave me a good view out one of the porthole windows. Apparently, we were the only passengers expected, because the stairs were up, the door was closed, and we were starting to taxi.

The flight attendant was back with a tall glass of ice, lime, and a bottle of San Pellegrino. She set the glass in front of me and poured. "I'm Tatiana. I'll get you whatever you need."

"Thank you."

The pilot came on and asked everyone to strap in for takeoff. I looked out and saw we were at the end of the runway, about to blast off. He said our flying time to Boston's Logan Airport would be approximately eight hours. At least I was going home.

I drank deeply from the glass, not realizing until I had consumed almost the whole thing how thirsty I had been and not caring much that gulping sparkling water would give me hiccups. I drained the glass, and Tatiana came over to pour the rest of the bottle. That's when I looked at her closely for the first time and recognized her.

"I know you," I said. "I saw you. You were at . . . you were . . ." She was the woman in the light raincoat from the ballroom and the sidewalk just before the cops had taken me down. "Who are you?"

"Cyrus will explain everything when he comes back."

"Where is he?"

"Flying the plane."

Of course. He not only owned the plane, he flew it. I watched Tatiana move around the cabin. She looked strong and toned, and something told me she was more than a flight attendant. A ninja flight attendant, perhaps, the kind of person we could have used more of back in my Majestic days.

"Put your seat belt on," she said. She could have used a little brushing up on her customer-service skills.

As I buckled in, she threw a lever on the side of my chair and locked it so it wouldn't swivel, which I assumed was required to keep the passengers from spinning like tops on liftoff. Then she strapped into the seat behind me.

The aircraft started to roll. I felt the g-forces climbing. The wheels left the ground, and we were flying. After about ten minutes, we were level and cruising. I heard Tatiana unhook herself. I needed a couple of moments alone to think, so I did what I always did when the seat-belt sign went off.

"Is the lav forward or aft?"

"It's in the back."

To get to it, I had to go through an office area and a small stateroom. The office had a TV, an exercise bike, a lot of stereo equipment, and a lit trophy case of some kind.

The bathroom was small but more than serviceable. I checked the mirror. Running for my life had generated a lot of sweat, which hadn't been kind to the cut on my forehead. It was throbbing and ugly, but it hadn't split open. I was going to have a nice scab for a while. I washed it and the rest of my face. The towels on the rack were all top quality. Each one had a small *BT* embroidered in the corner, and I had the absurd urge to steal one for Max Kraft, though it wasn't likely I'd ever see him again. I hoped he was safely on his way to wherever he went to hide.

My bag from the hotel had materialized on the bed in the stateroom. My backpack was there, as was my computer case. These people might have been dangerous, but they were organized. I went straight to my backpack to check for the flash drive and felt more relieved than I would have expected to find it right where I'd left it. I'd worked hard to get it. I pulled it out and stuck it in the pocket of my jeans. I pulled out a sweatshirt, the only clean top I had left. My jeans weren't exactly fresh, but my only other option was the pair of linen pants I had worn to the reunion.

While I pulled on the shirt, I tried to figure out what had just happened. I hadn't been taken by force, but I hadn't been given much choice, either. Thorne told me the *gendarmes* had picked me up in connection with the incident at the Novotel and that they considered me armed and dangerous. He had also told me he had gotten me out by claiming I was working for the CIA and taking me into his custody. Throughout this sequence of events, I had learned a few things: Cyrus Thorne had some kind of status with the Paris police, and possibly the CIA; he would have been happy to send me back to the *gendarmerie*, had I not agreed to go with him; and he wanted something from me. Knowing all that, my best option was to find out what it was and enjoy the ride home.

I started toward the main cabin, stopping on my way to notice some things I hadn't seen the first time through. The display case was not for trophies. It was to display a single item: a large crystal sculpture of a screaming eagle. The sculpture itself was beautiful, but with its claws forward and wings fully extended, so was the bird, in a brutal sort of way. It was a pure specimen from a perfect world where the strong eat the weak and there is no other law but that. It reminded me of Drazen. I reached out and touched one of the claws.

"Magnificent, isn't he?"

I whipped around to find Cyrus Thorne right behind me, squarely in my personal space. I hadn't sensed his presence at all. I took a step away from him. He looked different from when he'd been next to me in the car. The lighting in the cabin made his hair look more ginger than gray. He had changed out of a suit and into khakis and a golf shirt. It gave him a trim silhouette and didn't diminish in any way the attitude that the appropriate way to greet him was with a salute.

"It's very impressive," I said. "Where did it come from?"

"I had a bet with my partner."

"Who won?"

"I lost the bet, but Tony died winning."

"That must have been some bet."

He didn't seem to hear. "This is my tribute to him." I looked down at the inscription plate. "For Tony Blackmon." Below the name, all it said was "Get some."

It reminded me of what someone, probably Felix, had told me about Blackmon. I looked at Thorne. "Your partner was a marine."

"The best who ever lived . . . a good partner." He didn't exactly get misty-eyed, but there was sadness in his face as he looked at that eagle. It made him seem gentler.

"Let's go up front and talk." He turned and moved forward to the main cabin. We settled in at one of the tables, across from each other.

Thorne had a bag of cough drops sitting on the table next to him. He unsheathed one, popped it into his mouth, and peered at my head. "Do you need medical attention? Tatiana can help if you do. I have some experience as a field medic. I can do some things in a pinch."

He had a tinge of the South in his voice. If he were a car, he would have been a pickup truck, only tricked out with all the best military gear, especially battle armor. He seemed very well defended.

"I've already taken care of it, thank you." Something had occurred to me. "Who's flying the plane?"

"My copilot. Do you know who I am?"

"You're Cyrus Thorne, cofounder of Blackthorne and king of a vigilante army."

He seemed to like that. "That's very colorful. But I am no king, and we are not a vigilante army. I am a humble servant of the great and glorious country of the United States of America."

"Weren't those your fellow patriots firing on us at the Novotel?"

"They were overenthusiastic, I'll agree, and flawed in their tactical approach. We'll have to do some work on that." He looked around for Tatiana and nodded. She pulled an electronic organizer from her pocket, got out the stylus, and started tapping away. Turned out she was a ninja flight attendant and personal assistant. Cyrus turned back to our conversation.

"You did a good job handling a bad situation. I'm impressed."

"That was my goal, to impress the people who were trying to kill me."

He popped another cough drop. They were cherry, and he didn't suck them. He crunched them. Even sitting between two aircraft engines, I could hear him grind them to dust with his molars. "If they had been trying to kill you, you would be dead. Unfortunately, the target got away. That's why we're talking now."

"The target?"

"You know that I'm talking about Max Kraft." He put his arms on the table and leaned forward. "Let's be a little more direct in our communication."

"Sure." I sank a little deeper into my club chair. "Because we only have eight hours ahead of us."

"We should be able to get our business resolved well before we land in Boston, and I enjoy flying the plane."

"All right, let's do it. What do you want from me, and what happens if I don't give it to you?"

His gaze settled on me in a way that said he wasn't used to being the one answering the questions, but he would humor me. "Blackthorne is a preferred contractor to the U.S. government. We've worked for every branch of the military and multiple other departments and agencies. Most of the work we've done lately has been for the intelligence community."

"I guess that makes you a spy for hire."

"That's simplistic."

"I thought we were doing simple and direct."

"You do have a mouth, don't you?"

I just looked at him. I was locked up with him in an aircraft at 35,000 feet. There were at least three of them onboard to one of me. I was unarmed—Kraft's Baretta was one item that had not been returned—and something told me the captain and Tatiana weren't. If they wanted to hurt me, there wasn't much I could do. My attitude was about the only thing in the situation I could control.

He pulled a worn leather attaché onto the table and dug out a pair of utilitarian reading glasses and a file. He opened the file and perused it. "You're a private investigator from Boston, Massachusetts. You flew to Paris last night on Majestic Airlines. You sat in seat 4B. You were staying at the Hyatt in room 1200. Your partner is Harvey Baltimore, also of Boston. You've been partners for three"—he turned the page—"almost four years. Before that, you worked for Majestic."

"You checked me out."

"I'm in the information-gathering business." He took off the glasses and leaned back. "Your partner seems quite taken with his ex-wife. I find that to be charming. It says here that he's ill."

"That's a pretty thorough report." Tatiana, leaning against the bulkhead behind Thorne, shifted. I looked at her, and she offered a half-smile. Was there no end to this woman's talents?

"It's what we do," Thorne said.

It was what he planned to do *with* it that concerned me. "What do you want?"

"You like simple." He closed the file and took off his glasses. "Here it is. Max Kraft is a dangerous man. It is my job to find him. I want you to do it for me. Arrange a meeting with him so that we can intercept him. We'll take it from there."

"Kraft didn't strike me as particularly formidable."

"He has classified information. He's threatening to declassify it in the *New York Times*."

"You would kill him for that?"

"No one will print his story. We'll see to that." He waved his hand, as if the *New York Times* were some insignificant fly to be swatted away. The idea that he might really be able to do it was disturbing.

"If you can squash his story, then what are you so worried about?"

"Hoffmeyer."

"Stephen Hoffmeyer? From Salanna 809?"

"Yes."

I sat back and did a couple of small side-to-side swivels. Hoffmeyer, the dead guy who wasn't dead, which made Frank the crazy guy who wasn't crazy. Now I really had to focus. "Was Hoffmeyer CIA?"

"Hoffmeyer was with the Agency. Four years ago, he stole highly classified documents. He had them with him when the flight was hijacked. When we found out he was on the plane, beepers went off all over the world. At that point, we had a bunch of hostiles in possession of some of the country's most sensitive information. We don't know exactly what happened in the course of that hijacking, but we thought Hoffmeyer had gone down in the final assault. We thought the files had died with him. There are indications now that both the files and Hoffmeyer survived."

"Kraft has the files?"

"Max Kraft has those files. Our primary objective is to get them back. Our secondary objective is to make sure Hoffmeyer and the files never meet again."

"What would Hoffmeyer do with them if he got them back?"

"Sell them to the highest bidder, which will certainly include enemies of the United States. I'll tell you right now that will not happen. I won't let that happen."

"Is this more of that need-to-know information that I don't get to know? Because right now, I'm not taking anyone at his word."

"I can't tell you what it is, but know this." I hated people who said "know this." "As an American citizen, you do not want Kraft walking around with this information. You do not want Hoffmeyer to get it."

"Are you saying you'll kill Kraft to keep from letting Hoffmeyer get to him first?"

"If I have to."

"So, what you're asking me to do is help you kill a man."

"Yes." He started searching around for something, eventually locating it in a pouch on the side of his club chair. It was a remote control.

"Why am I supposed to trust you? You're a private contractor. You can't even show me a badge."

"No, but I can show you this."

He opened a little cabinet in the wall next to us. A flat-screen TV monitor was inside. As he pressed buttons on the remote, an image fluttered onto the screen. It was black-and-white and very sharp. The point of view was from above, probably close to the ceiling. I moved closer to the screen, because I knew what this was. A man held a woman down on a desk. He was big enough that she was almost completely obscured. I couldn't see her face, but I didn't have to.

I felt in my pocket for my flash drive. It was there. "Where did you get this?"

He hit pause. "From a translator who worked for Max Kraft." He nodded toward the screen. "Go ahead. You should see this. It's interesting stuff."

He restarted, and the incident proceeded as I would have expected. Vladi reached down to try to undo his belt. He was wobbly and uncoordinated. Had he not been draped over the desk, it wasn't clear to me he would have been able to stand. Rachel's hands were wrapped around his broad back. As he continued to struggle with the buckle, she withdrew her hands, only to push them around again, but this time under his jacket, where it was plainly visible that she was searching for the weapon. It was also clearly evident when she'd found it. Vladi straightened up quickly, stumbled back, and stood like an animal up on its hind legs. When she pointed the gun at him, his shoulders shook, his arms whipped around, and it was clear he was roaring at her. It hadn't occurred to me that there would be no sound.

Rachel also spoke as she pushed herself up from the desk and wiped her lips with the back of one hand, keeping him covered the whole time. He stumbled backward, clearly not in control of all motor functions, but then he advanced on her again with intent to do her real harm. She shot him twice in the chest. He kept coming, but she was able to step out of his way and slip around the desk. The way he went after her, you never would have guessed he had two slugs lodged in his chest. She raised the gun and shot him again. This time, he fell to his knees and hung there for a few seconds. Then he rolled gently forward, laid his head on the floor, and didn't move again.

It was a bit of a relief to see Rachel's hands shake as she set the pistol on the desk. She walked over to the wall farthest from the body and slumped against it. She slid down slowly to the floor, put her hands over her face, and cried. But almost as quickly as she started, she stopped, and from there the story took an unexpected turn, but it was one I should have seen coming.

She crawled over to where Vladislav had left a large briefcase. She laid it down flat and tried to unlatch it. Having no success, she crept over to Vladi's body and approached it as if it were electrified. She poked and pulled back and prodded and shied away. Getting no response, she pulled him over onto his back so she could rifle his pockets. She was fast and efficient. She never even looked at his face.

She extracted a set of keys and flipped through them until she found the one that worked. She opened the case and started pulling stuff out. Files, a flask, more files. When she found what she wanted, she demonstrated the universal sign for guilt, looking left and right. Apparently seeing that she was alone, save for the dead body behind her, she reached in and came out with a laptop. The billion-dollar machine. It had to be the one Roger had told Frank he'd stolen off a dead Russian—only Roger hadn't been the one who stole it.

On the screen, Rachel did what I now understood Rachel always did: she took a grievous situation and made it work to her benefit. She carried the laptop to her own bag and slipped it in. In some ways, I had to admire such a keen sense of survival.

Finding nothing else she wanted from Vladi, she did the whole thing in reverse, including putting the keys back into the dead man's pocket. Then she pulled out her cell phone and made a call. I imagined Harvey at the other end of that call, coming to the phone and rising about two feet off the ground when he heard Rachel's voice.

"Baby, come quick," she must have said. "I need your help." The screen went to blue.

Thorne put his glasses back on and consulted his file. "That was Vladislav Tishchenko. Brother of Drazen." He peered at me over the lenses. "You run with a dangerous crowd."

"Not usually."

"The woman is Rachel Ruffielo, your partner's ex-wife." He put the file aside. "From what I understand, Drazen is confused about the circumstances of his brother's death. This would clear it up for him. Ready to continue?"

He used the remote and started the show again. The screen stayed blue. There was a jump cut, and then my heart jumped, because Harvey was there. He was standing over the body in his suit with one hand on his forehead. He looked as if he were taking his own temperature. Thorne reached down and hit the fast-forward. It showed Rachel and Harvey talking and gesturing to each other. It showed Rachel leaving and coming back with the plastic bags, and the two of them straightening the corpse, and rolling it up. They were going at Buster Keaton speed, but it wasn't funny.

This time, Thorne hit the pause button and froze the two of them on the screen as they dragged Vladi's body across the floor.

My throat was dry, and his cough drops were looking good to me. "Can I have one of those?"

He set one on the table and pushed it across. I unwrapped it and popped it in. There was nothing special about it—I wasn't sure why he seemed so enamored of them—but it did the job. It got the saliva flowing again.

"That's your partner, isn't it?"

"Yes."

He placed the remote control on the table between us. "Here's how I think things will work. You continue your dialogue with Max Kraft. You get him to agree to meet you."

"We're not having a dialogue."

"You'll come up with something. At the appropriate time, we'll move in and take over. If you do that, no one you don't want to will ever see this."

He pointed at the screen. At that moment, Tatiana must have pulled the flash drive from the CPU in the back. On the screen, the system signaled its surprise by going to black and then announcing a fatal error.

24

IT WAS A LONG AND EXHAUSTING FLIGHT HOME. BY THE time I got back to Boston, I was jumping out of my skin. I called Harvey the minute I got to my car. When he didn't answer either of his phones, I knew it was because of Rachel. She had upset the natural order of things and taken a blowtorch to the delicate balance we had achieved. For anything that was amiss, I blamed Rachel.

Then I got to the house, where I found the two of them, sitting on the couch in the front room, ensconced in blissful domesticity. They were listening to music, oblivious to the world in general and me in particular.

I dropped my backpack. It hit the floor with a thud. They both looked up. Harvey had a haircut, and I'd never seen that shirt before, and those . . . were those khaki pants he was wearing? They'd been *shopping*, too?

"You don't answer phones around here anymore?"

Rachel raised a remote and pointed it at a stereo system that hadn't been there when I'd left. She turned the music down. "Did you get my video back?"

I pulled the flash drive from my pocket and tossed it in her direction. It landed on the couch next to her. As I watched her scrambling for it, all I could see was the image of her on the video, pawing through the possessions of the man she had just killed. All I could think about was how she had lied. She had lied to me, and I just knew she had lied to Harvey to make him love her, to get whatever she needed, whatever she wanted to take from him.

Harvey took the remote from her and turned the music off. "My apologies," he said. "We must have had the music playing too loudly. I should have been more careful."

"Harvey, can I speak to Rachel alone, please?"

"Why?"

"Girl talk."

Rachel looked at me as if I'd just slapped her. She knew what was coming. The defiance was already taking over her expression. Preemptive defensiveness, something any good liar needs in her toolbox.

"Harvey, baby, just give us a minute alone. It's all right. I can handle myself."

"Whether you can handle yourself is not the issue. It is more that—"

"Harvey, go."

He started to move forward on the couch so he could transfer himself to his chair. He paused, seemingly teetering on the edge. "No." He pushed back and planted himself firmly on the couch. "I am not leaving. I will not sit outside in my own house while the two of you discuss things that pertain to me as much as to either of you." He turned to Rachel. "You will not speak to me in that tone." He looked at me. "Carry on."

It seemed that the haircut wasn't all that was new about Harvey. I turned to Rachel. "You stole Vladi's computer."

She crossed her arms. "No, I did not."

"You pulled his keys off his dead body, unlocked his briefcase, pulled out the laptop, and stuck it in your own bag. Then you called Harvey. Did she happen to mention, Harvey, that she had stolen computer files worth a billion dollars?"

"A billion dollars." Rachel bolted out from behind the coffee table, stepping over Harvey's legs to do it. "Are you crazy? I don't know about any billion dollars."

"You're lying," I said. "You've been lying from the start. If you don't tell me the truth right now, I will take you to Drazen myself, and you can explain to him how you killed his brother and took his money."

"No. You will not." I ignored Harvey's stern command and hoped Rachel would get close enough for me to wring her neck, but she stayed on her own side of the room.

"I didn't know anything about any billion dollars. I swear—" She appealed to Harvey. "I swear to God, baby, I didn't know."

"Then why did you steal it? Why did you go straight for the laptop?"

"Because I knew it was worth something, but I didn't know it was that much."

"How did you know?"

"Roger told me. He said Vladi carried something around on his computer that was worth a lot of money. I didn't think about it until I saw his briefcase there. Whatever it was, I thought I could trade it to Drazen to get out from under his thumb."

"You didn't think Drazen would wonder where you got it?"

"I wasn't thinking about all that. I just . . . I had almost been raped. I had just killed a man. I wasn't thinking. I was just doing."

"That's bullshit. I saw you. You were thinking just fine."

She threw her hands up. "What do you want me to say? I figured if it was worth something, then Vladi owed it to me for making me shoot him. I knew it was going to screw up the rest of my life that I had to kill him, and it has."

"Why were you there at the office in the middle of the night in the first place?"

She reached up and pulled at the hair behind her ear. "I told you what I was doing there. I was covering my ass with Drazen. Roger set me up. He planned right from the start to steal their dirty money. I couldn't let Drazen think we were in it together."

"You're telling me you weren't?"

"I might be a lot of things, but I'm not stupid enough to scam Drazen Tishchenko. Then Vladi showed up, and you obviously saw the rest."

I went over to where the new stereo system sat. You didn't find them much these days with turntables. They must have had to look for a long time to find it. "Here's what I think happened." I turned to watch Rachel's face. "Roger tricked you into bringing Drazen into his company. Once Drazen was in, Roger stole his money. You went to the office that night to find proof. All of that was just as you said. But the proof wasn't to protect yourself from Drazen, it was to blackmail Roger. You wanted some of Drazen's money for yourself."

She upped the intensity on her glare, but she didn't deny it.

"Vladi showed up, you killed him, and everything went to hell, at least for you. For Roger, it was an incredible stroke of luck. He ended up with a video of you killing Vladi and the billion-dollar computer."

"I don't know how Vladi was carrying around a billion dollars. That doesn't make any sense. You have to be wrong about that."

"But right about everything else."

She swallowed and looked at Harvey. Any second, I expected her to go over and rub herself against him like a Siamese cat. "I didn't think any of it made any difference. Roger got what he wanted. He left with Vladi's cash and his computer. I got nothing that I wanted. Well, I got a little something. I went to Drazen and told him Roger had killed Vladi." She obviously enjoyed the memory.

"What kind of computer was it? What brand should I be looking for?"

"I don't know. A Dell, I think. Yeah, a Dell."

"What did Roger need to open the files on Vladi's computer?"

"I don't know. How should I know that?"

"Because you always know more than you're saying. What's on it that's worth a billion dollars?"

"I don't know. The brothers had cash stashed everywhere. It was probably some kind of access instructions. You know, where to look and how to get it. Vladi wasn't exactly a Harvard man. He would need something like that."

I looked down at Harvey, concerned about how all this might be sitting with him. He looked back. "Why is any of this important now?"

"What?"

"Regardless of its worth, why is the computer important if we have the video back?"

So much for his fragile psyche. "Cyrus Thorne has the video, or at least a copy of it."

"Who is Cyrus Thorne?"

"Remember Blackthorne? The private military guys who attacked Rachel and me up in Acton? That's his company. He's looking for Kraft. Because of Roger's e-mail, he thought Rachel knew where Kraft was. That's why he's been having her followed."

Harvey looked perplexed. I pulled over the ottoman so I could sit next to him. "The video came from a reporter I met in Paris named Max Kraft. He has a bunch of laptops that were taken from the 809 passengers, including Roger's. The e-mail Rachel got was from him, sort of. He hooked up Roger's computer and a message that had been sitting in Roger's out-box for four years was delivered."

"What?" Rachel was hovering.

"Apparently Roger's Internet account is still active. His wife probably kept it that way. She says she's over him, but I'm not buying it. She also thinks he's alive, which he's not."

"Roger is dead?" More eavesdropping from Rachel. "That doesn't make sense."

"He was hijacked and trapped in a burning aircraft. It makes all kinds of sense. The survivors of the hijacking knew Roger as Gilbert Bernays. He was on the plane all the way to the end. Frank Plume was another hostage. He told me he witnessed Roger's death. I believe him."

"Hold on." Rachel dispensed with the flitting around and plopped down on the couch next to Harvey. "You're saying Roger was on that plane. He died, and somehow this reporter, this Max Kraft, got his laptop? How does that work?"

"The hijackers collected all the computers from the passengers. Sometime during the ten days, all that stuff found its way off the plane and back to the hijackers' headquarters in Afghanistan. That's where Kraft got it.

When the marines got there and the terrorists abandoned their house, the townspeople got in and scavenged the laptops. Kraft found out. He went there and bought at least some of them."

Harvey nodded. "I understand. This Kraft must have been looking for a story."

"Which it seems that he got. According to him, it's a good one. I tend to believe him, since people are trying to kill him. He was attacked in Paris while I was there. He got away. I got picked up by Cyrus Thorne."

"Oh, dear." Harvey had managed to move himself to the edge of the couch, which slightly wrinkled his new slacks. He blinked at me with as much concern as he could comfortably show. "Are you all right?"

"Yeah. No. I mean, I'll be okay. It's just—"

"Hello?" Rachel called for our attention. "She's right here, Harvey. She's obviously fine. Can we talk about the video? Why does this Thorne person have the video? What does he have to do with it?"

I turned my attention back to Harvey. "Kraft wouldn't tell me what he was writing about, but he implied that Thorne is a bad guy and that his story will expose him. But Thorne says he's working for the U.S. government, that Kraft is in possession of classified files, and that it's his job to get them back. He wants me to contact Kraft again. He'll trade Kraft for the video."

"Why is that a bad thing?" Rachel asked. "That's a good thing, isn't it? We find this Kraft, turn him over to Blackthorne, they give us their copy of the video, and we totally destroy it forever. Then you tell Drazen that Roger killed Vladi. Roger is dead. He died in the hijacking, so justice has been served. We all go back to our lives of quiet desperation."

I was more conscious than ever of how much I disliked Rachel and this whole mess she had pulled us into. Also, she had yet to express one ounce of gratitude, but before I could pounce on her, Harvey took care of it.

"Rachel, please. You are not the only one involved in this." There was an edge in Harvey's tone. I loved the new Harvey. I just wondered where he'd been and why I had never seen him. Perhaps sensing that she was pushing her luck with the one person who could still stomach her, Rachel closed her mouth.

"First of all," I said, "Thorne told me a lot of things I'm not sure I believe. I'm not sure whether to believe Kraft. But I believe this: it is Thorne's intention to kill Kraft. I won't turn anyone over to be killed."

"Of course not," Harvey agreed.

"Second, we now have a new billion-dollar variable in the equation. Now we have to wonder if Drazen is looking for Roger because he wants revenge, or because he wants his money, or both. Something tells me he wants his money back."

"But we do not have it."

"That's true. At the moment, we don't have anything to give Drazen to make him happy—except the name of Vladi's real killer." I resisted the urge to wink at Rachel. "But maybe if we can find him his money, it will turn out he's not that concerned about revenge, and *then* we can all go back to our lives of quiet desperation."

"That's easy for you to say. You're not the one who will get your ovaries ripped out if you're wrong. How are we supposed to find the money?"

"If anyone has it, it's Kraft. He has the computers from Zormat."

"Can you call him?"

"He's a little hard to find." I tried to think of what I would say to him if I did. Then I remembered our conversation at the hotel just before the bullets started flying. "But I still have something he wants." The only question was whether or not I had it in me to betray Lyle Burquart.

25

I OPENED MY EYES THE NEXT MORNING AND DECIDED THE world wouldn't end while I went for a run. I hadn't been out in days, and the muscles in my back and shoulders felt as if they'd baked in a kiln. I got up and dressed and spent a good fifteen seconds stretching my hamstrings. When I got outside, I was pleased to find one of the first warm mornings of spring. I was not pleased to find that I had the lung capacity of a small bird. That's what happened when I slacked off.

Just past the turn to Memorial Drive, I noticed a car lingering off my left shoulder. It was easy to spot, keeping pace with me and not the rest of the vehicle traffic. No one trying to be stealthy would be caught dead following at that range. When the driver pulled up alongside and I saw who it was, I was annoyed more than anything. I couldn't even go running in peace. I was also on the verge of fainting, so I stopped and went over to lean in the window and see what Special Agent Eric Ling wanted.

"Hi there," he said. "How's it going?" He offered a steaming cup of Dunkin' Donuts coffee.

"Never touch the stuff. Thanks anyway."

He shrugged and fit the cup into a holder in the console between the seats. Government vehicles had all the snazzy features. He dropped his cool surfer shades and looked at me over the rims. "Get in. I'll drive you back."

"That kind of defeats the purpose."

"Maybe, but you weren't exactly burning up the course. I just wanted to ask you about this."

He pulled a photo from an envelope and held it up. It was a picture of Bo, ever the gentleman, holding the door for me at Grigorii's, the morning we had gone to meet Drazen Tishchenko.

He pointed at Bo. "Who's your friend?"

"Who says he's my friend?"

"We've been trying to identify him. We ran his plates, but that was a dead end."

That helped me feel marginally better. There was no end to the tricks Bo knew. It also explained why he was feeling so much heat.

Ling put the picture back into the envelope, then reached over and popped the door open. "Come on. Let's go somewhere and talk."

I looked down the path I wouldn't be running that morning and felt . . . relief. I opened the door and climbed in. He waited until I was buckled in, checked his side mirror, and pulled away from the curb. He turned at the next side street. There was no place to park, so he pulled up to a hydrant and killed the engine.

"Government plates," he said, not seeming all that bashful about it.

"I knew you had a team on me," I said.

"Sure." He twisted around in his seat so he was more or less facing me. "The Bureau has unlimited funds and manpower to spend following around a private investigator. That would be an easy sell."

He didn't actually say "two-bit private investigator," but it was implied. I knew they weren't up on Bo, and there had been only three people in the meeting. "Are you set up on Tishchenko?"

"We're up on Grigorii's. We have been for months. I got a call that an unknown female had wandered into the picture, which is pretty unusual for that place. I thought it must be Rachel, but it was you, and I asked myself, 'What would she be doing there?' I thought about it. Want to know what I came up with?"

"I'm all ears."

"It all comes back to Betelco. Everyone is connected through Betelco, including your partner. Harvey is connected through his ex-wife. His ex-wife is connected personally through Roger and professionally as the company's auditor. Tishchenko is connected because he was running dirty money through there. Right?"

"If you say so." I didn't see anything to argue with in there but didn't want to just agree with him. He could be tricky.

"Four years ago, Roger Fratello disappeared. He took Drazen's money with him. There's some indication he also killed Drazen's brother Vladi, but that's mostly rumor coming from his people. Drazen's been looking for Roger ever since. Are you with me?"

"I'm following along nicely, thank you."

"Good, because here's where you come in. Cut to right now. Traces of Roger start to show up again. Drazen Tishchenko ends up in Boston, and your partner gets grabbed."

"Didn't he say he was out shopping for a new wheel-chair?"

He smiled, indulging me. "Then I saw this." He tapped the envelope with the picture in it. "Lew and I started tossing around a few ideas for why you, a person with no prior connections to ROC, would be meeting with a high-priority ROC target."

"ROC?"

"Russian organized crime. That's what I do. I'm with a special unit."

I wanted to mention that Drazen was Ukrainian, but if he chased Russians for a living, it was a good bet he already knew.

"Anyway, even after all this time, Drazen is looking for Roger. If he thinks, for some reason, that Harvey can tell him where to find him, that's a good reason to snatch him up. If you want Harvey back, that's a good reason for you to visit with Drazen."

"That's a theory," I said. A pretty darn close theory.

"As you know, new information came up leading us to believe Roger had resurfaced, so we've also been looking for him."

"Right," I said. "He popped out of a terrorist's closet in Zormat."

"Well, I see that you *have* been following along nicely." Ling didn't look exactly impressed, more that I might not have been as two-bit as he'd thought. "We got a call from State. They had some items they couldn't identify. We started running prints for them and came up with a wallet belonging to fugitive Roger Fratello. We were pretty psyched about that development. Then we tracked a key from inside the wallet to the safety deposit box in Brussels, which is where we found your partner's prints. You see how that all works together?"

"I do."

"We came to see Harvey. We almost killed you. We left. We got the call from Harvey to come back. That's the part where the two of you lied to federal agents."

"Do you have some proof that we lied?"

"No, but I don't need it, because I don't really care about that. What I care about is Drazen Tishchenko, and since Harvey came back from his time out with head and hands intact, I have to think that you and Drazen worked something out. That's what I'm interested in."

"You're not after Harvey?"

"Are you kidding?"

"You're not after Roger?"

"We were," he said, "but he's dead. He died in the hijacking."

"You knew that?"

"We figured it out."

"How?"

"Probably the same way you did. We started asking some people."

"How come you guys didn't already know about that? The government is supposed to know things like that."

He shrugged. "We don't know a fraction of what we should know. Besides, we never knew he was on the Salanna plane until we got the prints from Zormat. Then we put it together. It's a bummer, too, because Roger was our best shot at getting Drazen."

I pointed at the envelope. "You obviously know where the guy is. Why don't you just go and pick him up?"

"Because I have nothing to charge him with, and if I did, no one would testify against him, and if they tried to, he would do the whole head-and-hands thing. We told you what happened to Walter Herald, and he did that knowing he was killing a fed. That sent a pretty strong message. Everyone at Betelco went running for cover after that."

"I could see how that would be discouraging to people."

"But let's be generous for the purpose of this exercise and assume I could pick him up and charge him with something. Do you know what he would do?"

"Call a lawyer?"

"Call the CIA."

"For what?"

"He has strong ties to the organization formerly known as the KGB. He knows state secrets. He says he does, anyway. The CIA swoops in, whispers something about the greater good, spirits him away, and the next time we see him, he's back doing exactly what we left him doing. Roger was our best chance. Not even the spooks would have had the guts to pull him out from under felony murder of a federal agent." He shook his head. He had the look of Charlie Brown after he'd tried again to kick the football, only to have the CIA snatch it away at the last minute. "I would have finally had him."

"All right, so your job is hard. What are we doing now? Right here, you and me?"

"We're talking about how you can help me with my job."

"Let me see if I'm following. Drazen is your big prize. You want him for the murder of Walter Herald. You needed Roger Fratello to get him. You wanted Harvey to get you to Roger, which, by the way, raises this question: How come you're just skipping over Rachel in this whole thing? Why aren't you after her?"

"We don't have Rachel's prints on Roger's money."

"You have pictures of her kissing Roger."

"That's not against the law."

"But you have to think she's involved." I couldn't just let her get away with it.

"We think she was responsible for bringing the Tishchenkos into Betelco and a number of companies in the area. Again, there aren't too many victims in this town—actually, in any town—willing to testify against the Russians."

"All right, fine. But now we all agree that Roger is ashes in Sudan." I looked for validation on that point. He gave me the nod. "Unless you want to nail him for lying about buying a wheelchair, doesn't that mean that Harvey is off the hook? He can't help you get Drazen on the agent's murder, because he had nothing to do with that. If he's off the hook, why would I help you?"

"Let me ask you something." His lighter tone suggested a new turn in the conversation. "How much do you know about the fall of the Soviet Union?"

Definitely a new turn. "Let's see, communism failed, the USSR crumbled and split apart. Now we have 220 countries competing at the Olympics instead of 180."

"The last time I checked in with Drazen Tishchenko, he was trying to sell a diesel-powered, ninety-foot-long, Foxtrot-class attack submarine to Pablo Escobar. Pablo needed a little something to run his product up and down the West Coast. Do you know where Drazen got it?"

"I'd have to think the only navy that wouldn't miss a sub would be the old Soviet navy, whatever it was called."

"He bought it in Kronstadt, which is where the Baltic fleet of the Red Navy went to die. We're taking about a hundred-million-dollar military vessel. Drazen paid five for it and had a deal to sell it for twenty."

"That would have been a fair return on investment."

"The thing about Russians is, they love money, they're scared of absolutely nothing, and they will sell anything. If you need it and you're willing to pay for it, Drazen Tishchenko will get it for you, and being who he is, he's plugged in. He knows party officials who know things. You know, like where the stocks of weaponized smallpox are kept. Where all the tactical nuclear weapons happen to be. They know where the weapons-grade fissionable material is, and they know how to get all that stuff out and into the hands of the people willing to pay for it and willing to use it. Any idea who those people might be?"

"People who don't like us?"

"That's correct. The submarine deal never happened, but only because the local *mafiya* back home blocked it. Drazen forgot to cut them in. Otherwise, the U.S. Navy would be chasing drug-running subs up and down the Pacific Coast. Are you starting to get my drift?"

We were still chatting amiably, but an undercurrent had crept in, something in his usually imperturbable tone that carried more weight than the words he was saying. That, by itself, felt like a pretty good case for helping him out.

He went on. "When Tishchenko decides to put a few tactical nukes out there, there's nothing to say we'll catch him then, either. Wouldn't it be better to just nip it in the bud?"

"I still don't know how I'm supposed to help you do that."

"I think you know where the fortune is."

"The what?"

"The lost fortune."

"His money has a name?"

"That's what people say when they talk about it." Having finished his own coffee, he reached down for the cup he'd brought for me and started peeling back the plastic flap. "According to legend, it's a billion dollars."

This was getting interesting, enough so that I couldn't hide it. "How does anyone misplace a billion dollars?"

"The better story is how he got it in the first place. Drazen owned a bank in Russia."

"He doesn't strike me as the banker type."

"I didn't say he was a banker. He's a gangster who owned a bank. That's all the rage in Russia these days. There's no real regulation of banks over there, so they buy them and use them as mattresses."

"Excuse me?"

"Mattresses. Places to keep their cash. Then they use the U.S. banking system to turn all that dirty money into clean U.S. currency. It's a beautiful thing. No one can accuse these gangsters of being stupid."

"I have to believe he didn't earn a billion dollars from ATM charges."

"He stole it from KGB agents."

"He stole it from the KGB? First of all, that sounds like a bad strategy. Second, where does the KGB get a billion dollars?"

"They stole it."

"From whom?"

"The Russian treasury." He glanced over, maybe to gauge my interest. This was probably the sort of thing that made most people's eyes glaze over. But I had a personal stake.

"I'm listening."

"The people who were most pissed off by the unraveling of the Soviet Union were KGB and party officials."

"That makes sense," I said. "The ones who benefited most from a corrupt system would be the ones with the most to lose. What did they do?"

"They stole the country."

"Stole the country?"

"Starting in 1992, for about eleven years, the KGB and other party officials pulled off the greatest looting of a country that the world has ever seen. It's hard to say how much money they took, but estimates run around six hundred billion."

"Jesus. How do you steal that much money?"

"The same way most people steal from their employers. They set up shell companies and false-flag bank accounts all over the world and sneak money into them. But there was so much money the KGB ran out of places to put it. They turned to the *mafiya*. But at that time, the *mafiya* wasn't sophisticated enough to handle it, so the KGB bought them what they needed to keep up."

"New BlackBerrys?"

"Computers and communications equipment. They gave them the most sophisticated and cutting-edge technical equipment available. It was a transforming moment for the bad guys."

"Bad guys? I don't hear any good guys in this tale."

"The worse guys. One of the worst is Drazen Tishchenko. The KGB gave him their money, and he took it."

"These KGB agents just sat around and let him take their hard-earned dough?"

"There was so much money moving so fast through so many accounts and countries and currencies that it was hard for anyone to keep up. By the time they figured it out, it was too late."

"Drazen was smart enough to do all that?"

"He had a guy."

Didn't they always? "Even if it was too late to get the money back, it wouldn't necessarily keep the KGB out of the complaint department, would it?"

"Anyone who came to the complaint department had to deal with his brother."

"Vladi?"

"In the Ukraine, Vladi was known as the man who couldn't be killed. He was shot seven times in four different incidents. Twice he took bullets for his brother. No one ever managed to kill him."

That was only because he had yet to run into Rachel. "Okay, but still, it's the KGB."

"When it got too hot, Drazen got his guy to give him a couple of maps—one for him and one for Vladi, so he could find the money."

"What kind of maps?"

"They're criminals, so he didn't put anything anywhere in their real names. It was in numbered accounts in places like Turks and Caicos, Liberia, the Seychelles, Nauru. Wherever he stashed it, he used fake names or numbered accounts. If he did have to stash some cash, he put it in safety deposit boxes, again under fake names. The map wasn't really a map but a list of files with the locations of accounts, names on the accounts, account numbers, passwords . . . things like that. After he got that, Drazen no longer needed his guy, so he killed him. Drazen and Vladi popped up in Israel next, where they offered to help Mossad track down former KGB agents."

"So, they got Mossad to take out their enemies." Crafty though not surprising that Drazen would be of the one-stone-two-birds school of criminal behavior. "And the computer that was stolen from Vladi had one of these financial maps on it?"

"According to legend."

It was a good legend, but there was a hole in the plot. "If you had a billion bucks stashed and someone found out where it was, wouldn't you move it? If the list was compromised, why wouldn't Drazen just move the money to new accounts?"

"That's never been explained, and it's one reason some

people don't buy the story. Drazen had his own list, so it's possible he did exactly what you're suggesting."

"In which case the computer would be worthless."

"And yet Drazen is here, and here he stays. I have to think he's waiting for something. Or someone?" He braced his arm against the sill of his door, leaned his head into the palm of his hand, and just stared at me.

"Tell me exactly what it is you need, Ling."

"I need information. I want to know what he's doing, why he's here. Anything you can tell me."

"He's here for his billion dollars. That's why he took Harvey. That's why he's done everything he's done while he's been here. He says he's looking for Roger, but I think it's the money."

He took off his shades. "Are you saying you really did find it?"

"I might know where it is, but I'm trying to make him go away happy, so I'm not sure we have the same objective. Besides that, I seem to have run into a hitch."

"What is it?"

"Blackthorne. Do you know them?"

"Yeah. They've done a lot of work for the military." He angled in my direction, as focused as a hunting dog on the scent. "Why? Have they approached you?"

I started to answer and stopped. Kraft had said that Thorne had supporters inside the government. I looked out my window at the college kids talking and laughing and hurrying to class. We were parked close to MIT. What was to say that Ling wasn't one? Maybe he had gone over to the dark side. Life sucks when you don't know whom to trust.

"I don't want you talking to them," he said, coming out of his comfortable slouch. He was agitated, as animated as I had seen him. "I am not getting screwed over again by the real spooks or the pseudo-spooks or anyone else. Are they working for the CIA? I heard they've been doing covert intelligence stuff."

"They don't want Drazen," I said, "and I'm not sure who they're working for on this one."

"How do you know?"

"Thorne told me."

He blinked a couple of times. "You met Cyrus Thorne?"

"Yeah, why?"

"Wow. He's kind of a legend around the Bureau. No one I know has ever met him, though."

"A legend in a good way or a bad way?"

"Good way. I don't know much about his company, but Thorne was the best analyzer of intelligence anyone has ever known. All this stuff that's happening now, the terrorism, attacks on the U.S., he saw it coming. What's he like?"

"Commanding. Listen, I'll do what I can to help you, but things are very complicated."

He hooked an index finger over the inside curve at six o'clock position on the steering wheel. "Can you say where the money is?"

I had to think about that. I assumed Kraft had it, but I didn't know for sure. I also didn't want to give Kraft up to the FBI, even if we were off the record . . . if that's what we were. After making such an issue out of protecting Lyle, I owed him that much. "I'm not sure where it is. I'm working on that."

Ling was smart. He knew I was lying, but I was determined not to feel guilty about it.

"All right." He straightened up, did as much of a stretch as the car would allow, and yawned. He put his cup back in the holder. He had downed two strong cups of Dunkin' Donuts brew, and he still looked as if he'd just rolled out of bed. "I have no leverage over you," he said. "I probably never did. But if you have his money, then you have leverage over Drazen, probably more than you know. All I'm asking you to do is to use it to help me get Drazen. He's a bad man. I think you know that."

He didn't wait for an answer before firing up the engine.

"Is that it?"

He put on his shades and turned to face me. With his dark glasses on, it was hard to read his expression. "I don't want you talking to anyone at Blackthorne again without letting me know, even if it's the man himself."

"Why not?"

"Because if they're working for the CIA, they could be playing you, and I'm not getting this close to Drazen just to have the goddamn Agency run in again and take my score."

"I see nine-eleven has done a lot to bring you guys together."

"Not really."

Ling dropped me off at my place. My running clothes were just sweaty enough to have to wash, which didn't seem fair given how far I hadn't run. I tossed them into the hamper, showered, and was getting into jeans when my cell phone rang. I followed the sound to my backpack and dug it out.

"Hello?"

"You are one lying, scheming bitch." Nothing like a friendly greeting from Max Kraft first thing in the morning.

"I guess you got my message. It's good to hear that you made it out of France."

"From what I hear, so did you. On the Blackthorne private jet." This wasn't how I'd envisioned our conversation starting off. It seemed he had spies of his own. "That whole thing in Paris where you pretended to save my life, what was that? A way to gain my trust?"

"Yeah. Also getting arrested and thrown in jail. Look, you're the one who dragged me into the Blackthorne portion of the program. I had my own problems to deal with, and now, because of you, I have to deal with Cyrus Thorne, and I have to deal with him because he has a copy of the video, the one you promised *I* had the only copy of."

"You asked for the video, I gave it to you. If you let it get away, that's your problem."

"I didn't let it get away. He got it from your translator. He knows you and I have talked, and he's willing to trade it back if I set you up. If I don't, I'm pretty sure he'll give it to Drazen. For a whole lot of reasons too tedious to go into, I can't have that."

"Is that—is that what this is?" He certainly wasn't in Paris anymore, but that's where I pictured Kraft, in his hotel on the Left Bank, peering out from behind closed curtains. That was what his voice sounded like. "Are they listening now? Are you setting me up right now?"

"I didn't call to set you up. I called to talk about a way I think we can all get through this, but you have to help."

"I'll help you. Sure. Why wouldn't I? You're working for the organization that wants me dead. Do you even hear yourself? What do you take me for?"

"It costs you nothing to listen."

"Unless Cyrus Thorne has someone triangulating the signal." I heard the sound of him sucking on a bottle and

wondered if he was having beer for breakfast. Then I realized I had no idea if it was breakfast time where he was.
He didn't hang up, so I forged ahead.

"We were right about Roger's computer—Roger's
other computer, the one that belonged to Vladi. Rachel
stole it. Roger took it from her because he knew there
were files on it worth a billion dollars. The files are like
a . . ." What was the term Ling had used? "A financial
map. Directions to the money." I waited for some sign
that he was there. Talking on the phone to Kraft was a lot
like talking to him over the Internet. He gave nothing
away. "Grunt if you're still alive."

"You're saying there really is a billion dollars that has
just been sitting out there for four years because,
what . . . the account numbers have been lost? I thought
that story was bullshit when you told me. You're saying
it's true?"

"The moral of the story is, always back up your files.
Do you have the Dell or not?"

"What if I do? What would a billion dollars buy me?"

"Your life, for one thing. I might be able to swing it
so that Drazen forgets about who killed Vladi in exchange for his money. That way, the video means nothing, and Thorne loses his leverage, and I don't have to
do what he says, and you can go on doing whatever it is
you do."

Measured pauses were not part of his speech pattern,
so when I heard one, it felt significant. I knew the wheels
were turning. "Let's just say for the hell of it that I have a
Dell. We can't really know if it's the right one—"

"We can if you open it up and find a game of Russian
Solitaire on it."

"Let me finish. The reason these laptops have value

to me is not because John or Joe or Mary's four-year-old grocery list is still on it."

"A billion dollars that will save someone's life is not a grocery list."

"That's not my point. It's because they were taken to Afghanistan and used by the Martyr's Brigade for years after the hijacking."

"So?"

"So there are hundreds of e-mails on those machines, and those e-mails are the foundation of my story. There is no way I'm giving this stuff up to you."

"I thought your story was on Blackthorne. Why would e-mails from the Martyrs be important?"

"If you knew that, you would have my story."

"I'm not trying to steal your story, Max. I'm trying to help you with it and I have a proposal."

"What?"

"You give me Vladi's Dell, and I'll give you the name of my Blackthorne source."

There was another long silence. "I'll think about it." *Click.*

I sat for a long time with the phone in my hand, trying to figure out what to do. The good news was that he had the Dell. At least a Dell. The bad news was that Lyle Burquart had made it clear he never wanted to see me again, and I had made him that promise. But it had been just as clear to me that the Salanna 809 survivors did not want Max Kraft to have their contact data. I had given it to him anyway. Why had I done that? I went into the bathroom and thought about it while I brushed my teeth. While I was flossing, I figured it out. It was because of what was at stake. The Salanna 809 survivors were trying to protect their privacy. I was trying to save

Rachel's life. There had been too much at stake not to have used the manifest to get the video, just as there was too much at stake not to at least ask Lyle if he would speak to Kraft. It sounded as if Kraft and he were both after the same thing anyway. Besides, what was one more betrayal?

26

THE SAME RECEPTIONIST WAS AT HER DESK AT THE WBRS radio station, thumbing through what could very well have been the same magazine. When she saw me coming, she opened a desk drawer and reached down into it with both hands. She came out with a goldenrod envelope. She hefted it up and offered it across the desk to me.

"What's this?"

"It's from Lyle. He said you'd be back."

She gave me a look of complete disdain, as though letting Lyle down meant letting her down, too.

"Thanks." I took it from her. It was heavy. "Is he back there?"

"He's gone."

The finality in her tone suggested that she didn't mean he had gone out for lunch. "Is he coming back?"

"No."

"Why not? What happened?"

With both hands flat on the desk, she leaned forward and looked up at me. "He left the day you came here and never came back to work."

The envelope in my hand suddenly seemed to have

more heft to it. "Is he all right? Has anyone spoken to him?"

"He called in. He said everything was fine and thanks and all that, but he wouldn't be back and not to look for him. He told us to donate his last check to the Jimmy Fund. He said he was leaving for good." She went back to her magazine.

I thought back to what he'd said in the control room about being fucked, about having some decisions to make. Apparently, he had made them, but I still had to wonder what would prompt a man to quit his job and uproot his family that way.

"He didn't leave any—"

"Forwarding information? No. He left that." She nodded to the envelope. I had the sense from her reaction that she had somehow been bruised by Lyle's departure.

"Were you friends?"

She had never taken her eyes from her magazine. "Good enough friends that I would never have expected him to leave town without so much as a goodbye." She turned the page but must have decided that more needed to be said.

"I hope you're happy with yourself. I hope it doesn't bother you that just when he was getting settled and things were getting back to normal, you came along and stirred it all up again."

I could tell she was one of those people who liked delivering bad news. It was right there on her face, and it made me uneasy. "Stirred up what?"

"His oldest son was run over by a truck and killed while his little brother watched.

I took a step back from the desk.

"That's why Lyle left the paper to come here. He

wanted to spend more time with Jeff. I guess now he'll be out looking for another job, thanks to you."

"Did they . . . was it an accident?"

"Hit and run. Never caught them."

I took another step back. It felt as if she'd just splashed acid in my face.

"He said to be careful with that."

"What?"

She nodded at the envelope that I was now hugging to my chest.

"And good luck." She turned the page to a new article. "He said be careful and good luck."

I sat in the car with the overstuffed envelope in my lap and both hands on the wheel, thinking about what she'd said and what it meant. I felt like one of those patients who wakes up in the middle of surgery—in pain and completely helpless. I tried breathing in through my nose and out through my mouth, but I couldn't catch my breath.

It was one thing to threaten an adult. Adults chose paths that sometimes went to scary places. But kids don't make those choices. A kid never had anything to do with anything. The thought that Lyle's son, trusting and vulnerable and feeling safe in his world, could have been run down and killed just for being his father's son hurt beyond words and made me want to kill someone.

Good luck, and be careful. That was Lyle's message. That was part of Lyle's message. The rest of it was in the envelope. I had to dig in to know the rest, but I had the strongest feeling that if I did, something bad would happen to me, too. I was certain of it. I brushed my fingers across the outside. It was soft and worn and well used. He had traded his job and his family's life in Boston for

me to have it. Perhaps not by choice, but that's how it had
turned out. I had to look inside.

I slipped my fingers in and pulled out a couple of
pages. They looked to be the middle pages in the draft of
a story. I pulled out a few more and found the beginning
of the article. It was called "The Private War of Cyrus
Thorne." With fewer pages stuffed inside, the envelope
had a little more give. I looked down and spotted a tiny
cassette tape. I pulled it out, and a second came tumbling
behind it. There was nothing on the labels except "1" and
"2." I had no way to play microcassettes in the car and
a suddenly burning desire to hear them right away, so
I started up the engine and drove to a nearby Staples. I
bought the cheapest microcassette player I could. I bought
batteries. I went back to the car, assembled everything,
and popped in tape number one. I didn't even bother to
rewind.

"—believe it was Pan Am 103?" That was Lyle's voice,
and I was immediately drawn in. Why was he talking
about Lockerbie?

"Without question, it was Pan Am 103." That was a
voice I didn't recognize. "There was a CIA team on that
flight. Five agents, including McKee. One of the best I
ever knew got blown out of the sky that day, and that was
the beginning of the end of it for Cyrus. He hung in with
the agency a few more years, but he never got over what
happened with Pan Am."

Best *I* ever knew. Was he CIA? The voice was not
deep yet had plenty of gravity. There was a bulldog quality about the way he powered forward, but strategic
pauses insinuated a wry sense of humor, even if he didn't
give it voice. I started glancing over the article as I listened.

"What happened?" Lyle asked.

"Cy was part of a team that investigated the incident. He came to believe 103 was targeted because McKee and his people were onboard."

"Why?"

"They had found out about a Syrian drug trafficker. He was swapping information for protection with the DEA and another CIA team in Germany. They were allowing him to bring drugs into the States. McKee found out. He thought it was bullshit. The Syrian heard, probably from other agents, that McKee was about to blow the whistle on his sweet deal. He blew up McKee instead."

"You're saying that, indirectly, the CIA and the DEA were responsible for Pan Am 103?"

"That's what Cyrus thought. To him, those agents were heroes, betrayed by their country, swept aside in some high-level cover-up. It drove him nuts. Then he got into counterterrorism, and that was the last straw."

"Any particular incident?"

"Everything taken together. He was one of the first to see the threat of the radical Muslims. He understood the socioeconomic drivers in third world countries, and he thought you could apply the domino theory to Muslim nations."

"Domino theory? Like LBJ's excuse for escalating Vietnam?"

"Exactly. But in Cy's nightmare, the first thing that happens is Pakistan falls to extremists. Then the princes in Saudi Arabia lose control, and the House of Saud falls. Osama comes out of the caves to lead his people. He has Saudi oil, and he has the bomb, and now the dominoes start to fall. Indonesia, the largest Muslim population in the world, the Philippines, Turkey, Syria, Somalia, and other African Muslim nations. Afghanistan goes back to the Taliban. The Palestinians get the muscle they need to plow Israel under. The ayatollahs in Iran are already developing their own bomb, and who the hell knows what Saddam really has in his backyard?"

I had to keep reminding myself that this was an old recording. It just made me realize how much the world had changed in a relatively short time.

"In Cy's world, what you end up with is a radical Islamic alliance with nuclear weapons lined up against Western nations with nuclear weapons."

"Armageddon."

"Yes, because, unlike the Soviets, religious jihadists are not afraid to die. There is nothing keeping their fingers off the buttons. Mass mutual destruction becomes a real possibility."

"But LBJ's theory never proved out." That was Lyle, arguing on behalf of sanity. "We pulled out of Vietnam, and the balance of power never shifted."

"True believers are not swayed by facts or historical precedents, and Cyrus is a true believer. He always was. Always will be. The more he learned about the threat, the louder he yelled. The louder he yelled, the more the powers that be wanted to shut him down. Eventually, they pushed him out."

"Then he didn't resign from the CIA." Lyle's tone suggested he'd suspected as much all along.

"That's why he started the business. He needed to regain control. Cyrus is big on control, and he had no problem finding fellow travelers to go with him. We had military officers, intelligence officers, special-ops types, force protection, people from some of these other security companies."

"Is that why you did it?"

"I was tired of the military. Cy was my best friend and my mentor, and I wanted to make some money."

I reached over and paused the tape, because a light had gone on in my brain, and I needed to look at what it was showing me. The voice on this tape was Tony Blackmon's. It was a tape of Lyle interviewing Cyrus's dead partner, the man who had started Blackthorne with him. The man who had probably known him best. Whatever he said had instant credibility, and what he'd said on this tape must have been what Thorne was so intent on keeping a secret. He had killed Lyle's son to keep it that way. Now he wanted to kill Kraft.

I pressed play. Blackmon continued.

"For a long time, it was just about getting the company up and running, but once we got going, for Cy it became all about the ideology. Everything that happened in the escalating pattern of violence and aggression—Khobar Towers, the *Cole,* the embassies in Africa—he took each one as evidence that the country was defended by morons, and if he, Cyrus Thorne, didn't do something, we were going to have the big fireball."

"Nuclear attack?"

"Right. It's the Thorne Mushroom-Cloud Defense. He can justify any behavior at all by invoking the image of that mushroom rising up over Washington or Manhattan. It's handy, because there's hardly anything Americans wouldn't do to stop that from happening."

I put the article and everything else aside to give my full attention to the tape.

"What sorts of things did he do?"

"He started sourcing bigger and riskier jobs. High-risk protection stuff that gave us access to diplomats and heads of state in the Middle East. Cy had contacts all over the world from his CIA officer days, so it wasn't hard. He also jumped on assignments in hot spots like Kosovo. It was great for business, but he was pushing the envelope more and more."

"In what way?"

"If we got called in on a kidnapping case down in Colombia, we'd get the victim released, but the kidnappers would all end up dead at the scene. Then we had to start finding ways to bury expenses, because we were going out on our own missions."

"You're saying Blackthorne initiated missions without being hired by a client."

"That's right. Isn't that what I just said?"

"I'm just being clear for the recording. You're saying Blackthorne became a vigilante organization disguised as a legitimate contractor." Blackmon didn't respond, so he went on. "Did you participate?"

"I can tell you right now, a lot of the things we were doing, they were things that needed to be done. People who needed to be dead. A Syrian gun runner selling weapons used against our troops. An Afghan war lord who sells drugs and on the side buys little boys to fondle and rape. A Palestinian telling a bunch of kids they've been chosen by Allah to have the great honor of strapping on some C4 and blowing themselves up."

Blackmon had to stop and take a rest here. I pictured him walking away from Lyle, trying to gather himself, and then coming back.

"The world is better off without these people, and if we had more of that kind of clear thinking in government, we wouldn't have half the problems we have today."

"You don't consider it murder?"

"It was murder. I am a murderer. But it was murder that needed to be done."

I didn't know if the long pause here meant Lyle was taking notes or trying to form a question. "If you believe in what he's doing, why are you talking to me?"

"Because the more we did, the more Cy wanted to do. He wanted more influence. He started taking money under the table from donors with foreign business interests, and those interests had to be protected. There were certain countries and governments that were more favorable to what we were doing, and their interests had to be considered. The decisions got more complicated, and pretty soon it wasn't about right and wrong." There was a real sense of loss in Blackmon's voice. Whether it was for his friend's loss of purpose or because he would miss going out and killing people once the article was published, it was hard to say. "Cy had created the thing he hated most."

"Thorne created his own politically driven bureaucracy."

Blackmon must have nodded, because Lyle told him he had to speak for the tape.

"That's what happened. I was ready to bail, but then nine-eleven happened." The silence that followed went on so long I checked to see if we'd come to the end of the tape. We hadn't, and eventually Blackmon began again. "Watching those towers fall . . . it did something to him."

"It did something to a lot of us."

"Cy felt responsible."

"Why?"

"Because he saw it coming, and he wasn't able to convince anyone. Because he felt like part of the failure, part of the useless and fucked-up government that had let things get to that point. He started taking a lot of black-bag jobs. Covert stuff. Illegal."

"Like what?"

"Political assassinations, kidnappings, torture—various other forms of violent persuasion aimed at targets of his choosing. Encouraging coups, training and arming insurgents, passing along classified information to where it's most needed."

"Where does he get access to classified intelligence?"

"You have to remember the core of the company was all ex-military, ex-CIA or DIA or NSA. We all had high-level clearance, and we all have friends who still do. There are a lot of people inside the intelligence community who believe the U.S. intelligence machine is inadequate to the job of defending the country."

"You have moles?"

"We get help here and there. Don't ask me for names. I'm not compromising those people. They're trying to do right. Most of us are trying to do right. But the jobs got bigger and riskier and harder to manage, and civilians started getting in the way. Cy's view is that everyone is a soldier in this war."

"Much like the radical Muslim point of view."

"That's what I keep telling him. 'Cy, you're no different from the people we're hunting.' He doesn't like to hear that. He considers himself a patriot, the country's last best chance. The hell of it is, he might be right. But when you start killing citizens, that's when I get off the train."

"What would he do if he knew you were talking to me?"

"Kill me."

The little recording machine turned itself off as the tape ended. I'd heard enough. If Thorne would have been willing to kill his partner over what was on that tape, he certainly must have killed Lyle's son, and there was no doubt he would kill Kraft.

I found Kraft's beeper number and called it. I figured I would beep him every thirty minutes until he called me back. When he did, I would tell him I had something to trade for Vladi's computer. Then I called Bo. When he answered, I didn't even bother with hello.

"I need to see Drazen," I said. "I need you to hook me up."

"Why?"

"I need a new deal."

27

DRAZEN TISHCHENKO WAS SEATED AT A TABLE IN THE back, a dark presence in the brightly lit fast-food emporium that was Wendy's. On his table were all the classic Wendy's accoutrements: orange tray, white plastic silverware, yellow paper napkins. He also had an impressive pile of Saltine packets to go with the chili he was scooping from a cardboard cup.

The way he held his cup offered a good look at the tattoos on his right hand. The biggest one, a black skull resting in a bed of leaves, was on the back of his hand. Elaborate symbols adorned the base of every finger. The one on his pinkie was a swastika. Just below each fingernail was a Cyrillic letter.

While I stared at his artwork, he stared up at me with those eyes, still as dead as the tattooed skull's. I didn't know how to greet him. I didn't know whether to sit. Last time, I had counted on Bo for all my etiquette cues, but Bo wasn't here this time, much to his chagrin. I'd had to work hard to convince him it was a good idea to meet with Drazen alone. As I stood in front of the man himself,

THE PANDORA KEY 261

I wasn't sure it had been the best strategy. I felt as if I had a swarm of wasps in my gut.

"Sit."

I pulled out the chair across from him and slid in.

"What do you want?" He'd turned back to his chili and was scraping the last of it from the bottom of the cup.

"I have news to report."

He put the cup down and wiped his mouth with one of the yellow napkins. "I like that the food at Wendy's in Denver is the same as the food at Wendy's in Boston. I don't like all American ideas, but that one was a good one."

"Roger Fratello is dead."

He balled up the soiled napkin and dropped it into the cup. "That would be convenient for you."

"Not especially. He died in a hijacking four years ago."

"What kind of hijacking?"

"Airplane. It was a Salanna Air flight from Paris to Johannesburg. He was traveling under the alias Gilbert Bernays." I had brought props to bolster my case—printouts of articles I'd been carrying around in my files. I slipped them across the table to him. Without taking his eyes from mine, he put his hand on them and pushed them right back. "Can you show me his bones?"

"There wasn't that much of him left. He burned to death when the Belgians stormed the plane. Nine hostages died. He was one of them."

"Again, that is all very handy for you."

"I'm not making this up. The FBI has come to the same conclusion. They've closed the case on Walter Herald's murder. That should be good news for you."

He was so quick I had no time to cover up when he reached across the table and slapped me hard across the face. The force snapped my head sideways. It stung enough to make my eyes tear. I covered my cheek. The skin felt hot where he'd made contact.

The only other patrons in the place were a few tables over. Two teenage boys wearing baggy jeans and a girl with oily eyelids and a spaghetti-strap top. They were looking at me with keen disinterest, as if the whole scene came straight out of a video game.

My nose had started to run. I dried it on the back of my hand and tried to pull myself together. "There's more. I think you'll want to hear it. It's about your brother's computer."

At first, Drazen went completely still, which made us a couple of statues, because I couldn't move, either. Everything rode on his next response. He flattened both hands on the table and canted forward, and I was encouraged. "What do you know of Vladi's computer?"

"I know that Roger took it. I know he was carrying it on the flight. I know if the files are intact, it's worth a lot of money, and I know it wasn't destroyed."

If a rattlesnake had eyelids, it would look the way Drazen did as he slowly blinked at me. "Where is it?"

When I didn't answer fast enough, he cocked his fist and reached over to grab my shirt. I pulled away and stood up, stumbling as I knocked my chair backward. At least I knew I was holding some cards, which made me feel surprisingly relieved and foolishly emboldened. "Don't touch me again."

I didn't have to turn around to know that one of his men was right behind me, probably the one who was holding my gun. Drazen had called him Anton, and he seemed to be his right-hand goon. I reevaluated.

"I can get the computer back for you, but I'm asking you, please, not to hit me again, so we can get through this conversation."

Drazen held his right hand in front of him and lined it up with his view of my throat, then he squeezed until his hand shook, as he must have imagined wringing the life from me. "The next time I touch you, it will not be to hit you."

"Give me your word," I said, "that if I sit down, you won't hurt me again."

I couldn't tell if his barely perceptible nod was for Anton or for me, but Anton set my chair upright and held it. I sat down again but kept my neck well out of Drazen's immediate radius.

"The plane was hijacked four years ago." I pointed to the printouts, still between us. "During the incident, the hijackers collected anything from the passengers they thought might be worth something. This included all the personal computers. Most of this stuff was found recently in Afghanistan by the U.S. military."

"The American army has my money?"

"No. The CIA was called, but the laptops were all pulled out before it got there. A private citizen has them."

"Who?"

Here was an interesting moment. I could give him Max Kraft's name, which meant he would have no reason to keep me alive. Or I could lie.

"The U.S. government is also looking for this man. If they find him first, your money is gone."

"The U.S. government does not scare me."

"They might not scare you, but they can take your money. At the moment, no one knows those files are there. If we do this right, no one ever needs to know."

He gave no indication either way, but I had to be right about this. I had to. There was no way he wanted the feds rooting around in his affairs.

I stiffened a little when he called Anton back to the table, but it was only to bring a pen. Drazen took it. Writing with his left hand, he scribbled something across the back of a Wendy's napkin. "This is the model and the serial number for Vladi's laptop computer." He pushed it toward me. When I took it, he didn't let go. "You find it, and you bring it to me and to no one else."

"I got that part."

I took the napkin and looked over the series of numbers and letters he had printed there. It was interesting that he had the long serial number memorized. "I can't guarantee the files will be on the unit."

"The files will be there."

"How can you be sure?"

"They cannot be moved." He pointed the pen at me. "Straight to me. No one else. Do you understand?"

"I understand. But if I do, I want—" My voice failed me. Even though I knew what I wanted to say, I couldn't get it out. He was such a remorseless creature. "I want something in return."

His gash of a mouth tightened. "You believe you are in a position to set terms with me?"

I made myself lean toward him, trying to pretend I wasn't scared. "A billion dollars is a lot of money. If Roger's been dead since he lost it, then he hasn't been around to spend any. It will be substantially more than it was when last you saw it. You lost it once. I can get it back for you, but I want to know that if I do, our deal will be finished. I want my partner and me to be released from all obligations to you." I was careful not to include Rachel. He would wonder about that.

I sat back and waited and hoped again that I had gambled right and he wanted the money more than he wanted revenge. Of course, there was nothing to say he wouldn't decide he was entitled to both. But he did have that whole thing about honoring commitments. I wanted to hear him say it.

He didn't say it. He didn't do anything. Maybe he was calculating. Maybe he was trying to restrain himself. It was hard to know with him. All I could do was wait and see if I had gone one demand too far.

He pushed the empty chili cup aside. "Let me tell you a sad story. When my brother and I lived in the Ukraine, we were successful businessmen. We had many people working for us all over the country. We had money. Our mother lived in a big house on a hill overlooking our town. We ate and drank and lived like kings. We had women, we had drugs, we had cars. Whatever we wanted. Then, one day, a man came to my door with seven other men, all with guns. Do you know what he wanted?"

"No."

"He wanted to take my life."

"To kill you?"

"No, to steal my life. He said he would kill my mother if I did not leave the country and let him move into my house. He wanted me to give him my cars and my businesses and all my money."

"Just like that?"

"It was wild times in the Ukraine after the fall of the Soviet Union. Worse than that happened. Much worse. This man thought that with a gun, he could take away everything I spent my life building. I have no doubt he would have killed my mother if I had not."

"If you had not killed him?"

He crossed his arms, which served to highlight the lovely tattoo that stretched the length of his right forearm. It was a feral-looking cat, wrapped in barbed wire and still on the prowl. He tipped his head and stared at me as if to say, "Try again."

I fought hard against the next, most logical conclusion, but I knew it was the truth. "You killed your mother."

"And then I killed him, but first I took him to his house, and I killed his wife and his mother in front of him." He leaned in. I could smell the chili on his breath. "No one takes my money."

I had to think that one through, but eventually I got to what I thought was the parable's message. He didn't give a shit about who killed Vladi. Someone had taken his money.

"All right, Sashen'ka. I will play your game. You bring me Vladi's computer with the files on it, and it will be done."

I felt the tiniest bit of tension bleed off.

"But there is another part. If you do not find it or you find it and do not bring it to me, we will have a settling of accounts, you and I, and I will kill your partner while you watch. Then I will kill you, too."

28

AFTER I LEFT WENDY'S, I COULDN'T GET TO FELIX'S FAST
enough. I would have called him, but I was busy beeping
Kraft. I did it three times before I pulled into the parking
lot of Felix's complex. On the last try, I punched in my
call-back number and followed it with 911. Surely he
couldn't ignore the universal code for near hysteria.

When the elevator at Felix's building proved too slow,
I took the stairs, climbing all seven stories without a
pause. By the time I hit five, my legs were jelly. By the
time I made it to his apartment and found Felix draped
across the lime-green beanbag chair, I could barely stand.

"Hey, Miss Shanahan." As soon as he saw me, he set
aside his laptop and popped to his feet. "Guess what?
Guess what I found out? I was looking into that stuff you
asked me about, the *vory*, and you know what? Do you
know what I found out? It's kind of hard to believe. I
don't know whether it's true or not. It could be true, I
guess."

"Felix . . ." I held up my hand—breathing was an
issue. I knew from experience that I had to stop him, or
at least slow him down, or he would just roll on and leave

me in the dust. Besides, I needed a moment to collect myself. "Give me a second, okay?" I poured myself into his only other seating option, a canvas chair, and closed my eyes. I'd raced over from Wendy's and Drazen so fast, I hadn't had a chance to think about what had just happened. When I started to think about it, to feel the enormity of what I was involved in, I decided I'd rather talk. I opened my eyes, and Felix was right there looking at me. Whatever he had to say, he was excited about it, but I had to get my piece said first.

"I just had a meeting with Tishchenko. He's not looking for Roger. He's looking for—"

"The lost fortune. I know. That's what I was trying to tell you about. The lost fortune of Drazen Tishchenko. Pretty cool, huh? Sounds like Lara Croft, Tomb Raider, or one of those really old Indiana Jones movies."

"Are you talking about the billion dollars that was supposedly on Vladi's laptop?"

"Hey! Miss Shanahan, you heard about this?"

"I did. How did you?"

"I found it in Russian chat rooms. They have them over there, too. You have to put all the pieces together, and a lot of it was in archived threads, and I had to use translation software, so I'm not sure I got all of it. Translation software is, like, so bogus. Half the time, it's completely wrong, and the other—"

"Felix, get to the good part."

"You asked me to check into the *vory,* and I did, and I thought they were really interesting with the tattoos and everything, and then you said you'd met one, and I was really curious about him, and so I checked him out. There's a lot out there on Drazen Tishchenko. He is one intense dude."

"It was on the laptop, right? A list of files . . . a map to the fortune . . . two copies . . . one for Drazen and one for his brother . . ." I trailed off so he could pick up the thread.

"Exactly. It was, like, a treasure map, because if you had the computer, it would lead you to the money, only Vladi's copy got lost when he disappeared."

Treasure map. I had used that phrase with Kraft, and he had laughed at me. "What do they say about Drazen's? What happened to his copy?"

"Eaten by a computer virus."

I had to smile. He had given me the first true moment of satisfaction I'd had in a long time. "You're kidding."

"I'm not kidding. After Vladi disappeared, Drazen went to find his list, and the file was corrupted. According to the story, Drazen loves porn, and you know what happens when you go to those porn sites. You're bound to catch something. He got some kind of virus that crashed his hard drive." He shook his head. "Should have used protection."

I looked over at him. He was trying to hide his grin, but his ears had turned red, which was his way of blushing. Dan was definitely rubbing off on this kid.

"I guess Drazen was a little hasty when he whacked his computer guy."

He went from blushing to stricken. "He whacked his computer guy?"

"More like his money guy. What does Russian urban legend say about how Vladi disappeared?"

"One night, he was visiting America and just vanished off the face of the earth. His billion dollars vanished with him."

"Not necessarily." I pulled out my Wendy's napkin with the model and serial number Drazen had given me. "This is the computer where the files resided four years ago. Tishchenko is confident they will still be there. He says they can't be moved. That's what I came to ask you about. What would make it so files can't be moved?"

He took the fast-food document and nodded as sagely as a twenty-something kid could. "That's how hardware-based encryption works."

"As opposed to software-based?"

"Right. Software encryption stores the critical information in memory, which means in the end, someone like me can go in and grab it."

"Critical information like a password?"

"Uh-huh. Hardware encryption encrypts every sector and byte, and it doesn't leave temporary files and directories unencrypted, which software usually does. In fact, if it's what I think it is . . ." He went back to the beanbag, pulled his laptop into position, and started pounding, referring to the napkin for the numbers. When the results came up on the screen, he took in a quick breath, sucking it through clenched teeth. "Oh, man."

"What?"

"First of all, that porno virus story can't be true, not with this kind of encryption."

"What kind?"

"I can't say for sure, but he could have used something like a KryptoDisk system, which would totally defend it from your average virus. It's military-grade encryption. The only thing that unlocks it is a cryptographic token."

"A token?"

"Four years ago, it probably looked like a thick credit card. Here, you can see." Sensing, perhaps, that he had more energy than I did, he brought his laptop over and showed me the photo on the screen. "You plug it into a slot in the side, the operating system loads, and everything comes up as normal."

"Is there any chance the files could have been erased or written over without the token?"

"No, except, well . . . usually, there's a recovery password in case you lose the key, because if you do, you're pretty much screwed. But you have to have one or the other or sometimes both to get in. It's also pretty—"

My phone started to twitter. I whipped it out of my front pocket. Private call, which was how Kraft's calls had been coming in. I flipped it open.

"Alex Shanahan."

"What the fuck do I have to do to keep you from calling me every half hour?"

Despite my dislike for Kraft and his battery-acid disposition, it was thrilling to hear his voice. I got up from the chair. Somehow, it made me feel more ready to deal with him if I was on my feet. "I have something you'll want. I can't put you in touch with the other reporter, but I have something better. I have his story and all his research notes."

"I don't believe you."

"Then fuck you. This man's son was murdered by Blackthorne, and he took a tremendous risk leaving this stuff with me right before he quit his job, packed up, and fled the city. So, if you want it, let's talk about a deal. If you don't, stop wasting my time."

He had no response to that. Maybe if he couldn't say something nasty, he said nothing at all.

"The research he gave me includes taped interviews with Tony Blackmon. I haven't heard all the material, but in what I heard, he talks about Thorne's background and the things that drove him over the cliff. He calls him Cy, by the way. Did you know that?"

Still no response. I had either shamed him into silence, which had to be hard to do, or he was interested.

"He talks about Thorne's motives and his own motives. According to the reporter's notes, he also gives names and dates and describes a bunch of the group's illegal operations. If this is what you're writing about, you want this stuff, and there is nowhere else to get it. Blackmon is dead."

I listened closely to the silence and heard what I had hoped to hear. He was breathing faster. He was interested.

"Can you at least let me hear some of it?"

I had brought the envelope with me. I had not let it out of my sight since I'd been entrusted with its care. I pulled the recorder from my backpack, turned it on, and let it run until I heard Blackmon's voice. I held the phone close to the speaker and let it run for about thirty seconds. I turned it off. "Convinced?"

"How much tape do you have?"

"Two tapes, probably four hours. Plus a lot of additional notes and research. You can have it all."

There was another long pause, and I was sick of hanging on his every word and breath, so I turned it back on him. "Do you have the Dell with the files?"

"I have the Dell and I looked for the files, but I didn't find anything that looked like them."

I went over to where Felix was working and found the Wendy's napkin. "Check the serial number on the unit." I read Drazen's notes to Kraft.

"That's it," he said.

That was troubling. The computer without the files would be very bad news, indeed. "You didn't find anything?"

"I looked."

"Hold on." I covered the phone. "Felix, if these files were on an encrypted hard drive, would you be able to see them without the token?"

"No. The operating system wouldn't even load."

Back to Kraft. "You wouldn't necessarily see them."

"Who are you talking to?"

"My computer guy, and don't even start with me. He is completely reliable. He believes Vladi's computer must have had an encrypted hard drive, which means you would need a key or a token to access them or even to see them." I went to look over Felix's shoulder. "Pull up that screen again, Felix."

He pulled up the picture of the KryptoDisk system. "Look on the side of the unit. Is there a slot there?"

"Yeah."

Felix cupped his hand to whisper to me. "It's just a standard PMC slot. That could be for a modem or a networking card or . . ."

I walked out of his range. I didn't need to complicate matters with the truth.

"If you don't have the key," I said, "you can't get to the files."

"Okay. Do you have the key?"

"No, but that shouldn't matter. It sounds as if Drazen has a way to get in. He wasn't concerned about the key, just the machine. Bring it to me in Boston, and I'll have all your materials waiting."

"I can't give you the computer, even if it does have your files. I already told you, it has the e-mails on it from the Martyr's Brigade. I need them for my story."

"Your story on Cyrus Thorne?"

"Yes."

I still didn't understand what e-mails from the Martyrs had to do with Thorne, and I was tired of being in the dark. "I need to know what you're writing about."

"No."

"Tell me what the story is about or, I swear—"

"I can't tell you."

"Swear to God, Kraft—"

"You don't want to know. Believe me, you don't."

"I swear to you I will burn this stuff to ashes and it will be gone forever because, let me just say this again, Tony Blackmon is dead."

He was going to give me the answer. I knew he would. I was just trying to make it sooner rather than later.

"Fine," he said. "You want to know the big secret?"

"Yes."

"Here it is. Here's the big secret." Even then, when he had me right on the edge, he waited.

"Kraft—"

"It was staged." The words popped out like a hiccup.

"What was staged?"

"The hijacking."

"The hi—" It sank in. "Salanna 809 was staged?"

"Planned, funded, and directed by Americans. The group that did it is Blackthorne. The e-mails prove it."

He didn't sound crazy. He was an award-winning investigative journalist, yet what he was saying sounded like crazy talk to me. "Are you making this up?"

"No."

"Why would Blackthorne hijack that plane?"

"They didn't. They hired the Martyr's Brigade to do it, and it wasn't really a hijacking. Thorne considered it an extraction. A complicated one, but an extraction nonetheless. It was called Operation Peloton."

"Who were they extracting?"

"Ali al-Badat. He was a prisoner in Pakistan."

Pakistan . . . al-Badat. This was familiar. I got out my notebook and flipped back to my conversation with Lyle. That seemed like years ago. "Right. I remember this.

They caught al-Badat when they were looking for some-one else."

"That's right. Musharraf had just declared his support for the U.S., which was about as popular with his Muslim constituency as bikinis. There was rioting in the streets, burning of the U.S. flag. The military opposed him. His in-telligence people were plotting against him. It was tense. In the middle of all this, he stumbled across al-Badat, the people's sheikh. He was popular, charismatic, articulate, and fully capable of destabilizing the pro-West secular gov-ernment of Pakistan. They couldn't put him on trial. They couldn't kill him and turn him into a martyr, and they couldn't let him walk. What do you do?"

"Organize a hijacking?"

"Right. Put on a bit of geopolitical theater and pretend to force Musharraf's hand."

Something was trying to make sense. "Was Stephen Hoffmeyer part of this?"

"Hoffmeyer was the Blackthorne operative onboard. It was his operation."

"Is that why Hoffmeyer disappeared?"

"What happened wasn't his fault. They had a mechan-ical problem with the plane—"

"Hydraulics."

"He ended up in the wrong country with no support. Thorne hung him out to dry."

"And because of him, nine innocent hostages died, a whole lot of other lives were screwed up, and a perfectly good aircraft was destroyed. Pardon me if I don't feel a lot of sympathy for the guy."

"Things got out of hand, obviously. That's what's in the files. It's post-operation communication between Black-thorne and the Martyrs. The terrorists took computers from the victims and used them for—"

"Their own purposes," I said. "I got all that a long time ago. What kind of communication?"

"Let's just say the Martyrs didn't plan on losing eight of their people. Thorne also wouldn't pay them the rest of their fee. He considered the operation a failure. You could say there was some cyber-discussion afterward between the Martyrs and Blackthorne."

"All right, look. I agree it's a big story. I'm all in favor of helping you take down Cyrus Thorne. So copy off your notes or your secret files or whatever, and let me take the computer. I'll even come to you. Tell me where you are."

"The computer is my story."

"You just said—"

"The fact that the evidence is on a computer carried by one of the hostages is part of the story. It's like a chain-of-custody thing. There is no way I'm separating those e-mails from that hard drive."

I felt a flash of anger, not so much at Kraft as at the fact that everything had to be so hard. But I had no problem taking it all out on him. "Here's the bottom line, Kraft. You can give the money files to me, or I can tell Drazen that you have them, and you can be on the run from Blackthorne *and* the Russian mob."

"The Russian mob does not scare me."

I went back to my chair and crumpled into it. How come no one was ever scared by all the things that scared me? I was running out of options, because in the end, he still held all the cards. "Are you willing to give me the files if I can figure out how to get them off your machine without messing with your evidence?"

"Yes."

"Fine. I'll call you back. When I do, please get back to me right away." This time, I got to hang up on him.

I looked at Felix. "He won't give me the computer, because it has some stuff on it for his story. E-mails and documents and things that were put on after the hijacking. Obviously, he's accessed them, so they're not encrypted. Is that possible, given this KryptoDisk hardware?"

"Maybe. There could be a slave drive functioning for stuff that doesn't need to be encrypted, but that would be a little funky. I'd have to look at it."

"That's what I'm hoping, that I can get it for you and you can hack around this need for a key or a token or whatever."

He shook his head. "No, ma'am. I can't hack it. That's what I was saying before he called. Anything over sixty-bit encryption is pretty unhackable, at least by me, unless you can give me, like, six or seven Crays to do it with."

"How many bits is this one?"

"It's probably 128- or 192-bit key strength. There's no way."

"All right, hacking's out, and he won't meet with me unless I can peel those files off. I think there's only one thing to do."

"Find the key?"

"Yep, and I'm not sure I'm going to like where I have to look for it."

There was construction in Kenmore Square where they were tearing down the bus shack. I had to detour around it to get to Harvey's. As I sat with all the rest of the detouring traffic, I got another call. The ID showed a private caller. I flipped open the phone.

"Alex Shanahan."

"This is Cyrus Thorne."

Just what I needed, Drazen and Cyrus within the span of two hours. "What can I do for you?"

"I haven't heard from you."

I had to shift my brain over to the Cyrus track to get straight what he knew and what he thought I knew. "I had to talk things over with my partner to get him on-board. He's not too keen on turning a man over to be executed."

"Did you convince him?"

"He thinks we're in over our heads, but he's in. Turns out he's more in love with Rachel than committed to his principles."

"Good. Have you made contact with Kraft?"

"Not yet, but I have figured out a way to get him to meet with me."

"How will you do it?"

"By promising that the two of us together can make bad things happen to you."

That produced a satisfied chuckle. I tried to say things to Cyrus that were true. He gave me the feeling that even over the phone, he could tell when I was lying.

"What about Hoffmeyer?" I asked. Maybe I could keep him on the defensive if I could make him have to lie to me. "Have you had any luck finding him?"

"We won't find him. He's been trained by the best. The only way we'll get to him is through Kraft. Then we'll have a shot at the big dog."

"Look, what if I can't get Kraft to come to Boston? Would your plane be available if I had to go to him?"

"Without hesitation. In fact, that might be preferable. When you're close to locking in your final plans, call me with the details, and I'll set the wheels in motion."

"Okay, good. Look, it's going to be a few days at least. Do you want me to call you, or do you want to check back with me? It's probably better if I call you." I waited. He said nothing, and I didn't know how to interpret the silence. "Do you still have my client's video?"

"It's in a safe place. How many days will you need?"

"How about if I call you the day after tomorrow?"

29

HARVEY WAS BY HIMSELF IN HIS OFFICE WHEN I GOT TO HIS house. He had on another new shirt, this one short-sleeved. I could not get used to seeing him in casual clothes, and I couldn't remember the last time I'd seen him wear something that bared his arms. I was surprised that his ex-wife wasn't fused to one of them.

"Where's Rachel?"

"I'm here." She came in from the kitchen with a big bowl of microwave popcorn. I hadn't noticed before, but the house was filled with the smell. With Rachel around, Harvey's house was always filled with something new.

"We need to talk." My preference would have been to talk things over with Harvey, but since the day's events affected Rachel rather substantially, it wouldn't have been fair to leave her out. The three of us sat down for a discussion. This time, I staked out the wingback. Rachel pushed Harvey up next to the couch.

"I just met with Drazen. The good news is, he wants the money, and if we can find it for him, we'll all be free and clear."

"Including me?" Rachel was barely able to contain her glee.

"Especially you. You're not even on his radar screen."

"Oh, thank God." She set the popcorn on the coffee table and collapsed onto the couch. "I have been living with this death sentence hanging over my head for I don't know how long."

"Four years," I said.

She looked at me. "What?"

"It's been four years since you killed Vladi and the money disappeared."

She sniffed. "It was—"

"Self-defense. You don't have to keep reminding me. Also good news, I think I know where the money is. I think Kraft has it. I know he has Vladi's computer. He's willing to trade it for this." I dug the heavy envelope from my backpack and dropped it onto the coffee table. The thud bounced the popcorn bowl. Rachel grabbed it and pulled it into her lap. "It's Lyle's story," I said.

"Who's Lyle?" She scooped out a handful of popcorn and passed the bowl to Harvey.

"Lyle Burquart. He was a local journalist who was trying to do what Kraft is doing. He wrote an article, an exposé on Blackthorne, four years ago. This must have been before the hijacking." I hadn't paid much attention to the dates. "Anyway, no one ever read it, because Thorne killed his son to keep him quiet."

"My God." Harvey reached for Rachel's hand. He looked pale.

"I went back to talk to Lyle, and he's gone. Packed up his family, left his job. But he left me all his notes." I took the microcassettes and player from my backpack and threw them out there as exhibit two. "These are interview tapes. The interviewee was Tony Blackmon, Cyrus

Thorne's partner. I haven't listened to everything, but
from what I heard, he disagreed with the direction
Thorne was taking and was ready to speak out about it."
A thought occurred to me as I was talking. "I wonder if
Thorne killed Blackmon."

"Why would he?" Harvey asked. "Is there an indication on the tapes that he was threatened?"

"The feeling comes more from Thorne. He told me
Blackmon died on a mission. He had this incredible crystal
eagle commissioned in his memory. It's like protesting too
much, you know? And it sounds as if Thorne is capable of
anything. But listen to the tapes. See what you think."

"Why do we have to listen to anything?" Rachel had
her feet on the table, her knees up, and the popcorn bowl
in her lap. "Let's just get this deal done and get on with it."

"I'm trying to, Rachel. There's just one problem. No
one can access the files without the key. Kraft won't show
up until we have the key."

"What key?"

"The key to accessing the money files. It's also called a
decryption token, and it looks like this." I reached into
my back pocket and pulled out the copy of the Krypto-
Disk page Felix had printed for me. "It's the size of a
credit card, only thicker. Here . . ." I unfolded the page
and handed it to her. "It slides into a PMC slot on the
side of the machine."

Harvey leaned over from his chair to see the picture.
Rachel handed it to him with barely a glance. "I didn't
know anything about a key or a token. How was I supposed to?"

"You stole the computer for the files. I have to think
you knew what was needed to access them."

She sat up straight and put her feet on the floor. "How
many times do I have to say this? I didn't steal the com-

puter for the files. I didn't even know about the files. I took it because Roger had said it was worth something."

"When Roger came to take it from you, did he try to boot it up?"

"He tried, but—" Her eyes widened. "He couldn't get it to work." She reached over to snatch the page back from Harvey. "Let me see that."

"Roger took it even though he knew he couldn't get in?"

"Sure he did. He was on the run, especially after that fed got killed. He said he would find a hacker to crack it."

"Felix told me there was no way to hack it. Roger probably had some hacker tell him he needed the key. You can't access the files without the key or the password."

"But we don't have the key," Rachel said, "which means we don't have the money, which means we must be planning on handing the reporter over to those Blackthorne people." She blinked up at me. "Right?"

"No, we can't do that."

"You just said if we can't give him the money, then Drazen comes looking for whoever killed Vladi. If he gets the video, he knows who to come looking for. Am I right?"

She was right, and it started to sink in that I might have overstepped my bounds just a tad. "When I made the deal, I didn't know I needed a key."

"But you did make the deal, which means you gambled my life on finding some key that has been lost for four years." She passed the bowl to Harvey and roared to her feet. "*How* in the *hell* do you make a deal like that?"

"Drazen has no idea you're even involved."

"If he gets the video, he'll know."

"Rachel, dear . . ." Harvey tried to calm her.

"How do you trade my life for something you don't even have, and have no real chance of getting?"

I looked past her to Harvey. I could see him struggling, torn between Rachel and reason. He wanted to please us both. He cleared his throat. "It seems the strategy you chose is very high-risk."

"Thorne will kill Kraft, and Hoffmeyer, too, if he can find him. We agreed we wouldn't facilitate something like that."

"But you're happy to hand me over."

"I didn't say that."

The room went quiet as we both waited for Harvey to answer. He stared down at the low coffee table and spoke slowly. "I am not disagreeing with the choice." He glanced up at me, then away. "But it was a choice that affected us all. You could have discussed it with us first is all we are suggesting."

All *we* are suggesting? Rachel could not have looked more smug. I got up and walked away from them, finding my way over to Harvey's bookcase. Some of the titles had been put back in upside down. Having to deal with all the interpersonal stuff on top of all the life-and-death stuff was getting to be too much, but they were right. I had made a somewhat large decision for the three of us. Perhaps they should have had some say.

I flipped a few of the titles right side up and turned around. Harvey was blinking at me intently, but Rachel stood with her arms folded and her head cocked to one side. She would not be easily placated.

"I'm sorry, okay? I got going too fast, and I didn't do things . . . right. You deserved more consideration than I gave you . . . both of you. We can talk about it now, but I still think a solution where no one gets killed is worth trying."

"I accept your apology," Harvey said. "And I agree with your reasoning."

"You're agreeing with her?" Rachel stood up and threw both hands in the air in disgust. "That's great. Just great. I'm so glad you're on my side."

"Rachel . . ." Harvey maneuvered his chair so he was facing Rachel. She had moved to a spot across the room from me and behind him. "We will take care of you. You must believe that."

"I know. I'm just . . ." She'd lost some of her self-righteous rage. She came over to him and encircled him from behind, hooking her hands together at his sternum. He pulled her hands close to his heart. She leaned down and laid her head on his shoulder. "I'm scared, Harvey. So many things could go wrong."

He turned back to me. "Are you sure this Kraft has the files?"

"No. That's why I think we should get Rachel out of town."

Harvey actually beat Rachel to the punch. "What? Why? Because you object to her?"

"Because you're right. Both of you. This is a very risky way to go. There are too many assumptions, and any one of them could be wrong. Even though Drazen has agreed to take the money and call it even, the biggest assumption of all is that he will keep his word. I think she's in danger if she stays here."

Harvey turned to Rachel, but a moment too late. She had already disengaged and moved away from him. She was across the room, plucking her tooth with that right thumbnail, working out the odds in her head. I knew what would happen next, and I didn't want to see.

"You two decide, but first, I need you to tell me where you buried Vladi."

Harvey was aghast. "For what?"

"I think Vladi took the key to his grave."

"How could you possibly know?"

"Roger didn't have it. Rachel here says she doesn't have it. I saw the video, and I never saw her take it off the body. I assume you didn't take it. We know Roger was looking for the body. It can't be the corpse he wanted. It has to be the key."

"How would he know?"

"He's the one who knew about the money to begin with. Of all of us, he would have had the best information. If he thought Vladi had it on him, then that's where I need to look."

"Dear God, there must be another way."

"There is. We could go and ask Drazen for his key. Presumably, he has a way to get in. Personally, I'd rather deal with the Tishchenko who's dead. Now, unless anyone else has a better idea, I need to know. Where is the body?"

30

DAN'S SHOVEL RIPPED INTO THE SHALLOW HOLE WE'D managed to scoop out over the course of three long hours. He dug up a dead body the same way he did everything else, with ferocious impatience.

"It goes without saying, Shanahan, that this is the creepiest fucking thing I've ever done."

"Digging up a four-year-old corpse in the woods would probably make most people's top ten."

We had waited until it was dark before striking out on our morbid mission, when the night was cool and the air thick as velvet with the smell of moss and fungus and decay. Harvey had buried Vladi in the forests overlooking the Quabbin Reservoir, thirty miles outside Boston, where it was very dark and very quiet.

I tried not to think too much about what we were doing. There was the whole physical aspect of having to handle the remains of a man long dead and buried. Then there were the spiritual implications. Was it not ignoble enough that Vladi had been dispatched with violence and disposed of with such indifference? Now he had to be disturbed for the purpose of retrieving the key to a fortune. They say you can't take it with you, but Vladi had, and now we were digging him up to wrench it back.

Dan stopped and dragged the back of his hand across his forehead. It wasn't that hot, but the work was arduous. "Are you sure this is the spot?"

"This is where Harvey's map said. We won't be sure until we hit something."

"Leave it to fucking Harvey to save the map to where he buried a dead man."

I stabbed the ground again with my shovel. The work was serving as a good anger management tool for me. I thought about Rachel with every rip and slice.

"And you're telling me this kryptonite thing will work after being buried for four years."

"It's a cryptographic token, and I can only go by what Felix told me. He says if it's in its protective case, it should be fine. It's fireproof and waterproof and every other kind of proof. According to him, you could run over it with a Humvee, and it would be fine, because if something happens to it, you're kind of screwed."

"Yeah." He leaned over to start shoveling again. "Instead of like we are now."

Two and a half backbreaking, arm-wearying hours later, my shovel cracked against something hard. Hard like a bone in the cod. Hard like an eggshell in the custard. I dropped my shovel and scrambled out of the pit, because I knew I was standing on the body of Vladislav Tishchenko.

I tried to walk it off, pacing among the trees, but every time I tried to get back in that hole, I wanted to vomit. Then I did. I leaned against a tree and puked my guts out. All this just at the thought of pulling the remains out of that hole. I hadn't seen anything yet. Oh, for a glass of cool water to splash in my face and rinse the taste of death from my mouth. I straightened up and looked to the sky. It was clear. There were stars in the universe, twinkling down on us as we dug a man from his grave. Some things just shouldn't be.

"Are you coming back? Or do I have to do this sick fucking thing by myself?"

Dan, who had not stopped to vomit, had apparently uncovered the body. He climbed out and popped another chemical light stick. I went to my bag of supplies and pulled out a set of gloves. They were heavy-duty fisherman's gloves that came up to my elbows. I tossed a pair to Dan. Then I pulled out two pairs of surgical gloves and a couple of surgical face masks. Having been wrapped in plastic bags before he was planted, Vladi could be a skeleton or a still-rotting puddle of putrid tissue, but I figured one way or the other, there would be something bad to smell. We put on our masks, and I joined him at the side of the pit.

What Dan had dug out looked like a giant, mud-encrusted cocoon. "Do you think we have to pull him all the way out?"

He snapped on his first set of gloves. "What else would we do?"

"Slice open the plastic and dig around until we find his wallet. That way, we don't have to see that much."

"Right. We just have to stick our hands into it. Come on, Shanahan. How bad can it be?" He pulled on the heavier gloves and dropped down into the hole. "You didn't happen to bring any rope, did you?"

"Uh, no."

He shrugged. "I'll push from down here. You pull from up there."

He grabbed the feet end and yanked hard, dislodging the body from where it had been embedded for four

years. Loose soil fell from around the roll of plastic.
When he had it mostly worked out, he paused for a moment, perhaps to see if any ghosts came forth. If they
had, they had arrived in silence. I crouched down. When
he put the feet into my hands, only one thing came to
mind. Vladi wasn't a skeleton yet.

I started to pull. Dan moved along the body toward
the head, pushing as he went. The fact that neither of us
wanted to touch the thing was problematic.

"Grab him," he said, huffing through his nose. *"Grab*
him. Don't let him roll the fuck back on me."

"I'm trying. I can't get a good . . . grip."

The body wasn't heavy as much as awkward and hard
to hold. We teetered at one point with the mass hanging
half in and half out, until I found a better way to grasp it.
Unfortunately, the better way required me to put my arm
around it. Dan gave one last shove and pushed the shoulders ashore. I rolled the mass away from the ledge and
sat back on my butt. Dan climbed out and sank down
next to me. The two of us sat there, sweating, breathing
fast, eyes fixed on the task in front of us.

"We should get on with it," I said after a few shallow
breaths.

"Yeah."

"Before someone comes and finds us."

"I know."

"This would be hard to explain."

"No doubt."

Neither of us moved. I could smell his exertion. I'm
sure he could smell me. It was hard, dirty, tedious work,
this grave robbing.

I stood up, reached down, and offered a hand. He
grabbed it and pulled himself up. Then he surveyed the
cigar-shaped package at our feet.

"I'll take the head," he said.

"No. You're doing this as a favor to me."

"For Harvey, Shanahan. I'm doing this for Harvey."

"Whatever. I'll take the head."

I didn't have to tell him twice. We took our positions and crouched. I found the place where the edge separated from the roll and nodded to him. The plastic was wrapped tightly around the corpse but not fastened in any way. As we started to unroll it, I had the absurd image of a crescent roll. The plastic was thick and dried out. It cracked and complained as we unwound Vladi's shroud.

"We need to anchor the end," I said. "Or it will just wrap itself again."

Dan looked around and found a couple of heavy rocks. We used them as weights and kept unrolling. We went slowly, inch by inch, both of us drawing away as far as we could without losing contact. Nine-foot arms would have been useful.

"Jesus *fucking* Christ." Dan was staring at the first thing to fall out at his end. It was a foot. Actually, it was a leather O. J. Simpson loafer with a foot in it. The shoe was stuck to the plastic, as if it had gum on the bottom, which meant it stopped as the rest of the body had rolled forward.

I sped up. Better to just take it in all at once and not piece by gruesome piece. One last roll, and there he was. Displayed on the ground in front of us were the earthly remains of Vladislav Tishchenko.

I had hoped for skeletonized. No such luck. The plastic, much like a large freezer bag, must have preserved him. He looked like Beetlejuice. His skull was partially covered with skin and random tufts of hair. There were no eyeballs, only sockets staring up at me. His suit was

mostly still there. It was a double-breasted affair, probably brown, but it was being worn by only half a body or
less. He had been wearing a gold chain, which was now
draped around his spine.

"Shanahan."

"What?"

"Get the wallet. Let's plant this guy and get the fuck
out of here."

I moved around to where his waist was . . . had been.
My outer gloves were too bulky to rifle through his pockets, so I took one off, leaving only the surgical glove. I
started to reach and recoiled. It was instinctive. I had to
concentrate really hard to reach down and lift his suit
jacket. But once I had broken the barrier, once I had
touched him, I couldn't move fast enough. I turned him
slightly to reach into his back pants pocket. I tried not to
notice how the corpse moved under my hands. Parts of it
around the waist felt somewhat solid but spongy. Other
parts felt like what they were: a bag of bones. I tried his
side pocket. Loose change and some keys. I pulled everything out and dumped it in the dirt behind me. No wallet.

I stepped across him to stand on the plastic and try the
other side. I didn't look at him. I didn't think about what
I was doing. I forced every ounce of concentration I had
into the few square inches where my hand was searching.
His cell phone was in his other side pocket. I took it.
There was nothing in the back pocket.

"*Shit*. It's not here. It's not *here*."

Dan was standing at his post near the feet. "Breast
pocket," was all he said.

Like an experienced necro-pickpocket, I lifted his
jacket, reached in with just the tips of my thumb and
index finger, and extracted a long, flat leather wallet. I
took it over to where I'd dumped the other stuff. I

whipped off the other big glove and started rifling. There was money. I pulled it out. It was a stack of hundreds. Driver's license. No credit cards. Some kind of identification card written in Russian and what looked like a stack of food stamps, probably stolen. Here was a man who stole millions, maybe billions, and he felt a need to steal food stamps.

That was it. There was nothing else. There was no card or case or token. Nothing. I rocked back and sat on the ground.

"Maybe it's one of these keys," Dan said, poking at the key chain.

"It's not a key. Not a real key. It's a card the size of a credit card. I was sure it would have been in his wallet." Dan went back to Vladi. Without hesitating, he reached down and patted down the entire body, starting at the shoulders. He found it in one of the pant legs, the one that still had a foot attached. He pulled out his knife, cut open the pants, and came out with a sleek carrying case, like a business card holder, only slightly bigger. He tossed it over.

"Oh, my God." I couldn't believe it. "This is it. This has to be it."

"Must have been strapped to his leg."

The case looked as if it might have been brass. I looked for the mechanism to open it but couldn't find it. No buttons or slots or hinges. There must have been a trick. While I was looking, Dan was busy trying to roll up Vladi.

"A little help here?"

I gathered all the stuff we'd collected and dropped it into a plastic bag. I put the bag into my backpack. I pulled on my fisherman's gloves and went back to work. The body made a soft thud when it landed in the bottom of the grave. We grabbed our shovels. Compared with digging him up, it took hardly any time to bury him. Still, it was almost five in the morning when we'd finished. The last of the glow sticks had gone out, but the sky was brightening when I turned to take one last look at Vladi's final resting place.

31

THE SUN WAS COMING UP AS WE DROVE INTO BOSTON. Dan had to get home and get cleaned up for work. I dropped him off at his place. Then I drove over to Felix's house of electronics, figuring to head off any Kraft requests before he even made them. Felix used his digital camera to take photos of the token. The one I liked best showed it lying on the front page of the *Boston Globe* right next to the date. Then he used his scanner to scan it in and his computer to send it to an e-mail address Kraft had provided. In the process of doing all that, I learned how to open the damned case.

When I got back to Harvey's, I was covered in mud and sweat and smelled as if I'd marinated in a swamp. Not surprisingly, Rachel was the first to greet me.

"Did you get it?"

"I got it."

"Oh, my God. Where is it? Let me see it."

I opened my backpack, pulled out the plastic bag with the token in it, and held it up. She reached for it, but I snatched it back.

"No one touches this but Felix."

Harvey was in his office. The empty popcorn bowl was still on the coffee table.

"Harvey, are you okay?"

"Did you have success?"

"We did." I found myself feeling good, for a change, that I had actually accomplished something I'd set out to do, something important. "I beeped Kraft. We should hear from him soon."

"She won't let me see it." Rachel had followed me in. I took out the second bag, the one with Vladi's personal items—the pinkie ring, the wallet, and the chain from around his neck—and tossed it to her. She held it for a matter of seconds before she figured out what it was and dropped it onto a side table. She glared at me, and I couldn't help but enjoy it a little. For someone as tough as she was, she seemed awfully delicate sometimes.

"I'm going upstairs, babe, to finish packing."

I needed to get showered, too, but it was pretty clear Harvey was upset, probably about the packing. I decided to sit with him for a few minutes. I was about to collapse into the wingback before remembering my encrusted condition. I sat on the floor and leaned against the couch. I dropped my head back and closed my eyes and enjoyed for a few moments not having Rachel sitting between us. There were few of those moments left to enjoy anymore.

"There is not much left of us," Harvey said, "after we are gone."

I opened my eyes and looked at him. He had found his way over to the side table and was holding the bag that Rachel had dropped. He studied each item carefully through the plastic as a blind man might—with the tips of his fingers.

"There was more of Vladi left than I would have preferred."

"I am not speaking in terms of the material things or the biological matter we leave behind."

I put my head back again. "I suppose what you do with your life is more important than how much stuff you leave behind, even if it is a lot of stuff. Vladi Tishchenko left a billion dollars behind, yet he's in a grave where no one will ever visit because of the life he lived and the things he did."

I heard him pushing his chair closer. The wheels still needed oil. I knew I should have gotten up and done it right then—I would never remember to do it when I actually had the time—but I was too exhausted.

"Did you know that I was drafted to go to Vietnam?"

That woke me up. Harvey hardly ever told me anything personal about himself, and he never reminisced. I lifted my head to look at him. "You were drafted?"

"In 1968, I was eighteen years old."

I did know that, but not in the way you really *know* things. I knew how old Harvey was, but I had never considered him to be anything but the middle-aged guy who wore glasses and drank tea.

He smiled a little. "The answer to your question is no, I did not serve. I requested and received a deferment, and then I enrolled in college." He shrugged and looked down at me. "Accounting."

It was odd being the one looking up at him. "Sounds like a good decision. You're lucky you had a choice."

"It was an exciting time to be young and away from home for the first time. Everyone had an opinion on absolutely everything, as you might well imagine. It was an age of debate and discussion. I listened and read and tried to inform myself, and I began to develop my own opinions." His voice had taken on a warmth and verve that made him sound like a much younger man. "I cannot express to you what a wondrous thing it was to have an opinion of my own. One of the things I was drawn to was the peace movement."

"Really? You were a peacenik?"

"Not the violent antiwar radicals but those making reasoned arguments against U.S. involvement in a region of the world that neither wanted nor needed our help. The arguments of those who wanted peace seemed more compelling to me than the logic of those defending the war." He put his elbow on his armrest and rested his chin in his hand, as if thinking it through all over again. "I also could not see a way to win, which meant men . . . boys were dying for nothing. And so I became an activist for peace."

Had I given it any thought, I would have had him hanging out at the library, working as a proctor, afraid to talk to girls. I almost smiled as I pictured him with long hair, granny glasses, and a bong. "Did you march?"

"I did everything that was asked of me that was not violent in any way. I was not a leader but a follower, a fact that my father was gracious enough to point out on more than one occasion."

"You father didn't approve?"

"He was desperately disappointed in me, in the things I believed in, the things that I did. He accused me of intellectualizing my fear, of making up an argument to justify a decision that came from cowardice. He called it postdated conviction." His voice had developed a sharp edge, and the warmth was gone.

"He wanted you to go to Vietnam and get mowed down in the jungle? Or addicted to heroin? Or so damaged by your experiences you could never be a fully functioning member of society again?"

"My great-grandfather came from Poland to settle

here. Several members of the extended family, particularly on my mother's side, came over before and after World War II. Other family members—aunts and uncles, older cousins—were lost in the camps. Another uncle died in the Warsaw uprising. He is a hero to them . . . to us, as he should be. My father believed we should give back because this country had given us so much."

"And he was willing to offer up your life to pay the family debt? Screw that."

He didn't respond. He didn't even seem to hear me. I was participating in a conversation he was having with himself, maybe had been having for years.

"Postdated conviction," he said. "I have never forgotten that term. All my life, I have never truly known if he was right."

"No, Harvey, you are not a coward, and fuck your father."

He looked at me. "What did you say?"

"It takes a lot of courage to stand up to your father for the things you believe. There's nothing you need to do to prove yourself to me or your father or . . . or Rachel or anyone else."

Dust and dried mud rained down from my jeans as I unwound myself and got up from the floor. It took me a good thirty seconds to straighten up with my lower back so stiff, but I had to get up and pace around, because Harvey couldn't, and his father had pissed me off.

"Fuck all fathers. Mine, too. Mine especially. Kids are sitting ducks to bad fathers. They believe everything Daddy tells them because they don't know any better. It doesn't make it true. It makes them cowards."

He fiddled with the loose pad on the armrest, something else I should have fixed. "She has decided to leave.

That is what would be safest for her, would it not? To leave Boston?"

He looked up at me with this futile hope in his eyes, and I realized he meant for me to disagree. I couldn't.

"Yes, it would be safest for her to get out of Boston. At least for now. Maybe later, she can—"

"Yes, of course."

I really needed to get cleaned up, but I didn't want to leave him alone this way. For the first time—maybe the first time ever—I wished Rachel were there. I pulled my watch from my pocket, and he noticed. "Go and do whatever it is you must do. I will be fine."

"I'll just be upstairs in the shower. Call me if you need anything."

He had made his way over to his desk and his computer. He pulled up a game of Minesweeper. Rachel wasn't even gone, and the old Harvey was back.

32

WHEN I CAME OUT OF THE SHOWER, THE DIRTY JEANS I'D
left on the floor had been replaced by a clean pair, laid
out on the bed. If I hadn't already known they were
Rachel's, I would have guessed when I lifted them up and
saw they were the style that came only to mid-calf. I was
a few inches taller than she, so when I put them on, I was
relieved to see they made it that far. The long-sleeved
cotton shirt she'd left buttoned down the front. The fit
was a little tight for me. Baggy worked better for someone trying to conceal a waist holster and a weapon.

Rachel came in just as I was buttoning up and laid a
blow-dryer on the bed. "I thought you might want to use
mine. Harvey doesn't have any around the house. I also
put your clothes in the wash."

"Thank you." She was being nice, which meant there
had to be something in it for her. "Did you talk to Harvey
before you came up here?"

"Why?"

"He seems . . ."

"Sad?"

"Deeply sad," I said. "Sadder than I've ever seen him."

"That's because he thinks he's about to die."

"What are you talking about?"

She shrugged casually. "I think that's what he means. He keeps saying he feels a darkness."

"He told you that?"

"Yes."

"When?"

"I don't know. In the past few days."

"Here I thought he was sad because you dumped him once and he's about to lose you again." When I sat up to face the mirror, she was there, too, standing with her arms crossed, her face pulled into a sulk, and one foot thrust forward in case she felt the urge to start tapping.

"I resent the implications."

"This from a woman who ran around on a man with a critical illness. Pardon me for being skeptical."

"Is that what you think? You *would* think that."

"Tell me you weren't running around on him before you dumped him."

"I wasn't."

I stared at her in the mirror. She blinked first, coming out of her fighting stance to drop down onto the bed. The pills on the worn chenille bedspread suddenly held great fascination for her. I went back to my grooming task. Getting the knots out of my hair was easier than getting the truth out of her, and I had some serious knots.

"I wasn't out looking, is what I'm saying, but by the time I met Gary, I already knew it wasn't going to happen between Harvey and me, so what was I supposed to do? Pass on Gary and end up with neither one? Nuh-uh."

"How do people like you get to be people like you?"

"You mean someone who takes care of herself?"

"That would be one way to look at it, I suppose." I leaned forward to check out my face more closely. My skin was stressed and dry. The circles under my eyes had grown a darker shade of dark, and the hints of wrinkles around my mouth were turning to fact. A long weekend at a spa would have helped a lot.

"I worked my ass off to get where I am. How many people in my family do you think graduated from college? None. Not until me. No one in my family had ever even lived outside of Brooklyn. I went to college. I graduated. I earned every penny of my own tuition. I didn't get any help from anyone."

"Earned it how?"

"I did the books for my pop's construction company. I managed the office. I did a little estimating. Whatever he had time to teach me I learned, because that was the real world, and he taught me more than any professor ever did. Do you know how you work construction in New York and New Jersey?"

She was into it now, leaning forward on the bed, schooling me in the catechism of Rachel Ruffielo.

"You make deals. You talk to this guy. You talk to that guy. Another guy comes to see you. Down there, *union* is just another word for mob, and everyone has their hand out—the local city councilman, the cops, the feds, the zoning commissioner, the building inspectors. If you don't play, someone comes and burns down your building." Her voice had grown strong and robust and the New York accent more overt. She was demonstrating the parts she could, holding out her hand for a bribe. "That's what I learned from my pop. You're paying one way or the other; it's a cost of doing business, so just pick your poison and close your eyes."

I swung around on my bench to face her directly. My hair was just going to have to dry itself. "Everyone makes compromises in life. That's survival. It doesn't explain why you have to treat someone who loved you as much as Harvey did—and inexplicably still does—the way you did."

She looked at me with genuine surprise. "What did I do to him that was so bad?"

"You dumped him. You got tired of him and walked out and married a younger man."

"Are you so sure that was such a bad thing?"

"I think he would tell you it was a watershed moment in his life, and not in a good way."

She blinked a few times and looked stricken, but she got over it. She stood and walked over to a framed photo on the wall, a black-and-white of Harvey's grandfather from a long time ago. Her arms were crossed again, but more in contemplation than defense.

"The first time I ever met Harvey, he looked at me with those big cow eyes. I didn't want anything to do with him. But then there was this one time when my whole department went out to a little club down the street from the office where we liked to go sometimes. Here comes Harvey, out of the blue, dressed in a gray suit and a low-key tie, looking like some kind of undertaker at a wedding."

Her head tipped ever so slightly to go with the tinge of wistfulness that had crept into her voice. If I could have seen her face, I probably would have seen a smile. But when she turned to slouch against the wall, all she showed me was her poker face.

"He asked me to dance. I couldn't believe it. This schleppy guy with toner on his fingers and a suit that didn't fit had the balls to come up and ask me to dance. I was hot, too, back then." She put her shoulders back and thrust out her chest. "I mean, what's he doing there in the first place? It's not like anyone asked him to come. I sure as hell didn't ask him. So, I decided I was going to teach him a lesson. Take him out on the dance floor and show him up so he would never come near me again."

She was talking to me now as if we were old pals sharing the warm and funny stories from our past. I hated her for it. I understood how hard it must have been for Harvey to follow her to that bar. I hated her for wanting to punish and humiliate him for it. I hated her more for expecting me to laugh about it with her.

"Anyway, we went out on that dance floor, and he just . . . he blew me away. Have you ever seen Harvey dance?"

I had barely ever seen him walk.

"Harvey has moves. When he was coming up, they had sock hops and school dances and stuff like that, and he really took to it. So, here we were out on the floor doing twirls and dips, and I was having fun with this mope if I just kept my eyes shut. And then he asked me out on a date."

That might have been even harder to fathom than Harvey dancing.

"He caught me in a moment of weakness. I said, 'Yeah, what the hell,' figuring we'd go dancing again and I wouldn't have to talk to him. Do you know what he did?"

In spite of myself, I leaned forward, waiting for the next verse.

"He showed up at my house with this big bouquet of flowers. He was wearing one of his dopey suits, but he walked me to his car and opened the door for me. He bought me dinner and poured my wine. Then he took me to this little jazz club I had mentioned I always wanted to go to. They had a trio playing there. We danced for hours. Then he took me home and gave me a sweet little peck on the cheek."

"It sounds nice."

"I had fun." She shook her head and smiled, just thinking about it. "With him, it was never like 'Let's get a pizza, go to your place, and fuck like rabbits.' He was sweet to me." She reached back to touch the hair on the back of her head, then left her hand clamped around her neck. "He was always sweet to me."

"So, you just had to throw him over for a younger stud."

The smile faded, and whatever image she had in her mind was gone. "I was thirty-three years old. I didn't have that many years left to attract a man."

"You had a man."

"A man who would stay with me."

"Oh, come *on*. You can't tell me you believed Harvey would walk on you."

"I didn't believe it. I knew it."

"Well, that just strikes me as so much horseshit."

She drifted back to the photograph. I didn't know if it held a specific fascination or if it was just something to focus on. "I wouldn't have given him any choice. I would have made it so hard on him that he would have had to leave me."

"What, you were possessed?"

"If I had stayed with Harvey, I would have just ended up hurting him. The nicer he was to me, the more I would hurt him."

"Why?"

"Because I hurt people. That's what I do. I couldn't stand knowing how much he loved me and knowing how much I was going to hurt him. Every day it got harder. I couldn't stand it, so I left."

This time, when she turned to look at me, I saw something in her eyes that might have passed for pain. I never knew with her what was purposeful manipulation and what was genuine, but I did know what she was talking about. I was on to that theory of hurting someone before they had a chance to hurt you first. She had, however, let him down in the most brutal possible way.

"If you were trying to make him stop loving you, you failed."

"Story of my life. I couldn't even do that right. But I give myself credit. At least I was smart enough to figure it out and leave before I hurt him any worse."

"I don't think there is a way you could have hurt him any worse." I started to turn back to the mirror but had another thought. "I take that back. There was one thing you could have done to hurt him worse."

"What would that be?"

"Come back. You never should have come back."

33

BY THE TIME I'D FINISHED DRYING MY HAIR, IT HAD BEEN half an hour, so I did my Max Kraft routine, beeping him and putting in my number and 911, just in case he needed a reminder to check his e-mail. I called Felix and told him he was on standby. Then I tried Bo again and finally got him. He was still in Philadelphia and would be until things in Boston cooled down. Timon was with him for the same reason. I felt bad for having dragged him into it. He told me not to worry, that he had done what he did for Harvey. He gave me detailed instructions on how to reach Radik if I needed help.

Harvey had spent most of the night before going through Lyle's research. He had organized it and put it all into a nifty leather portfolio. I should have tried to sleep, but I was too wired. Besides, there was no way I wasn't going to listen to more of what Tony Blackmon had to say. I unzipped the portfolio and pulled the contents out. Harvey would have come up with some kind of index or summary. I sifted through the stack and found it. The tapes were there, one still in the small player I'd bought from Staples. It was at the end of the B-side of the second tape, which meant Harvey must have listened all the way through. He was thorough that way.

I found the A-side of the first tape, which had been re-wound, dropped it in, and started listening. After a very short time, it was clear that Cyrus had gone over to the dark side early on. What was interesting was to hear Blackmon, the nonpsychopath, struggle with the pinpoint effectiveness of vigilantism versus the slow grind of due process. He talked about Mossad and its efforts after the 1972 Olympics to hunt down and murder every terrorist involved in that bloody fiasco. He talked about Pablo Escobar and how the only reason he was ever caught was that the vigilante group Los Pepes had turned the tables on him, kidnapping his family and friends, killing members of his crew, and using all manner of violence to persuade people not to help him. He made the point that Los Pepes was very likely made up of moonlighting police and military officers who followed the rules by day and made the real progress at night. He made a persuasive argument for the ends justifying the means, at least in the case of terrorists determined to nuke us all to kingdom come.

I was at the beginning of the first tape, side A, when my phone rang. Private call. It was either Thorne or Kraft. I flipped it open and answered.

"I got your e-mail. I'm on my way there."

It was Kraft. I checked my watch. It was just about nine in the morning. "How long?"

"It will be a few hours. When I got closer, we can decide where to meet. Keep the key with you, and we need a safe word."

"What do you mean?"

"If I call and for any reason you need to tell me not to come in, use the word *quiet,* and I'll know. I'll call you."

Click.

I hated how he did that—kept all the power over our communication. Still, the news was good, and I wanted to share it. I went downstairs to tell Harvey.

From the top of the stairs, I heard the unmistakable razor-blades-and-vodka voice of Tom Waits. I slipped quietly down, trying to stay under the sound of "Jersey Girl," one of the all-time great songs about being in love when it's easy. Its gently swooping sha-la-las and quietly strutting acoustic guitar sounded like boardwalks and striped cabanas and ice cream that drips out of the cone and down your hand, the sweet cream mixing with the taste of salt on your skin.

A set of packed bags was at the bottom of the stairs, and Harvey and Rachel were in the front room, the one with the new sound system. Neither noticed me, but the planet could have fallen into the sun and they wouldn't have noticed, because Harvey was on his feet, and Rachel was in his arms, and they were dancing.

They weren't moving much; it was more like swaying. But it was enough to imagine them years before on a dance floor somewhere, when Harvey had his legs under him and could do what he loved to do and move the way he wanted to move.

Harvey had been a good dancer. I could see it in the way he held Rachel, with one hand flat against the small of her back, his wrist cocked just so. His other hand, with hers in it, was high in the air, in case he was struck with the impulse to spin her. Rachel's head was tucked under his chin, and his eyes were closed, and all that weight that he carried around in his life was just . . . gone. He was floating. That's what she did for him. No matter what she was, no matter what she said or how I felt about her, some part of her loved him, and every part of him loved her beyond words. She made him dance.

Watching them together, holding each other, made it easy to understand why he would do anything for her. It also made me wonder what it would be like to be loved that way.

> *Nothing else matters in this whole wide world,*
> *When you're in love with a Jersey girl . . .*

They were saying goodbye to each other. I sat down on the steps and waited for their music to end.

34

I DIDN'T REMEMBER RACHEL HAVING AS MANY BAGS AS I had to load into the Durango or that they were that heavy. I thought about checking for silverware, but that might have been considered inflammatory.

Rachel had wanted to take a cab to the airport, but Harvey insisted that I drive her.

"I wish you would go with us," I said to him. Rachel was in the car waiting.

"I cannot," was all he would say.

"You shouldn't be here alone."

"It is unlikely that Mr. Kraft will call before you get back. Besides, you have your phone with you and the key. If he calls, you can make arrangements to meet somewhere."

He was right. It had been just a little over an hour since Kraft and I had spoken. He wasn't likely to check back in before I got back. Besides, if it made Harvey feel better to know that Rachel was safely on her way, it was worth the effort. I just didn't want to leave him alone. I had tried to call Radik and got his voice mail.

"Give me your phone."

He reached into his saddlebag and pulled out his cell. I programmed in Radik's number. "Keep checking with him. If you can get him and you can communicate, ask him to come over. If the land line rings, don't answer it."

I checked my watch. Ninety minutes to her departure time, and she still had to get to the airport, check in, and clear security. I could get Felix or Dan to move her through, but even with that advantage, we had no time to waste. I had to go. I gave him the phone back. "Are you sure—"

"I will be fine. Please, this is hard enough. Just go."

Rachel didn't even look at me when I got in and buckled up. Her attention was focused on whatever she saw out her own window. I checked to see that she was strapped in and started the car, and we drove for several miles in silence. While she continued her vigil, I paid attention to the traffic. I still wasn't accustomed to all the changes the Big Dig had wrought. If I didn't read the signs, I always ended up somewhere I didn't want to be.

Eventually, the heavy silence started to feel childish. "Harvey said you're going to Hawaii."

"Uh-huh."

"I didn't travel a lot when I was with Majestic, but that was one place I always found a way to get to."

"Uh-huh."

"Dan will probably move you up to first class, which is nice on such a long haul."

She didn't answer. Screw it. At least I gave it a shot. But then she turned her head, and I happened to catch just a glimpse of what was going on. She blinked the tears out of her eyes and wiped them with a swipe of her thumb.

"I don't want to go."

"Harvey said you always wanted to go to Hawaii."

"Not like this." She turned away again, slipped on a pair of shades, and didn't say another word until we pulled up to the Majestic curb. We got out and met at the trunk, where a skycap was already pulling out her bags.

"Where to, Miss?"

"Molokai." She tried to hand him the ticket.

"You'll have to check in at the counter." He nodded to a kiosk set up down the curb, then took the bags over and put them in line for her. I slammed the trunk closed and pulled out my phone to call Dan.

"What are you doing?"

"I'm getting someone to come and take care of you."

She shook her head and gave me a smile tinged with something that looked like remorse. "I'm used to taking care of myself."

I put the phone away and went to get back behind the wheel. I took a last look at her across the roof of the car.

"Rachel?"

In the permanent twilight of the covered curbside, she had taken off her sunglasses to dig in her bag, probably for ID, so when she looked up at me, I could see it. She knew she had left something really good behind.

"Be safe."

I took every yellow light and time-shaving maneuver I could to get back to the house quickly. When I walked back in, something was different. I felt it. The old cliché was true, that you didn't know how much you missed someone until they were gone. I couldn't say I missed Rachel, but I did feel that something had shifted. I walked past that seldom-used front room, stopped, and had to come back. It wasn't the absence of Rachel I was feeling but the presence of someone who shouldn't have been there.

Cyrus Thorne was on the couch. He was leaning back with one foot propped on the corner of the table in front of him. He had his glasses on and was reading the top page of a stack that was in his lap. On the table in front of him were a big, black, large-caliber semiautomatic hand-gun and the leather portfolio that held Lyle's notes. There was also a bag of cherry cough drops. He was sucking on one, rolling it around in his mouth.

Harvey was there, still in his wheelchair. His wrists were tied to the arms of the chair.

Cyrus pointed to the stack of Lyle's notes and smiled. "Are you writing a book?"

"Someone gave that to me. I haven't had a chance to look at it yet."

"There are taped interviews, too." Without changing position, he reached out for one of the cassettes and managed to snag it with just the tips of his fingers. "Do you know who's on this tape? My late partner, Mr. Tony Blackmon."

"No kidding." I kept my eye on his weapon and tried to look around casually. I knew he wasn't alone, but I couldn't see anyone else. "I guess you didn't believe me when I told you I needed more time."

"That's because you were lying." He got up and came toward me. "Mr. Kraft is on his way."

I looked at Harvey. "How would you know something like that?"

He reached around my waist, and the sweet smell of his cherry cough drop was right in my face. I could hear it clacking around his molars. He found the key in my back pocket. "He's coming for this." While he was back there, he took the Glock. "He'll call you for location, and as long as you don't say the word *quiet,* he will feel safe to meet you."

He smiled, and I had a deflating feeling that only flattened me more when he took my phone from my hand, held it up next to his ear, and whispered, "We've been listening."

35

I WAS CONFUSED FOR ABOUT TWO SECONDS, AND THEN I was mortified by my own stupidity. While I was on the Blackthorne plane, Thorne and Tatiana had had access to my cell phone, my computer, and everything else I'd had with me. And they were spooks. Of course they'd been listening. Probably tracking me, too. No wonder I had never seen anyone tailing me.

Here was one of the problems with being in so far over your head. You didn't even know what you didn't know.

Thorne's gaze shifted to a spot over my right shoulder. "Red."

I thought he was talking in code, but then a voice came from behind me. "Sir?"

I turned to find one of Cyrus's soldiers. He looked very young, and he wasn't called Red because of his hair. It was dark and cut close to his scalp.

"Did you clear the house?"

"Upstairs and down, sir."

"Excellent. Take care of her, then make sure we stay clear in the back. I don't want any surprises."

"You got it, sir." Either Thorne's men had learned not to argue with the boss, or he really commanded their respect.

There was a tense moment when I could feel Red behind me and I didn't know what "take care of her" meant. But all he did was pull my wrists together and secure them with plastic cuffs. He took me over toward Harvey and put me on the ottoman next to him.

"Are you all right?" I asked him.

"Yes. Are you?"

"I'm fine."

He glanced at Thorne and lowered his voice to lip-reading volume. "Did you get her off?"

I nodded, and he slumped in his chair. It almost seemed as if his concern for Rachel had been the only thing keeping him upright.

An unfamiliar ring tone called out. Cyrus answered a phone he pulled from his gear bag and launched into a conversation in a different language. It was hard and guttural and sounded something like Bo when he spoke to Timon or Radik. Thinking about Bo reminded me that he wasn't coming and that Thorne knew that, too. As he'd said, he'd been listening. I leaned over to talk to Harvey. "Did you ever reach Radik?"

"Unfortunately, no."

"I don't suppose you left a message?" Harvey wasn't big on those. He shook his head.

No one was coming.

Harvey nodded toward Thorne. "He is here to intercept Mr. Kraft and likely kill him. Once he has accomplished that, he will very likely kill us as well."

That summed it up.

"What do you think will happen to the video of Rachel's incident?" he asked.

"It's not on my list of things to worry about right now."

"She will not know. Drazen will come for her, and she will not know to run."

"Rachel takes pretty good care of herself. Right now, I'm worried about our own situation." Thorne was still on the phone. He'd left my cell sitting on the table next to the portfolio. "He's been listening to all my calls, so he knows about the money files. He took the key, so he must plan on taking the money, too. That will make a nice and unexpected bonus."

"Indeed." Harvey's chin dropped to his chest, and he looked the way he did when he'd taken too much medication. But after a minute or so, he seemed to wake up. "Yes. He will want the money. That is undoubtedly true."

"Who wouldn't want a billion dollars free and clear? He can plow it back into his company."

"But he must get to it first."

"He's got the key. All he needs is the computer, and it's on the way."

"Listen to me." Harvey turned as far as he could toward me, given that his arms were lashed to the chair. "Before she left, Rachel and I talked. I will tell you what I told her." He took a difficult breath, but one that seemed to calm him. "I am through being afraid. I am through being manipulated. I will do what I think is right, what I think is best."

He was remarkably composed. It always freaked me out when Harvey was less nervous and more measured than I was. I was desperate to hear more, but my cell phone rang.

Thorne finished his call and radioed for Red. Then he came over, grabbed me, and pulled me over to the couch. The ringing seemed louder than normal. He put a second cell down next to mine, and I understood why. The two of them were ringing, but not exactly together, which made for almost continuous bleating.

"It's a clone," he said, "and it's been most helpful. If you don't follow the plan, your partner will become another casualty of war."

The private war of Cyrus Thorne.

Red showed up, and Thorne nodded to him. He walked over and put the barrel of his rifle against the back of Harvey's skull. The phone kept ringing. I looked at Harvey's face. He wouldn't look at me. I could tell he was trying not to be scared, but his chin was trembling. He closed his eyes, and pretty soon, urine started dribbling down the struts of his wheelchair.

"If it's not Kraft, get rid of the call. If it is, you know what to do."

Thorne flipped open both phones at the same time, and the incessant ringing stopped. He put one to my ear and the other to his.

"Alex Shanahan."

"Max Kraft."

It was a relief to hear his voice. I needed something to be easy.

"I'm glad to hear from you," I said. "Are you all right?"

"Fine. Tell me where you are. I'll come to you."

I gave him the address and directions from the turnpike, which was how he was coming into town. "How far out are you?"

"Half an hour."

He waited a beat, and I knew he was giving me a chance to warn him off.

"Park a couple of blocks away," I said. "And come to the back door and knock. I'll be waiting for you."

Thirty minutes seemed like thirty hours. I didn't want Harvey soaking in his own piss, but the most they would let me do for him was get towels from the bathroom and try to clean him up. Red cut off our restraints. Harvey held out his arms, and I pulled him up.

"I want you to listen to me." He braced himself against my arms and leaned closer. "I believe you can survive this."

Cyrus had dug out Lyle's microcassettes and settled down with his own little player and earbuds to listen to what his late partner had said about him. Red was assigned to watch us, which meant there was at least a third person in the house.

"I have an idea," he whispered, holding my arms as tightly as he could. "And when I see the opportunity, you will know. You must take it."

His grip was not strong. I managed to transfer it to the handles of the wheelchair so I could work on drying his pants, not easy since he still had them on. The most I could do was dab at them with a towel. He didn't seem the least bit embarrassed to have me do it. When I was done, I kept a hand towel for myself, folded the rest, and put them in the seat of his chair.

I transferred his weight back to me and eased him down into the chair. "What about you?"

"One of us has to stay."

"For what? To be killed?"

He didn't answer. As I wiped off my own hands, I saw that he was actually serious. "Harvey, I'm not leaving without you."

"You must."

"No." I leaned down with the hand towel to dry the underside of the chair. I wanted to appear busy so Red wouldn't tie me up again. Cyrus, who would know better, seemed riveted by the Blackmon tapes. "Why would you even consider something like that? Why would you ask me to consider something like that?"

"God granted me this opportunity. I know it. I promised myself that when it came, I would not turn away, and I will not."

"Whatever it is you have in mind, let me do it. You're too weak. I'll have a better chance than you would."

"No."

I had already wiped every inch of the chair's undercarriage. I sat down next to the right wheel and started on the spokes. "This is all because of Rachel. She's got you all confused. You don't have to prove yourself to her or to anyone else."

"I have done many things for Rachel, some that she deserved and many that she did not. But this I am doing for myself. Now, please, for once, just this once, do as I ask."

He didn't sound like himself, he didn't look like himself, and I had the sick, panicky feeling that the Harvey I knew was already receding from my life. I reached over and adjusted his towel. "Harvey—"

"Sir?"

It was Red, holding his fingers to one ear. Thorne took out his own earbuds. "What?"

"He's here."

Harvey leaned down and whispered, "Listen for your chance. When it comes, take it."

Thorne was on his feet, gathering his weapons. He also grabbed a radio and mounted it on his ear. It had a small, graceful microphone that arced out in front of his mouth. The two men escorted me to the kitchen and took up positions on either side of the door. It was dark and quiet. The porch light was on. I heard footsteps on the other side of the door, then the knock.

Thorne nodded to me.

The blood rushed to my face and seemed to pool there, throbbing with each beat of my heart, because all Thorne wanted was Kraft and maybe the money. If Kraft had Vladi's computer with him, he would have them both, and he wouldn't need Harvey and me anymore. "Who is it?"

"Kraft. Open up, goddammit. Let me in."

I unbolted the door and opened it. He brushed past and into the kitchen. When he turned and saw the two weapons pointed at him, he looked surprised, and then he looked disappointed, and then he looked at me with such deep loathing I could feel it on me like a wet sheet.

"I'm sorry."

Red reached out for his bag. Kraft tried to fight him for it. Thorne stepped up and whacked him in the temple with the butt of his rifle. Kraft went down and stayed there.

Thorne grabbed the bag and left Red with Kraft.

"Come to Daddy," he said, and then held it up to look at his prize. "Finally."

36

THORNE TOOK ME BACK WITH HIM TO THE FRONT ROOM.
Red came a few minutes later, dragging Kraft next to
him. He had tied his hands and feet with the plastic cuffs.
He tied my hands but left my feet free. He didn't bother
with Harvey, probably thinking him too weak to fight.

Thorne had the computer out of its case and in front
of him on the coffee table. He handed the cord to Red.
"Find a plug." The kid crawled around until he found a
wall socket under a side table next to the couch. If
Cyrus's inner soldier was a four-star general, Red's must
have been a buck private—happy to be told what to do
and happier to do it.

"Okay, it's in."

Cyrus searched for the power switch, found it, and
flicked it on. He sat back with both arms out, like a man
waiting for his lover to come into his arms. He blinked a
few times, waited some more, and then smiled. He
rubbed his hands together and leaned forward. Just as he
was about to hit the keyboard, his forehead creased. I
couldn't see the monitor, but I heard the familiar whine
of a laptop going black and shutting itself down.

Thorne went through the whole routine again. After it shut down the second time, he looked as if he wanted to bash the uncooperative machine. Instead, he picked up his radio and called for someone else to come. We hadn't seen anyone else, so it could have been anyone. It turned out to be Tatiana. She seemed to pop up wherever the action was. Or maybe it was wherever Thorne was.

Tatiana was dressed in jeans, polo shirt, and Kevlar vest, and she was bristling with weapons—just like one of the boys. Her quasi-soldier gear showed off strong biceps and broad shoulders that I hadn't noticed on the plane.

"What's up?"

"It doesn't work. It keeps shutting itself down."

"Let me see."

Tatiana sat on the couch next to Thorne. He slid the laptop over and then hovered. "What's wrong with it?"

"I don't know. It might be the battery. Go away and let me work." She was far less deferential than she had been on the plane, which meant her subservient act must have been for my benefit.

While all this was under way, Kraft stirred. First he turned over on his back and stared at the ceiling. When it occurred to him that he wasn't in the room alone, he managed to sit up. With feet together and hands behind him, it took a few tries. He looked at me. He might have had a concussion. He might have forgotten his own name. He had not forgotten how much he despised me. He treated Harvey as if he weren't there and spoke to Thorne.

"You won't stop the story."

Thorne lunged across the room, grabbed Kraft at the collar and under one armpit. He dragged him to the laptop and practically pushed his head through the monitor.

"What did you do to this thing?"

Kraft laughed at him. "Go to hell."

Cyrus reached down between Kraft's legs, grabbed his balls, and squeezed. Kraft let out a high-pitched yowl as he tried, without use of arms and legs, to twist out of his grip. Judging by the bright red hue of Kraft's face and the escalating screaming, Thorne only squeezed tighter. It went on long enough that I started to feel sick.

"Okay . . ." *Wheeze, wheeze.* "Okay, you—" *Cough, cough.* "You asshole." Drooling and choking, Kraft barely got the words out. "Let *go.*"

Thorne released him, and Kraft collapsed with his knees on the floor and his face on the couch. As he tried to catch his breath, Tatiana grabbed him by his scruffy hair and lifted his head. "What's the deal?"

"The battery's dead."

"It's plugged in. Why would that make any difference?"

"The power runs through the battery. If the battery is completely dead, it doesn't matter. You can't get power to it."

"How have you been running it?"

"I haven't. It worked long enough to print out the documents I needed. I think it will run on an auxiliary battery, but I haven't run it since. I didn't want to mess with it." Tatiana let go. Kraft dropped to the floor and immediately drew his knees up, either for protection or for relief.

"What does it look like?" Thorne grabbed Kraft's bag and dumped the contents. "This auxiliary battery."

"I don't have one." Which begged the important question of how he had expected us to get our files off. It seemed to be a moot point.

Thorne went over and sat next to Tatiana. "There are auxiliary power sources you can buy," she said. Then she lowered her voice, and the two of them conferred, glancing over at us and probably deciding whether to deal with the problem right then or take the machine back to the crack staff in Falls Church. I was voting for right then, because it meant we got to live a little longer.

Thorne closed his eyes and rubbed his forehead. He unwrapped a cough drop and plunked it in. Then he came over and stood in front of me. "Where's a Radio Shack around here, and if you give me any crap, I'll shoot Piss-Boy over here. I don't really need him."

I didn't know the answer. Why didn't he just check the phone book? "I can tell you where there's a Staples." I gave Tatiana driving instructions. She geared down and left.

Red was apparently still walking post, so that left Thorne and the three of us. He decided not to waste the time. He pulled a straight-backed chair in from the dining room and dropped Kraft into it.

"Where's Hoffmeyer?"

"Dead. He died in the Salanna 809 hijacking. Didn't you hear?"

"He's the only one who could have told you the name of Operation Peloton."

"I got it from the e-mails."

"It wouldn't be in any third-party communication. There were only two of us who knew the name of the operation. We never told the Martyrs."

"How do you know Hoffmeyer didn't give them the name? You left him out there to die. Why would you expect him to keep your secrets after that?" Kraft nodded toward the computer. It was sitting on the table, as useful as a rock in its current state. "You should have paid up. There would have been a lot less chatter."

"I don't pay for failure. Operation Peloton was a spectacular failure, and the objective was never accomplished. How do you contact Hoffmeyer?"

"He contacts me every time he gets a new chapter done."

"Chapter?" Thorne tried not to look concerned, but the cough drop crunching pace increased considerably.

Kraft smiled. "I should have a Pulitzer and a best seller by the time it's all over, and you will either be in jail or you'll have oversight committees crawling up your ass. Knowing you, as I feel I do now, you might prefer prison to that." Kraft was annoying to me, and we were supposed to be on the same side.

"So, you believe bringing me down will make the world a better place?"

With his hands clutched behind him and his eyes on the three of us, Thorne seemed to be calculating whether we were worth the effort. He must have decided we were.

"Who do you think is protecting you, reporter, and your right to print whatever left-wing, radical, uninformed drivel you come up with? Your elected officials?" Kraft tried to respond. Thorne rolled right over him. "No, they are not, and I'll tell you why."

I kept an eye on the door, watching for Tatiana. Once he had the money, Thorne would have no more use for Harvey or me.

"The U.S. government is filled with men who follow rules. It takes no imagination to follow the rules. It takes imagination to think up a plan to fly planes into a building, to conceive of a plan that was so elegant in its simplicity, so bold in its execution, and so unquestionably effective. Do you think our public servants are up to the task of hunting down people like that?"

Kraft rolled his eyes. "I hate people like you."

"Of course you do. Power flows to those who can take it, friend. That means away from quibblers like you and into the hands of men like me, men who can make the tough choices and take responsibility for the outcome. I understand why you would hate me."

I was checking the door again when Thorne planted himself right in my line of sight. "What about you? What do you think?"

"That we should all take up arms and start our own militias. Maybe we can organize ourselves into tribes and aspire to be like Rwanda or Zimbabwe."

"Do you know how many nuclear weapons North Korea has built?"

"Not a clue."

"Nor has a single one of our crack intelligence agencies. They don't know how far along the Iranians are with their program. They didn't know that Dr. Khan was selling the secrets to designing and building a bomb to anyone who would pay him." He pulled a cough drop from his pocket and offered it to me. When I declined, he unwrapped it and popped it into his own mouth. "Let's bring it down to something more personal. Would the world be better off without Drazen Tishchenko in it?"

"That's not my call."

"Here is a man who shoots his own mother, who trades nuclear weapons like baseball cards." Thorne knelt down and put his hand on Harvey's knee. It was an odd and inappropriate gesture. Harvey was aghast at being touched, which was probably why Thorne had done it. It was undoubtedly some kind of interrogation technique. "He will kill Rachel, you know. After I show him the video, he will hunt her down, and he will murder her, and he will take his time doing it. Surely, if you had the chance, you would put a bullet through this man's brain."

Harvey looked as though he would put a bullet through Thorne's brain if someone would give him a gun and he had strength in his arms to lift it. But then he sat back and looked across at me, and a calm seemed to come over him. All he said was, "No."

"What if I told you he could be responsible for the deaths of millions of Americans if you didn't? What if I told you he had access to several transportable nuclear devices from the old Soviet arsenal and that he had them out for bid?"

"I would ask you to prove it in a court of law, and even then, I am not sure the penalty would be a bullet to the brain."

"Then you probably believe that old canard, 'It is better for one hundred guilty men to go free than for one innocent man to go to prison.'"

"Or to have a bullet put through his brain."

"But what if one of those one hundred guilty men develops a way to smuggle a nuclear bomb into Manhattan? Does that equation still work? Is it better for a million Americans to die than for a thousand innocent men to go to jail?"

"Perhaps it depends on whether you or your brother or your father or your son is one of those innocent men."

"Or if you or your brother or your father or your child is incinerated in a nuclear blast. That is the crux of the matter, isn't it? How do we balance the needs of the many against the needs of the few?"

"Due process," Harvey said, "is what keeps us from being terrorists ourselves."

"That's a quaint idea, old man, but not very workable in these days of weaponized anthrax and transportable nuclear devices."

"I suppose," Harvey said, "one can justify any behavior using the mushroom-cloud defense."

Thorne removed his hand from Harvey's knee. "Where did you hear that term?"

"From your late partner."

"How did you know Tony?"

He didn't, but he had listened to him talking to Lyle on tape for four hours.

Harvey went on. "He was quite conflicted over the things you did and the person you became. Was he one of the difficult decisions you had to make?"

Thorne looked profoundly spooked. His skin had lost some of its ruddiness. He pushed his hand through his hair as he turned away. Kraft, ever the reporter, was keenly interested.

"Is that true, Thorne? Did you kill your own partner?"

Tatiana broke the tension when she came through the door. "I'm back," she said, dumping a Staples bag on the couch. "I got exactly what we need."

37

TATIANA GOT THE LAPTOP HUMMING. CYRUS HAD PUT the key back into its protective case. He removed it from its shell, and handed it to her. She carefully slotted it into the side of the unit. Then the two of them stared at the screen, mesmerized with anticipation. We all stared at them, waiting to see what would happen. They waited. They waited some more. For Cyrus, the anticipation turned to frustration and then anger.

"Goddammit, what now?"

Tatiana was calmer. She seemed more intrigued than angry. "I don't know." She worked the token in and out a few times. That didn't seem to do the trick, so she pulled it out and checked the receptors, wiping them clean with the sleeve of her shirt. That didn't work, either.

"Is it the right computer?"

She turned it over and checked the back of the laptop against the back of a business card Cyrus handed her. It took me a few seconds to realize where he'd gotten the serial number. I had read it to Kraft over my phone. There wasn't much I knew that they didn't.

"The computer is fine," Kraft said. "If there's something wrong, it has to be the key."

Everyone turned, and now the spotlight was on me. "I dug the key out of Vladi's grave. It can't be the wrong key. It might be old or damaged, but it's the right key."

Kraft started to bat that one back, but Harvey interrupted. "It requires a password." The room went quiet. Now everyone was focused on him.

Thorne walked over and gave Harvey his best commander's stare. "What did you say?"

"My ex-wife knew how to get into it. She and Roger Fratello believed the password would be enough. They did not understand that it required both the key and the password. She told me the password." He took a breath and set his shoulders. "Let my partner and Mr. Kraft go, and I will give you what you need."

"Is he telling the truth?" Thorne looked at me, and so did Harvey, and I knew what was happening. Here was the chance he had spoken of. Here was the opportunity that I was supposed to take.

Tendrils of panic made their way up from my gut and started to wrap themselves around my heart and my lungs. I didn't know if what Harvey was claiming was true. I knew this. If I contradicted Harvey, Cyrus had no reason to keep either Harvey or me breathing. If I supported his story, it at least bought us some time.

"Yes . . . he's right. Rachel was supposed to call back with the password once she felt safe. She must have given it to him before she left. I didn't know."

Thorne looked to Tatiana. "Is that possible?"

She shrugged. "It could be configured that way."

Thorne knelt again in front of Harvey so they were eye-to-eye. "Give me the password."

"First, let them go."

"You know, I've learned a few things in my time about how to make people talk, a few interesting techniques."

"I am already a dying man, and I have learned to live with pain."

Thorne rose slowly and wandered over behind my chair. I felt his hands on my shoulders. "I'm not talking about physical pain."

"If you hurt her, you will never get the password. Never."

Harvey sounded less afraid than I felt. He was playing his last hand, and he was all in. The moment was both thrilling and devastatingly sad, and I didn't know what I was supposed to feel.

"You let them walk away, and I will give you the means to open the files. Whatever else is there, there is more than a billion dollars available to the one who gets there first."

Thorne didn't move. Harvey kept going, more anxious this time. "I know of no cause that would not benefit from the infusion of a billion dollars in cash that is free and clear. No one knows about this money."

Again, the heavy silence. I didn't think Thorne would let Kraft go, a situation that had its own implications, but it seemed he was considering some kind of deal.

Tatiana broke the silence. "He's lying."

Harvey looked stunned. He tried to stutter a response, but Tatiana rolled over him.

"There's nothing here that looks like money. No hidden files. No encrypted files. No account numbers or serial numbers or passwords. I looked for anything in English or Russian. There's nothing like that on here."

Cyrus was crunching cough drops like mad, one after another. He probably wasn't used to dealing with something as frustrating and mundane as computer problems. "But the serial number matched."

"I think someone must have swapped out the hard drive. The one that's in there now is not even encryption hardware. It doesn't need the key. There's nothing on the drive except the Martyrs' documents, and those were moved onto it a couple of days ago."

I looked at Kraft. "You swapped out the drive?" Drazen had said the files could not be removed from the drive without the key. He had said nothing about the drive being removed.

"No. Fuck, no." He squirmed to sit up straighter. "That can't be right. Those files should be three and a half to four years old. It's the key. It's the damn key. If it's been buried for four years with a decomposing body, it's got to have gone bad."

We stared at each other, and Thorne stared at us, and Harvey just looked lost. Someone had pulled the stopper out of the floor, and we were all fighting to keep from swirling down the drain.

Thorne turned to Harvey. "It was a noble effort, friend. As a soldier, I appreciate what you tried to do. But I don't believe you."

Harvey seemed genuinely confused. He studied the floor as if he could read the answer there. "No. I am telling the truth. Please—"

Thorne picked up the radio and called for Red. The eager soldier came quickly and stood, waiting for orders.

"Red, start packing the gear. We're going." He looked at Tatiana and nodded in our direction. "Take them down to the basement."

I could see in the way they looked at each other what

that meant. We were going down to the basement and never coming back up.

"Wait." Harvey tried to stand and almost pitched straight forward. Thorne pushed him back with one hand.

Tatiana hadn't geared back up since coming back from Staples. She did it now, slipping into her vest and throwing her rifle strap over her head. She swung the rifle around to free her hands, then she lifted Harvey out of his chair. As she carried him in her arms, she made a face. "You stink, old man."

I could hear Harvey wheezing all the way down the basement stairs, and I was afraid Tatiana would kill him and I would get down there and find his dead body.

"Cyrus . . ." I tried to climb out of the chair, but Red pushed me back. "You're talking about a billion dollars. Probably more." I tried to look around Red so I could see Thorne. "Isn't that worth a few more hours? No one would ever come looking for it. We can figure this out. Harvey is telling the truth. He never lies."

But the truth was, I didn't know if he was lying or not. He was certainly clever enough to have made up the password story. Rachel was also clever enough to have kept one last secret for herself. It didn't matter either way, because Thorne and Red were talking as if I didn't exist.

Tatiana took Kraft next, easily hoisting him over her shoulder and carrying him the way a fireman would. He spewed venom at her all the way down the stairs, using his best weapon—words.

When she came for me, I fought her, at least as much as I could with my hands tied. I couldn't stand not to at least make it hard for her. I fought her all the way down to the basement. At the bottom of the steps, she dropped me onto the concrete. With no hands or feet to break my fall, my hipbone and the side of my knee took the worst of it, hitting the concrete with blunt force. It hurt like hell, but at least I managed not to land on my head.

Harvey was on the ground on his left side facing me. I hoped he hadn't been dropped. The only evidence that he might have was that his glasses were somewhere beside his face. His breathing was level. His wheezing had stopped. He was calm, which meant he'd already given up. That pissed me off.

"I am sorry," he said. "I could not even do that right."

Tatiana was checking her weapon.

"Don't shoot us like this," I said, trying any means of delay. "At least let us up on our knees. Let us go out with a little dignity."

All I heard was the sound of her cranking the rifle, getting ready to finish us off. I twisted around so I could look past her. When I rolled up to a sitting position, I saw something, or thought I did, in the dark corner behind her, something moving. "Come on, what do you care? What difference does it make how you kill us?"

"Exactly. You're going to hell just the same whether you're lying on your back or up on your knees, so say your last, and—"

She dropped her rifle. Her eyes flew open. Both hands went to her throat, and even though her mouth was opened wide, no sound came out. I couldn't see what was around her throat, but it was killing her, and she knew it. She tried to twist around, to shove her elbow into the midsection of her attacker. She tried to kick backward. With rising panic, she tried to grab the rifle hanging by the strap around her neck. She tried everything a dying woman would try to save her life, but her legs shuddered and twitched. It took a long time for her to die, and even though she had been on the cusp of killing me, it wasn't easy to watch. She went limp and fell to the floor. The man who had garroted her came out of the shadows. With his finger to his lips, he signaled me to be quiet.

"What . . . what is happening?" Harvey asked. "Who is there?"

"Harvey," I said. "Be quiet."

"What?"

"Shut up, Harvey."

The attacker crouched next to the woman he'd just killed, pulling weapons and ammo from every pocket. Her radio crackled. Cyrus was calling to her.

"Unit two, unit one, come in. Unit two, come in." There was a short space for a response, then "Unit two?" Another pause, then "Tatiana, come in." The radio went silent.

Our savior continued digging through his victim's gear and came out with a gas mask, and none too soon. I heard the door upstairs open, and Cyrus's voice came floating down.

"Tatiana?"

After a pause, I heard the sound of a canister clattering down the steps and the door slamming shut. My eyes immediately began to water. I squeezed them shut and tried not to breathe in as the musty basement filled with gas. I heard things going on around me. I knew I had to get out, but I couldn't think of anything except trying to keep that gas out of my lungs.

Harvey was hacking and coughing and sounding as if he were dying. Someone cut my restraints. I felt a weapon and a mask in my hand and heard someone yelling at me to put the mask on Harvey and take him upstairs. I was so lost I needed someone to tell me what to do.

I felt my way across the floor to Harvey and fit the mask over his face. I felt for Kraft where I thought he had been. I couldn't find him, so I went back to Harvey. Without bothering to cut him loose, I pulled his arms over my head. With my back to him, I started to lift. My thigh muscles screamed, my hip felt as if it might pop right out of its socket, but I kept pressing and managed to stand up with him draped over my back. I staggered to where I thought the stairs might be, one hand in front, feeling my way. Halfway up the stairs, my foot caught on something. A body. It was either Red or Thorne. Two down. At least one left upstairs. I leaned one shoulder into the wall and pushed my way up, one step at a time. My hand finally reached the door. I pushed on it, and we fell through the doorway to the relief on the other side.

The two of us lay there for a few seconds. I knew we weren't alone in that house, but I couldn't move. Except for my ears, every orifice in my head was leaking. My eyes were tearing, my nose was running, I was drooling and coughing. I pulled myself up, grabbed Harvey, and dragged him to a kitchen chair. Then I went straight to the sink, turned on the water, and splashed my face with handful after handful. I slid down to the floor and sat with my back against the cabinet, half hacking and half crying. If I'd had a third half, it would have been dying.

It was the voices from the other room that got me moving. I pulled myself to my feet. The pistol was still in my waistband. The knife I'd used in the basement was nowhere to be found. I used kitchen cutlery to free Harvey's hands and feet.

"Should I take the mask off?"

He nodded, so I did. I got him a damp dish towel and told him to wipe his face, then weaved my way back into the living room to see what was going on.

Kraft was on the couch, hands and feet still tied. He looked like a big cat with his face in a throw pillow, trying, no doubt, to keep his eyes from dripping out of his head.

Our anonymous rescuer was standing over Thorne, who was unconscious in a heap on the floor.

"Is he dead?"

He shook his head.

I raised the weapon and took aim. "Put your hands up and turn around."

He didn't say anything, but then he had a gas mask on. *"Do it."*

He did. I stepped forward and took the semiautomatic sticking out of his waistband. I popped out the mag, and it dropped to the floor. I tossed the empty pistol onto a chair. I searched him and took away everything he had scavenged off Tatiana's body and threw it onto the chair, hoping he didn't notice my clammy, sweaty palms. Then I took a step back. "Take off your mask."

He did that and turned around. He seemed familiar, though there was no reason he would. I had never seen his picture. No one had.

"Mr. Hoffmeyer, I presume?"

38

IT WAS BEGINNING TO DAWN ON ME THAT BLAND WAS THE look of choice for spies, and Stephen Hoffmeyer, or whatever his name was, was no exception. He had on a white open-collared shirt, tan pants, and a well-used black leather jacket. Everything else about him was average. Sandy hair, blue eyes, average build. I didn't know if I could pick him out of a lineup, and I was looking right at him. He did have a nice tan.

"Stay cool," he said. "I didn't come here to do harm."

"What did you come here to do?"

"You have something I need. I have something you need. I came to do business."

"Take off your jacket."

He shrugged the leather jacket from his shoulders and let it slide down his arms. In one smooth move, he caught it in his right hand and offered it to me.

"Drop it on the floor, get down on your knees, and put your hands back on your head."

Harvey appeared in the doorway. He had made his way down the hall, using the kitchen chair as a walker.

"What is this?" He looked, as I probably did, as if he'd

been weeping for a week. "What is happening? Who is this man?"

"This is Hoffmeyer."

"How do you know?" With one arm, I helped him to his wheelchair.

"It's the only person it could be. Isn't that right, Kraft?"

Kraft didn't bother to answer. He had managed to get himself to a sitting position. I had no reason to untie him. For the moment, I had enough balls in the air.

"Check this." I picked up Hoffmeyer's jacket and laid it across Harvey's lap. Hoffmeyer didn't move, but something told me he was humoring me, letting me keep him under control. I stepped back and positioned myself so I could watch both him and the doorway.

Harvey pulled a long, flat wallet from the pile of leather and opened it. Without his glasses, he had to hold it at arm's length to head it. "Joseph Hildebrandt of Tucson, Arizona."

"Where did you come from?" I asked him. "Don't say Arizona."

"Check my bag." He nodded to a black gym bag on the floor near the door.

I went over and got it and put it on Harvey's lap. "Take a look."

"What am I looking for?"

"Take out the Mylar envelope," he said, "and open it."

Harvey reached in and pulled out a silver bag. It rustled and crinkled as he handled it. Then he opened it and pulled out a hard-drive unit that looked as if it would slide right into the computer Kraft had brought us.

"That's the lock," he said. "All I need is the key."

Vladi's laptop was still on the coffee table. It had been

powered down and unplugged. Thorne or Red must have been packing it up to go.

I looked at Hoffmeyer, still on his knees in the center of the room. "What happened to Red?"

"Was he the second man down the stairs?"

"Yeah, he must have been."

"I broke his neck."

If he was psychologically scarred by having done it, he hid it well. That made two dead in the basement—Tatiana and Red—and Cyrus, still breathing but not moving, next to Hoffmeyer. Dead bodies . . . spies . . . tear gas . . . How would we explain all this? I couldn't think about it. I had to think about what was right in front of me.

"Let me have the drive, Harvey."

He gave it to me, and I went to the couch and sat down. Kraft must have felt the shift. "Cut these goddamn things off of me." He was fighting the cuffs, which only made it worse for him. "My eyes are killing me."

"I know. I'm sorry. Hang on for just a few more minutes."

"Goddammit. You are such an amateur."

It was so tempting to reach over and smack him across the face, but it would have been bad form to do that to a man with his hands tied behind him.

I had never swapped out a hard drive before, though I had watched Felix do it once. To get to it, I would have to take apart the laptop's housing.

"Harvey, I need you to go to your desk and get a—"

"Phillips-head screwdriver?" Hoffmeyer was still down on his knees with his hands on his head. "I've got everything you need in my gear."

"Where's your gear?"

He pointed to a corner, where a black backpack was nestled in a basket of magazines. He must have tossed it there in the heat of the moment. Harvey had maneuvered his chair closer to the couch. I checked with him for his input. "He did save us," he said. "In rather dramatic fashion."

He had also killed two people in rather dramatic fashion. Had he wanted us dead, though, he could have waited five more minutes, and Tatiana would have done the job for him.

"Okay. Go ahead."

Hoffmeyer stood up and took a moment to shake out his left shoulder. He kept rotating it as he stepped over Thorne. He brought the pack over and dug around until he found something that looked like a manicure case. He unzipped it, and it turned out to be a case full of small tools, one of which was exactly the one I needed. He extracted it and handed it to me.

"Thank you."

"You're welcome. What do you want to do about Cy?" Thorne had begun to stir.

My nose and my eyes were still running, causing the scene to go blurry every few minutes. I used the sleeve of my shirt to dry my eyes.

"How about if I cuff him?"

"Yeah," I said. "That's good."

He went off to do that, and Kraft started agitating again, albeit with his eyes squeezed shut. "What about me? You trust him and not me? He wouldn't even be here if it wasn't for me."

I watched Hoffmeyer tie up Thorne. He was efficient but almost deferential as he lifted him to a sitting position against the side chair where I had been tied up. He was a hard guy to figure out. I didn't want to use my last brain cells trying. He dragged over a chair and sat, letting out a big sigh as he did.

"I'm getting too old for this."

I wasn't afraid of him. I wasn't really afraid of Kraft, either. Hoffmeyer had a lock blade in his pack. I borrowed it and cut Kraft's restraints. He got up and stumbled out of the room, presumably in search of water for his face.

Hoffmeyer sat across from me, staring coolly back. The laptop was on the low table between us. I had that feeling again that I was in charge only because he permitted it. "Who are you, really? Why are you here?"

"You can call me Hoffmeyer. I'm here for the money."

"Drazen's money?"

"I think of it more as my money."

That was the straightest answer I'd gotten from anyone since the whole thing had begun. "Where did you get the hard drive?"

"From Kraft. We've spent a lot of time together. We're collaborating on a book about Blackthorne. Political exposés are hot now. I think we have a shot at getting published."

"So I heard." I couldn't tell if he was genuinely excited or being ironic. Either way, things just kept getting more surreal.

"Anyway, I swapped it out one night when Max was asleep."

"You did what?" Kraft had found his way back. He was standing in the doorway, dabbing at his eyes with the same damp towel I'd given Harvey. I knew it was the tear gas, but he looked as though he were crying over the betrayal.

"I'm sorry, man. I couldn't let you carry that thing around with you. It wasn't safe. I knew Cy was around.

Then you told me about the Russian. I copied over all your stuff."

"You told me you didn't know what was on it."

"Yeah, I lied. Roger told me what was on it while we were on the plane."

"Roger Fratello?" I asked. "You knew him as Roger and not Gilbert Bernays?"

"He told me his real name. He told me everything." He sat back and rubbed his left shoulder, which was clearly bothering him. "Those are the kinds of things you share when you're hostages together. No matter how positive you try to be, you don't really know how much time you have left. Lies become meaningless. Artifice slips away." He shook his head. "Roger caught a bad break."

"Roger made his own bad breaks." I had no sympathy for him. "He was an embezzler. According to the FBI, he was also responsible for the murder of an FBI agent. He told Drazen the guy was working undercover, and Drazen murdered him."

Hoffmeyer nodded. "I believe that he did feel some remorse over that. He said the Russian scared him. He was looking for a way out of town. That was the biggest chip he had to bargain with." He nodded and smiled at Kraft, who had reclaimed his spot on the couch next to me. "This is going to be a great story, man."

"Pulitzer Prize, baby. I'm telling you. *Oprah, Larry King, Today* show . . . well, me, not you. But we can't miss with this."

"Could we hold off on the victory parade for a few minutes?" I said. I looked at Hoffmeyer, who seemed far more interested in the money than in Oprah. "How did you know the drive needed a key? Did Roger know about that?"

"Roger couldn't figure out why he couldn't get to the files. He didn't know anything about hardware encryption, but I did. I told him he needed a token. That was disappointing for him."

"I'm sure it was."

Harvey weighed in from the wheelchair. "Can we please begin at the beginning? I am deeply confused."

Hoffmeyer leaned forward and tapped the laptop's monitor. "Find the money. Nothing happens here until you do." He was perfectly polite, but with a titanium edge underneath. Maybe that impression came from having watched him kill Tatiana.

"You can't take this money." I was confused about a lot of things as well, but not about that. "Drazen will kill us if we don't return it to him."

"Find it first. Then we'll talk about how to handle Drazen."

He seemed so confident and reasonable and in charge, it was hard not to just follow along. Again, I looked to Harvey.

"One way or another," he said, "we need to know what is on the drive, do we not?"

39

I SWAPPED THE TWO HARD DRIVES WITHOUT ANY COMPLI-
cations. Harvey, Hoffmeyer, and Kraft watched closely
as I did it. Kraft plugged in the auxiliary battery Tatiana
had bought, and they all continued the vigil as I turned
it on. When it got to the point where the operating system was supposed to load, everything stopped. The
token was still on the table. I fit it into the slot and
pushed. When it engaged, the system began to load. It
was so quiet in the room, all I could hear was the low
whistle in Harvey's breathing and the sound of the computer at work.

The system loaded, and when it got to the next screen,
I looked over at Harvey and smiled. I shouldn't have
been surprised. Harvey never lied, and Rachel had, in
fact, held back one last secret. "What's the password?"

"Yaryna." He spelled it for me.

"Who is that, Vladi's girlfriend?"

"His mother." An idea that carried its own special
meaning, given that his brother had shot her to death.

When the computer was ready to go, it looked like any
other used by every other schlub in the world who used

Windows. This one ran Windows 2000. It had a desktop screen with icons and not a single clue to what might lie beneath its bland exterior.

I started working through the directory. All the files had cryptic names like 104bkl2sign. There were columns of them, one after another. I didn't know what I was looking for, so it would be hard to know if I'd found it. What would the financial files look like? Would the information be in code? I scavenged around in the cyber-haystack, clicking files randomly, hoping one would be the needle. I gave up and went to the search function.

"Harvey, if you were putting together a map to a financial fortune, what would it look like?"

"It would have the names of banks, the addresses, the names and numbers of contacts at those banks. It would have account numbers and passwords. Unless the money is all in cash, it would have a list of investment interests and investment vehicles."

"Bearer bonds? Like that?" I typed in "bearer bonds" and hit enter. Nothing. I tried "serial number." A list of files came up. That was a hopeful sign. I started opening them. They were Excel documents, spreadsheets with exactly the information Harvey had described. Locations, account numbers, passwords, and, best of all, balances.

"I found it." Everyone knew that, because they were clustered around behind me watching the screen, but I had to say it anyway. I couldn't help but feel excited.

"Well done," Harvey said.

Hoffmeyer tapped me on the shoulder. He wanted to cut in. We switched places. He emptied a bag on the desk next to the machine and went to work. There was a three-and-a-half-inch disk, what felt like a relic now. There were a couple of jewel boxes for CDs and what looked like a load of different kinds of adapters and batteries. He had come prepared to attack that machine in whatever way necessary. As it turned out, it had a USB port, so all he needed was a flash drive. He had several and the software to make the computer recognize it. I could have used it in Paris.

He started to close all the files I'd opened but paused on the last one. He produced a notepad and a pencil and copied down three random account numbers with passwords and contact information. He tore off the page and passed it to Harvey.

"Would you mind checking these accounts? I'd like to make sure it's all there."

I found the cordless phone and gave it to Harvey. God only knew where all the cell phones had gone to. Hoffmeyer was copying the files to the flash drive. About ten minutes passed as he worked through all the files. He typed quickly and clearly knew his way around a computer.

Harvey finished his call. "It is all there and more. The money has compounded quite nicely over the past four years. I have written the new balances here. I think you can expect the same from all the investments."

He passed the paper back to Hoffmeyer, who folded it in half and slipped it into his front breast pocket.

"Can I ask you a question?"

"What?"

"Were you a hostage, or were you part of it?"

"Buy the book," Kraft said. He had found the bag Thorne had taken from him, pulled out his reporter's notebook, and started scribbling. He was no longer tied up, and it did cross my mind that it would not have been out of line to smack him.

"I was both," Hoffmeyer said.

"I don't understand what that means."

"The whole thing was a bad idea from the start, a low-percentage play." He nodded in Thorne's direction. "I told him that. But he was doing it no matter what I thought. He liked the intricacy of the plan, the elegance of the solution. He was going to send someone else, but I decided to go. I went to make sure no citizens got hurt."

"The hijackers didn't know you were part of it?"

"I had my reasons for not identifying myself to the Martyrs Brigade. Isn't that right, Cy?"

He had been the first to notice that Thorne's eyes were fluttering open. It took two tries before he could get his chin off his chest and was in a position to take in what was going on around him. He saw Hoffmeyer and blinked a few times. A sly smile broke across his face. "Am I looking at a ghost?"

"Hello, Cy. I wish I could say it was good to see you."

"Are you going to kill me?"

"Thinking about it."

Thorne didn't seem too worked up by the concept. He adjusted his weight from one side to the other and winced as he did it.

Hoffmeyer was keeping one eye on his files and one on Thorne. "Still having problems with that hip?"

"No more than I ever did. What are you calling yourself these days?"

"The consensus in the room is Hoffmeyer."

Thorne let his head loll back and roll around until his neck cracked like a big knuckle. Then he straightened up and yawned. "Where have you been keeping yourself?"

"I was surprised that you never came looking."

"You were officially dead. We sent Carmopolis to check. Remember him?"

"He was a fuckup."

"Yeah, he's dead. He told us he had a positive ID on you. I found out later he spent that week in Thailand shacked up with a hooker and never even checked. It's hard to find good people." His expression turned almost wistful. "Somehow, I knew you were alive. All those years it nagged at me. When the Zormat thing hit, it opened everything up again. I got a little misty."

"You missed me?"

"I didn't think I would, but we were friends for twenty years. I did miss you. I made a nice tribute to your memory. I hope you get to see it sometime."

I looked at Hoffmeyer, and I realized what had been familiar about him. It wasn't his face. It was his voice. I had heard it before—on Lyle's interview tapes. "You're Tony Blackmon."

"Not for a long, long time now."

"I thought—" Back to Thorne. "You said—"

"He was dead? He was supposed to be." He looked at Hoffmeyer. "But I have to admit, it is good to see you."

"How's Maggie?"

Thorne gave a *que será será* shrug.

"Have you seen your kids?" Hoffmeyer offered a sad smile and shook his head. "Or do you still consider them to be a liability?"

That piqued Harvey's interest. "How so?"

"Over time, Cy came to see his family as a vulnerability. He never wanted any of his enemies to use them against him. Cy can't be vulnerable, so he created a lot of distance from them."

"Blackthorne is my family. It used to be yours. Why didn't you come back?"

"And give you another crack?"

"I expected you'd be back to kill me."

"I'm not like you, Cy."

"You used to be."

Harvey and I looked at Kraft, but it was clear the only people in the room who knew what they were talking about were Thorne and Hoffmeyer. Kraft stopped his scribbling long enough to ask what we all wanted to know. "Another crack at what, Hoff?"

"Cy had a side deal with the Martyrs. Besides hijacking the plane, they were also supposed to kill me."

I reached over and tapped the arm of Harvey's chair. "I knew it. Didn't I tell you that?"

"I shouldn't have done that." Thorne looked contrite. "It wasn't smart. But you would have gone down as a hero. You should see the crystal eagle I had commissioned for you." He gave me the chin. "She was impressed. Go ahead, tell him."

"It's impressive. Why didn't the Martyrs kill you?"

"Because I was the only one who knew what to do when everything went all to hell. They couldn't kill me. Every terrorist group and insurgency in that part of the world started showing up and trying to hijack the hijacking. It was a circus."

"One of the hostages told me you tried to save them."

"I did what I could. It never should have happened. I can't defend my part in it, or in any of the other things we did. But when it was all over, I didn't want to do it anymore. I had the chance to disappear, and I took it."

"I never took you to be weak-willed, Tony."

"One man's conscience is another's weak will. I had a lot of time to think while I was on that plane. I spent time talking to those people. They weren't soldiers, Cy. They were citizens, and they were scared. They had no way of dealing with what was happening to them. The ones who died burned to death. It was ugly, and it wasn't right." He shook his head. "It wasn't right."

"You should have come in for counseling. Or you should have stayed dead."

"You're right. I should have stayed dead. But then Max came to see me, and we started talking about the book. I liked that idea. I figured I owed you one."

"It wasn't the billion dollars that flushed you out?"

"It makes for a nice bonus." He opened and checked more of the files. He'd been working as he talked to Thorne. They must have been the last, because he pulled out the flash drive and put that into the pocket of his trousers. Just when I thought he'd made a mistake and left copies on the laptop, he pulled out a second flash drive and made a backup copy, this time moving all the files off the hard drive. Had Drazen and Vladi done the same, they would have avoided a lot of trouble. "Friends," he said, zipping his bag. "It's been a pleasure. Max, do you need a ride somewhere?"

"Just get me someplace where I can write. Where are you going? Can we go over some of this?"

"Wait a second." I got caught on the handles of Harvey's wheelchair trying to get out from where I'd been wedged behind it and the couch.

Hoffmeyer was collecting himself to leave. "Do you mind if I retrieve my weapons?"

"No, go ahead. Look . . ." I pushed Harvey forward a few inches and freed myself to charge out into the middle of the room. "You can't leave. What about Drazen? You're taking the money we're supposed to give him."

"Right, right. Sorry." He reached into his breast pocket and pulled out a business card. "Call the FBI. Tell them to look in this safety deposit box. They'll find the weapon used to murder the FBI agent. It has Drazen Tishchenko's fingerprints all over it. Or if you want, you can strike a deal with Drazen. Tell him to forget about the money or you'll take what you know to the feds. Either should work."

He handed me the card. There were notes scrawled on the back. When I turned it over, it was Roger Fratello's business card from Betelco. Holding it gave me chills.

For a dead man, Roger was very busy. "Where did you—"

The unmistakable click of a round being chambered interrupted, and I looked up to see Hoffmeyer about to shoot Thorne in the head.

"What are you doing? Don't kill him."

"He'll come after me."

Thorne, again, seemed wholly unconcerned. "He's right."

"You can't just kill him."

"I can."

"Don't."

"Why not?"

"Because . . . " I thought about what Harvey had said, that there had to be a difference between us and them. Maybe that was true, maybe it wasn't. All I knew was I didn't want him to shoot a man who had his hands tied behind him. "Because you're not like him anymore."

Hoffmeyer tilted his head. I watched him caress the trigger. Without moving the gun, he crouched down next to Thorne. "I won't kill you today, but that doesn't mean I won't kill you. And don't ever forget that I know Maggie, and I know your kids, and I can find them if I have to. Grandkids, too."

Thorne tried not to show it, but his casual expression grew just a shade more forced.

"Don't come after me, Cy."

Hoffmeyer stood up and backed off, but his shoulders

tensed, and he spun around and aimed at the doorway a
split second before I saw what he had either heard or felt.
No one had been watching the door, which explained
how Drazen Tishchenko and his man Anton were able to
materialize right in our midst.

40

EVERYONE WITH A WEAPON, INCLUDING ME, HAD IT OUT. Everyone had at least one bull's-eye on him. If it went wrong, most of us would be shot. At least some of us would be dead, and that seemed like a waste.

"Drazen, what are you doing here?"

He looked around the room, seeming remarkably unperturbed by the situation. "Who is Thorne?" he asked.

"That's me. I called him. Did I forget to mention that?"

I remembered the phone call he had made as we had waited for Kraft. He had apparently been speaking Russian.

"He said he had my money. He said he could tell me who killed Vladi."

Cyrus said something to Drazen in Russian that made Drazen shift his focus to Hoffmeyer. Then Hoffmeyer joined their discussion. Now I couldn't understand any of them.

"How about we speak a language we can all understand?"

Hoffmeyer obliged. "I was just telling Mr. Tishchenko that Cy undoubtedly brought him here to kill him."

"That's not true. My intention was to take him back to Virginia and kill him. But first I had planned to see what he would tell me about the black market for rogue nuclear weapons."

Not surprisingly, Drazen seemed confused by Thorne. "You are U.S. government?"

"It doesn't matter who he is," I said. "He's not taking you anywhere, and we're not talking about who killed your brother. Our deal was if I gave you the money, none of that would ever come up again." I glanced at the table where the computer had been. It was gone. I took a few steps back so I could include Kraft in my field of vision. He was clutching the machine to his chest. "Give me that."

"You can't let him have this."

"He's not interested in your story. Give it to me, or I'll shoot you."

Reluctantly, he passed it over. I held it up to show Drazen. "Vladi's laptop. This is the reporter who had it. Here it is. Everything is happening exactly as I told you it would."

I set the machine back on the table before anyone could notice my hands shaking. I had absolutely no plan. I was going with the flow.

Drazen's eyes brightened. "The money is there? You have it?"

Hoffmeyer held up the flash drive. "Your money is here."

Drazen put both hands on his pistol and aimed carefully at Hoffmeyer. "This is a trick. The files were on the computer. They couldn't be moved."

"They couldn't be moved without the key," I said. "But we found the key."

"Show me."

The token was still in its socket. I reached down to pull it out, held it up for him to see, then tossed it at him. He caught it with one hand. He looked at it and clearly recognized it.

"We used that key to copy the files onto that flash drive. We checked some of the balances. The files are good."

Drazen turned to Anton to show him the key. They talked quietly. Cyrus and Hoffmeyer leaned in to hear. I watched their faces for some secondhand clue to what was being said, which might tell me what would happen next. But they were spies. They looked like the more dour half of Mount Rushmore.

"Do you not wish to know where we found that key?"

Everyone turned toward me, but I hadn't said anything. They were looking behind me to where the voice had come from. The only person behind me was Harvey. I didn't want to turn my back on anyone, but I could hear him laboring, and I knew he was trying to push himself out of the corner.

"Harvey, stop. Stay back."

But he didn't stop, kept pushing, and eventually made it across to the center of the room. That put him pretty much in everyone's line of fire. I could hear in his breathing how scared he was. I reached over to touch his arm. "Harvey, what are you doing?" He pushed my hand away.

Drazen seemed as surprised as anyone to see a man in a wheelchair before him. "Who are you, gimpy man?"

Harvey smiled slightly. "I am the gimpy man who killed your brother."

The room had already been tense, but now I started to feel panicky. I was now convinced that there were people in the room who weren't getting out alive and that Harvey was volunteering to be one.

Drazen shifted his aim to where he was looking, right at Harvey's heart. "You?" He laughed. "Who cannot even stand on his own two feet? Vladi would never have allowed himself to be killed by you."

Harvey fumbled open the flap on his saddlebag. When he reached into it, Anton took notice. He was covering Hoffmeyer, but he watched Harvey closely. Harvey didn't seem to care. He pulled something from his bag. Trying to look casual, he tossed it toward Drazen but didn't put enough on the throw, and it ended up on the floor between them. Anton leaned over and picked it up. He gave it a little shake before handing it to Drazen. It was the bag of Vladi's personal items, the ones I had dug from his grave.

Drazen stared at the bag for a few seconds before telling Anton to open it. Anton did so and offered it to Drazen. Maintaining his bead on Harvey, Drazen pulled out the gold chain I had taken from around Vladi's neck . . . spine, actually. He looked down at Harvey. "Where did you get these?"

"Leave now, do not hurt anyone, and I will take you to him."

I was starting to feel sick at the thought of where this was going. "Harvey, don't—"

"*Quiet.*" He turned his head just slightly to deal with me in case I didn't follow directions. Then he rubbed his eyes. He didn't have his glasses on. That was probably a good thing. "Please, do not interfere."

Drazen took a step toward him, which put the barrel of his gun about six inches closer to Harvey's heart. "How did you get Vladi's possessions?"

"I told you, I killed him."

"Vladi was strong. You cannot even stand."

"Strong, yes, but not bulletproof, and I have not always been in this chair."

"Why would you kill him?"

"Because he attacked my wife."

Drazen had to think about that, but then he seemed to know he was talking about Rachel. "She is not your wife. She is no one's wife."

"She was once my wife, and to me, she always will be." Harvey leaned in toward the barrel of the weapon. His voice was getting stronger. "Your brother tried to rape her. I shot him three times in the chest to stop him. I put him in the trunk of his gold Lexus. I drove him out of town. I dug his grave and rolled him into it. I covered him over with dirt, and that is where he lay until I learned about the token. My colleague discovered that he had been carrying the key to a fortune when he died. I went to the place where I buried him, I dug him up, and I found the token you hold in your hand." He nodded toward Anton. "And those items."

Drazen looked as if he were struggling with the idea but at the same time wanting to believe it. "No. You are too weak to do this thing." He looked at me. "She did it."

Harvey gave me no opening to respond. "For one billion dollars, a man can find the strength he needs. I did not want to share the money. I told no one. If it is vengeance you came for, take me."

Drazen seemed unsure. "Who are these men?"

"It is not important who they are. Their business is with each other. Your business is with me."

"He's lying," Cyrus said. "It wasn't—"

"Shut up, Cy." Hoffmeyer had produced a second piece, which he now held flush against Thorne's skull.

"Again," Harvey said, "leave now, and I will take you to Vladi's grave."

Drazen stepped back to have another quiet chat with Anton. They both nodded, seemingly in agreement.

"I accept your offer," Drazen said. "I will take you and my money."

"No." I stepped in next to Harvey. "That is not the deal. Here's the deal. This man"—I nodded to Hoffmeyer—"has the money on that flash drive. If he wanted to walk out of here with it and leave you in a pool of blood, he could, and I would have no problem with him doing it." I tried to keep my breathing level and to make the words slide out and not tumble. "But I promised you a copy of your files. He has two. Here's what I propose. Hoffmeyer, you give him one copy and keep one, and whoever gets to the money first wins. More than likely, you'll each get some, and there's plenty to go around."

"No." Thorne tried to get up, but Hoffmeyer stepped on his thigh. "You can't give money to that terrorist. You can't do it. Kill him now. He's a cancer. He's evil. He will sell weapons to our enemies. It's treason if you don't kill him or at least take him prisoner. It's aiding and abetting, it's—"

"Shut up," I said. "You don't have a weapon, which makes you not part of this discussion." I looked at Drazen. "Honor and commitment. I made you a promise, and I'm keeping it. In return, you must forgive all debts. No matter who killed your brother, no one in this room owes you anything, and we will never see you again. That's the best deal you're getting today, and if you kill Harvey, you'll have to kill all of us. Bloodshed means police. Much bloodshed means more police, more coverage in the news, more pressure to find the killers. Others know of our dealings with you. An FBI agent, for one."

Drazen chewed at the corner of his bottom lip. When he looked at Hoffmeyer, he seemed to be sizing him up. Hoffmeyer looked right back, and when he spoke to me, his eyes never left Drazen. "Whatever I get to first, I keep? That's the deal?"

"That's the deal."

He shrugged. "Okay."

It was Drazen's move. "I want one more thing." He twisted his brother's chain around his fist and held it up. "Tell me where to find Vladislav."

"And then you're in?"

"Yes."

Harvey still had the pad and pen he had used to write down Hoffmeyer's accounts. He was already writing.

"All right. I'm not walking into anyone's line of fire, so everyone lower your weapons." No one moved. "Me first."

I set the Glock down on the coffee table next to the laptop. Then I waited. I happened to catch Kraft out of the corner of my eye. Even he had a small revolver. He must have picked it up from Tatiana or Red. "Kraft, put that down."

He hesitated, and it pissed me off. We didn't have trouble enough? *"Now."* He set it next to mine. Hoffmeyer set down the weapon he'd had on Thorne, but he kept a bead on Drazen, who was still aiming at Harvey. Hoffmeyer said something again in Russian. It must have been about Anton, because Drazen nodded, and Anton holstered his cannon. Then Hoffmeyer and Drazen watched each other lower his, and we had a room with no weapons pointed at anyone. Amazing.

Very slowly, I stepped around Harvey and went to Hoffmeyer. "I'm sorry," I said to him, "but I need the files."

He looked at the flash drive. "Grass huts on the beach don't cost that much." He put the drive in my hand. I looped around Harvey again and offered it to Drazen.

He looked at it. "I have your word these are my brother's files."

I looked back at Hoffmeyer. He could have handed me a decoy drive, and I wouldn't have known, but he nodded, and I believed him. "You have my word."

I carefully made my way around to stand next to Harvey. It was so quiet I could almost hear his pen gliding across the page. When he was finished, he tore the page out and handed it to me. It was filled with his careful script, a little more shaky than normal. I handed it to Drazen. He looked it over, then passed it back to Anton.

"We're finished now," I said. "Leave."

He did. No goodbye. No thanks a billion. No nothing.

"You'll regret that," Thorne said. "It was a big mistake."

Kraft collapsed onto the couch. Hoffmeyer put down his bag and pulled out his own laptop, no doubt looking to get a head start in the race for the billion dollars. I followed the exit of our most recent guests to make sure they'd left. I was reaching to lock the front door when it popped opened and almost cracked me in the head. I stepped back, drew the Glock once again, and took aim. I was so fried and so close to the edge, I almost fired. If I had, I would have killed Rachel.

The door opened wide, and Rachel backed in, dragging one of her many bags with both hands. "Can someone help me here? Can someone—*hey!*" She'd turned, spotted me, and nearly tumbled over backward. "What the hell are you doing pointing that thing at me?"

"Sorry. I—"

"Rachel?" It was Harvey, calling from the other room. "Is that you?"

"I'm here, baby. I came back." She looked at me over her shoulder. "Would you get my bags?"

I closed the door, pushing her bag outside to do it, and locked it. I followed her into the front room, where she was on her way into Harvey's arms. She took two steps toward him and pitched forward, tripped up by Cyrus's outstretched legs. Almost before she was down, he had her. His arms were free. He scooped her up with them, pulled her in close to his body, and held a knife to her throat.

"Now I have a weapon."

41

THORNE STRUGGLED TO HIS FEET, NEVER LETTING RACHEL move enough to expose him. Hoffmeyer's gun was back out. He was to the left of Thorne. I was to his right. Kraft was still on the couch. Harvey had the desperately disappointed look of someone who had made it to within two feet of the finish line and fallen down.

"What do you want, Cy?"

"What I came for. The reporter and his files and you, Tony. I can't let you leave here. Not now."

"I knew I should have killed you." Hoffmeyer looked at me. "What did I tell you?"

Harvey was still in his chair almost directly in front of Thorne, eight or ten feet away. "Let her go."

"Not a chance. Roll back, Piss-Boy."

"Take me instead of her. She has nothing to do with this."

"I don't give a shit."

Harvey kept moving forward. "Once you kill her, you are dead. Do you want to die, or do you want to keep up your good works? Who will fight the war if you die here today? Take the money and go. But do not take any more lives."

"I don't plan to die here today."

Thorne was talking to Harvey but keeping his eye on the other dangerous man in the room. Hoffmeyer was inching around to Thorne's right.

"Don't try it, Tony. You're out of practice."

"She's a citizen, Cy. Let her go. Let all of them go. We'll settle this between us."

Thorne's gaze tracked across the room in a very calculated fashion. He looked from Hoffmeyer on his left to Kraft and Harvey right in front of him. When he got to me, standing to his left, my heart was going so fast I thought it would pull me down face-first, because I knew he was about to try something, and I didn't know what to do.

"Why don't you come and join us?" he said to me.

"What?" I could see Hoffmeyer in the background, inching closer to him, but I made myself not look at him.

"I've been impressed," he said. "I think you would be a good addition to the group. We can always use more women, especially since I'm down one. With the proper training, you could be good. Virginia's not a bad place. You'd be traveling a lot, of course, but—"

In an instant, he pushed Rachel at Harvey and turned and flung the knife at Hoffmeyer. Hoffmeyer fired as he fell back. I squeezed off a round, but Thorne was already on me. He grabbed my wrist and pushed it straight up. He twisted until I lost the grip and the Glock fell to the floor. Still holding my arm, he turned and tried to flip me over his back, but I kept my center of gravity and hooked my other hand around his face. I dug in my nails, hoping for eye, but caught mostly nose. When he turned his head, I yanked him back and kneed him in the kidneys. He was bigger than I was and much better trained, so I had to make up for it with imagination and sheer, wild-eyed force of will. I kicked and twisted and bit and slashed and ducked and made myself generally hard to grab hold of. He did manage to throw me over onto my back. It hurt a lot, but when he reached down for the gun, I shoved the heel of my hand into his throat. When he pulled away, I got up and drove my shoulder into his balls. At least, I tried to, but he moved, and I went head-first into a side table and fell. When I staggered to my feet, he had my Glock. He was going to kill me with my own gun.

"Maybe," he said, breathing hard, "you're not so good after all."

As he raised the weapon, someone shot him in the back. I looked over for Hoffmeyer, but it wasn't him. It was Harvey, holding Hoffmeyer's gun. Harvey fired again. Thorne spun around but stayed on his feet. I got up, staggered forward, and threw myself into the backs of his knees. Thorne fired two shots on his way down. Rachel screamed. I landed a few feet away. The Glock landed between Thorne and me. He reached for it. I was faster. I picked it up and pointed it at his chest.

"Stop. Stop moving. Put your hands on top of your head. Put them up. Put them on your head. Get them up." I couldn't stop yelling. If I was breathing, I was yelling, adrenaline pushing the words out. "Don't move. Don't you move. Don't . . ."

"Shoot me," he said. "Can you do that? Go ahead. Put one in my chest. Right here." His left arm hung limp at his side. Blood ran down his arm and dribbled off his fingertips to the floor. But his other arm still worked. He used it to point to his chest, to show me where to shoot him.

The three shots were fast and quiet, right into his

chest, right where he had pointed. Cyrus Thorne fell back and died with his eyes wide open.

I swung around, looking for Harvey. I wanted to tell him I hadn't thought he could shoot that well. I found Hoffmeyer, holding the wound in his side.

"He needed to die," he said. "It shouldn't have been you that had to kill him." He started to wobble, but Kraft was right there to help him.

"Harvey? *Harvey*?" I turned around. Rachel was kneeling with Harvey. She had blood on her hands as she looked up at me. "What should I do?"

I crawled over to her. "Are you hit?"

"No. It's Harvey. He's bleeding. What should I do?"

"Hey . . ." I put my hand on his back to roll him toward me and felt something warm and wet. I pulled my hand away. There was a burgeoning stain on the back of his new shirt. It was a shoulder wound, an in-and-out. Painful but definitely survivable. I turned him as gently as I could in case the bullet had broken his shoulder blade. That was when I saw that the entire front of his shirt, one of his brand-new shirts, was also turning red, stained with the blood from a different wound. He'd been hit in the side, just beneath his rib cage. This one didn't look survivable.

"Call an ambulance." I said it to anyone who was still around and still alive. "Call 911."

I turned his face toward me. "Harvey. Don't go to sleep. *Harvey, stay awake.*" His lids were fluttering, but there was life in his eyes. I could see it. I laid him flat on his back and kneeled next to him so I could put pressure on the wound. I covered it with the heel of my hand and pressed hard. I could make the bleeding stop. I knew I could. If I pressed hard enough, the bleeding would stop, and the ambulance would come, and the

EMTs would stabilize him, and he could beat it. He could live.

"Harvey. Don't close your eyes." He was drifting off. *"Harvey."* His head lolled back, and he opened his eyes. "You have to stay awake. You have to fight. Rachel, make him stay awake."

She took his face in her hands as I pressed harder on his side, but the blood oozed up between my fingers and ran over my hand. I couldn't make it stop. I didn't know what to do. I didn't . . . I looked around for something to press over the wound, and I couldn't find anything, and when I looked down again, he was looking up at me, and his lips were quivering. I leaned down, put my ear to his lips, and felt the words as much as heard them, because I knew in my heart what he wanted to say.

"Let . . . me . . . go."

With one hand supporting his head and the other on his chest, I couldn't wipe my tears. They ran in a furious stream down my face and dripped from the tip of my chin onto his collar.

I took my hand from his side. Rachel was crying, too, trying to get her arms around him. I lifted him enough that she could put his head and his shoulders in her lap and hold him. "I came back," she said. "I didn't want to leave you. I came back for you, baby." She held him tight. "I love you, baby. I love you."

Somehow, he found the strength to lift his hand and reach for mine. I took it and held on. I held on to him as tightly as I'd ever held on to anything, and I regretted every moment I had shut him out or held him distant and not let him close to me. I looked into his face, his soft, sweet face that had so often been etched with fear and doubt and pain and bleak acceptance, and I wondered if the meaning of a man's life could be found in one moment, if his whole life could be lived for the purpose of getting to that single moment—a moment without fear.

He closed his eyes, and I reached down and touched his cheek with the back of my finger. I smiled, because he had shaved, which meant it had been a good day.

42

WE DROVE DOWN TO THE CAPE ONE MORNING IN EARLY April to spread Harvey's ashes. We'd had a hard time picking the spot. The only times I had ever seen him completely at peace were when he'd been reading, so I suggested Widener Library in Harvard Yard or Copley Square across from the Boston Public Library.

Too boring, Rachel had said. Harvey was a lot more fun than that.

"What's your idea?"

"I don't know."

"Where did you get married?"

"In a synagogue in Brooklyn, but that was because my mother insisted. He would have been fine with a justice of the peace."

"First date?"

"That jazz club I told you about. It's been gone for years."

"Favorite date?"

She had to think about it, but then I could see in her face that we had our place.

We took the Truro exit and drove down toward Wellfleet. She couldn't remember the address, but she remembered the street and thought she could recognize the house. After driving around for ten minutes, winding in and out among the expensive homes, she spotted it.

"There. That's it. I remember that rooster wind thing on top."

I parked on the next block. We walked back to the house, the scene of Harvey and Rachel's favorite date years before. They'd come to a wedding of a friend of Rachel's at this house on a warm Saturday night in August, toward the end of the season. They had danced under a tent on the beach, and that's where she wanted Harvey's final resting place to be, the only problem being that it was a private beach. It said so on the sign hanging on the big gate with the chain and the heavy padlock.

I looked back at the house. No lights on. No one stirring. There had been no cars in the driveway. I checked the fence for wires. No visible signs of an alarm.

"Screw it," I said. We were about to break the law anyway by scattering human remains on a beach belonging to someone else. I handed the urn to Rachel, found a good foothold on the wooden gate, and climbed over. She handed Harvey across, then scrambled over behind me.

The walk to the beach was a long one, over a planked bridge that spanned the rolling dunes. The sound of the surf grew louder as we walked toward it. By the time we'd reached the steps down to the beach, the rest of the world had fallen away.

Being a private beach at 10:00 A.M. on a workday, it was deserted. The smell of seaweed was in the steady, cool breeze. Seagulls dipped and whirled overhead, while smaller shore birds played chicken with the waves, scavenging the wet sand they left behind. But it was easy to picture the place in the summer with umbrellas and canvas chairs and kids and suntan oil.

Rachel stood in the sand with her eyes shaded against the morning glare. The sun was trying to break through the mighty steel bands of clouds that had wrapped us tightly since October.

"It was a big wedding," she said. "Harvey said he wouldn't come, but then I told him about the entertainment. They hired a big band to play live. They put the whole thing up over there, this big white tent with a dance floor inside. I'd never seen anything like that. Harvey had such a good time dancing that night. I think we were the last to go home."

I offered the urn to her. She looked at it, then pulled the sleeves of her sweater down to keep her hands warm and wrapped her arms around her. She turned to face the wind and said, "You do it."

"Do you want to say anything?"

"I wish we'd brought champagne. We had champagne that night."

"Do you think he'd like the water or the sand?"

"The sand," she said. "Most definitely."

"Then we should turn around."

We turned and faced the dunes. The wind from behind whipped my hair around and into my face. I took the lid off and handed it to her. With my back to the ocean, I spread Harvey's remains along the beach. They call it ashes, but it was heavier than that, and grainier with small bits of bone. I painted a wide swath where Harvey and Rachel had danced and drunk champagne, and I was glad that Harvey had wanted to be cremated, because I never bought into that whole thing where you put the body someplace—in a hole in the ground or a stone mausoleum—so you can come and visit, because after the soul departs, the body doesn't matter anymore. You might as well be ashes, and who would want to picture Harvey for all eternity the way he was at the end?

I pictured Harvey wearing lightweight linen pants, a short-sleeved sport shirt you might see in the 1940s, and a thin woven belt around a slim waist. I pictured him dancing on the beach with his girl, nimble and graceful and happy. I had never seen it myself, but I could imagine it.

As we walked back to the car, there was the slightest thinning in the cloud cover off to the west. It wasn't much, but just enough to let us know that winter would eventually let go.

Take a white-knuckled ride with these thrillers from Pocket Books.

Heretic
Joseph Nassise
The Vatican has a secret weapon. His name is Cade. And he's the last defense in the war between good and evil.

Blood Memory
Greg Iles
Memory fades. But murder lasts forever.

Puppet
Joy Fielding
She cut the ties to her past. But someone won't let her forget...

The Unforgiven
Patricia McDonald
She swore she was innocent of murdering her lover. But someone doesn't believe her—and wants her to pay.

The Black Jack Conspiracy
A Department 30 Novel
David Kent
When secret government agency Department 30 is involved, the stakes are always life and death. But this time the game is fixed.

Voices Carry
Mariah Stewart
Her memories are flooding back. With a vengeance.

Available wherever books are sold or at www.simonsays.com.   13450